Crimson Awakening

First Line Series

By Leticia Edghill

This is a work of fiction. Temples, long-standing institutions, and agencies are mentioned but characters, except one, are entirely imaginary. The deity mentioned is part of Egyptian mythology, but much of her personality and actions were created by the author. Other businesses, events, and incidents are the products of the author's imagination. Any resemblance to actual persons, living or dead, or actual events are purely coincidental.

Ebook ISBN 979-8-3507-3023-4

Printed Book ISBN 979-8-3507-3022-7

Cover Design: Franchon Hurt

I would like to thank all of those who have supported me in my writing journey. My mom, who read and edited the first copy of my manuscript. My writers group, Writers Critique Group in New York for helping me to grow as a writer and reading and editing my earlier manuscripts. Catja who helped me edit the entire manuscript. And of course the many of you who told me to keep going and those who enjoyed reading my many mistakes copy.

Thank you

To my children Khari and Tiy, the dream is real. Keep on dreaming.

CONTENTS

Chapter 1

Her manicured nails sparkled in the sun as she slowly stirred and sipped her chocolate martini. She sat at her favorite table by herself, hidden away in the back of her favorite restaurant on sixty ninth street and Broadway. Lena loved being able to watch the Broadway traffic and watch the trees sway in the wind. She was dressed to impress in her taupe pencil skirt and cream strap around the ankle stilettos to match her long sleeve blouse. The colors complimented her golden caramel skin.

Tulips bloomed in tiny gardens on the sidewalk and in the middle of the streets. She couldn't remember what they called those concrete sections. Lena sighed. Restaurant patrons were sparse despite the sunny day. Still, Lena was glad for the quiet moment as she surveilled the few passersby and waited for Theo.

"Well," she whispered, "another beautiful spring day in New York City."

"Talking to yourself?" Theo asked as he walked over to her table. "You couldn't have known I was here since you're backing the door."

She rolled her chocolate brown eyes and continued to twist a lock of her tightly curled hair around her fingers as her best friend sat down. "You know me, Theo." She shrugged as she continued to peer at the man in front of the eatery window. He wasn't strange, she thought to herself. She sensed that she had seen him before. No, she knew that she had seen him several times. Still, she couldn't be one hundred percent sure, she had never seen his face. Lena thought he was beautiful and tall, his muscles pressed through his black sweater. She couldn't help but think the weather was too warm for a wool sweater, but he didn't look the least bit bothered. His thick, bone-straight, blue-black hair hung over his face, so all she espied was his full carnation pink lips as he pulled on the cigarette.

"Darling, I could give you something to put in your mouth," she whispered as she sipped her drink.

"I'ma pretend I didn't hear that. City traffic coming downtown was horrible. I should have taken the train." He stilled when she didn't reply. "Lena, what are you looking at? You haven't looked at me since I walked in. Where's my usual greeting?"

Lena regarded at him and smiled. "Hey, Theo. How are you? Looking customarily beautiful." He was dressed similarly to the man standing outside but in an Armani sweater and jeans. The black shirt seemed to make Theo's mahogany skin glow. He was about to reply, but Lena didn't give him a chance. "Now, have you seen him before?" She asked as she pointed out of the window. "I can't help but think he's been following me. I keep seeing him almost every time I go out."

Lena heard Theo huff before he sipped his drink. She glanced at him briefly before he glimpsed who she regarded. He had to clasp his hand over his mouth to stop himself from spitting his drink all over the table. "So you know him?" Theo didn't answer and Lena didn't glance his way. She swore his reaction became guarded. He swallowed and took a deep breath.

"I'm sure it's just a coincidence. Maybe you should ask him if he recognizes you," he replied with a painful smile.

Lena stared at him before she answered. "Grandma used to say there's no such thing as a coincidence."

Theo shrugged. "He seems harmless. Hope you haven't been waiting long. I had some issues at the office." Theo took another sip.

"Don't they all seem harmless?" Lena sighed, "Should we invite him to dine with us," Lena asked as she glared at Theo. She swore he turned puce. Did Black people turn puce? Still, he said nothing. "I'm going to take the fact that we're not running for the hills that he is harmless. Don't think I'll forget," she stated as she continued to watch the man outside. Finally turning to Theo with her mouth twisted, her eyes wide and brows raised, Lena said, "I ordered our usual to start figuring we could order the main course when you arrived. Is there anything you wanna say? I'm all ears," she stated turning back to watch the stranger.

"Not as long as you keep looking out of the window."

Lena blew air out of her mouth and turned to Theo. "Whatever, if he wasn't so alluring, I'd be creeped out."

"So only ugly people are stalkers?"

"Yep, all the big ones, ugly and you know," she replied rubbing her finger over the inside of her hand. "Never seen one that looks as good as him."

"I wish I was getting half the attention you're paying to your beguiling stalker."

Lena snickered. "Sorry, I'm all yours." The waiter brought their appetizers. "So what's up? It's been a while since I've seen you."

"Oh, now you care. You've been ghosting me for over a week."

"You know I have a deadline coming up and I'm stuck."

"Is that why you're in a mood?" He paused to watch her reaction before signing. "I miss my bestie. Anyway, I'm good. Work is the same and so is my social life."

"Yes. So, your social life, what about it? Who are you dating and how long has it been?"

Theo didn't say a word. His eyes caste down at his hands before taking another sip. Then he said, "It's fine. Nothing major happening. What about yours? Still hanging with Angelo?"

"Eh, a bit here and there. No strings. I'm trying to distance myself anyway."

"Alright Lena."

"Theo, are you going to that club anytime soon? I so want to join you?"

"What club?"

"You know where my guy showed up. What's it called again?" Lena paused and pushed out her lips, pretending she didn't know the name.

"You playin' me right now, right?"

"Yep, Zoe's. I wanna go with you and the girls. When are you going?"

"I'm not sure." Theo was quiet for a moment before he turned to look out the window. "It seems like your friend is gone." His shoulders relaxed as he picked up his drink. Theo took a long sip before spraying it over the table and window.

"Theo, what the hell?" Lena pushed back her chair a little before she turned to regard what Theo was looking at, but she saw no one. "Are you okay?"

"I'm good. Are you ready to go?"

"What? No dish. Tell me what made you so gross. You have more manners than the queen. What happened?"

"I want Korean BBQ."

"Since when? Every time I ask you, you say you don't like spicy food."

"Let's try now." Theo waved to get the waiter's attention to get the check.

"The best place is across town. I'm hungry now."

"I'll make it up to you. Besides, you ate your appetizers," he said pointing to her plate. "You're good for the ride."

"You took too long and I was hungry. But seriously?" Lena stared at Theo, who sulked like he had swallowed something nasty. She observed as he put on a smile and gestured for the waitstaff to bring the check. Then she scrutinized him as he paled and the smile vanished. Lena finally turned to see what happened. She watched as a tall brown skin man in a black suit walked toward the table with the check in hand. His shoulder length brown curls bounced as he walked. She was sure he wasn't their waiter, she would have noticed.

"Good Evening, nice to see you again, Theo." Lena beamed up at him.

"Hey, I wasn't expecting you to be here," Theo responded nonchalantly.

The man shrugged his shoulders. "Leaving so soon?"

"I changed my mind."

Theo had totally ignored Lena. She couldn't believe that he would not introduce her. The guy wasn't only handsome, but his baritone voice vibrated through her. "Hi," Lena said smiling up at him once again.

He smiled and replied hello, but didn't say anything else. She couldn't help but think that was odd. Most men at least smile and stare as they try to think of something to say.

As Theo got up after paying, so did Lena. She followed him to the door which was held open by the same guy who brought them their check. They walked some distance before she said anything. "Was that weird? He only said hello. Didn't ask me my name or anything. And you didn't introduce me. Theo, he was just my type."

"He was probably too tongue-tied to say anything."

"Please, looking like that."

"Lena."

"Theo, you could have said, 'hey whatever his name was, this is my girl, Lena. Would that have been so hard? Trust, I would have been charming. I wouldn't have embarrassed you."

"Lena, leave him alone. Avoid Sanju, avoid."

Lena sucked her teeth and glared at Theo sideways. "You lucky we been friends for so long, I swear," Lena muttered. He just used her line from her favorite movie, she thought. She didn't believe that a guy who twinkled like that was bad enough for him to use that line. If it were her she would have introduced him. So rude, she thought.

"I'm going home. You've ruin my mood." Theo just gaped at her as she kept walking toward seventieth street. Theo walked by her side, but they didn't speak.

"I have to go back to work anyway," he replied before she got off at her stop on the train and headed to her favorite pizzeria. Nothing like a warm slice straight out of the oven.

It wasn't a long walk from the train station. Lena admired what little of the sunset she could see among the towering buildings all around. "Hi, how are you?"

"I'm good. Didn't think you'd drop by today."

Lena shrugged. "I just need some comfort food."

"You want your regular slice or sandwich?"

"Good question. Sandwich, let me get the eggplant parm, but I'm gonna take it home."

"I could have had Angelo deliver it," he said with a wink. Lena only gave a slight smile as he finished ringing her order up and looked at the slip on the counter. "In fact, I have an order going to your building in a half hour. So no need to wait. I make it special just the way you like it."

"You're the best. What I owe you?"

"Anything for the girl who put our shop back on the map. Ten even and I'll throw in your favorite drink."

"Thanks, see you Saturday."

"Any time, beautiful." Lena turned back again to wave before she made a beeline for her apartment. It wasn't far, just a few blocks. Perfect for admiring the strange daffodils on her street. She could have waited for her order. Perhaps, Angelo had mentioned something to him and wanted to hang out.

Lena took a deep breath as she walked the final hundred feet to her doorstep. She wished she had someone to come home to. It was cool to hook up with Angelo, but there wasn't anything worthwhile there. Just the perfect buddy.

As she walked in the door of her apartment her phone rang. "Hello....Hey mom, how are you?..... I'm fine. Totally on for Saturday. I can't wait.....Yes, I reached out to my sisters, no response. Guess no one wants to hang out with their baby sister.....I know.....No, I'm not dating anyone...I wouldn't call that dating." Just then the doorbell rang. "By mom, my order's here."

She hung up the receiver and answered her door. "Hey, Angelo. Has it been thirty minutes already?"

"Give or take. Can I come in?"

"You got time? No other orders?"

"I delivered it and now I'm on my lunch break. Besides, pops knows we're I am."

"It's six o'clock in the evening."

"It's fine. So we can't just chill?"

"You said, please keep that in mind. Come in."

It was late afternoon when a tall tanned gentleman approached the guy Lena had been watching through the restaurant window. "Did you have to stand right in front of the restaurant? You should've been a bit more conspicuous."

"Well, Ren, being this close let's me hear what she's saying. She wants to give me something to put in my mouth besides my cigarette. Not sure you have a chance after that confession."

"Kyoshi, we've spoken about this. Still, you won't have to baby sit her much longer. Not as often anyway."

"You're sure she knows nothing? She doesn't know about her mates or you? Nothing?

"No, her mom didn't tell her anything. Make sure to check her building before she gets home. If Theo see's me he probably won't stay so she'll get something from the pizzeria and spend time with the owner's son. Make sure she's safe."

"That needs to end. So below her."

"You mean beneath?"

"No, below. I'm sure he's been beneath her a few times," he stated staring straight at Ren. It wasn't long before he started to shake from laughing. "I can't believe you fell straight into that one," He heckled in between breaths.

"Why am I having this conversation with you? Just make sure she's safe. I'll leave here and check the hospital." Ren watched his lieutenant walk off before he started to smile. Kyoshi's jokes were bad but it was one of the only times Ren witnessed him smile. He turned to walk around the corner and into the restaurant. It was his usual check-in. He had never seen Lena when he arrived at the restaurant. He knew Theo's sentiment towards him and wondered if he would be rude.

He walked through the doors of the restaurant. "Mr. Arias glad to see you," he was greeted by one of the staff. Ren nodded and smiled. He walked into these doors more often now. He wanted to make sure that things were running smoothly in spite of the constant threat. As he passed by she stepped closer and whispered, "she's here sir." He didn't need anyone to tell him that, but he smiled and nodded as he headed to the back of the restaurant. A server stepped to the side and slightly bowed. He had told them a dozen times that wasn't necessary.

"Mr. Arias, sir. She's."

Ren didn't allow him to finish at all. "I know, thank you." He snatched the check presenter and walked toward the farthest back table. He knew that he made it clear that she was off limits to every vampire but they didn't need to remind him and watch her so closely. He damped down the frustration as he approached the table.

He greeted Theo and to Ren's surprise, Theo was polite to a fault. Still, he didn't introduce Lena to him. As she smiled up at him and said hello, he was dazzled. He had never been this close to her. She was beautiful. It was as if the distance between them and the glass that he often looked through had skewed her beauty. He was so dazzled that he barely responded. All he managed was a brief hello and a smile in return.

He couldn't help but think that she was so close. It was no longer just a dream or an endeavor. She was close to his world and him. She breached the distance with every meeting. His eyes followed her as she walked with Theo down the sidewalk. Ren knew that Theo was shaken by him showing up when he was with Lena. He would eventually have a talk with Theo. Lena could not be kept from him. Ren blinked, gathering himself. He had work to do. He turned from the door and walked around the restaurant greeting the customers as was customary when he frequented his restaurant, Ariana. He had named it after his first wife. Now hundreds of years later he would have another. His only love. After greeting his guest Ren went to check the small kitchen in the back.

When he finally walked out of Ariana's doors he headed downtown. He had one more stop. He would head to the hospital. He had no doubt that his business partner would go in without him. He was already aware of what to expect without going inside. The numbers were increasing. He didn't know how much longer he'd wait for her. As it was, she would enter his life at a perilous time.

Ren pulled up the collar of his jacket as the people passing stared. It was a windy April night. Even the flowers he was sure that Lena noticed, bobbed and swayed in the breeze. Still, it didn't make a difference to him, but he didn't want to draw more unwanted attention. Ren was over six feet tall and muscular. His large curls whipped around his long angular face as he walked. Finally, he decided to wait across the street. This side of town had no flowers and very few trees remained. A true concrete jungle.

He had been business partners with Marcellus, Cell for short, since his arrival in New York. It helped that they had grown up together. Who would have thought that they would be vampires together as well? "So, how many do we have tonight," Ren asked when he saw the glint of the chain Cell wore on his jeans. He stepped from the doorway and folded his arms across his broad chest.

Ren saw Cell look up before making a beeline toward him. "More than I wish to say. It's become worse. We need to find these vampires. They will ruin everything."

"I'm aware, but how do we track them? They are excellent at hiding. I went to Queen's Hospital. Renee seems to have her hands full as well."

"We should use our soldiers."

"That would lead to disaster. We've already cut the training time in half. The soldiers could create more of a problem than solve it."

"Where is she?"

"She should be at home. She hasn't been out much lately."

"Ren, why don't you go to her? You've been tracking her for years. Just create a situation to meet. You say she still wears that necklace you gave her."

"She doesn't remember who gave her the necklace. I took care of that memory the day we met. I didn't want her trying to find me before I had fulfilled her mother's wishes."

"How long before you'll meet her?"

"She comes closer every day. I just saw her at the restaurant. Make sure everyone knows Lena is mine."

"You got it."

Chapter 2

Lena woke up disoriented. She squeezed her eyes shut against the morning sun which was streaming into her living room. "What am I doing in the living room," she asked herself out loud. She opened her eyes, sat up, and pulled the afghan off of her. Damn, she thought. She fell asleep while Angelo was there, again. He must have let himself out sometime after the first movie. She had to admit he wasn't alluring. His father owned the pizzeria she frequented and he was cute. But that's it. She sighed and stretched. He was sweet though. He had made sure she was comfortable. He even spread her blanket over her. Lena put her feet on the floor and ran her hands over her face. Then she noticed the note.

"Guess you're tired. Maybe we can go out next time," signed Angelo.

Like she said, he's sweet. But not her dream guy. She wanted more. Before she got up from the couch, the phone rang. She grabbed the receiver from the square table next to the couch.

"Hello....Hi mom...Mom, I just got up...No I haven't gotten a chance today...Mom, I'm the youngest, they should call to check up on me....Yes, we're still on for brunch on Saturday. Can we try a new place?...Yes, I have one in mind...Okay, love you too...By mom."

Lena got up to look for her phone book. If she didn't call now, she wouldn't. She probably should have memorized her sisters' numbers but it wasn't like she called often. And Amen forbid they call her. She always thought the older siblings should take care of the baby.

The phone just rang and rang. She hated leaving messages, they sounded so lame. Hey Yazzy/Yo-yo, this is your sister again. I'm checking in with you. How are you? You should call your sister at some point. Then she hung up and put the phone on the stand. Lena wondered if her mom thought that they would be close if she gave them all names that started with Y. Yolanda aka Yo-yo, Yazmine aka Yazzy, and her's Yalena. Her nickname was Lena and she was glad. What other nickname could she make? She shook at the thought.

She should show her mom her phone log of all the times she called and received no answer. Yo-yo was one thing, she's not even in the country. But Yazzy lived less than 3 miles from her. For heaven's sake, they both lived in the city. Lena rolled her eyes and plopped down in the chair at her desk.

"Okay, Lena, focus," she whispered before staring at the screen. It would have been cool if staring at a blank screen would make the words flow from her brain to the computer. She sat for an hour and nothing came. So she got up and decided to clean up from last night and get something to eat. Surely a shower. It sounded good to her. Then maybe, just maybe the words would come.

It hadn't taken more than a couple of hours to clean up her small apartment, get something to eat, and shower. Then she sat for another few hours staring at the screen and reading what she had already written. It was good, but the ending was vague. She got up and sat in the window seat and stared at the passers by. Perchance creating stories for strangers would help.

"Sweet." Lena's eyes glittered, looking in the full-length mirror as she twirled. "Why have I been hiding all this?" She had been dying to wear this outfit. The dress fit better than when she tried it for the first time. Looking in the mirror she couldn't help but admire how she glittered in her fitted black dress. She loved that it showed off her shapely caramel legs while the outfit concealed and teased from the back. It was short and sleeveless, with three triangle cutouts on each side. She loved how the dress accentuated her curves. Lena gathered her hair in a messy bun before she accessorized it with red bangles and chandelier earrings along with her red strap around the ankle stilettos. She was sexy.

How much longer would she have to endure this place? Lena blew out a breath, as she stared at the pages strewn across her writing desk in the far corner of her room. Her book should have gone to her editor. This was the final step before the novel went to print, but Lena didn't like the ending and tried to change it, yet nothing seemed to work. She had given up writing after her third try and decided to go to Zoe's. She needed a break. Certainly dancing would break up whatever was blocking her creativity. She tried calling her sisters earlier that day, but neither Yolanda nor Yazmine had answered their phones. She pondered if she had been calling too often. Was she being the nagging little sister? She finally decided to unwind at this club she overheard was all the rage. Her friends bragged about the club for months. They said that all the cutest guys and girls went to this club. It didn't matter if you were gay or straight; this was the place to be.

When her friends called and told her that her favorite actor and DJ had made a guest appearance, she knew she had to go. Why had it taken her this long? She thought about going before, but Theo always discouraged her. Even when they were all together, he'd direct them somewhere else. She was determined to go tonight. Thursday night was Caribbean night, and they played all the latest reggae, soca, and calypso. That was her kind of music; her parents were from Los Barbados, after all.

While she thought she was hot, she went next door to check with her bestie. So she grabbed her crocheted bolero and headed out the door. Lena was just about to knock when the door opened.

"Hey, Theo."

"Hey, yourself. Aren't you hot?" Theo's blue eyes looked her up and down; Lena just smiled.

"Just checking to make sure I'm totally sizzling. Going to Zoe's."

"Ooh, Zoe's. They're not so hot anymore. There is another club we can go to. So glad I caught you. You would be bored, trust and believe." At first, she hadn't realized that Theo was dressed to party. She stood back and regarded him; his black pants fit perfectly, and a thin silk sweater lay snug over his muscled chest. He had slicked and pulled back his brown mass of curls into a short ponytail at the nape of his neck. "Let's go, girl. The party is about to be blazing."

"Don't you have to go to the office in the morning?"

"Hmmm," Theo cocked his head to the side and curled his lips, "like that's gonna stop me." They walked down the stairs and out the front door. As soon as they stepped outside, a tall man waved at them.

"Theo, you called a cab?"

"You thought I was going to walk? I'm saving my energy."
Theo stopped at the end of the steps as he stared at a tall gentleman
with straight black hair who stepped out of the car. The man
walked a few steps and opened the back door.

"Hello Theo, Cell thought you might want a ride tonight."
Theo's eyes widened as he stiffened.

"Now you're sent a private car." Lena laughed and rolled her
eyes as she skipped down the steps. Truth be told, she was glad she
wasn't walking. Her feet would be sore enough from the dancing.
The driver took her hand as she climbed into the car and she
thanked him. The driver seemed so familiar. But she couldn't make
out the figure in the dim light of the street lamps. She needed to
report that so it could be fixed, she thought. Once Theo got into the
car there was a tense silence. Lena wondered what was wrong with
him. She called his name but he didn't respond so she watched the
streets and people they passed. They even got out of the car in
anxious silence.

The club must have been packed because the line outside went
down West fourth and down to Seventh Avenue then doubled back.
The music inside was blasting. They didn't get in line. Theo
walked right up to the huge steel doors. What luck she thought
when they were waved inside. She was glad she had stopped by his
apartment.

"I thought we were going to another club."

"Well, they sent a car, so here we are. That is what happens when you're a regular," Theo said as they stepped from the entrance hall into the club. Then he stopped. "Now, Ms. Lena, you are not allowed here by yourself."

"You must have inhaled a hallucinogen," Lena murmured. She didn't know what was wrong with Theo, but this place was so her, she thought. The dance hall music beckoned her as she walked down the long hall to the security area. Finally, she thought as they two stepped through the curtains. She stopped with Theo but looked up and all around, enchanted by the atmosphere. The place had white walls, black furniture, and sheer curtains that divided the small sitting rooms from the dance level.

"Is that a bed? What do they do inside? I mean, what are they doing?"

"Never you mind. You are not ready for all that right now. And did you hear what I said?" Theo grabbed her and turned her towards him to make sure she stood and listened to him. "Lena, did you hear me? You are not allowed in here without me."

"Why? This place is me. And who is that?" As she spoke, her gaze surveyed the club and stopped at the DJ booth that hung over the crowd. She peered into the booth, and there he was, tall, tanned, and hot. And if she didn't know any better, she would swear that his watchful gaze guarded her.

"And, do not think of making him your next boy toy. He is not for you."

"What, he's totally a beefcake, and I think he's watching me. But, I need more than a toy, and he may be a good candidate."

"Of course, he's watching; you are fresh meat and a hot tamale. And no, you don't need to date or marry him."

"Marry? I just want to appreciate him." Lena grinned, still regarding the DJ booth.

Theo scoffed. "You're not even listening." Theo threw his hands up in the air. "Lena, let's dance," he said, as he grabbed her hand.

She followed Theo to the dance floor but didn't take her eyes off the booth. The man stared at the crowd before turning to talk to someone in the room with him. Then he disappeared.

Theo and Lena danced for what seemed like hours. There was no way she'd sit down with the DJ playing jam after jam. Then the same man who picked them up came to retrieve Theo, leaving her dancing. She continued to dance for a song or two. Until it seemed like all the women that surrounded her were asked to dance but her. She wondered if she was making more of it than she should. Undoubtedly, the men were intimidated. Or they figured she was too much upkeep. The girls didn't ask her to dance either. She sighed; she just wanted to dance.Eventually, she decided to sit down after the fourth girl was taken to dance and a curtained room.

She sat at the bar and ordered a pineapple cosmopolitan. She sized it up and decided she liked Zoe's. It was a cool place. A great place to bring her girls.

Funny, she thought, she had never been to a club with white walls. As she inspected the club see noticed there was little light. The only lights she saw were in the far corners of the club. Strange, but it is a club, she thought. The lighting should be dark. Instead, it all glittered from the disco ball that hung in the center of the room. What little light the lamps gave off was amplified by the ball.

She glanced at her watch; Theo had been gone for almost an hour. The music was a nice mix, and so was the environment. The rooms are definitely weird. It looked like people were making out behind the sheer curtains. Not exactly where she would kiss a guy and have him rub up on her, but to each his own. Still, impressive. Guy-girl couples danced and a guy on guy and girl on girl. She liked a place where people needed no facades. Lena despised pretense. One reason, among others, many men weren't in and out of her life. She kept things real and didn't want to deal with a lot of bull.

Sitting there with no one to talk to was as lonely as if she had stayed at home. She thought going with Theo would have been the perfect time to catch up with her best friend. "Just delightful," she mumbled to herself.

Chapter 3

Lena decided to pay for her drink and order another, but the bartender wouldn't let her. He said that her money wasn't any good here, and she could have anything she wanted. Odd but cool, she thought. She's had men buy her drinks. Usually, the bartender says, 'these drinks are from him.' She wondered who was treating her so well. She ordered the same cocktail and decided to sit at a table near the dance floor. She wanted to be in plain sight when Theo decided to grace her with his presence again.

"I hope you're enjoying the drinks," a large shadow passed in front of her. She couldn't see his face. He was all dark angles. Lena was about to thank him and say that she wasn't interested when he bowed. "Sorry for disturbing you," he growled and choked as he bent over and walked away. That was odd, she thought, but when she glanced up again it was him, the guy from the booth.

He floated over to her table. Not literally, but his movement appeared so fluid, the man appeared to be afloat, still there he was.

Lena gazed at him as he walked through the crowd. He radiated confidence as he took long, sure strides toward her. He wore black slacks and a creme long-sleeved collared shirt. Two shirt buttons were opened, and his sleeves were rolled up to the middle of his forearm. That's when she realized. He was the guy from the restaurant. He wasn't their waiter but brought them their check. Lena wondered if he frequented the club.

As he walked through the crowd women stared after him. A couple of women grabbed his arm to get his attention. One woman stood in front of him and whispered in his ear. He smiled. He whispered something quickly before walking around her. He was tall, several inches over six feet tall, handsome and muscular, but not too much muscle. His big brown curls cascaded around his angular oval face. His eyes were dark, and his lips full.

"Hello, beautiful lady. It's nice to see you again. I am Lorenzo Arias. You can call me Ren."

"Hi," Lena replied smiling. "I am Yalena; you can call me Lena." Funny to meet him here, Lena thought, Just then, her favorite song came on, and she danced in her seat.

"Would you like to dance, Lena?"   Lena nodded and smiled. She got her wish to meet this gorgeous man. She wondered if he was the one who paid for her drinks.

"Is this your first time here?"

"Yes, I came with Theo."

"Theo? He may not be too happy with us dancing."

"Certainly. How do you know Theo," Lena asked

"Theo is a regular here and I make it a point to get to know all our regulars."

"Our regulars? You're one of the owners of Zoe's?"

"Yes, I am partners with my friend Cell. He's our main DJ."

"Oh, wow. Love the mixes. Some are hypnotic."

"Yes, some are." The music continued to play as they danced.

At times Lena would step back a little to look at Ren. She wanted to burn his image on her retinas. If she never saw him again, she would be happy. Lena gave a soft snort as she laughed at herself in her head. Who was she kidding? She wanted him. If she had a type, he was definitely her type. She raised her gaze from his smooth, mocha chest and glanced up. Their eyes locked, and they smiled at each other. His gaze sent shivers down her spine. She swore that he imbibed her.

Then the music changed again. This time it sounded like a horn section playing. She looked toward the band on stage. Ren circled her as the horns played. Then he held one hand and took two more steps. She knew that song. She loved that song. Her hips moved to the rhythm and dropped to the beat. This was her jam, but if you couldn't dance, this was the tell. A man had to be able to dance.

Ren started to move with her, a two-step. She couldn't help but wonder about him. Then he spun her around bringing her to stand in front of him. They shifted together. Ren started to move them around the dance floor and people moved to the side to watch them. Lena was excited. She hoped to soar as she glided with him. As the beat ran through her she was sure it ran through him. His gaze was intense. Then he placed a hand on her back and guided her to spin under his arm picking her up to whorl together. Yes, Lena thought this was it. People didn't really dance like this anymore. Especially not at most clubs. How old was this guy?

He drew her closer with the right hand that was placed on her lower back as they glided around the dance floor together. Her dad had taught her to dance like this, but she never thought a guy Ren's age would move this way. They spun again and he twirled her. Their torsos pressed together and rotated before the music paused. His dip was right on time. They held it. When the music started again, Ren brought her up and they were kind of face to face. He was several inches taller than her so perhaps eyes to chin. She breathed hard and smiled as they stood there before she stepped over each foot and twisted from side to side. Lena took a step and turned right in front of him. Everyone clapped, but she ignored them as they started the two-step and quick turns all over again. He was it. She knew her dream guy had to be able to glide with her.

"You're a pretty good dancer. You should come on Latin night. I think you'd like the music."

"Maybe." She was still breathing heavily, but he wasn't out of breath at all. The music slowed, and people walked back on the dance floor. Ren drew her close to him. His scent was intoxicating. Lena put her arms around his neck and he pulled her closer. "If I didn't know any better, I would think you just wanted to dance with me again."

"You would be right in that assumption," he whispered in her ear. "That would be tomorrow, by the way."

"Possibly...." When the song ended, he took her hand to lead her back to the table.

"Would you like something to eat? We have some delicious seafood dishes. You look like a lady that would enjoy crab cakes or coconut shrimp. My treat."

"Okay, I'll let you buy me something to eat. You choose; you would know what's good. But don't expect anything in return."

"I won't take that last statement personally. You must have met some trifling men. I am a gentleman and am not looking to take advantage of a beautiful lady. I will have your order sent as soon as it is ready. And I will see you tomorrow," he replied as he raised her hand and gently brushed his lips against her soft skin.

"Tomorrow, Ren." As Ren was leaving, Theo was walking toward her out of the crowd on the dance floor. Both Ren and Theo appeared to have paused, Theo side eyeing Ren. Lena wondered what that was all about. First, he didn't want her to even consider him. Now he was staring daggers at Ren before he disappeared into the crowd.

Lena eyed Theo as he approached her. She didn't remember ever seeing his beautiful mahogany skin so pale. She wondered what had happened. "Theo, what was that about?"

"Nothing, you need to stay away from him."

"Why? He seems nice enough. Besides, it seems like you hung out with him. He can't be that bad."

"He's not bad, probably the nicer of the two owners. But he's not what he seems."

"What? Anyway, where were you? For someone who didn't want me to meet him, you didn't stay to keep me from him."

"I had to go visit Cell. He works here."

"Oh, the DJ? How do you know these people?"

"Yes." Theo faltered. "I'm Ren and Cell's accountant. They are the ones who invited me down here." Theo hesitated before he mumbled.

"What?"

"Nothing." Before he said anymore, the food arrived. Ren must have known that Theo would be hungry because he sent two plates instead of one. They ate and didn't stay much longer. Theo was in quite a hurry to leave the club. He complained that he was tired and ready to go, and he refused to let her stay without him. So they took a cab back to the apartment building.

Early the next morning, as Lena sat in bed, she couldn't help but think she had met Ren before. Maybe she had seen him before the restaurant; she wasn't sure. But, of course, if she had seen him, wouldn't she have remembered? She didn't understand why she was so drawn to him.She did attend Latin night. Nothing was different. She and Theo walked to the front of the line, and, of course, the spot was packed. She didn't have to pay for anything. Lena glared as the women tried to attract Ren's attention. She danced for a while to salsa and meringue with Ren, while Theo spent time with Cell. When Theo came back, Ren disappeared, but not without the two of them eyeing each other. Then the food was placed in front of them. Seafood paella this time. After eating, they went home. Again, Theo was in a hurry to leave.

Each time Lena went, Ren would spend more time with her than before. She always enjoyed her time with him. It wasn't all night, but he would stay a couple of hours with her. She did learn that he was from Argentina, and his parents died many years ago. He owned a building on Park Avenue and lived on one of the top floors. It seemed like the club was his life, and all the people who worked there knew him for years before.

Another Saturday afternoon, Lena thought. She wished the day was really just another day. She was coming closer to her deadline and had only half completed the section she wanted to change. Lena huffed right before hearing the door slam in the hallway. It had to be Theo, she thought. She was about to open the door but heard Theo's voice and decided to listen to a bit before doing so.

"Come on, Marc."

Marc sighed. "Theo, why are we here? I thought you were not interested. That you have someone.""Not for me. My friend Lena. The one I have been trying to get you to meet for months now."

Lean crossed her arms and leaned against the door. Theo had someone, she thought. He never told her. She missed the rest of what they said before the knock. She thought she'd better give them a few seconds, or they would know she was listening. Then she heard Theo's voice. "Lena, darling. I know you're home."

Lena came to the door in a crochet romper, her hair, in a curly, messy bun. "Yes, Theo," she said opening the door. But before Theo could introduce him, Marc moved Theo aside and took Lena's hand, planted a kiss."Hello, beautiful Lena. I am Marc. I'm honored to meet you."

Lena snatched back her hand as she surveyed Marc. "Theo, why are you bringing different men to my apartment?"

"I thought you wanted to meet a nice guy. You and Marc can hang out and keep each other company. He has a life and dreams.

He's the best at his firm." Lena stared at her friend. She couldn't believe this.

"Theo, when I asked you to hook me up with one of your guy friends, you hem and hawed. Now each day before we go to the club you bring a guy to meet me. He's the fifth guy. Please stop."

"I'll stop when you meet a nice guy." Lena huffed and slammed the door in their faces. Theo was fuckin' unbelievable, she yelled and then mumbled. What was so wrong with Ren that he was blocking, she wondered as she returned to her desk. If he hadn't been her ride or die since high school she would truly tell him where to go. Lena groaned as she tried to refocus and write.

For weeks, going to Zoe's to visit Ren was the highlight of her week. She enjoyed seeing him and being held in his arms. Tonight was no different. She dressed to entice. She wore a sleeveless black knitted off the shoulder top and black capri pants, and black kitten heel pumps. Her hair was swept up into a bun to show her long graceful neck and accentuated with gold hoop earrings. Classic and sexy was her goal. Her reward when she walked through security was the immediate attention of Ren. As soon as she and Theo walked through the curtain, Ren walked towards them. Theo gave her an evil look and pushed through the crowd. He didn't want her there and begrudgingly came with her every time.

"Glad you decided to attend," Ren murmured into her ear as he gave her a one-armed hug.

"I'm glad to be here." Lena beamed, sensing the slight pressure of Ren's arm around her waist. He guided her to a table by the bar.

"How are you? Did you finish your book?"

"I'm well and no. My editor and agent are pissed, but I got an extension because the publisher agreed with me." Ren pulled out her seat at the table between the bar and the dance floor. Once the two were seated, Lena gazed at Ren as his eyes swept the club.

As much as Lena loved to sit close to the action, the loud music was way too loud for an in-depth discussion. She had hoped that they would sit in the love seats on the other side, behind the curtain. But when she thought of it, the sofa was cozier then she wanted to be with Ren at the moment.

They sat for a moment before a wait staff brought their drinks to the table. "I thought you'd like this." Lena nodded and smiled. Then someone came up to Ren and whispered in his ear. He nodded. "Lena, I'll be back shortly."

Lena sat and regarded the people dance for longer than she wanted to. She would rather dance with Theo than be by herself again. She sighed before taking a sip; it was good. It wasn't a pineapple cosmo but something with pineapple. She scanned the floor a bit longer and thought she saw a man lick and kiss a woman's neck, but before she saw anything else, Ren was standing in front of her. He drew the chair closer.

"What do you think of the club?" Ren asked as he sat next to Lena. "I assumed you enjoyed it because you kept coming back." Ren smiled.

Lena chuckled. "I'm not much of a club-goer, but I do like it. The atmosphere and energy here are inviting. Although, had it not been for the present company," Lena said, looking at Ren. "I doubt I would have returned so soon."

Ren smiled as he took her hand, turned it over, and kissed her palm. "I am grateful for your beautiful company." Lena's eyebrows rose. She had never had a man press his lips to the inside of her palm and wasn't sure what it meant, but she could guess. The way she felt at the moment, she wanted to get cozy with him. Sitting on a loveseat, perhaps, would be nice.   "Shall we dance?" Ren asked as he stood, holding her hand. So he wanted to nestle her as well, she thought.

"Maybe a little while." Lena gleamed, rising from her seat. Lena cherished the time that she spent with Ren. But she wanted more. They had a good time, they reveled in each other's company. Still, the club wasn't the best place to learn about someone. She wanted to get to know Ren. He seemed so mysterious, and that drew her to him. It appeared he finally got the hint because he asked her to go out on a date with him.

Finally! She thought.

Chapter 4

It was quiet. Only a few staff members organized the club. The floors and the sitting area needed to be cleaned. Bar glasses washed. Unlike other times, Ren stood by the bar, directing Cell on what needed to be observed continuously. He wanted the entire set up done before he left to wine and dine, Lena.

As Ren regarded his busy staff, he couldn't help but think that he had to win Lena's heart before telling her his true identity. He was nervous. How weird was that? Why was he worried? He was a vampire. Could vampires be neurotic? He could make her love him if he wanted to. Why should he be apprehensive? Yet, he desired to win her affection. For some strange reason, she enticed him. No other woman, or feeder, had ever stirred such emotions or such arousal in him.

"Ren, man, do you really think that this is such a good idea? How do you know that she is of the first bloodline? She could just be another feeder. It seems as though she'd be more than willing to provide you with her blood's sustenance."

"Cell, you seem to be resistant to my choice of mate. You know that our mate has a celestial connection to us. Besides, do we not all start as feeders? And is that what Theo is to you and Marcia? Is he just food?"

"I have nothing against Yalena. But, I'm starting to think that the concept of a mate is just a lot of bull. I've been searching for over three centuries and have yet to find her. Marcia is just a someone to pass the time. She's a good buddy. And no, he's not just food. You know, Marcia and I only feed from a few people. It's hard to explain. We're attached to him, but it's hard to say if it's his love or his blood. We relish the flavor of him. And unlike our other three feeders, he doesn't seem to want to be one of us. He just wants to be with us as long as he can. But Yalena will want it all. Can you not perceive this in her eyes? She wants you, and only you."

Ren didn't remind Cell of how long he had waited for a mate. "Yes, I'm aware. That's how it should be. That is how I want it to be. I just hope that Lena will still want me when I tell her what I am." He paused for a moment. Lost in thoughts of watching her over the last decade and then finally, holding her as they moved across the same floor he was now walking across. "I long for her. It doesn't even matter if she's the first line or not. You make sure everyone is aware that she's under my protection, off the menu. She will be mine."

"We need her to be the first line. Things are getting rough around here."

"You let me agonize over that." Ren walked into the cellar to get drinks for the bar when they heard banging on the door.

"I'll get it, Ren." Cell was not expecting to receive Theo so early. "Theo?"

"Is Ren here? I must speak with him."

"He is." Cell sighed. "What no hi Cell, how are you?" Theo was about to speak but Cell held up his hand.

"What do you want with Ren?"

"I must speak with him."

"But you won't tell me what about? Should I be jealous?" Theo said no more as Cell walked toward the cellar to call for Ren. "Ren, Theo is here for you." Ren came up the steps with the liquor box in one hand and a glass of red liquid in the other.

"Hey man, you're going to see her tonight. Why are you drinking the reserve? You're starting to torment me, Ren. You haven't fed since she started coming to the club."

"And I am not feeding on her tonight either. It's not yet time." Ren placed the box on the bar and turned toward Theo before leaning on it. "What do you want, Thelonious?" Ren asked as he casually sipped the contents of the glass.

Theo kept his distance but faced Ren. "How many times have I said, don't call me that? No one calls me that."

"Is Thelonious not your name? Like the magnificent jazz musician?"

"I like to be called Theo."

Ren smiled. He enjoyed needling Theo, especially since Theo had a problem with him dating Lena. "He was a good friend. You should be proud to carry his name."

Theo rolled his eyes. "I don't want you to see her. Don't make her part of this."

"Don't worry, Lena will be well taken care of. She will be my queen."

"No," Theo blurted before he caught himself; he took a step back and quickly averted his gaze.

Ren had set the glass on the counter and taken a step forward. Theo lowered his voice. Ren noticed Theo take a breath and swallowed before he continued.

"She's an innocent, Ren. She doesn't belong in your dark world."

"Does your world not have its own darkness?" Of course, it does, Ren thought. There can never be light without the dark. "I believe that it's up to her. Is it not?" Then it dawned on him. "Isn't this a conversation you should be having with Yalena?" Ren dreaded the thought of Lena pulling away from him. Would Theo try to stand in his way?

"She's ignoring me. She won't listen to reason, and it's not like I can explain why I am warning her."

Under his calm exterior, Ren was secretly glad that Theo hadn't managed to dissuade Lena. "You seem perfectly happy with this world."

"I am happy. My love is here, but it's so restricted; it ends when the party ends."

"She will not have to deal with the club if she does not desire to do so. I will not take her away from the life she lives now unless she desires me to."

"Yeah, right. You know Lena will sink right in. So I'm begging you, please leave her be."

Ren scoffed before he stepped closer. He brought his face close to Theo's as he spoke. "And if I do not, Thelonious? Will you tell her tales of Zoe's and make her afraid of me and the life I live?" Ren remained close for a few seconds as he glared at Theo. Theo lowered his eyes. Then Ren walked back to the bar and picked up his drink. He couldn't help but think he had softened over the years of dealing with humans. He had never honestly had the cruelty of most vampires, but this was tiring. He should make Theo tell Lena beautiful things about him so she will give in to his every whim. Ren sighed. That he wouldn't do.

"So, what's your decision, Theo? I'm growing impatient. Will you keep the real club a secret? Tell me that you won't tell her before I am ready."

"It's up to her, I guess."

"Good boy," Ren replied. "You should go to Cell's room, I'm sure Marcia would love to see you."

"Tell her I will see her tonight. I have to get back to work."

"I will. Don't worry, Lena will be happy with me."

"Of course, she will." Theo gave a faint smile, hung his head, and headed back into the sunlight.

Ren downed what was left of his drink. "Cell, I am going to Lena."

"Ren, so soon?"

"I promised her the day. This is our first actual date. I'm sure I'll be back before it starts. Find me a sweet one and keep her. I will need to feed when I return. And don't taste her or let anyone else feed from her."

"Yes, your majesty." They both looked at each other and laughed. "I'll see you later tonight." With that, Ren put on his sunglasses, walked through the steel doors, and out into the sun. It was a beautiful day to be with his mate. He was promised that she would be his.

Every so often, when Ren walked in the sunlight, he had to chuckle. He remembered how many times he had seen movies where the vampire cowered and burned to death in the sun. If people only knew, it wasn't that easy to kill them. Ren couldn't help but smile. As woman thought he was smiling at her and said hello. Ren past her a card for Zoe's without a word and kept walking. She would be a welcomed treat for one of his clients., Ren thought. If humans were aware of how close they lived to vampires, they would be terrified. Of course, Ren would never tell.

He walked briskly through the Village to Soho, where Lena lived. Ren had never dreamed that it would turn into a trendy place next to an artistic one when he bought the club's property. Charming place to be, he thought. Even if the village had also been a place for strange people.

He wondered if he would let her invite him in today. Ren knew that had to be avoided for a while. At least until he was sure that he could control himself if she got really close. He would savor each drop of her sweet blood when Lena did allow him to feed and lay with her. The thought of her made his mouth water, and his fangs lengthened. He fought internally to regain his composure. He gulped as he walked up the brownstone's steps to ring the buzzer.

Lena's body jackknifed and her eyes shot open as she looked around. "What the fuck?" She muttered as she squeezed her eyes shut while she rested her head on her knees and tried to catch her breath. "Did I drink too much last night? Why am I dreaming about that old woman again," she asked out loud. Lena envisioned the woman laughing with delight. Her skin was a mahogany brown, and her long white dreadlocks hung all around her. She sat in a full lotus, her hands relaxed as if she was meditating. She spoke in another language most of the time.

Lena thought she had heard the speech before. It had to be an ancient language, not spoken now. She remembered the woman saying, "you like him, you should like him. You were born for him, born to rule his world." Lena knew she should call her mother. She hadn't had that dream in almost a decade. The last time she had, it was after her sweet sixteen. Who was he the woman was laughing about?

Lena was about to reach for the phone when she remembered the scowl on her mom's face. "No, let's just relax." Lena took a deep breath as she got out of bed and walked over to her CD collection. "Let's see, what am I in the mood for?" She picked one and loaded it into the six disc changer. "Yes," Lena said as the music played, and she swayed and two stepped to the bathroom.

Swaddled in her towel, her hair wrapped in a T-shirt, Lena sang along with Babyface as she went through her closet for clothes she could wear. She couldn't decide. Finally, she laid out three outfits. She eyed them smiling as she threw on her oversized t-shirt and unwrapped her hair. At least one of those would work she thought. Now it was time to write she said to no one as she headed to her writing desk.Before Ren arrived, Lena had tried on several dresses and outfits that she laid out over her bed and her fluffy chair. So why is it, she asked herself, that none were to her satisfaction?

"How do you dress on a date with a man you like but barely know?" She said aloud as she pursed her lips and looked in the mirror at her light pink cropped long sleeve sweater top and her low rise jeans. It was one of her favorite outfits. "This will have to do." Face screwed up; she pulled at the sundress she wanted to put on. It wasn't warm enough for that, Lena thought. If she only picked up her cropped jacket from the cleaners yesterday. Lena sighed. You would think she never dated before.

She grabbed her sparkly beige kitten heels and pushed her foot in. As she slipped on her shoes, the buzzer rang.

"Lena, it's me. Are you ready?" Ren's deep voice came through on the intercom.

"Sure, be right down," Lena pressed the button and responded before she grabbed her favorite bag, and her leather jacket and headed out the door. Ren was here. She was so excited her heart was racing. Lena swore it was pounding so hard that someone standing next to her could hear it. She tried to calm herself by taking deep breaths as she walked down the flight of stairs. It helped, she thought, by the time she opened the door to where Ren was standing.

They both smiled at first sight of each other. For a moment, they both seemed enchanted. Each frozen in their place. Neither of them spoke. His scent overwhelmed her, and Lena couldn't seem to catch herself. She wasn't sure what was going on in his mind, but he seemed rooted to his spot.

Ren parted his lips to speak, then closed them. She wondered if he was having a hard time as she was. Lena gazed at him as his eyes glided over her hourglass form. He was transparent, she thought and hoped her desire for him wasn't all over her face. Lena's top was draped over her torso, hugging her substantial bosom and giving a glimpse of her slim waist. The pink sweater just glanced the top of her jeans, which were form-fitting.

"You look beautiful, Lena."

It took her a moment to find her voice. "Thank you, Ren. You look handsome." What she thought was that he looked delicious and utterly delectable. Ren also wore blue denim but with a beige sweater underneath his leather jacket.

"Hey, Lena! Ren, I didn't think I would see you here." Both Ren and Lena glanced at each other as Theo approached with two tall, muscular men.

"Wanna go for lunch?"

Lena glowered at Theo in disbelief as he stepped between her and Ren. "Theo, I told you I had plans." Lena was beyond frustrated. What was his deal?

"Was that today? My gosh, where is my head?"

"Keep it up, and it will be removed from your shoulders," Ren whispered from behind Theo.

Theo tried to ignore Ren, but Lena saw him go pale. Theo stepped behind Lena and whispered, "Mocha and muscular just like you like them."

"I can hear you, Thelonious," said Ren. Theo gazed downward.

Lena closed her eyes and schooled her features. When she opened them, Ren held out his hand. She smiled and took it. They walked away from the group. "See you later, Theo."

Lena saw the two guys before they came to stand in front of Theo. "You neglected to tell us that Ren was who she was dating."

"Yeah." chimed the other. "Are you trying to get us killed?"

"You must have a death wish,". the first stated before they both walked in the opposite direction of Ren and Lena, leaving Theo to watch the couple alone.

Ren glimpsed down and smiled. "So, what do you want to do?"

"I have you for the whole day?" Lena asked smiling up at him.

"As promised. You've got me as long as you want me."

What came to mind, Lena wouldn't voice. Instead, she smiled, musing over the possibilities. "How about the MET? I thought we'd go there since you said you know so much about art history."

"You got it." Ren put out his hand; Lena took it and nodded as the cab turned the corner. Now that was strange, she thought. If she wanted to catch a cab, she would have to walk a few blocks to Sixth Avenue. But Lena figured it happened by chance.

The drive uptown took a bit of time. Sitting so close to Ren heightened her desire for him, as though his scent was drawing her in. Lena had been chest to chest with Ren at Zoe's. She didn't discern why she was overwhelmed. Finally, Lena decided to open the window a little. The breeze and her admiration for the trees may dispel her urge to give him a lap dance.

"Are you okay, Lena?"

"Yes, just needed some air." He nodded and smiled, but he seemed to feel the same way. He cracked the window on his side and turned slightly toward it. Lena glanced at him, wondering what was going through his mind. Was he overwhelmed by the desire to return to her home? No man had ever evoked such a sensation that she couldn't control her emotions or herself. Lena took a piece of dark chocolate out of her pocketbook and began to nibble. That seemed to release the tension.

"Is it that bad?" He asked as he laughed. "Come here." She smirked but didn't move immediately. Instead, she shook her head no, not wanting to appear fast. And definitely didn't want to be close enough to be engulfed by his cologne or whatever he was wearing. But Ren asked again, so Lena obliged and sat close to him, his arm around her.

"No woman has been so alluring in all my life. You must be some lady."

How sweet of him, she thought. Would she explain that she foresaw a link between them, drawing her closer to him as it awakened every desire? "Yes, I am. Then, I could say the same. No man has ever enticed me as you do. The things going through my mind a lady doesn't speak of." Lena swallowed. Did she just tell him that? Why is it easy to talk to him? There was some sort of connection. How? Is it even possible to experience such comfort with someone you barely know?

"I wasn't expecting such honesty from you," Ren chuckled at her response.

"Oh, I don't believe in facades or lies." She cleared her throat. A bit of mystery on my part would be nice she thought. He smiled but didn't respond. Every once in a while, she noted he would turn towards her and take a deep breath. Lena smiled and rested her head on his chest. Ren began to shift in his seat, so Lena sat up. She thought surely she was pushing it until he took her hand in his. His skin was smooth and soft, yet his hand felt tepid, not warm. Lena thought back to the club and how his hands felt. She didn't notice before. Well, at least they weren't cold. She wasn't sure why that caught her attention.

They finally made it to the museum. Ren helped her out of the cab, and they held hands as they walked up the steps. Lena wanted to see what kind of man he was, so she pulled out her wallet when they reached the cashier.

Ren turned to Lena, looking at her with disbelief. He placed his hand over hers, and he shook his head before turning back to the cashier.

"I apologize. I've dated all kinds."

"That's fine, just don't do it again. It's insulting." His reply was stern, which caught Lena off guard. He squeezed her shoulders and winked as he gave a slight smile. Then he stepped closer to the booth and paid the cashier for the two of them.

After returning to her side, Ren placed his arm around her shoulder and guided her towards the hall. Her heels clicked over the marble floors. "Isn't this beautiful?"

"Yes, it is," Lena said. She loved visiting museums, especially art museums. There was so much beauty in one place and you could learn so much about other cultures. "Do you have a preference? Each country has its own style."

"Hard questions, perhaps I like Chinese art the most. Chinese culture and the philosophy of Confucius influenced many Asian cultures. I especially appreciate seeing the artist's perception of

Asia." They passed a few people as they walked further into the hall.

Then Ren asked, "have you ever been to Asia?"

"No. Have you?" Lena asked.

"I must admit it has been some time since I've been, but, yes, Hong Kong and Shanghai, China, and parts of Japan."

"That's awesome," Lena responded before noticing that Ren was deep in thought. "Ren are you okay? What are you thinking about?"

"It's been a while since I've seen my Sifu."

"You have a Sifu? Cool, why don't you just go visit him? Where is he?" Boy, she thought so chatty Lena.

"He past some time ago. I often miss his sage advice." They walked a few more steps in silence. "Next time I go to Asia, I will take you with me."

"I'm sorry to hear that" Lena paused for a moment she didn't want to sound too excited after finding out he lost someone. " Of course, I'm in to travel." Lena wondered if she would really go with Ren. At that moment, she could picture herself with him forever. Lena smiled for a moment and then seemed to come back to herself. She couldn't help but ask herself why she was thinking that way.

"I want to show you something before we leave this section."

"What is it?" She asked as she followed him towards the end of the hall.

"Here it is. It's called a damaru."

"What is it used for?"

"It's a drum. The Tibetan monks believe that the vibration of the drum would protect against evil. Think you can guess what it is made from?"

"No clue. It can't be pottery; the color is too light."

"Take a guess."

"Ren, don't do that. Just tell me what the drum is made from."

"A human skull."

"Seriously?" Yelena scrunched up her face and shook a bit. The thought gave her goosebumps.

"Yes."

"That's absolutely abhorrent." With disgust on her face, Lena kept looking at it. It was hard not to stare at it. Finally, she said, "I wonder what it sounds like."

"I've never heard the sound; I'm not that old." Ren paused to view the date on the plaque in front of the damaru. "Well, maybe, I am." Ren turned to her; his eyes gleamed before he reached out and pulled her into his arms.

"There is no way," she said, still chuckling.

"When I stayed at one of the shrines in Tibet, they had one. They don't use them anymore, but it is kept to remind the monks of their history. The monks there weren't old enough to have heard the sound either. No one could tell me why they thought using the skull was important. Guess too many years had past."

Lena just stared at him for a moment. She wondered what was with the I'm old comments. He couldn't be older than thirty, maybe thirty-five. Then she asked, "where to next?"

"How about the French exhibit?"

Lena nodded and smiled as they walked out of one exhibit and down the hall. She wondered what tales Ren would tell next.

"The Palace of Versailles was something to behold. It was designed for King Louis XIV. Well, more like he demanded it be built. He did have the knack for throwing a tantrum. King Louis was not a man you wanted to enrage. I was the king's personal favorite. I had lunch with him and dignitaries from all over the world on more than one occasion. The gardens were the most lavish and beautiful in all of Europe at the time. You can search for pictures of it, but they don't do justice to the palace's gardens. The birds created the most beautiful sound before you got to the water fountain. Many of the creatures in the garden were never seen by most people before they visited. Those were some of the better times I spent in Europe."

"Now cut that out," Lena chided, turning toward Ren. "You're telling a story. There is no way you're old enough to experience the gardens at the Palace of Versailles with King Louis XIV."

"Perhaps?" Ren smiled at Lena.

Lena wondered why he kept alluding to his age. It was more than odd. She was starting to recall the tales her grandmother told when she was a child. Accounts she would rather not remember. Once upon a time, she believed them, but she thought it was just a story to scare her and her sisters as she grew up. Were they real? Lena gave herself a bit of distance from Ren. She needed a moment away from his enchantment. At least for a bit, she thought with a smile.

They walked and talked their way through the museum, laughing and squeezing each other's hands. From time to time, he would put his arm around her and squeeze her shoulders. He told her about Greek and Roman art from the classical period. Of course, there was always a joke to go with it. They took their time exploring the museum. Lena had been there plenty of times but this was special. Her first date with him to her favorite place. She smiled.

Lena wanted the day to last as long as possible, and she kept thinking that it was too good to be true. He was sweet, intelligent, handsome, and wealthy. How Lena loved that day. She wasn't sure how long she could keep him at bay, though. The sexual tension between them could be sheared through. Lena knew that she only had one quick denial in her. If he asked more than once, Lena would be all his. But why was this happening so quickly?

They spent most of the day at the museum. By the time the two left, the sun was setting. She paused on the step admiring the sunsets orange haze above the row of brightly colored trees. Lena took a deep breath and sighed.

"Would you like to go get something to eat?"

"Yes, I'm famished."

"Okay, I know a pleasant place. It's not too far. We can walk on this beautiful late fall evening."

They walked a little further. It was a good thing Lena had worn comfortable heels. Otherwise, he would have had to carry her to the restaurant. Not that she would mind him sweeping her off her feet. She had not persisted in maintaining her distance from him. It was as if they had known each other for years. When their eyes locked, it was magnetic. Lena didn't hesitate to take his hand or walk close to him.

She agreed with Ren; it was a beautiful autumn evening, perfect for a walk. It was a while before he said anything. Yet, Ren didn't let go of her hand for most of the day. Now his arm was around her waist as he held her hand.

"So, what is your favorite food, Lena?"

"I like a variety of foods."

"Pick the one you would eat every day if you had to."

"Wow, okay. Jamaican and Japanese food are my top favorites."

"You have a diverse palette."

Yalena nodded. "I like to taste different foods. One day I'd like to eat my way through the world."

Ren shook his head and smiled. "Here we are."

"Really, this is my favorite place. My friends and I do lunch here."

Ren smiled. "Have you ever had dinner here?"

"Actually, now that you mention it, Theo always convinces us to go elsewhere for dinner. They served mainly Italian dishes, but also they serve dishes that contained the spices of different countries."

"Well, that's okay; it means I am the first to take you to dinner here." He held the door for her to enter. The young lady to her right greeted them.

"Good night. Mr. Arias, good to see you."

"Ms. Charleston, how are things going here tonight."

"Quite well, sir. Your table is ready. Right, this way." Lena followed her past the bar on the left and through the main dining room. After the small bar, the raised section was to her left. The lights were dim like candlelight. Ms. Charleston led them to the back of the restaurant. When Lena reached the back room's archway, the restaurant's small section was alight by candles. The back of the restaurant was a quarter of the size. It held four tables with two chairs each. Each table except theirs had several lit candles of different sizes and a beautiful water bowl with a floating candle or two. It was beautiful. Small room was painted a midnight blue. Lena knew that because this was her favorite section when she met for lunch with Theo. The ceiling was specked with white, silver and gold paint, giving the appearance of the stars and galaxies. The sconces on the wall added to the glitter. The room now aglow with so many candles gave a feeling of a star lit night that was lighted by the moon. When she approached the table she saw a bowl of floating rose-shaped candles. She smiled.

Once they were settled, their waiter approached. "Good Evening, I am Robert, and I will be your waiter tonight. Mr. Arias, the pinot grigio you ordered, sir." He showed Ren the bottle; Ren nodded, and Robert proceeded to pour a glass for each of them. "I am told to tell you that your appetizers and food will be sent out as requested."

"Thank you, Robert," Ren returned.Lena was speechless. Had he set all this up for her? He was definitely pulling out all the stops.

"I see you trying to impress me. How often do you come here?"

"Not really, just once or twice a day." Lena had such a puzzled look on her face that Ren chuckled. "I own this restaurant, Lena."

"Oh...Really." He nodded in response. "Cool." It was quiet for a while. Lena was at a loss for words. She began to sip on her wine and fill her mouth with the savory appetizers he had them bring to the table. Lena loved it even more at night. But that could have something to do with the company she was keeping. If he only knew, he didn't have to work so hard. She felt as though she belonged to him.

That caught her off guard. Lena had never belonged to anyone. She had dated. Even the man she was once serious about had never made her feel like she belonged to him. Around and around, she thought about how Ren made her feel but came up with nothing. To her, he was just a nice guy, a stranger. She had no recollection of ever meeting him. Still, he felt so familiar to her, as though they were promised to each other. She wanted to groan, her mind thinking of seeing the old woman in her dreams.

"So, have I succeeded in impressing you?"

Lena gave a small smile. "A little."

"Let me guess. You want to know more about me."

"What are you, a mind reader?" Lena thought. "Yes, more than what you have told me so far, of course."

"Let's see, I am much older than you."

"This again?" Ren made no reply. "By how much?"

"Hmmm, how old are you?"

"Hey, I thought we were going to talk about you?"

"Yes. Just answer the question."

"Twenty six."

"Well, that makes me about nine hundred and fifty-three years older than you."

"Okay, Ren, not funny. There is no way you're that old." Lena couldn't help but wonder if he really was that old. She mentally shook herself and thought, get a grip, Lena. Those were just stories.

"No? Well, I am older than you by ten years."

"Does everything have to be so difficult?" He gave a full smile, and for the first time, she noticed his beautiful white teeth. Lena thought that his eye teeth were particularly pointy and long. She was starting to believe that she was losing it. "You have gorgeous teeth, and they're so white."

"Thanks. I have had a sublime day with you, Yalena."

"I enjoyed the day too, Lorenzo. You are a pleasure to be with." He leaned over and took her hand in his.

"The pleasure is all mine. You're a lot of fun," he said as he kissed the back of her hand. Lena felt sparks where his lips had touched.

Lena enjoyed the dinner with Ren. She thought that the wine and the food were delightful, as well as the small chocolate dessert he picked for her. They talked for a long time. He finally told her what it was like to grow up in Argentina. He told her about Argentina's history as though he lived it.

Lena had enjoyed the restaurant, even after she became aware that he ate very little of anything. Instead, all he did was nurse what Lena thought was a bloody mary.

It had been a long day, but so beautiful. Lena didn't want it to end, but she knew it had to. They left his restaurant pretty late, and he got them a cab to her apartment. It was relatively quiet in the back of the cab. Quite serene. She sat close to him, his arm around her and her head on his shoulder.

"I had a wonderful time today, Ren."

"We did that part at the restaurant," He replied with a smile. "Can we go out again tomorrow, then?"

"Sure." They stopped at her apartment, and Ren paid the driver before he got out of the cab and came around to let her out.

"I would like to walk my lady to her door, so I'm sure you're safely at home."

"That's fine. Your lady, huh?"

"You noticed that?"

"I'm sentient. We shall see if you're worthy of being part of my life." Lena couldn't help but smile as she took the first step of the stairs. He was definitely making his agenda quite clear.

"Let me have your key, so I can open the door for you." And that he did. She lingered at the doorway and looked into his eyes. Ren's eyes seemed so intense as he gazed into hers.

"Well, I guess this is good night Ren, even though I don't want it to end."

"I don't want it to be over either, my love. You can invite me in."

"Mmmm, no, not tonight. I don't think I could control myself, and that would my three-month rule."

"Three months rule?"

"Yeah, I have to be seeing a guy for at least ninety days or three months before I bring him into my home or my bed."

"And how long have we been seeing each other?"

"Eighty-five and a half days," Lena replies.

"Eleven weeks, two days, and twelve hours."

"Ren you've been keeping track?"

"Yes. I didn't think it would take me this long to kiss you."

"You haven't..." Lena didn't get to finish saying that he hadn't kissed her before he leaned over and pulled her to him. He lightly placed his finger on her lips. Then pulled her closer as if they couldn't get close enough. He held her face in one hand and the other around her waist as he softly kissed her lips. His tongue teased her at first as Ren licked her top and bottom lip, coaxing her to open her mouth.

It was a good thing he held her tight because her knees began to bend, and he had to hold her up if he wanted to finish their kiss. His lips were soft and full, and his long, tantalizing kiss sent shivers through her. After they stopped kissing, he didn't let go. He just held her close, their gaze intense. She couldn't find her voice, so she just smiled.

"I will count the hours until I kiss you again." His lips twitched as he kissed her cheek, and then he whispered in her ear. "You have no idea how strong the urge to ravage you." Then he turned away. Lena was left leaning on the wall. Her breath caught. Lena wanted him to come with her to her bed. Lord knows it had been over a year since she let a man touch her. Lena wanted him to feel her. However, she didn't call him back. And she wouldn't refuse him again.

Lena stepped into her apartment and leaned on the closed door. She was floating on cloud nine. The heat of his arm around her and his hand on her cheek radiated through her. She evoked the feeling of his kiss.

Lena felt nothing like she had imagined. She was happy to have some time alone with him outside of the club. She knew now that she had fallen in love with Ren. He was handsome, loving, warm, tall, dark, and striking. Lena couldn't help but think she had met him before. Presumably in a dream.

Chapter 5

The next day, Ren walked to Lena's home. He rang the buzzer just as he had done yesterday. "Can you come up? I need a few minutes," uttered Lena as she buzzed him in. Lena stood by her apartment door, watching him walk up the stairs. She smiled as their eyes locked.

"Hi," she said. She beckoned him into the apartment, "come in and have a seat." He nodded before his eyes possessively glided over her. Lena glimpsed the hunger in his gaze. Surely, she was mistaken, she thought. She blinked, and the look was gone. She gave a crooked smile. She had enjoyed her time with him the day before and looked forward to today.

Lena closed the door behind him before she walked into his open arms. The warmth that enveloped her and his kiss made her melt inside. She delighted in the hunger that poured into the gentle way his lips touched hers. She sensed the urgency and passion in his lips, the way his tongue teased her mouth open, and then twirled inside. She couldn't help but put her hands in his hair and hold on to his neck. "You keep kissing me like that, and I won't be able to wait another minute," her voice was a husky whisper. As she gazed into his eyes, she became aware of the molten desire that stirred and disappeared.

"I have mixed feelings about your ninety-day rule," he remarked, loosening his hold of her. "I respect a woman who heeds her own principles, Lena, but I thirst to feel your skin against mine." She smiled and reached up to gently kiss him once more. Knowing his longing was as much as hers seemed to strengthen her resolve. Lena eased her arms down to rest on his chest as he held her.

"Let me grab my shoes and bag." Ren nodded

As they walked out of her apartment, Lena turned and locked the door; Ren's left hand slid into the back pocket of her jeans. Lena slowly pulled his hand from her pocket and placed it around her waist. "That is something I will never accept in public."

Ren cleared his throat. "So, any ideas for today's agenda?"

"I thought the South Street Seaport would be alluring on this beautiful fall day. And of course, before the end of the day, I'd like to hit the Fulton Market. They have a great selection of edibles and kitchen items. Does that sound good to you?"

"Sounds good," Ren responded as he ushered her into the Mercedes.

"I like your car. Any particular reason you drove today?"

"I wanted time alone with you." She smiled at him.

"We could've walked."

"This is easier, don't you think?"

"Possibly," she replied.

"Walking may be unpleasant if you decide to shop." Lena smiled as she turned to peer at the people who passed the window. They drove for a while in silence.

Yalena thought of what she should buy since she didn't have to take a cab home, and she had Ren to help her. Well, maybe only a few things, she thought. It was good that the traffic was moving well today, she murmured to herself.

Once Ren parked, they began to walk toward the seaport. It was a beautiful but chilly day. The sun was bright in the sky, and the air was crisp coming off the water. Lena wanted to explore the mall before walking the port. It seemed almost empty as they passed the shops.

"Does anything stand out?"

"Nothing I want to buy. I have a ton of clothes. I just wanted to see what stores were here."

"Our next stop?"

"No clue. Seems too early to head to the market or dinner."

"We can walk the port."

Lena and Ren spent the rest of the day window shopping, taking in the fresh air and looking out across the water. The weather was sublime. Just as the day before, they walked hand in hand or with his arm around her. He would nuzzle her cheek or the top of her head from time to time, but no passionate kisses like the night before. Lena realized that he would help her make her ninety-day mark.

They stop and watch the water from time to time. She was happy to be close to him, he felt like her shelter in a storm and she wondered if he would be around long enough for her to be sure that he was. They spoke from time to time but seemed to relish the closeness and presence of each other. It was near evening before Lena noticed that being close to him brought her no physical warmth. How strange Lena thought.

The hours seemed to glide past and as they stepped out of the Seaport museum the sky was a beautiful pink and orange.

"Are you ready for dinner?"

"Do you own an eatery by the pier as well?"

"It never crossed my mind to attain property here." Ren smiled and winked at her. "Even so, I know a place."

"Since you selected the restaurant, I'll pick the dessert. There's a grand ice cream parlor, well two, but I think one is better than the other."

"Agreed, if you wish, we can peruse the market after dinner.

As she slowly ate her favorite rum raisin ice cream, Lena walked with Ren through the market. She hadn't bought any new clothes or shoes to her surprise, but she knew that there were several items she wanted from the grocers there. Ren carried the small shopping basket as they walked the isles. She grabbed fresh lasagna noodles and the store brand marinara.

"I didn't peg you for a store brand kind of girl."

Lena smiled. "I'm not but the sauce here is fresh and delicious. I've had it before. I feel like making lasagna later this week."

"Okay, so you'll need ricotta and mozzarella."

"No, I hate ricotta. I use parmesan cheese instead. And lots of it."Lena guided him toward the cheese section and picked up a huge lock of the imported cheese. Ren had walked down to the end of the refrigerated section and picked up a well known American brand. "No, Ren not that one."

"But it's cheaper."

Lena rolled her eyes. "Don't pretend to know my taste or pocketbook." The man behind the cheese counter chuckled and Lena smiled. "Lets taste them." She poked a small piece of cheese with a toothpick from each small container. "Taste the American brand first. Ren looked put off. "Come on. You expect me to buy that, you need to taste the two and tell me which you'd prefer."

Ren put down the cheese and walked over to Lena. He tasted the first piece Lena offered. "It's good." Lena rolled her eyes and Ren tasted the second piece which was the imported parmesan. "Wow, there is a difference."

"Of course there is. As my mom used to say, 'you get what you pay for.'"

"Fine, you're right."

"Whether you thought so or not, she's right. You'll be happier accepting that now," the grocer chimed in as he chuckled and walked away.

Ren laughed and nodded his head. "Do you need anything else?"

"I just had ice cream so I shouldn't, but they have great cannolis."

"I don't think it will make much of a difference."

"Good answer," Lena replied as she laughed.

It was after nine when they reached her building. Ren walked her up to the ornate front door. His smooch was soft and sweet, but not sultry and passionate. Lena guessed they both wouldn't need much encouragement after a passionate kiss. However, after that night, she felt Ren persisted in maintaining the distance between them despite their mounting sexual tension.

She didn't see him or speak to him for four days. Lena couldn't help but think that times had changed. Still, she didn't want to call first. They didn't have a phone relationship. She couldn't think of one time they spoke on the phone. Still, he could call, she thought.

Lena elected to go to Zoe's the next night to see him. She was hoping it would appear natural since she hadn't made arrangements to visit the club before. But after not even seeing him at Zoe's, Lena became melancholy. She was disappointed. She thought things were going well. He didn't seem like the kind of person who would brush her off. She could not imagine what would make him a put berth between them. Lena thought, perhaps he stayed away because he couldn't control himself, but Ren wouldn't have had to if he had shown up at her door. Lena didn't remain long that Thursday night; she didn't even eat. She was surprised when an arduous, thin, muscled man carrying a bag of what she presumed was her food, met her at the door before Lena tread outside.

He handed her the bag. "I'm told to tell you to give him another day." Without another word, he turned and walked away, leaving Lena dumbfounded. Theo was huffing and puffing behind her because he wanted to stay. He whined the entire cab ride home. When Lena got back to her apartment, she put the food in the refrigerator and went to bed. She wasn't sure what was going on. Lena appreciated that they were abiding by her precepts. But she was crushed not to have his company.

Sitting in the DJ booth, Ren's thoughts were of his beloved. He couldn't believe how beautiful Lena had grown up to be. She was tall, about five foot eight inches. Her curvy build made him yearn for her even more. Things were their usual, except for Ren. He sat on the loveseat near the DJ booth entrance, staring at a spot on the burgundy rug. A beautiful blonde draped across his lap. She was more than eager to be his comfort and feed for the rest of the night, but he had barely fed from her. He didn't move or speak until Cell came back upstairs.

"She took the bag, but she was doleful. Ren, she spent her time here looking for you. She sat in the same seat as when she first came here. She did not order a drink or anything to eat. She's brooding. And if you do not feed, you're going to kill her when you finally entice her."

Cell didn't have to say anymore. Ren wrapped his arms around her; his incisors lengthened before sinking deep into the supple skin of her neck. She didn't scream, but one could briefly see her pain in the contraction of her frame. Cell had not turned around to face Ren, but spoke into the dark. "Ren, let her up, man."

Ren did as asked. He had fed longer than he should have. He knew that he needed to feed but he had no desire for anyone other than Lena. Ren had not regularly fed since he started dating Lena. Once he stopped feeding the guards were at the door. One collected the girl from Ren's lap, and the other grabbed up her things. Another beautiful girl walked in and sat on Ren's lap, as they exited. She took the scarf from her neck and tilted her head to the side. For the first time that night, Ren spoke

"I haven't see you in a while."

"I've been buried at work," she replied with a smile. You remember me?"

"I recognize all my regulars." Before she said another word, he held her and began to feed again. He didn't realize how ravenous his body had become. He was so consumed with thoughts of Lena he hadn't acknowledged his starving body. Feeding seemed to quench the thirst but not the yearning for the woman he had yet to claim. It wasn't necessary for Cell to tell him to stop this time. He just did, and she sat up, wiped off the excess blood with her handkerchief, tied her scarf, and got up. She couldn't help winking at him before she left.

"Cell, keep an eye on things here. I need to go see Lena."

"You think so?" Ren thought that was an odd thing for Cell to say. He walked toward where Cell stood looking out over the crowd from the DJ's booth.

"Who are those ugly burly guys?"

"According to Kiyoshi, they came with Woods," Cell replied.

"Are those soldiers?"

"Seth's version of soldiers anyway."

Seth Woods was the son of one of the council members. Ren was waiting for a move against him. He knew that there would be repercussions after butchering one of the council members, even if it were a righteous kill. Ren had never dreamed they would take this long. Now Seth was strutting around their club with soldiers.

"They dare show themselves here. Is this not a peaceful place?"

"You cannot be that sprung. You have yet to take Lena, but you challenged them, Ren."

"What nonsense are you spouting?"

"The night you laid claim to her, you challenged them. You said no vampire could touch her. Later, I found out Seth had taken a fancy to her and was going to snatch her on the way home until you said that. Amusing how he adhered to that warning but none of the others."

"He is not worthy to breathe the same air."

"I agree with you, but he believes he's equal to you." Ren turned to Cell, waiting for him to continue. "There's talk around the club, people think you need to be brought down, that you think you're better than us. I've known you for centuries and I know that you earn your place everyday your here. I acknowledge that you are the leader of this family and sovereign of this clan, and I respect that. The problem is that vampires outside our family are not okay with you giving decrees that affect them." Cell paused for a moment before he continued. "There are whispers that some may challenge you. People ask how you became ruler and why you get to make calls like that."

Ren disregarded what Cell said. "The earlier years were easier to govern them. Vampires were obedient. These vampires are wild and unruly. They have no charm or manners." Even though Ren didn't continue to speak, he proceeded to revel in the days past. It was silent for several moments before he spoke again. "None can better me so far. I am the only one who decides how we live in this city. I have been doing it for more than two centuries. And I am the one who has to deal with the backlash from any problems." He paced for a minute to contemplate how to handle such an intrusion. "How many soldiers, and where is Seth?"

Cell watched the crowded club for their soldiers. Finally, two men gestured above the crowd. "According to our guards, we've identified eight, so he may have up to sixteen. And he is in your bed. The one you used to take women to before connecting with her a few months ago."

Ren ignored his last comment. "Have them eliminate all eight. But be subtle; I don't want Seth to sense that he's under attack. And when the snakes rear their heads after the others disappear, take them out."

"Are you sure you want to start this war? You haven't even fed from her. Is she worth it?"

"This is not just about Yalena. How many have turned up in Marcia's ward this week?"

"What are you talking about?"

"How many, Cell? How many men and women with bites who don't remember what happened to them and how many dead."

"Five died last week, totally drained. So far, ten a week who have no clue, and two who turned."

"These fools, do what they should not. Superfluous hunting and problems. Why are the young yearning for experiences they are ignorant of? We are part of the modern world. We have places that provide feeding. Why does Seth want to destroy that? If this keeps up, we'll have to shut down Zoe's and Ariana's. I like it here. We've made it work for over three hundred years. I will not have some disrespectful toddler dismantle all we have built."

"Listen, we do not want this to end here. I didn't mean to make it sound like we're not behind you. You're our leader, but there is going to be some rebellion in the ranks, Ren. If they're not part of us, they want to make their own rules to live by."

"Then, they need to be within the parameters I set."

Cell nodded and returned his gaze to the dance floor. "It is done. There is only one left, but Seth doesn't realize it. And you better reach him before the soldier tries to check in."

"Fine, seal off the club and take out the last one."

"Sure." Before Cell could retort, Ren was gone. He headed to the hallway that led to the room where he used to feed. It wasn't long ago that Ren would call women to bed where he lay in front of the dance floor under the DJ booth. It had remained shut since the night Yalena showed up, and he wasn't sure how Seth opened the room. He reached right before Seth's man got to him. Seth had just finished feeding and sat looking out over the club. Ren shut the automatic hatch before Seth could react or move. Then he wrenched Seth from the circular bed.

Seth seemed shocked. "Get the fuck off me," he said, struggling to remove Ren's grip. Seth searched in vain for his soldiers, but he was abandoned by all but Ren. Ren wondered if Seth knew that his soldiers could do nothing even if they were alive. The club's doors were impenetrable for most vampires, just as the inner sanctums were also dense steel. Ren didn't think Seth understood that he was taking a chance by bringing them here and sitting in his seat, Ren was sure Seth had surveyed the club and understood that the room right under the DJ's booth was perfect.

They both glared at each other. It was easy to read the other's disdain. Ren couldn't help but think of Seth's father, Pierre. His son was nothing like him in strength or grace. But Seth had always been a sickly child. Not many dhampirs were formidable and healthy. Now Seth stood before him, challenging Ren for the throne. Ren's lips curled into a smile as he threw Seth against the opposite wall.

"This is not your club or room," Ren's voice rumbled, but Seth said nothing. His hateful expression didn't change in the slightest as he scowled at Ren. Ren scrutinized his opponent. Seth's complexion was pallet at best. His hair, a muted dark chestnut, didn't have the sheen of his mother's raven hair. Ren had heard the rumors, and it appeared that it was true.

"Have you lost your mind?" Ren almost growled. "Zoe's is my place. You do not come in here to take over or threaten me." Seth laughed, and so did Ren. Ren smiled as he moved to grab Seth's collar and raised him from the floor as he plunged a silver stiletto through his stomach, sliding it upward to his rib cage. Blood began to pour down and pool on the travertine floors before Seth. "Now, laugh."

Ren let go and withdrew the knife. He glared as Seth cowered on the floor. "You've ruined pristine floors," Ren said, looking at the mess and Seth with disgust. "Seth, this is my place of business. New York is my city. You have a problem with my decrees; live somewhere else." Ren's voice was hardly above a whisper. "I will not tolerate disobedience or dissension in my ranks. You may not be part of my family, but you are part of my clan, and you live in my city, You will live within the statutes made for our survival and the survival of those we feed on."

Ren seized Seth by his neck, lifting him so that they were eye to eye. Seth's feet dangled beneath him. As the two stared daggers into each other's eyes, Ren witnessed the hatred and venom pooling in Seth's eyes. He knew that this was just the beginning of their war. Ren was not looking forward to the battle. He would have to go to the council before he could get rid of Seth.For now, Seth was all that was left. Ren's men had disposed of Seth's soldiers. Finally, Ren had Seth escorted out with orders that he could not return before Ren could speak with the council. Ren accepted that nothing would come of the conference. Still, he had no choice. He would reprimand and punish anyone who didn't observe protocol. In the end, he would rid himself and the clan of Seth. Ren was just hoping it wouldn't cost him more than just killing him there and then.   Seth was thrown out for everyone to see. He bared his fangs in the direction of security and walked to the corner across the street.   As Ren walked back to the DJ booth, his mind reverted to the woman he had avoided. The only thing he wanted was his Lena. He wanted her every desire to come true. Even if she was mad at him for lying, he hoped it wouldn't be long before forgiving him. He would help clean up the club and prepare for the council before seeing her.

"Cell, we may have to start over soon. This is how it started when we were in Rio de la Plata."

"So, we'll move to someplace else. You perceived it was inevitable, Ren."

"I do not think Lena will be ready to move."

"Like it matters where she lives. She's a writer. She can work anywhere. Not like she's going to actually work."

"It's too soon."

"If she wants to be with you, she'll move. You need to go to her. I guarantee that if you do not connect her to you soon, and you catch what I mean, we will not be able to protect her much longer. Like not inviting anyone into your home that you don't know."

"You are right, Cell. I will go to Lena after we clean up."

Chapter 6

It was late afternoon the next day when Ren left the club to visit her. He rang the buzzer. "Lena, I'd like to take you somewhere?"

She rolled her eyes. Lena was still upset with him, so she decided not to ask him to come upstairs to wait for her. "That'll teach him to stand her up, she muttered." She couldn't help but wonder what he was talking about. She pressed the button to respond, "fine."

The buzzer rang again. "Dress comfortably, we're going to workout."

She pressed the intercom button to respond. Was this how he was going to make up to her? What kind of make up is this? Lena couldn't help but wonder what they were going to do. He hadn't shown up for days and now he wanted to take her somewhere to work out? She should be upset that he expected her to be available.

Extraordinary how he had perfect timing, she thought. She had thrown on her hoodie to go to the brick oven pizzeria. She took a deep breath and looked into the mirror. She wasn't expecting Ren at all. Guess she was dressed for a workout. But what kind of workout? Were her sweats okay or should she have on a different outfit? Lena couldn't help but think she should switch to something better. She decided to change into her black track pants, her burgundy exercise bra, and a matching black racerback crop tank top. She pulled on her hooded cardigan before pulling her curly mane into a ponytail. She slipped on her leather jacket before she picked up her handbag and her pink sunglasses as she stepped out and locked the door. When Lena caught sight of him through the glass door, her heart skipped a beat. She just didn't want him to know it.

Ren wore the men's version of her pants with a red hoodie and his leather jacket. Did he read her mind? "Hey," Lena said as she opened the main door. She sauntered down the stairs and stood a few feet before Ren. He took a few steps to bridge the gap between them. Then he put his arm around her and kissed her cheek before they started walking.

"Oh, are we best buds again? I wasn't sure after not seeing you for a few days, and then you stood me up at your club." He stopped walking and turned to her to face him. He removed his sunglasses before hers, held her face in his hands, and gently kissed her lips.

"Lena, it was the only way for you to make your ninety-day rule. We wuld have never made it had we spent any more time together before your imaginary date line." Lena rolled her eyes as she gave a slight smile before giving him a quick peck on the lips.

They walked to the end of her block before she said anything. "Where are we going and how are we getting there?"

"You'll see when you get there and we can walk or hop on the train."

"Guess it isn't a short walk." Lena stopped mid-stride. "You take the train. Mr. Let's drive to the seaport." Ren didn't respond but took her hand in his.

He smiled and put his arm around her neck. "Yes, I take the train, but rarely. There is next to little parking there so the car wouldn't work and the traffic going to the Village is never fun." Lena stared at him for a moment. "Come on, you won't regret it. I promise."

As they waited for the train they needed, Ren whispered to Lena. "I still remember when they started building the network of trains. I believe my first ride was from lower manhattan to Grand Central Station. It was a wondrous sight."

Lena poked him with her elbow. "Stop that." Ren laughed and Lena scowled at him.

After leaving the train station, they walked up the block quickly. Lena wondered all the way where they were going. "Ren, where is this place? And what are we doing?"

"You'll see soon. We're not far. Just a few blocks from the station. They only walked a bit further before stopping in front of a recently remodeled building. "It's upstairs," Ren said before pulling her arm to walk into the building.

"I was reading the sign," she squealed.

Ren winked but didn't reply. He continued to walk up the flight of stairs. There was one sign but when Lena tried to stop and read it, he pulled her. She couldn't imagine what he wanted her to see so badly or what he was trying to hide. When they reached the landing, before Lena was able to observe what was going on through the glass door, Ren covered her eyes and walked her into the room. "Since you are a martial artist, I thought you'd like to learn a new style," Ren whispered as he removed his hand.

Lena was silent for several moments, a bit in shock. Did he bring her to a dojo? The floors were wooded and mirrors were across from them on the far wall. Lena wondered how he knew she wanted to learn a new style. She watched the man and woman cartwheel and flip back and forth across the floor. She had seen several capoeira performances but had never considered taking classes. She turned to Ren.

"What made you want to give me martial arts lessons?"

Ren shrugged, "I thought it was something we could learn together."

Lena smirked and nodded before turning to the two approaching people. "Welcome to our dojo." The lady spoke but they both smiled. "I'm Josie and this is Carlos. We'll be your instructors for today."

Lena smiled and nodded, saying hello to both of them.

Carlos turned to her. "Ren told us that you were a martial artist. What styles have you studied?"

"I've studied several styles of Kung fu." Lena paused. She didn't discuss the specific styles she had studied with anyone. When no one said anything and both the instructors watched her expectantly, she continued. "Tai chi is the one I mostly practice." Most people had no clue how deadly tai chi could be, so when asked she would only volunteer that style. She didn't like strangers knowing her capabilities. It seemed strange now that she thought about it. It was as if she was expecting people to pick a fight all the time if she said any other form.

"Nice, I like Tai chi. Which form?" Lena wasn't expecting him to be a Tai chi practitioner.

"Chen style." Lena would say no more. Why did it matter she wondered? She was there to learn a new one.

"Wow, beautiful," Josie replied. "You both are dressed comfortably so just take off your shoes and we'll get started. Also, unless you have non-slip socks, please remove them also." We all bowed to each other before she sat and slipped off her shoes and socks. Ren did the same.

There was no one else in the dojo. No other classes going on. It was amazing to get the full attention of the instructors. They explain the rules and a bit of the history of Capoiera before they started. Then they learned the basics before practicing the form of a battle. Lena was sure they moved quickly because of her experience. It definitely moved too quickly for a novice.

It was fun sparing with Ren. The spins and kicks were a cool trick to combine with her forms. It kind of reminded her of monkey style. Lena wasn't good at that style, she disliked the form so much that she wouldn't practice long enough to master it. She was glad Capoiera wasn't as similar.

When they finished the lesson, Lena glanced at her watch. Several hours had passed since they entered the dojo. She was hungry and hoped they would head straight to a restaurant. They both put on their shoes and socks and retraced their steps out of the building.

When they stepped outside a black hybrid sat out front with a tall male leaning by the door. As the building door opened he looked up.

"It took you long enough." He called to them.

"Thank you for waiting Kiyoshi," Ren replied as they walked down the steps. Then Ren place a hand on her back and guided her towards the car. "I hope you didn't think I would make you walk back after such a workout." Lena just smiled. She was glad he had a car pick them up.

The gentleman opened the door and even took Lena's hand to help her inside. She had seen him before, but she waited until Ren got in and they were off before saying anything.

"Has he been following me?"

"I'm sure you're mistaken."

"I'm pretty sure that I've seen him, Kiyoshi, multiple times. He looks like a model, there's no way I'm mistaken."

"We'll talk soon. He's a precaution. He is there to protect you."

"Now you're not making any sense."

"Not the place for that conversation, soon."

Chapter 7

Lena was more than aware that he was avoiding her question. He did that sometimes and Lena wondered why. What was he into that he needed to sidestep her questions? Was that why Theo had warned her off of dating Ren? She didn't say anything else, not another word before they pulled up at the pizzeria. Lena got out and headed for the door without waiting for Ren. She didn't like when people hid things. But she kept wondering if she was being paranoid because she had a appalling imagination. In her stories, there was always a hidden agenda and she started to think real people were quite similar to those she wrote about. Why would she need security? She had been fine all her life. Did he notice something she didn't?

She walked into a restaurant not far from her place. It was late afternoon, and the lunch rush was over. Still, there were a few people. Several tables sat empty. Lena stood at the counter trying to decide what she wanted while she waited for Ren. She ordered two slices of the margherita pizza and walked away from the counter toward the back of the small eatery.

Lena admitted that it felt good to have waited, and it felt even better that he made her pause. Still, she had a few questions. Questions he had not yet answered. Before that, she decided to have the talk with him. The wry thing was, he beat her to the punch. "Lorenzo, can I be frank with you?"

"You sensed it too?"

"Sorry?" Lena had no idea what he was talking about."

"The pull we seem to have towards one another." Lena smiled sheepishly. He kind of chuckled at her response before he said anything.

"I am looking for someone special, true love. A kind of love that would last more than seven lifetimes."

The last statement shocked her. Lena usually told her dates the same thing when she wanted to scrutinize if they would make up some lame excuse and leave. But, honestly, Lena hadn't dated anyone who hadn't disappeared after that, whether it had been three months or six. Had Lena seen him before and not noticed?

Ren took her hands in his. "Lena, I feel like you are that woman. I want you to be a part of my life. I believe we have a great connection." Lena thought that was something she would definitely not say.

"Ren, have you been talking to Theo?"

"No. Theo won't tell me anything about you. He would prefer that we didn't date each other."

"Yeah, he told me not to go out with you. I can't figure out why he's so against it. You seem like a great guy, and I'm attracted to you. There is a magnetism between us. A lot. If, I told you what I wanted to do when you were sitting next to me in the cab."

"Me too."

"I, I'm a little scared to act on what I'm experiencing."

"When you're ready, Lena. There is plenty of time for you to be at ease with who I am."

"So, who are you? I have talked to people. And no one can tell me more than you've told me. Or should I say no one chose to?"

"Were you that curious about me?"

"I just wanted to make sure you're not a pedophile or psychotic, or criminal. I was trying to figure out why Theo didn't want me with you."

"Theo is a bit overprotective. He desires the best for you."

"It's more than that. Theo won't even give me reasons. He always has reasons."

"He will reveal his doubts soon enough. Please stay here. I will return."

"What? Why?" Ren didn't respond, just motioned for her to remain at the table. Lena watched him as he walked out of the pizzeria and stopped on the other side of the door. But Lena couldn't see any more than that.

She sat for a while, eating the pizza the waiter brought right after Ren left the restaurant. She thought it was strange that he left her by herself. Since she couldn't figure out why he walked away, she decided to think about her book and how she would write the ending. Lena was so deep in thought she didn't notice anyone approaching the table until the squeaking of the chair.

"Mind if I sit?" A man asked. "Your friend appears occupied at the moment, so I thought you needed company." Lena tried to look around the man.

"Sorry, who are you? Don't bother, I'm here with someone. So, yes, I mind. Please sit at one of the other vacant tables." He didn't react. Lena glared at him, her eyebrows furrowed. She'd never encountered him; why would he sit down at her table? "I don't sit and chat with people I've never been introduced to. Leave."

"Sure, I'll leave if you'll join me."

Lena couldn't believe how brazen he was. She scrunched up her face in disgust. Was he daft, she wondered? "I don't think so. I don't know you." Was he serious? And where was Ren? She twisted in her seat to look around the restaurant. But she couldn't identify him at all. So what in the world was going on?

"I don't understand why Ren would leave you all by your lonesome. The world is so treacherous." He laughed. "Let me introduce myself." He reached out his hand, "I am Seth, an archenemy of your boyfriend who is the ruler of our world."

Lena overlooked the outstretched hand. She was even more confused. Ruler? What in the world? Wait, is he an associate of Ren? She had never seen him at the club. Wait, he said, archenemy. What in the world, she thought? Undeniably high out of his mind.

"I'll explain it all on our way. Let's go."

"No thank you. I'll stay here."

"Going to make this difficult, are we?" He motioned to whoever sat at the table behind her, and Lena turned in that direction. Two elephantine men got up and approached her. "Please, Lena, get up. Let's not make a scene."

Lena stared blankly. "How could you possibly know my name?" She hadn't meant to ask what she was thinking. She surveyed the pizzeria again. Desperately, searching the doorway and window to find Ren. She had no idea what was going on, but she wanted no part of it. She would have to fight them off. Lena pushed her seat back, still settled, and planted her feet flat on the floor, her hands clenched into a fist. Able to see past Seth this time, she saw Ren walk through the door. She relaxed a bit.

When Lena looked towards the door, Seth followed her gaze, flinched, and reached for his side. Seth slowly backed away as Ren neared the table. He strode directly in front of Seth, facing Lena.

"Lena, did you want to go clubbing tonight?"

"I thought we were taking a break from Zoe's?"

"That was the agreement, but can we go there? I'll make it up to you later."

"Okay." Lena reckoned there was no point in arguing. Plus, she wanted to avoid creepy and crew. Ren helped her up. She tried to act nonchalant, but inside she was shaking. She had no clue what was going on and didn't feel safe going directly home. Luckily, or on purpose, they were only a few blocks from the club. Lena had never realized how close she lived to Zoe's. It was as though she was being pulled into his life.

It was dark outside when they left the pizza place, and Ren held on to her so tight that Lena thought she would break. "Ren, what is going on? Why did that man approach me?" Ren didn't respond. Lena walked a little more. "How did he know my name?" Still, Ren said nothing to her. "Ren, why are you holding on to me so tight?"

"Am I holding you too tight? Sorry." He loosened his grip a little but refused to comment on any of her questions. Lena let it slide until they got to Zoe's.

Ren opened a large steel door a few feet from the club's entrance. "Ren, we weren't expecting you." Lena glanced around, not sure where they were. It was just a large hall. The red carpet ran the length of it.

"I wasn't expecting to be here, Cell. We've got trouble."

"Hey Lena, Theo is upstairs in the DJ booth." Lena stared at Cell. He was different, she thought. He was clothed in jeans and an Ed Hardy t-shirt that loosely hung on his athletic frame. When Lena did not move, Cell turned toward her again. "You can join him. Just go with Kiyoshi."

Lena rolled her eyes. "Cell, is that your way of asking me to leave? And is anyone going to tell me what's going on?" He smiled at her, and Ren nodded. "Seriously?" Lena stood a few more seconds to see if anyone would say anything to her. When neither reacted nor paid her the slightest attention, she turned towards the tall thin muscled gentleman. "Fine, lead the way." Kiyoshi nodded and turned away from Ren and Cell. Lena stared at Kiyoshi's back as she followed; he had broad shoulders and was tall. Most men around the club were muscular or athletic. Kiyoshi was no different. His blue-black hair hung straight down, partially hiding his eyes.

"Kiyoshi, is that your name?" Kiyoshi turned his head a fraction and nodded. Lena concluded that he wouldn't give any more information. But as she glared at his back going up the stairs, she remembered. "Wait a minute. You were the guy following me." He kept walking, not reacting to her question at all. "Why were you watching me?" Again Kiyoshi didn't acknowledge her question. Lena marveled why no one reacted to her questions. "Where's Theo?" She guessed that he was in the booth but wanted to hear him speak. He said nothing. He didn't even turn to face her. Kiyoshi just kept walking; he never said a word to her. He barely acknowledged her presence. They walked into the DJ booth as they came out of the stairwell.

"Hey, it looks like you've moved up in the world," stated Theo. "Thank you, Kiyoshi." Kiyoshi huffed and turned around to leave the booth.

"Don't joke. Theo, he was the guy following me." Theo did not comment. "What's with him?"

"That's just Kiyoshi. He's the strong silent type. I heard him speak once and almost fell out of my chair. He has a sultry baritone voice. I would have jumped him, but he's not gay; pulls all the sexy women in here when he's off."

Lena walked to the window and peered out over the dance floor. So this is what he sees, she thought. She walked around the booth running her fingers over wood-framed equipment. There were few places to sit but lots of screens that showed different parts of the club. Finally, she turned to Theo, who patted the space next to him on the sofa.

"How were your dates with Ren?"

"I've seen him before, I spotted him following me." Lena hesitated a second, thinking about where she may have seen him. Finally, she turned back to Theo. "Kismet." Lena glanced around the booth. "Damn, this place is dark. How do they even see to play the music?"

"Makes sense; he's Patrick's Lieutenant. There are a few lights over the turn tables and a lamp in the corner, but they're only on when the club is running. So, what are you doing here?"

"What do you mean, Patrick's Lieutenant? Who the hell is Patrick?" Lena paused, "I'm not sure. Some guy named Seth waltzed over to my table after Ren walked outside. He wanted me to go with him. After Ren came back, we jetted back here."

"If he believed that he needed to bring you here, they threatened you."

"What? Ren didn't speak with Seth. And he didn't threaten me. Creepy as fuck and tried to make me go with him. I was ready to fight. Anyway, who are they? And I never met the guy."

"Other...people. You don't have to know them. Look, Lena, everyone here knows Ren has had his eye on you. And I'm aware because Cell has made comments about it that Ren told everyone hands-off from the time you walked through the door. He wanted you."

"Wow, I'm flattered."

"You shouldn't be. It's a dangerous world they live in. We're not just talking about you being Ren's date for a few nights. He craves you to be his."

Was being with Ren a death sentence? Theo had definitely been acting like that. But Ren was a superb guy. "Is he a thief? A polygamist? Has baby mamma drama or gets around?"

"Well, no, no, and definitely not."

"Murderer, gangster, or rapist? A drug dealer or addict?"

"Well, no drugs and not a rapist."

"He's a murderer and a gangster?!"

"Not a gangster. As for murder and not in that sense of the word, he's defended himself."

"Against whom? About what?" Lena begins to yell at Theo. "Thelonious Bartolomeu Jones, can you tell me what's stuck in your craw from the first moment you saw Ren looking at me?"

"I need people to stop fuckin' saying my full name." He broke off, took a breath, and exhaled. "I can't tell you anymore."

"What do you mean you can't tell me anymore? You haven't told me anything. Are you under some legal restriction?"

"No, I'm not his attorney."

"So spill."

"Can't; he wants to tell you himself." An uneasy tension kept building in the room. Lena's mind was whirling. Then, just as she started asking a question, Kiyoshi walked back into the room.

"I don't mean to break up the lovers' quarrel, but Theo, you're wanted. Usual room." Theo got up without a word. He glanced back at her sadly and walked out.

"Kiyoshi." He stopped and turned his head to the side. "Where is Ren?"

Still backing her, Kiyoshi took a deep breath before replying. "He will come for you when he can."

When he can, Lena thought. Lena sat back on the sofa. Yep, his voice makes a girl wanna swoon, she thought as she examined the room again. State of the art turntables and mixing platform, a stool, and this sofa. She sighed as she put her bag on her lap. Lena examined her nails for a moment. She couldn't help but think she needed to go to the salon. Then she put her bag next to her and crossed her legs. I need to stop carrying so much in my bag, she thought. She ran over the events in her mind. So, she was greeted by men, she'd never crossed paths with them, but they know her. "This is ridiculous," she mumbled to herself before getting up. Lena mumbled as she walked out of the room and turned left.

Lena walked down the hall, looking around. She passed two doors. She started to wonder if she had walked by them before. After hearing Theo's voice, she turned around and walked back to the second door. It was slightly ajar. She was about to knock when she saw someone's bared back. She hesitated. Lena knew she should have walked away, but to go where. She wasn't familiar with the building. Lena stepped forward again with her arm raised to knock. But she didn't. Lena stood transfixed, watching Cell get onto the bed with Theo. There was also a woman. Lena's mind wondered who she was. She professed Theo to be her best friend. Yet she knew so little about him, she thought. Then she saw the woman kissing Theo's neck. Lena's hand lowered, but she didn't look away. Something dark dripped and ran down Theo's chest. She gasped and quickly covered her mouth as she backed away. What was she seeing? When she took her eyes off the door, she looked up and saw Ren. Her eyes widened, one hand still over her mouth; she pointed with the other. Ren nodded and put a finger over his lips. Lena stared as he shut the door and walked over to her. Her mind was spinning. This couldn't be real.

Before she could move, Ren was there. He leaned toward her and muttered in her ear. "Let's talk, my love." Placing his hand on the small of her back to guide her up the stairs and down the hall. Lena noticed that in this hall the doors were either black or grey. Before she could think about the oddity any further, Ren opened a black door and gestured for her to enter. The room was sparsely furnished. Only a bed and one chair were there. Ren gestured for her to sit; he stood in front of Lena before squatting down. He took her hands, and it seemed like he couldn't find the words. "Yalena, I'm not sure what you saw. I wanted to tell you, but..."

This can't be it, Lena thought before speaking. "Is that what you were hiding from me?"

"I've been waiting for the right time to tell you."

"You're him."

"I beg your pardon."

"I should have known. My grandmother used to tell my sisters and me these freakish tales. She said we were descended from an ancient line and that one day a vampire would come to claim one of my sisters or me. My mother said she crossed paths with you when she was young. But you never came for any of us. You're him. You're claiming me?"

He sat next to her. "I've been stalling. I thought you were oblivious." Ren hesitated and looked at her. "I've wanted to tell you, but I was afraid you would run from me. Yalena, I have fallen in love with you. I have wanted you from the moment I held you. I want you to be mine."

"I've fallen in love with you, as well. But this is happening way too fast. I thought all of those stories were just tales."

"They are real, Lena. It wasn't supposed to be, but I am running out of time."

"What?"

"Do you want to be my beloved?"

"Yes, I believe that now."

"I need you..." Lena gazed into his eyes. For the first time, the desire that swirled for only a moment stayed as he returned her gaze.

"What? Ren, you're going to have to fill in a lot of blanks. It's been so long since I've heard about your kind. I thought they were just stories." Lena got up from the bed and paced the room.

Lena's grandmother once told her that she or her sister would marry one. She and Yazzy would argue over which one of them it would be. But, Lena stopped believing in vampires before she was twelve. She often tried to remember why her grandmother had told her and her sisters the tales. Now she knew. If, she could only remember the stories. Her next thought was if they were real, there must be so many other tangible things that she didn't want to think about. But, she couldn't help but think that there was something about her situation that she was supposed to remember. Lena turned toward Ren. "Will you feed from me as that girl did from Theo?

"Yes. Your fragrance has made me want you from the first time I was close to you. I crave to have your body and your blood. I yearn to treasure your body and mind."

"Will it hurt when you feed from me?" Did she just say that out loud? Damn, she thought. Why did she want him so badly? Why was she so willing to be a part of this?

"Probably, making love helps to distract one from the pain." He reached for her once more; this time, Lena didn't move away. She couldn't move. Her body was frozen, rooted to the spot. She wasn't sure if it was more fear of what she had gotten into or the shock of what she had seen and was becoming a part of. The feeling of him behind her made her melt into him. "Lena, can I have you right now?"

"Why rush? Why now?"

"I am fighting for you. It would be nice if you felt the same."

"Are you mine?"

"From the moment our eyes locked."

"What do you mean you're fighting for me."

"The night you walked into my club, I declared that no vampire could touch you. You were mine. I was unaware that your scent would attract so many vampires that night. That would include one who thinks he is my equal. So he threatened to take you from me before I could feed. That is why I brought you here after what happened in the restaurant. He may not seem like much, but he is resourceful."

"Before you could feed?"

"What difference would that make?"

"You, allowing me to feed on your blood, would connect us. It would not be easy for Seth to take you from me without me knowing that you were in trouble."

"Okay. So, who's the woman?"

"We need to feed on blood to stay alive. That is Marcia. She and Cell are a couple. The three of them have developed a loving relationship in addition to feeding."

"Is that what you want for us?"

"I want more than just an emotional connection and an exchange of blood."

"What do you want?"

"You forever, or as long as we live."

"I always imagined myself with children."

"That's not impossible. It may be fatal for you, though. If, the children are mine anyway."

Lena smiled for a moment and pondered how crazy she was even to contemplate this. She was trying to remember the myths that her grandmother told her, but it had been so long she could barely remember bits and pieces. If vampires did exist, what else in the world of fiction was real? Lena shuddered to think of such horrors, and he encircled his arms around her.

"I need to feed, Yalena. Will I be with you?"

"I need time. I want you so badly, but this scares me."

"It should. I understand if you need some time. However, I will have to leave you. I need to feed before the club opens. And I need you and Theo to stay here. When we close up, you'll go home with me."

"I would like to go home."

"That may no longer be possible. It's not safe." Lena gauged she wasn't going anywhere, so she plopped down on the bed, and she had a thought.

"Hey, does Cell feed on Theo too?"

"Yes, that's why he's a little off when you're with him at the end of the night. Theo is not the only one. There is a girl who comes to be with them when Theo isn't here. You will probably meet her tomorrow."

"Ren why do humans let vampires feed?"

"When we feed our body secrets a chemical into the body that gives them a euphoria. Some just want to be around vampires. Our body's pheromones give a high to those around us for long periods. We'll talk later. I will see you in a few minutes."

"Before you go. Will you make love to her while you are feeding?"

Ren smiled. "It makes it more fun, but no. I will make love to no one but you unless you say otherwise." Lena couldn't help but smile. He kissed her on the temple and inhaled. Then Ren stood up. He was about to walk to the door, but Lena gripped a handful of his shirt and just wouldn't let go.

Lena wanted Ren to hold her. She was stepping into a new world to be with him. The fact that she was so willing unnerved her a little. She felt she should have had a strong resistance. Yet, she could voice none of her doubts or emotions. All she managed to say was, "please stay with me."

Ren knelt in front of her and kissed her lips longingly. "Lena, the first feeding between mates solidifies the bond. It would be as though married." He kissed her forehead. "I will be back." He got up, but Lena would not let go. "Lena, I need to feed. Things can grow perilous for you if I do not feed." Lena regarded him, not able to do much else. She want to say that she was his. That she needed him, but her voice became lighter than a whisper and then was stuck like a bone in her throat. She bowed her head and let go of Ren's sleeve. She shrugged out of her sweater and tossed it aside before she slid back on the bed, and laid her head on the pillow.

As he knelt next to her, he smiled. "You do not have to do this now. We have some time. You are taking this all to calmly. That worries me."

Lena propped herself up on her elbows. The moment had passed and she found her voice. "I know I should be scared, but I'm not; well, not of you anyway. I'm not sure how to explain it." Lena paused before she continued. "Ren, you've had so many opportunities to have me or abuse me. You could have had your way with me, and yet you waited for it to be my choice. I'm sure you won't willingly harm me and that life is a risk. I want this. I want you." Ren smiled and kissed her as he slowly pushed her back onto the pillow. "Two more things, Ren."

"What is it?"

"Is this your room, and will you change me after we have children?"

"Yes, this is my room here. And yes, I will transform you when I feel we're ready. I told you I want you for more than seven lifetimes, as long as we live." He smiled as he lowered his head to kiss her lips. "We're not done talking. There is so much I must tell you. And we must finish the ritual that connects us." He stopped talking and caressed her neck, and then her cheek, as his thumb feather over her lips. His hand wandered all over her body as he kissed her, and her body tingled.

Lena took both of her hands and held his face to hers. Ren pulled her hands away and winked as he pulled down her pants. He pulled at his shirt, stretching and almost tearing it as he took it off. Lena wasn't disappointed by his rippling sculpted muscles and wrenched her top over her head. Ren smiled at her as he unbuttoned his pants and removed them along with his boots before he returned his attention to her. He sat next to her and ran his index finger over her torso. Lena giggled a little as his finger tickled her.

"Ticklish, are we?" Lena shook her head, yes, and he began to poke her to force her to laugh. "We are going to have so much fun before I turn you."

"Oh?"

"Yes, I plan to enjoy feeding from you because once I turn you, I will have to find feeders for both of us." He passed his hand over her bosom before yanking her shirt over her head. Ren kissed her lips, then slowly moved to nestle her neck. Ren pulled at her bra closure before he slowly pulled it from her and put her nipple in his mouth. Lena couldn't help but moan as he nibbled gently, raking his teeth over each nipple while watching her face. Lena could see his teeth elongate right before her eyes. She closed her eyes tightly. Then Lena felt the pinch as he bit her breast.

"Just a small bite." He whispered to her. "You okay?"

Lena opened her eyes and peered up at Ren. "Yes." He smiled as he intermittently sucked on the tiny cut, then plunged his tongue into her mouth. Lena could taste her blood on his tongue as he kissed her. As his fingers pinched and caressed the flesh between her thighs her body bowed. He glided two fingers inside and played with her, massaging her clit as his fingers moved in and out of her. Lena moaned loudly. Then she heard the rumble at the back of his throat.

"You are so wet," he whispered as he removed his fingers and plunged himself into her. Lena didn't think her body could take all of him, but he pushed into her deeper and deeper. Sounds rumbled in Ren's chest she had never heard before. It sounded somewhat like a growl but so much more feral. Lena watched his face until he began to kiss her neck. As he pushed deep into her, his teeth pierced her skin. The pain was dulled by the pleasure between her legs and the heat that burned inside her.

"Ohhhh, Lorenzo." He pulled back and looked into her eyes. His lips were smeared with her blood.

"Are you all right?"

"As okay as I could be with blood oozing out of the side of my neck." He smiled faintly before returning to feeding. She closed her eyes. Overwhelmed by the feeling of him and of their lovemaking. Lena moaned before he stopped feeding and kissed her. Again she encountered her blood upon his tongue and lips. It was warm still and had a metal and salty tang to it. As he kissed her, he thrust deep inside her. Lena had given her body and blood to him now. There was no turning back.

"Yalena?"

"Yes," she remarked as he licked the excess blood from her neck. "I take it; my blood tastes as wonderful as you imagined."

"More so." He growled satisfyingly before moving to lie next to her. "I will do anything to protect you, my Queen."

"My King." They kissed again with such passion as he held her tightly in his arms. He felt so warm as her blood coursed through his body. Lena rested her head upon his chest to see if the stories were true. He chuckled.

"How's my heartbeat?"

"It's so faint, but I hear it. It's very light, almost like a flutter rather than a thump. Your heart's rhythm is so slow."

"Bet you thought I didn't have a heartbeat. But something has got to circulate your blood through my body." He grinned again as he squeezed her. "Go into that bathroom, clean up, and get dressed. Theo will be here soon to take you to a room that would be more relaxed."

Lena ran her hand next to her to gather her clothes before she held them up for him to see. "It would appear that my clothes didn't fair well with our passion." Her shirt was stretched past wearing with buttons missing; her bra had no hooks.

"You'll find a bag of clothes in the bathroom. I hope you like what I have selected for you." Lena sat up a bit too quickly and held her head. "I should have told you to sit up carefully. You're going to be a bit light-headed. I apologize; I got a little greedy."

"Try not to do that often." He smiled and nodded. Lena straddled him and kissed his lips.

He turned his head to whisper in her ear as he held her. "Not sure that I could make love to you again and not feed. Let's not risk it."

"That's too bad. I am insatiable."

"After I turn you, I will gladly make love to you until the sun rises or sets. Not before. I am not sure I have enough mastery over myself to make love to you without draining you dry." He eyed her more severely as he said the last few words and moved her from his lap. Her head had stopped spinning, so Lena got up and went into the bathroom.

As she stood by the door, she asked, "who was that man that tried to get me to go with him?"

"He's the one I told you about. His name is Seth. Avoid him. He's hazardous."

"Ah, I didn't go looking for him."

"No, you didn't," murmured Ren. "You won't have to worry about him for now."

Lena waited a second before she turned to contemplate herself in the mirror for several moments. She examined the marks on her breast and her neck. Minuscule holes were left. The wounds had sealed, but she could see them if she looked near. She was sure they would show a bruise soon. Lena sighed. "So, I am to be his mate after all," Lena murmured to herself. She searched through the bag resting on the toilet seat. She approved of what he chose for her. It all seemed so leisurely and felt soft to the touch. As she took the items out of the bag, she surveyed them. She rubbed her thumb over the threads. She could see he liked quality things, she thought as she dressed. She wondered where he bought them from. The bag had no name. After she dressed, she examined herself in the mirror. She adored it. Cute and comfy. By the time she finished cleaning up and getting dressed, Ren was not in the room, but Theo sat at the edge of the bed staring at the wall.

"You just wouldn't listen to me and leave him alone." Theo stared at her, a worried expression on his face. "You had to have him, didn't you? So was it worth it?"

"Relax. You're not my father," she replied in a whisper as though she were pacifying a cat. "And, hmmm, lovely. It was ecstasy. I wish to be in his arms again."

"And feeding."

"Painful, but sex took my mind off of it. Rather, erotic. Speaking of erotic and sexy, where is my amorous vampire?"

"You called." As Lena asked for him, he walked through the door and stood before her. Dressed, but so sexy. She stood for a moment, undressing him with her eyes, knowing what lay beneath his sweater and slacks made her body react--remembering the man that hovered over her not long ago. Lena put her arms around his neck and kissed him longingly. "Do not worry; I am yours for eternity." He kissed her lips one more time and pulled her arms from around his neck. "I must go. I will come to collect you when I am ready to go to the penthouse." Lena nodded, and he disappeared in the blink of an eye.

"Shall we go, Lena?"

"Where are we going, Theo?"

"A room on the third floor. It's pretty cool. They have already sent food and drinks up. One of the drinks you'll have to get accustomed to."

"That dark thing, you and the rest of the club drink?"

"Yes, it's just a concoction that Ren created. It's supposed to nourish the body and help replenish the blood. He has a knack for cooking. Weird right? Vampires don't eat."

When they entered the room, their food was already there, and so were their drinks. Theo was right. It appeared they planned on them being there for a while. But it was cozy. There were comfy chairs and a large TV.

"Does this often happen, Theo?"

"Only when the council comes. Relax, it may be a couple of hours."

This was genuinely crazy, Lena thought. Her mind was racing as she paced back and forth. She really had no clue what was going on in the city where she lived. Lena often preferred to be secluded in her home, away from the rest of the world. When she wrote, she blocked out everything so that she could focus. She hated watching the news, but sometimes the reports and being up on the latest movies were her only link to the outside world. Lena read a lot; she loved books. She liked to understand what was going through other authors' minds. She had been fascinated with the vampire world for a while. At the time, she thought it was fantasy. Lena had no knowledge of its actual existence. Her mom had advised her that her fascination with them was detrimental. Now, Lena knew why.

Theo and Lena settled in the theater room. The walls were dark, and several home theater chairs were arranged in two sets in front of the big screen. Lena wondered where the vampires would gather. Theo told her about the conference room located on the first floor. He said it was in the corner of the building and was used for nothing else. Lena asked what it looked like, and he offered to sneak her down another night while their men were occupied.

Chapter 8

Ren sat in his office watching the monitors of the club and the conference room. As a mix of house and hip-hop pumped through the building's first floor, the vampire council assembled in the conference room. The room was simple. It was a white-walled room with an extra-long cherry oak table in the center. Fifteen seats were set around the table for each member, their mates, and feeder, two places at the table's head for him and his queen. Cell and Marcia would sit on either side of them. Despite the white walls, the room seemed rather dark. There were no windows in the room, and it was lit by lanterns in each corner.

Once they had gathered to enter the room, Ren decided it was time to go down. He didn't need to make them sit and wait. It never made this easier but seem to make them more cruel. The vampires were ushered in, and all took their seats around the table. No vampire came unattended. Each came with a companion and a feeder. Once everyone was settled, the double doors were barred by one of Ren's men. Ren had one guard posted for each entry that led to the building on council meeting nights. Finally, Ren encroached into the room and everyone stood until told to sit down.

"Why are we here, Arias? Why did you call an assembly? It is not time for us to meet."

Ren had yet to reach his seat when the question was posed. "Well, Lockington, I didn't want to banish or silence one of the council members' children without giving his maker and him a chance to voice an opinion."

"Please tell me this is not about the little girl you have been chasing and haven't yet fed from," said Jon. He feigned a yawn, his thin lips stretching. Ren knew he was trying to hide his interest.

Ren tried to calm his rabid temper. How dare he? How dare they? "I see Seth has taken time to fill your heads with misconceptions."

"Is it a misconception?" Seth decided to chime in with a question.

Naturally, Seth used any opportunity to undermine him, or at least he thought he did. Ren was now utterly aware that he will not win this one. He should have beheaded Seth in his club room under

the DJ room. They would have been upset, but Lena would be safe.
Now he would play a dangerous game. "This is not about my
Queen."

"So you have fed," uttered Lockington.

Ren sat up straight in his seat and addressed the council calmly.
"This is early assembly is about Seth's disrespect of me and my
authority as your sovereign. It will not be tolerated." Ren knew he
was fighting a losing battle and paused to repose his temper. He
leaned back in his chair and steepled his hand. Ren stared at Seth
for a moment. He was wearing a t-shirt underneath a leather jacket
and a flannel shirt tied around his waist. "Did you know that there
have been corpses drained of blood showing up at hospitals across
the city? Also, people drained of blood with no memory, and two
who had been changed. This happens every week."

"You can't expect me to supervise all my children," responded
a woman next to Seth.

"I didn't single anyone out," Ren chided as their eyes met.

"Madeline, you can't be for real. We all have children, and the
others and I manage to watch and guide them if they get out of
line. Yours seem to be the only ones whose behavior is never
checked by you," said the portly man across the table.

Madeline Pierre hated to be put on the spot. She was the type
of vampire who gladly faded into the background. If she were lost
in the environment, no one would remember her or what happened.

She was stark, and there was really nothing particular about her to remember other than possibly her raven black hair.

"Seth, what do you have to say for yourself," asked Lockington.

"I don't like the laws. You have all these decrees. Only feed in particular places. Should be willing to feeders. No killing, no hunting. Where is the fun in that?"

"Son, you weren't born in the time of vampires hunting. What do you know of it? We haven't hunted in centuries, hunted people anyway. Some of us choose to hunt animals now and again to keep our skills and senses sharp. If you want to hunt and kill, join those groups."

Seth turned to his mother. "Don't you get it, Maddie? I just don't like rules. I don't like him; he's not my sovereign."

"Insolence."

"Woods, you would do better to clam up in his presence. He is not a vampire to be trifled with," Jon plainly voiced.

"Please, what is grandfather going to do?" Seth replied.

"Viste?" Before Seth could manage to respond to what Ren had said, Ren slit his throat and pulled him out of the chair next to Madeline. "Sos un boludo. ¿Como no vas a entender algo tan simple?" Still, Ren didn't think it was enough to show his strength, so he ran him through with the same silver stiletto he had wielded before. Seth was suspended in mid-air by that same blade. Seth's feet violently shook below him, almost a foot above the ground. Blood rushed from his body as his flesh began to smolder from the silver blade stuck in his chest. "Learn respect," Ren said with a calm voice as he leered into Seth's eyes. Ren was fuming. He took a few seconds to calm himself. Then he turned to Madeline, "I will not continue to tolerate such contumacious behavior, Madeline." As he held him in the air, he calculated it was the superior time to tell them about the soldiers. Seth's body began to shudder with pain as his body healed around the blade, only to burn again. "Did I tell you about the soldiers he brought into Zoe's? Not just one or two but sixteen soldiers where other vampires were feeding. Sixteen savage killers, where our feeders were."

"Soldiers!" Lockington repeated. All members at the table gaped at Madeline and Seth.

"No one even makes them anymore except out Liege. It's a well kept secret", chimed Lockington.

"I got my sources," said Seth weakly, sitting on the floor in a pool of his blood as the last of the healing continued.

"Lleva los meses quemándose la cabeza,' Ren said as he wiped the blood from his hands and threw the handkerchief in Seth's face. He walked to the front of the room to watch the council's faces.

"So, what do you want to do with him?" Madeline Pierre asked. Ren knew she would be nervous. If they kept pushing, she would lose her only son from her human womb. They were playing a baleful game.

"That's why you're all here. Seth's fate is in your hands. If we have any more problems, I will solve it; permanently."

"May we be introduced to the Lady who seems to be the center of all this?"

"Akbar, I had no intention of bringing her here this eve."

"Is it, not our custom to bring our mates to the first council meeting after the union has taken place?" asked Jon.

"It is Jon," confirmed Ren

"So when will we meet her? She's probably one of the two humans in the room a couple of floors above us."

"Very observant, Lockington." Ren glared at him. He never liked the way Lockington always played close to the vest. Way too close. Now he would have to go get Lena.

"You tried to hide her, but the old nose still works."

Old nose my ass, thought Ren. "While you discuss what to do with Woods, I will get her. I warn you all; I have not completed the ritual, and the aroma of her blood seems to arouse most vampires."

"Please, you speak of common vampires, not us. Please waste no more time. We wish to convene with our Queen," chimed Akbar.

"Very well, I will get her. Cell and Marcia, get him out of here," he said pointing at Seth. "And have someone clean this up and check on the club for me. Make sure the club is running smoothly." With a simple nod, Cell, and Marcia, left the room.

As the events occurred, Theo and Lena had been watching them in the theater. Lena was in shock. She could not believe that she had mated herself to one of the most preeminent vampires on this side of the globe.

"I can't believe you didn't figure that out. You have always managed to find the most prominent person in the room and attach yourself to them. He is no different from the men you normally pull. Well, except he's not human, is he? Well, not entirely anyway."

"No, he's not totally, is he? But such speed, such strength; influential men do turn me on."

"Oh boy, if you weren't in love before, you are now." Theo began to laugh. Lena didn't think it was quite so funny. She threw a pillow at him. That is when Ren came into the theater.

"Theo, what have you been doing to vex my queen?

"Just making her see the truth about herself."

"And it is?"

"She has a thing for powerful men. And you, sir, are an illustrious man."

Ren stared at Theo. "Well, be that as it may, Lena, I need you to come to the council meeting. You will take your place after today by my side at the table. But today, it's just an introduction. I did not want to take you to the conclave before I spoke to you. If you want to change your mind, now is the time. Once you are introduced to the council, the game changes, and there is no way out." Lena didn't reply; she slowly walked up to him with a smile on her face and reached up to kiss his lips. The kiss felt like the beginning of a beautiful night. He pulled away and clasped her hands. "Come, they have been talking long enough, and I don't like where their conversation is headed. And Theo, you shouldn't have encouraged her to watch the surveillance camera."

"Yes, your liege."

"Am I dressed well enough?"

"You know what you regard as casual others consider to be almost dressy. I hope that isn't your biggest fear now."

"No, a nervous habit." Ren nodded his head and whisked her to the elevator.

They took it to the first floor and walked to the room where all the vampires sat around the table. Everyone was silent when they entered the room. Ren immediately walked Lena over to the head of the table. It was a simple room, white walls, and scones in the corners. As she walked, Lena looked at all the faces around the table. She didn't know that so many vampires were involved in running the city.

Everyone was quiet for a moment. Lena felt like she was suddenly under a microscope, and she didn't like it. This was grating against her senses. Then the vampire closest to her took a deep breath and smiled. Lena was repulsed. But she tried to school her features to a nonchalant calm. She thought of her first audience with the publishing companies' execs and how she remained calm.

"Ladies, gentlemen, and mates, this is my queen and yours, Yalena."

"Mademoiselle, Yalena, I am Gordon Lockington," greeting Lena with a strong French accent. Lena recognized him as soon as she saw him. She would never forget her grandfather's dark brown wavy mass of curls with one sand colored patch in the front. He was sitting straight up in his chair, his almost black skin radiant as always. Still, she believed it was better to behave as though she didn't know him. She wasn't sure what her response should be when meeting the council, so she nodded and gave a slight smile.

As Ren said, each name of the council, Lena smiled at them, and they gave a slight bow. "There is also Madeline Pierre." Yalena looked the woman directly in the eye, a small smile on her face as she bowed her head ever so slightly. Madeline's face was stern, she did not return Yalena's smile, and her bow was almost imperceptible. "Jonathan Dunne, we call him Jon." Dunne looked like an average white man; he wasn't fat or skinny. His eyes were brown, as well as his hair. There was nothing distinctive about him. "And Mohamed Akbar." As she greeted Akbar with a smile, he acknowledged her greeting. Dressed in a dark suit, he was a tan and portly man with his eyes reflecting warmth. "Yalena, they are the council along with their mates."

Lockington cleared his throat. "Forgive me for being so blunt, Ren, but I now understand why there is all the fuss. She smells so sweet and delightful. And since we know that Seth cannot master himself, it is natural that he wanted her." Lena knew Lockington wasn't the least bothered by her smell. She was his blood.

"I agree with you, Lockington; my mouth is watering just by the scent of her. Ren, I believe you should take her back to the room she was in. It could get ugly down here."

"Thank you, Jon. I believe that is best."

"Before you go, has she fed?"

"No, Jon, I am not ready to turn her yet."

"Hmm, that could get dangerous, Arias, for her."

"I can assure you that you will not have to worry about that. I will get the council's decision when I return." He led Lena out of the room rather quickly.

As they exited the elevator, Lena pulled away from Ren. "What was that about? Why did you drag me down there only to leave so soon? And why did he ask you if I fed already?"

"Can we speak in the room?"

"Why not now?"

"Now, who's being difficult?"

"Ren!"

"Walls have ears and all." When that didn't seem to move her, he stepped closer and whispered in her ear.

"The rooms here are soundproof. Exceptional hearing and all."

"Oh," Only then did she let him take her into the room.

"And please do me a favor."

"Yes?"

"If you are going to question me, wait until we're behind closed doors."

"Yes, of course, my King," she stated a bit sarcastically. Once they reached the room, he let go of her and shut the door behind them. Lena glanced around to see where Theo was, but she and Ren were absolutely alone.

"Where is Theo?"

"Probably on the dance floor."

"I'll to join him after we speak."

"You shouldn't leave this room. Everything you need is here."

"And the reason I shouldn't leave this room," Lena asked as she crossed her arms over her chest.

"Theo is not in danger from a rebel vampire who will not follow the edits already set. And he is under Cell's protection. You, on the other hand, are my responsibility. And until I train and turn you, you cannot club when the others are here."

Lena wondered what training he thought she needed. He'd already seen her in action. "So, even though they know I belong to you, they would still try to kill me?"

"Yes, there is talk going around about a legend. The myth is about the Egyptian vampire goddess."

"Who do they consider a vampire deity?"

"Sekhmet."

"Why would they say Sekhmet was a vampire goddess?" He chuckled when Lena asked. "What's so comical?"

"You've heard of Sekhmet, and there is nothing about her that would make you think vampire."

"I never really thought about it like that. I suppose. She was bloodthirsty; it is said that she drank blood and had to be tricked by Amen and Mut into drinking a blood potion that ended her blood lust. Some say that it transformed her into the goddess Het Heru."

"You use their Khemetic names instead of the Greek."

"That's what I was taught. My mom believed that using the original names gave them more power than the Greek ones."

"As Shakespeare would say, 'what is in a name?'"

"Sometimes, everything is in a name. Vibrations have power."

Ren smiled. "And I know Het Heru's number is 5, and that is your favorite number."

"Stop teasing and tell me already, Ren."

"Well, Lena, in the legend, the first bloodline of the goddess still exists. Her descendant is a woman. The vampire who makes her his queen will be one of the most illustrious of all vampires. It is said that all vampires will unite under him to command this earth. They believe that you are that first line. If I am the one to turn you and make you my mate, I will be the one to rule this earth. To them, that means the life we live now, hidden. Many don't want to be hidden; they want to dominate humans and enslave them. While I don't want to be hidden, I feel that it is best. We have been hunted before, and it is not a pleasant event for humans or vampires alike. It is better to live a life where those who seek us find us. We live a good life, a part of society. I think that is quite beautiful."

"What makes them think I am the first line."

"Your willingness to be with me and their greed to covet you. No mass of vampires had ever been drawn to one human. Your smell attracts them. You may find that they may listen to you, a mere mortal if you speak. Whether they want to or not."

"And you; do you have that same feeling?

"Desire you, yes. But it is said that her true mate will be the only one to have dominion over her and will not succumb to her will or whim."

"And yes, you do have some sway over me."

"Do I?"

"I'm accustomed to getting what I want when I want. I have never had a man talk to me with such authority, and I actually listen and consent. I am normally the rebel. But I'm not sure if that is because you are a vampire or not."

"We can test that," Ren reacted with raised eyebrows. But I need to get back to my meeting. The council is planning a coup. They were all in on the scheme, and they will try again."

"What plan, Ren? How do you know all of this." He moved his hair out of the way to show his ears, and there it was a small earpiece.

"The room has the equipment."

"Yes, most of the rooms here are soundproof. How else is a vampire supposed to know if his subjects plot to overthrow him?" He winked at her as he left the room. Lena turned on the surveillance feed to see what the council was up to in the conference room. And as Lena would have it, they were talking about her.

"So Jon, do you think she is the first line," asked '

"It does seem so, doesn't it? We shall see, I guess."

Mohamed chimed in. "We can't wait to see. We need not take any chances. We need to be rid of her. I say we let Seth try one last time."

"But if he gets caught, Mohamed, Ren will eliminate him."

"And that is my problem, how? Besides, it's for the greater good. Without her, we can overthrow Ren, and we can rule."

"We are talking about my only son. My son from my womb before Ren killed his father. Besides, how do we know we'll be able to overthrow him? He is the most puissant and cunning of us. He has gained and maintained governance for over two centuries."

Jon sat in silence for several moments. "Pierre deserved it. What did he think Ren would do to him if he were caught?"

Lockington rolled his eyes. "And yet we sit here plotting his demise." With the twist of the doorknob, the room fell silent. Cell and Ren intruded.

"So, what have you all deliberated?"

"Arias, I believe I can speak for the group, and we decided that we should chalk it up to growing pains," replied Lockington. "You know youngsters, always rebellious."

"If that is your choice. It would have been safer and better to exile Seth for some time. But your decision stands; I will not overrule you. I will explain to you one thing. Should he, at any time, offend or try to abuse my Queen, or should he disrespect me, I will end him without your consent."

Jon took a deep breath and blew it out through his mouth. "We understand your liege."

"And thank you for giving Woods another chance."

"Fine. Madeline, keep him out of my way. I warn you all, there will be no second chances."

"Will everyone be staying?"

"No, Cell, we are all going back to our side of town."

"Speak for yourself; I will stay and enjoy the festivities downstairs. I can still cut a mean rug."

"Well, Lockington, you are welcome to stay. There are plenty of beautiful women downstairs."

"I'm sure there are none as tempting as your Yalena."

"You've got me there. None as tempting for me anyway."

Chapter 9

As they rode to Ren's Park Avenue home, Lena sat quietly in the taxi. The day had been incredibly long, and Lena looked forward to the much needed rest. Her mind reeling after all that occurred. Yet, she had so many questions about how her life would change. She wasn't even sure how she was taking it all so well. Granted, as a child, she was told of vampires and that they lived all around them. She even remembered the tale her grandmother told of one visiting the family from time to time looking for his partner. But never did she think they were more than stories. She couldn't help but wonder if he had come to her house.

Lena was in awe of Lorenzo. She gave little consideration to what would develop. Now, she was the wife of a vampire, Queen to the tribe and family. She didn't even want to think of herself having children that might kill her. She had no concept of what it would be like to live centuries. On top of it all, she and Ren were mates for what may eventually feel like an eternity, even if it wasn't. Did vampires break up? The movies always made it seem like forever. This was enormous. If that wasn't enough, her life was threatened by people or vampires, she had never encountered until today. And for what reason?

"Long day."

"Who are you telling;" Lena retorted. She hugged him and rested her head on his chest. "I watched the room after you left me."

"We will discuss that at home. I just want to make sure you are okay."

"As well as can be expected after the day I've had," Lena stated as she reached up to kiss him. He squeezed her and then held her a little closer the rest of the way.

When the car stopped, Ren got out and walked around to open her door. As she waited, Lena shifted her head to look up at the building. The gray stone building was several stories tall. As they approached the building, a gentleman in a dark suit greeted them and opened the door. Ren took her hand and led her down a short hallway. They took an elevator to the top floor.

Finally, she thought. She pondered why Ren lived so far from his business. She followed him into a short foyer and where he gestured for her to sit down. "I don't wear shoes in my home. Slippers are underneath the bench unless you'd like to go barefoot. I should warn you the marble floors are cold. But most of the rooms are carpeted." Ren bent down and pulled out a pair of pink ballet slippers. "I thought you'd like these."

Lena smiled. "Thank you. You're taking such good care of me, Ren."

He nodded and smiled. Lena slid off her ankle boots, and Ren slipped the slippers on her feet before taking off his and putting his feet into slippers of his own.

Lena followed Ren through his home, looking around as she went. The first room she viewed was the living room, across from the foyer. She was shocked by it all. She didn't predict the home would be large and definitely not warm and comfy. She wasn't sure what to expect. The fireplace came to a flaming roar when they entered the room where Ren said he had recently spent most of his time. The room was almost bare, although the carpet was a silky, shag lilac carpet, a pile of large pillows rested against the wall, and a futon in the corner with a colorful decorative cover and pillows. He turned on some jazz, Lena grabbed a sizable pink cushion and sat by the fire.

"I think this will be my most cherished room. I could write here. I like the mood, the ambiance. Plus, there's something freeing about sitting on the floor."

"I am delighted. It was empty until about two weeks ago. I had it decorated with you in mind. I wanted to give you a place in my home that was all you and would be deemed comfortable. Of course, I did not fathom that this would turn into our home so soon. Things have moved quite hastily for us." Ren came and sat behind her on another pillow. He embraced her, and she leaned back on him. "I love you, Yalena. I noticed you when you walked into Zoe's with Theo. I make a habit of watching the door from the booth; never have I had my breath taken away as when I glimpsed you. You looked so beautiful that night. Then our eyes met when you looked up to the DJ booth."

"Ren, when I saw you, I was curious as to who you were. But Theo wouldn't tell me anything. He wanted me to stay away from you. I wasn't aware you were watching me, but I presumed that I caught your eye. Especially when you came to talk to me."

"I had to find out who you were. I had to know you, even if it was for a night or a week."

"Yeah, who would have thought that I would be mated to you for an eternity."

"You say it as though you are not happy about this."

"Hundreds of years is a long time. Most people can't be married for half of a lifetime. Just wondering if we will tire of each other."

"We can cross that bridge when we come to it. Vampires tend to feel things with such intensity, hatred, revenge, love. We tend to love our mates for our whole life. I am acquainted with many vampires who fell in love, but the one they loved did not want this life or them after discovering who or what they were. They have never mated again. We have one companion for our lifetime, however long that is. Once you have turned, you will understand."

It was quiet for several moments. Lena took her time assimilating the information. Finally, she took a deep breath and leaned further back on Ren. He cocooned her tighter in his arms and kissed the top of her head. "Lena, do you even want me to turn you? Maybe you want to stay as you are?"

"I hadn't really thought there could be any other way. Your world is a danger to me. When we spoke earlier, you said that I would have children. But how would I protect our children if I am not like you."

"You will always be protected, my Queen. You do not have to transform just to experience safety."

"Then, of course, I will grow old and wrinkled. I will leave you behind much sooner if you don't change me."

"I'm sure you'll still be just as beautiful as you are now. You would leave me sooner than I would like. I have lived so many centuries without you. Still, this is your decision, Lena. It works well for me either way. Of course, I desire for you to eventually want to be like me. I want to spend more than one lifetime with you."

Hearing those words warmed her heart. She took one of Ren's hands and kissed it. With him, she was enveloped in peace. A serenity and love Lena hadn't received from any of her other lovers. "One of your council members mentioned something about me feeding. What was he talking about?"

"To assent the bond between us, you must drink of my blood. It laces us together. I will official become your consort and you mine. I did not request the binding because I wanted to give you a chance to revise your decision. Though we live for a long time, this life is not easy. I was unsure what your reaction would eventually be. You were so calm and unfazed when I told you who I was, it scared me. I thought that when the knowledge sank in, you would run in the other direction. That may be what you should do."

"No, my love. By the time you told me, I had already given you my heart. I accepted that I belonged with you before you said anything. I wasn't willing to run away from what my heart seemed to have found for me." As Lena spoke, she reached up to caress his face and ran her thumb over his lips. "I was told of you and your world when I was young. It is only after you showed me who you were that I realized I was not told tales."

"I only wish we had found each other earlier. This is a risky time. The council is planning my downfall as we speak. While I have no fear that I will live on, I fear for you, my love. They can be quite treacherous, and the lengths they will go through to make sure you are not mine scares me. I am not sure what I would do to them if anything happened to you. And I do not want to live without you."

"Will our exchange of blood alter their decision?"

"No, it would just mean that we're getting nearer to me changing you. And that is what the council fears the most."

"I heard them today. They really want me dead. Seth is going to try again. Madeline wasn't happy, but they are going to risk his life." Yalena drew closer to Ren

"I am mindful. They are petrified that you are from that line."

"Do you believe that I am her, the descendant of the line of Sekhmet?"

"Yes."

"How do you know so much? We're talking about a line that is older than the world's knowledge."

"My sire told me a lot. He also helped me find some of the ancient scrolls."

Lena nodded. She couldn't help but think that she would like to meet this sire. She has a lot of questions for him. Especially where he ascertained his knowledge. "Ren, can you tell me more about that line? What's so special about it?"

"Well, although you may not be a full vampire or born to any vampire parents, the line we speak of is a line of pure vampires. Sekhmet is the Khemetic line. And if you are one of her descendants, you are part of the first line."

"I'm not sure I understand."

"If the legend is right, Sekhmet was a vampire. She had three children. Two of her three children were from her mate Ptah. The first of her children, a female not many were cognizant of or even comprehended. She was conceived during one of her rampages. Before the marriage to Ptah, the nameless girl child was conceived and born before Amen could transform her. The blood potion that Amen tricked her into consuming, changed her whole being. But her very first child was born of two vampire parents."

"But two vampires can't have children."

"That is true about today's vampires. If that were true then, she shouldn't have had children at all, but she did. We are talking about a true immortal. According to the Khemetic religion, Sekhmet was the daughter of the creator, Amen, and his wife Mut; she was a goddess. She was sent to earth to rid it of the unrighteous, but she became bloodthirsty. So she would be no normal vampire. That is what makes this legend so incredible. Not only did she manage to have two other children, but a full fledged vampire. That is why the first line legend is so important. Whoever is mated to the descendant of a pure vampire line will have the power to rule our world and end those who will not comply with rules that allow us to live with our feeders."

"Big deal, huh?"

"Yep."

"What are the signs?"

"Like I told you before, the attraction to you that vampires can't seem to help. The scent of your blood being hard for vampires to resist."

"We've seen that. What else?"

"Even though you may not change physically after your feeding, the first line heir have a proclivity to exhibit some vampire traits. You will not be as strong as other vampires but stronger than your human counterparts. Also, your senses will be heightened, and you may grow fangs. While mine lengthen before I feed, yours will stay until I turn you if you are of the first line. Actually, they are supposed to come in after the binding ritual."

"Really! Anything else I should grasp?"

"Most human women die in childbirth to have one dhampir. The descendant of the first line will bear at least three children. There will absolutely be two pregnancies; one set will be twins. The legend doesn't say exactly how many children."

"Not sure I should be scared, happy, or mortified." Lena chuckled a little and then sighed. She knew that he mentioned it but it was still a daunting thought. Having children is such a dangerous life event. One wonders why women have the desire to give birth. "I never really pictured myself with more than two children." Ren couldn't help but chuckle at her reaction. "Will you love me even if I am not her?" Lena paused again and turned slightly towards Ren. "So you mean to tell me, that if I am not the line, I will die after my first birth to your children?"

"I will not lose you, Lena. Should your pregnancy put you in danger, I will transform you."

It was silent for a little while. Lena needed some time to absorb what she was just told. She truly cared about Ren. She had started to love him from the moment he held her in his arms. She wished it was that simple. If he were only, just human. "We should finish the ritual and bind ourselves to each other."

"I must warn you; some people become violently ill if they feed on our blood. That's why most mates haven't had children. They were turned by their lover for fear of losing them."

"Is that why you haven't transformed me."

"Yes, I told you I want to give you every wish your heart desires. And I understand that children mean a lot to you."

"Think you can make love to me without draining me dry."

"Yes." Lena grinned at his reaction, and she turned to face him. Kissing his cheek before she turned and knelt on the pillow before him, removed her shirt, and untied her wrap skirt.

"God, you are gorgeous," Lena said as she unbuttoned his shirt and kissed his full lips. She ran her hands down the rippling muscles of his chest.

Ren carried her over to the futon with such fluid motion she was unaware of their movement while kissing him. Lena gazed in heat as Ren unbuckled his pants and dropped them to the floor before taking off his boxers. Lena quickly removed her panties for fear that he would rip them in the haste of trying to grasp what he wanted the most. Ren chuckled at her actions. As they kissed again, he hovered over her and removed her bra. He wasted no time with foreplay but slid into her body.

"Lorenzo," Lena sighed He kissed her lips and slowly pushed himself deeper inside.

"Yalena, my love." He used his fingernail to slit his wrist and held it to her mouth. His blood was syrupy and warm. As she fed she hear him say. "Te doy mi sangre, para que te conviertas en parte de mí. Cuando tomas mi sangre, estás atado a mi costado y no estoy atado a ningún otro. Tú eres mi consorte y yo la tuya. Nada vendrá delante de nosotros." Lena felt as though there were fine strings lacing her to Ren and nurturing her. The cords seemed to tighten ever so slightly as he bit her side. This time it wasn't as painful as the first time. Lena was unsure if that was because she was drinking his blood or their entanglement. Sooner than Lena wanted him to, he pulled his arm away from her mouth.

"Lena, are you ok." He was looking directly into her eyes. Lena took his face in her hands and kissed his lips. He continued the fluid motion, pushing further into her with each stroke. His caress emulated heaven throughout her body, she thought as she moaned loudly.

"I wasn't sated. But I am fine. Just tired, Ren." It was dawn now. Lena had been up for almost twenty-four hours, and she started to crash.

"What was it you said to me? It felt like I was being tied to you."

"You were. But it was more like I was being anchored to your side." He smiled slightly and kissed her cheek as he whispered. "What I said to you was 'I give you my blood, so that you become part of me. As you take my blood, you are fastened to my side and I am bound to no other. You are my consort and I yours. Nothing shall come before us."

"How beautiful, Ren." Lena brought his head closer to her and kissed him longingly. "I feel like I should have said something."

"When you feel the time is right, you will anchor yourself to me as well. How do you feel?"

"Like I am ready to pass out. I usually don't sleep much past sunrise, so just let me rest. I will probably leave the club early tonight and go home."

"You seek to leave me already?" Ren chided before he continued. I'm sure you didn't think you would move in so soon. But, no, you can't go home." Her eyes shot open "I can send someone for your things, but you can't go home. Not now. It is not safe. This is your home now. Any of your friends you want to keep in contact with, just tell them where you are. They can come to visit, but you can not go to your apartment."

"This is more severe than I realize?"

"I'm afraid so. Get some rest. I have some things to handle, but I will be here. Do you mind if I take a look around your apartment?"

"No, of course not. Got to make sure your men bring everything. Just stay with me 'til I fall asleep. My gums hurt."

"Hmm, I will stay until then." And he did. She slumbered in his strong arms.

He fixated, his eyes unblinking as her stared at her for moments at a time. She was in his arms. Ren smiled and kissed Lena's forehead. Then he stared as she smiled slightly and mumbled before turning away from him. He didn't know that she talked in her sleep. Well, not talk, she murmured. Ren smiled before getting up. He wanted nothing more than to keep a vigil next to her. Still, he couldn't watch her all night. Even though he was tempted to stay, he decided to leave the room.

It had taken him over nine hundred years to encounter his beloved. Then he had to wait over a decade to even hold her again. Now she was in his home. He had made love to her and tasted her blood. She was his mate. Ren had never thought that he would experience real love. He had never known any vampire who had waited as long as he had for their mate. There was only one tale of a god who had waited ten thousand years. Ren was glad his wait had not been that long. Lena had brought him the feelings and pressures of love. His only regret right now was that he hadn't been totally honest about her role in all this. Ren took a breath. He hated that he twisted the prophecy. He wanted her to know everything, but from what he had learned of his Lena, she needed to acclimate to her environment. Telling her that the world he curated was not to be his may be too much for her. He would tell her soon, that this world was hers. Their clan and family would return to their matriarchal way of life.

Ren sat in his chair reeling in the knowledge of it all. All that he had been taught and what he suffered was in preparation for this. Lockington had promised him Yalena, and now she was his. He smiled. Ren glanced at the clock before the phone rang.

"Hello," he said after picking up on the first ring. He didn't want to wake Lena. "I thought you would have called sooner," he said to the person on the other line. "Lockington, she's fine and yes she's asleep. Shouldn't you be also?.... "And what kind of gratitude do you deserve after putting myself and your granddaughter in harm's way?" Ren got up from his chair. This was just the thing he needed to get himself going. "Listen, I've got to check out Lena's apartment....I'll keep in touch." Ren slammed the phone onto the cradle. He was glad she was nothing like Lockington. Promise or none, he could not love such a woman.

"So much for work," Ren said to no one an hour later. He sent some of his men and Kiyoshi to Lena's apartment to move her things and bring some here, but that was all he did. He would head over and see what they found. He didn't want to leave anything behind that she might need.

Lena wasn't a late sleeper, even if she was exhausted. But this day, Lena rose in the afternoon. And she woke up the same way she fell asleep, in his arms. Lena smiled to see him when she opened her eyes. He kissed her forehead and smiled.

"I see your fangs came in."

"Stop playing. My gums are quite sore." This was really happening, she thought. She had wondered why her grandfather had taken such a shine to her. When her mom had stopped talking to her about this lineage, her grandfather still told her bits and pieces of his history.

"Your fangs did indeed grow in last night. And they are only a little longer than your normal eye teeth. They don't look bad." Lena touched her fangs to see if he was telling the truth. Her mouth felt strange, but the room had no mirror to see what had changed.

"Ouch, they're sharp." Lena sucked the blood that oozed out of her finger. "Guess I am the first line. Or maybe from another ancient blood line. The Khemetic line cannot be the only one, can it?" Lena knew that Khemits history was ancient, but she also knew there were histories that were older. Ancient Khemit was a culmination of African history. People from all over African migrated from other southern cultures to create it. There had to be deities from those cultures.

"We shall see. Until then, you must eat. Here is your breakfast."

"I knew I smelt something cooking. Smells good."

"Thanks. Your clothes are in the bedroom, and your desk is in the office set up with your laptop and other computer items from your apartment."

"All of my things? When did the guys bring them?" She guess this was really it. He did say that she couldn't go home, but to move her home.

"I had people moving things from your apartment after leaving your side. Your furniture will be in storage until we move or figure out what to do. I had them bring your dresser; your belongings are in our room. All your things have been put away. And the shoe closet is right outside the bathroom in our room."

"Really, that's, well, it's a lot." When Ren didn't reply she continued. "Was I asleep that long? I didn't hear people moving about. I was expecting to go home tonight. I, I didn't think we would move this fast."

Ren smiled gently at her. "I know it's a lot and I didn't ask. Still, you're safer here and your safety is my priority," he said as he pushed a curl behind her ear. "Our bedroom is on the other side of the apartment. How is your breakfast?"

"Great, thanks, Ren."

"My pleasure. Now I have to check in at the restaurant and the club. So I will be gone for the day. If you decide to leave the house at night, you should take Patrick with you. Or he'll arrange for Charlie. They are both here but tend to make themselves scarce. If you need Patrick, just call his name."

"Who is Patrick?"

"The main soldier that is in charge of your safety. He prefers not to go out in the sunlight, though. You can just tell him where you're going. When you need him, he'll be there. Patrick's great that way."

"I thought that you didn't keep soldiers anymore."

"In peaceful times, only the head of the clan is allowed to keep soldiers."

"Ren, you were trying to tell me about your real age before, weren't you?"

"Yes."

"And how old are you?"

"Nine hundred and seventy-nine."

"Seriously? So, you are an old pervert." Lena had to say something sardonic. He smiled a sly smile and was by her side in an eye blink.

"Lena, are you saying I'm too old for you?"

"Way, way, way, way, way, waaaay too old." Lena laughed. Ren pushed aside the breakfast tray, and hovered over her, baring his teeth.

"My love, you look so delicious. Do you mind if I drink your blood, blah?" Lena laid back in the bed, but she was still laughing. Ren removed the sheet and parted her legs before beginning to use his tongue to explore her. Lena couldn't help but moan as he tickled her inside. She was in heaven. Then he replaced his tongue with two of his fingers and bit into her thigh. She tensed up as she came with his head and hands between her legs.

"Still think I'm too old for you?" He asked as he gently eased himself into her. Her body quivered under his as he kissed her lips.

The taste and aroma of her blood on his tongue and lips. She couldn't respond verbally. But she was sure that her body's rise to him was more than satisfactory. He stopped kissing her to run his tongue along her fangs. She guessed he would approve. While he wouldn't tell her, she was sure that he was happy events were proving that she descended from the first line. As he gave her such pleasure, she stopped thinking all thoughts. Lena moaned and called his name.

"Is this what you vampires do all night?"

"We have only just begun, my love." And as he said that, he pushed more forcefully and deeper into her. Lena screamed before he covered her mouth. Then, Lena bit into his hand without even thinking, and a smile spread across his face.

"Am I going to have to ascertain a feeder?"

"Sorry, it just felt so right. Not sure I want anyone else's blood circulating through my body right now." He moved his hand and kissed her. Lena gave in to the urge and her teeth pierced his tongue. His blood was sweet, and Lena couldn't seem to help herself.

"I will have to keep reminding myself that you are not a full vampire yet. You are really playful and insatiable." It was sublime to make love to him as often as Lena wanted. Then he had to ruin the mood by reminding her that he had to go. "I will leave you in a little while."

"Just hold me for a while." And that he did. It was silent for several minutes. Lena just had to know more about the council's decision "Now, why didn't the council exile, Seth?"

"They need him here. None of them can really move against me, but Seth wants my predominance, and he figures he can take it. So the council can hide behind him. They think I am none the wiser."

"So basically, they are willing to sacrifice him."

"Yes, they are. All except for Madeline. She will be infuriated with me when I slaughter him."

"You think you will have to?"

"It may not happen soon, but he will try to reach me through you, and I will eliminate him. That will start the war, and we will probably have to move someplace else."

"Wherever you go, I go." He kissed her when she said that. Lena presumed that he was happy to know that she was with him whatever happened. Lena wondered why she was so willing to be with him. Why was she so drawn to him, come what may?

"Now, get up and get dressed. This morning, your publisher called and said that your latest book deadline is coming up."

"How did she?" Before she could finish, Ren answered.

"I had your calls forwarded."

"Oh." She guess he thought of everything. She hadn't had time. "It's almost done. I'm just editing the last chapter." Lena finished eating before she got up to figure out where furnishings and possessions were. This was her new home. It was unimaginable. She still couldn't believe all that had happened. What was she going to tell her mother?

Chapter 10

Sitting at her writing desk in the office, packing her manuscript for the delivery service. Lena finally completed writing the final book to her thriller. It had taken her several months to be satisfied with the ending. Her agent was ready to kill her; she changed the end so many times. She had spoken to her agent and editor several times and just couldn't settle. Then several other changes needed to be made.

She was unable to concentrate with all that had been happening to her. Lena's mind was racing. Lena longed for someone to talk to. She missed her grandmother. Since she passed away, Lena would talk to her mom. She sighed, tapping her fingernails on the desk. In this case, that would probably not be the best idea. Lena still didn't know what to tell her. Should she even tell her? It's not like she could just cut her off. They were too close for that. Her mom had already acknowledged the calls started to wane. She would call Theo and show up at Lena's door soon. Perhaps, Lena could go out for brunch, but how would she explain that her canine teeth had extended significantly past the rest. Would she have to explain? Of course, she thought. Lena liked them, and of course, Ren loved the fact that they came in. That meant that he would attain his desire to rule the world of vampires. Lena had no clue how safe it was to have lunch or even visit with her mom. Would she be putting her in danger? She figured that her best thing was to call Theo.

"Hey, Theo. What are you doing?"

"Working, of course, stranger. Not everyone has a wealthy counterpart. What are you up to?"

"Very funny. I have a career, thank you.Just concluded my final edit, and I miss my friend. But, you sound upset with me."

"Like you don't know why. But we can't talk about this now."

"I understand. I haven't called in a while, and I've been a hermit. I had to finish my book. I just had it delivered to my agent. Come celebrate with me. I'll have Ren send something over from the restaurant."

"Why don't we just go the place? We can have lunch with Jen and Kelly."

"I don't fee like leaving the house right now. Not sure if would be safe to."

"Oh."

"You can't invite Jen or Kelly here today. Just you. I can have a cab pick you up and bring you here."

"You're at the penthouse? I have been dying to see the inside of that place. You don't have to send a cab; I can get one and bill the taxi to Cell's credit card. I will be there in an hour, and you better have lunch ready."

"I'll call when I get off the phone with you. See you soon." Lena was so excited, but why? It's not like Theo didn't comprehend what was going on. But she appreciated that she would have someone to talk to. Lena got up from her desk in the office and headed to their bedroom. She walked through the bathroom to the closet before she remembered the food. She sat on the side of the bed and called the restaurant before taking a shower. Lena couldn't wait until Theo saw her teeth. She was sure he wasn't anticipating this. Shoot, she wasn't expecting this either.

When the bell rang, Lena was dressed in an aqua velour tracksuit, her hair neatly pulled back in a ponytail. Lena was excited about the prospect of telling everything to someone. She ran to the door, but it was only the delivery guy. Well, at least the food was here, she thought. Lena gave him a tip, shut the door, and walked to the kitchen to put down the food. She hadn't cooked in the kitchen while living with Ren. She barely even ate in there. Lena stood for a minute and admired the gorgeous gourmet kitchen. Amazing, she thought, he had an 8 burner stove with two oven doors. Why would he need all of this? He didn't strike her as much of an entertainer. Still, she loved it. The white cabinets with some glass fronts were classic, she thought. Ren had a floor to ceiling freezer and refrigerator, including a full wine rack. Then she thought of how spoiled she was; she didn't need to cook. What she needed was pretty much laid out for her or delivered. All Lena had to do was warm the food up. Funny, she hadn't glimpsed how beautiful the kitchen was. Then it dawned on her. Why did a vampire need a gourmet kitchen? And where did he learn to cook? He was indeed a splendid chef.

Wow, how weird. Lena inspected the kitchen, its cabinets, and the fridge. They were definitely stocked to fulfill her heart's cravings. There were crackers and peanut butter, the cookies and tea she was fond of, and different kinds of pasta in the cupboard. The refrigerator was filled with prepared meals Ren left for her. There were lots of fish, seafood, and vegetables in the freezer, and her favorite pints of Haagan Daz ice cream, swiss almond vanilla, and macadamia brittle. Lena poured herself a glass of pinot noir and surveyed the rest of the refrigerator and cabinets. She guessed he wanted to keep her as content as possible. Great food, great love; Lena was indeed satisfied.

As she stood there leaning on the counter, lost in thought, the doorbell rang. There was her, Theo. Lena drained the last drop of wine and headed to the door. There he stood, his usual fabulous self. Lena looked her friend up and down. Theo was dressed in his gray Armani suit with a knit sweater underneath. His hair was pulled back as usual. Theo's green-gold eyes sparkled as he took her in. Lena gave Theo a big hug and pulled him into the house. "I love seeing you on your workdays."

"So you don't like my tracksuits?"

Lena shook her head. "Theo, I'm so happy you came. I am just bursting at the seams. I gotta talk to someone."

"Well, hello to you too. I'm just delighted to get out of the office, really. I was not enjoying it today. I was wondering what was going on over here." Lena stopped walking shortly after she passed the bench. "First, you must remove your shoes. There are slippers in the basket underneath if you'd like. No shoes in the house."

"Okay, we," Theo replied as he walked back and sat down. When he finally put on the slippers, Lena seized his hand and pulled him towards the kitchen. "Come on, we can eat at the kitchen counter and chat."

"No, you are going to take me on a tour of this place first."

"Wait, you're for real, you've never been here."

"No, I haven't. Anything I need to talk to Ren and Cell about, I go to the club. Besides, Ren is a very private person. I don't think anyone but Cell has been here. And he sure wasn't inviting a feeder here." That's when Lena punched his arm. "Ouch, and what was that for."

"I can't believe you never told me. In fact, you weren't ever going to tell me? If it weren't for the fact that I am now Ren's mate, I would never have known about your relationship with Cell and Marcia. Now I know why you kept turning down all those dates I set up for you. And they were some sexy men too. Anyway, I am hungry; let's eat."

Theo took off his jacket and hung it on the back of the stool. "Fine. But I couldn't tell you. I didn't want you in this world. Not as I am. I am just food to Cell and Marcia."

"Are you sure? Cell seems pretty in love with you and Marcia. Actually, I'm surprised that they haven't asked you to become one of them."

"Cell has offered, but I don't think Marcia is in favor of the competition. She's the jealous type. As a feeder, I don't pose a threat to her, and Cell can still have me."

"Wow. Maybe you should find someone else."

"I believe I told you to do the same thing. Besides, I'm kind of addicted to it now. Lena, I look forward to being with them both. I enjoy making love to them; I even relish the feeding now. That's mainly why I didn't want you to know of it or succumb to anyone. I had no idea Ren would fall for you, and you would be Queen of the whole damn thing. Damn you. I am so jealous. You're lucky; Ren isn't gay."

"Oh yeah, he likes pussy, and he craves my body and my blood."

"Oooh, alright, bitch." Theo grinned at her before looking her up and down and laughing. "You go, girl, make him addicted to the stuff." Theo reached over and gave her a hug. "I'm glad you're not just a feeder."

"Me too."

"Pause, smile for me." As he asked, she obliged, and there they were, her fangs long, bright, and shiny. "You are the one he's been looking for."

"What do you mean looking for," Lena asked as they walked to the kitchen.

"He has been looking for the first line for several hundred years. Well, him and a lot of other vampires."

"By the way, Theo, I hope you wanted your favorite because that's what I ordered." Theo nods. "What is the big deal with this first line anyway? What difference will it make?"

"As far as I understand, it is what the first line of Sekhmet symbolizes. She was sent with the power of the creator to control or put an end to the unrighteous. She represents preeminence. No one would dare question her or her line."

"So, I am a status symbol," Lena replies, licking the sauce from her finger. She loves the lobster and avocado sandwiches from the restaurant.

"Surely. I'm privy to some things Ren and Cell. But that would only be a part of it. I mean, as you have seen, Ren is no one to be trifled with. But you are supposed to have her power and her skills."

"So, I am a trophy, breeder, and warrior for the kind."

"Don't forget, Queen."

"Yeah, starting to wish I did listen to you, Theo."

"Too late."

"Humph.."

"Are you serious?"

"Yes, actually. I wouldn't mind having Ren without all this stuff.

"Have you told him that you are not the helpless damsel he thinks you are?"

"No, actually. Odd, isn't it? I've been training almost all my life for a role I didn't know existed. I'm sure he has found them, though."

"Your swords?"

"Yeah, he hasn't let me go home, and he had some guys move my things from my apartment. And I mean everything. Theo, my life has changed drastically in a few days. I had no idea that when I started seeing him, that my life would mutate this much. Not to mention so soon.

"Lena, I warned you when you saw him."

"Only because you thought I would be a feeder. It's part of my job description for now, though."

"Have you found the swords anywhere?"

"I haven't looked, actually. I didn't really think about it until I started talking to you. I've been so wrapped up in getting that book finished. That's all I did for the last month in addition to eat, shit and fuck." Lena huffs and slouches a bit over the counter. "I wonder what Ren thought when his men showed him."

"Probably that you were more than he bargained for. Lunch was a delight; now you have got to take me on a tour of this place." Lena smiled, wiped her hands, and got up from the stool.

Lena started with the side of the apartment where the bedrooms were. She hadn't actually walked through the whole house in the weeks that she had been there. Exploring the apartment with Theo was fun. They talked about the apartment being more massive than expected and didn't discern the reason a vampire needed so many rooms. While exploring the apartment, they found two locked doors. Lena hadn't been in the penthouse long enough to ask about that room. Up until that point, she was clueless to its existence. Showing him around made Lena feel like she had been operating in a daze for almost a month. Lena hadn't noted any other room than those she frequently habituated and only barely. They walked back down the hall.

"The house is lovely. I just have one question." Lena glared at Theo with raised eyebrows. "Why is the office so dark? The kitchen is black and white, and the master and bathroom are candescent with their cream walls, cherry floors, and royal blue curtains. The house is bright and airy. What's with the office?"

"What?"

"The office is so oppressive and dark. If I were you, I'd get rid of the paneling.Lena laughed as she pulled Theo toward the other end of the house. "No, I'll leave Ren with his room." She laughed again as she said, "this is the room I'm most fond."

"I can see why. The colors are lovely and then the large pillows. You're the person that this room emanates. I bet you sexed him in this room, your first night in the place," Theo states as he moves the pillows to sit on the futon.

Lena sits next to him. "I don't know what you're talking about."

"Oh, yeah, you did. Judging from the way you behave, he rocks your world."

"Yes, he does. I am in love with Ren. I have been from our first dance."

"I'm guessing, all of this a little more than you bargained for," he stated as he gestured around them.

"That is an understatement," she retorted with a smile and a chuckle.

"Hey, stand up and turn around for me."

"What? Why?" Theo didn't answer her, just gestured for her to rise and then twirl his finger. As Lena did, a smirk came to his face, and he shook his head. "What is it? Why do you have that look on your face?"

"You haven't observed a little roundness in your stomach?"

"Well, I noted a little yesterday. I thought that I was just overeating Ren's cooking."

"Hhmm, you think that's what it is, do you? It could be something else."

Lena didn't answer. She just stood still. Her head to the side and one hand holding her arm. When she realized what Theo was alluding to, Lena plopped down on the futon. Lena couldn't believe it. She had enough to contend with, considering her love was a vampire; she was descended from a goddess, and people or vampires wanted her dead. Now a baby. No way.

"Can't believe it. It's not a year yet, and you are knocked up already. Did you forget to suit up or suit him up?"

"You real close to being cussed out. Married women don't get knocked up," Lena rebutted miffed. "Being married, I didn't think I need to. I didn't think it would happen so promptly. I mean people try for years sometimes. We didn't use protection. He's a vampire and I'm clean. Would condoms even stop vampire sperm?"

Theo laughed. "When did you get married?"

"For being part of this world, there are some things you don't know?" Lena watched Theo. He seemed clueless. "The mating ritual between a vampire and his mate is a private affair. Still, you are married or mated after that. No big hubbub or a lot of money spent. I guess you could if you wanted to. But, I'm good. We made promises to each other and that's enough."

Theo smiled and patted her hand. "Sounds beautiful. You'll be fine. On another note, have you selected an outfit for the All Hallows Eve celebration tomorrow?"

"Okay, one thing at a time. I just found out I am probably expecting. I'm not thinking about partying? Wait, what celebration? I didn't know anything about it."

"Oh, you're pregnant. Were you even planning to have children with him?" Lena nodded in agreement. "Lena, you can't be serious? Are you even aware of what month and day today is?"

"October. But it can't be Halloween already."

"Tomorrow. And Zoe's always has a big event for Halloween. You're the mistress of the club and the clan; you have to be there. And I have been here long enough. It's been fun. I love you. But I am going to Zoe's tonight with Jen and Kelly." Theo got up from the futon and walked back down the hall. Lena followed.

"Do they know?"

"They are feeders for other family members. And they will be there. I haven't told them anything, but they have asked why Ren hasn't circulated for new blood. I didn't say more than he has found a nice lady. They're curious."

"Well, at least I will finally be able to go to the club. Ren hasn't really wanted me there lately. Not like I'm too upset. I guess I'll see you at Zoe's?"

He slid his feet in his wingtips, took his jacket from Lena, and pulled it on. "Definitely. So what are you about to do?"

"Please, I am going to sleep. I've been up early and really late working on that book. I am tired, and my husband returns home in the wee hours of the morning. I need my strength."

"I wager you do." Theo smiled his dazzling smile and winked at her. "Later, chica."

As soon as he left, Lena did indeed go to bed. She was so tired, but it took a while for her to fall asleep. She kept thinking about being pregnant. She knew little of the children of vampires and humans other than they were called dhampirs. The thought of being pregnant didn't scare her, after all she wasn't a teenager, she was twenty six. She had a decent job, some money saved and she was married, not single. Note to mention, her partner was well off. She wondered if her pregnancy would show up on a pregnancy test. Lena sighed. Well, she thought, she would ignore it for a few more days, and make sure she didn't drink anymore. She drifted to sleep trying to imagine what their children would look like.

When Ren walked through the door, Lena opened her eyes and sat up. She yawned and stretched, listening for him. His voice was barely a whisper, but Lena heard him. She guessed her senses were keen now. He was talking to someone, yet Lena couldn't tell who it was. So she decided to try to sneak up on him. She quietly ran towards the door, jumped on his back, and kissed his cheek. Ren barely moved.

"Did I wake you up, my love?"

"Yes, but I was taking a nap so that I could be up for you. You've had a long day. Let me take your mind off things." Lena got down off his back and wrapped her arms around his waist.

"Just a minute. You haven't left the house since you've come here. You should meet Patrick; after all, he is your personal bodyguard." He opened the door a little wider, and out of thin air appeared a large, dark skinned black man. He was clean-cut and had the physic of a pro wrestler, his muscles straining through his suit. "Patrick, my Queen Yalena, we call her Lena. Lena, this is Patrick."

"Hi, Patrick." He had a handsome face. His hair cut close to his scalp.

"Queen Yalena, nice to meet you." Patrick bowed slightly, and then his golden smiling eyes met hers.

"Were you invisible before, or am I seeing things?"

"Your eyes do not deceive you, my Queen," responded Ren. "My soldiers each have exceptional talent. Yours can be invisible. I thought that would be a good thing for you."

"Thank you, my love. Patrick, it was nice to meet you. Sorry, I'm not really that exciting. I like things pretty quiet."

"Not an issue. It makes my job easier. Mr. Arias, will that be all?"

"Yes, actually. You can retire for the night. I'll keep an eye on her. Remember, tomorrow she goes to the club."

"Yes, sir. Goodnight, Mr. and Mrs. Arias."

"Good night Patrick," They said in unison. Then Ren closed the door and turned to her, kissing her lips. "Missed you today," stated Ren.

"It's only been a few hours of my love."

"I don't desire to be without you for more than several minutes."

"Ren, you sweet talker." He picked her up in his arms and carried her to the bed."

"I am thirsty."

"You didn't drink at Zoe's."

"It wasn't enough." Lena immediately tried to jump out of his arms, but he held her even tighter.

"You fed at the club." He laughed for a moment and gently laid her on the bed.

"I guess I haven't told you about the reserve."

"No, what reserve?"

"In case of an emergency, we keep a reserve of blood in the club's basement. One never knows. We must always be prepared to not feed. There is also a special reserve here. Actually, there are two. One is in the locked room you no doubt found today."

"Yes, I found it. But there is no knob or lock or anything. How do you get in?"

"Fingerprints. I haven't programmed it for you yet. I will when you need it."

She nodded and smiled. Lena couldn't help but watch Ren as he removed his suit. She wanted to peel him out of his clothes. "You were saying something about being thirsty. And I am craving the stroke of my king right now." He climbed on the bed and sat next to her. He kissed her neck, and cheek and put his head in her lap.

"I just want to be near to you right now. I love you very much, Yalena."

"I love you too, Lorenzo."

"I wouldn't do anything to hurt you; well, other than turn you."

"I perceived as much."

"Lena, is there anything you want to tell me?"

"You found my swords." Lena smiled as she looked down at Ren and ran her fingers through his mass of curls. "Where are they?"

"Yes, they were in your closet at your apartment. The guys brought the case and everything here. They burned me when I touched them."

"I was wondering today if you were going to ask me. I had forgotten about my blades over the last few weeks with all that had happened. I have been training in Kung Fu since I was about seven or eight. Those swords were specially made for me. Oddly enough, my mom had the master fold silver into each blade, and the thread of the handle has silver in it. I never really knew why. But I love the way they feel in my hands."

"So you are not as helpless as I thought. You are indeed my warrior Queen. I would love to see you in action."

"You would think that you've never seen me in action. One of our dates was to a dojo."

"I could see that you were good but I had no idea how good. I think you put on a show, as though you didn't want me to know how good you were."

"We hadn't had our talk yet. No one had even gotten close enough to know that I would enjoy a lesson. Anyway, can't exactly fight or practice with a blade in here."

"There is a dojo on the second floor."

"I thought you wanted to feed."

"Never said I won't. Let me retrieve them, and you can show me how good you are." He went into the closet, pulled back the rug, opened the door in the floor, and lifted out a carved box. He brought the whole container to her.

"If you're as good as they say at your temple, you will train our children."

"You knew."

"When the box showed up, I decided to find out about them and you. It seems you are the best swordsman in the temple."

"Now, I'm not sure I can live up to all the praise." He put the box on the bed, and Lena opened it. They were still coruscated from the light, as if untouched.

"You won't be able to touch them once I change you."

"Nonsense. I will just cover the handles with something else." Lena gazed at the swords and ran her fingers along the hilt. Then she looked up at Ren. "So, lead the way." He grabbed the box and headed for the other side of the house past her favorite room, and on the opposite side was an elevator door. There were no buttons at all, just a square screen. When Ren put his hand over it, the doors opened.

"The hand pad has already been programmed for you. So you can use it any time you wish. I would want you to practice when you have the zeal to."

How could he have already programmed it for her, she thought. Lena sighed, she had been at Ren's for a while now. She hadn't even left the building. Practice that is something Lena hadn't done in days. But it had been long since she touched her blades, let alone practiced her swordplay. How could Lena have neglected them, forgotten about them? Well, at least now, she could practice as much as the pregnancy would let her. Pregnancy? Lena still couldn't believe that she could be. When should she tell him? Not yet, she thought. She still needed time to process to make sure. Then Lena wondered if he was cognizant of it. When should she tell him?

The elevator stopped, opening onto a large room. The wooden floors were glossy, and different weapons aligned the walls. Lena thought it was great and that she would love working out here. They walked through the threshold, and Ren stopped to remove his shoes before entering the room. Lena did the same. They were standing in a small area, around five feet squared. There was a bench on one side and small cubbies lined the entrance wall with flat shoes.

Ren laid the sword box in front of Lena. "We leave these soft shoes here just for the dojo." Ren handed Lena a pair before slipping his feet into a set.

She had missed them. It had been longer than a few days now that Lena thought about it a little more. Time had flown as she worked on her novel each day. It had been quite a few weeks since she held the swords, which was longer than usual. Lena practiced a form at least once a day since she was given the blades on her sixteen birthday. For as long as she could remember, martial arts had been the most important thing to her after her education. Lena felt that she'd become adept in several styles, and her teacher agreed. She had developed into a master at twenty-one.

Lena grasped the swords, then loosened and tightened her grip to feel comfortable again. Afterwards, she shifted from sided to side. Her teacher always said it looked funny but it was her way of centering herself before she began. Lena closed her eyes briefly and became one with the blades. Holding both of them, the weight seemed to diminish as she moved. With each movement you could hear the staccato of a whoosh before silence as the blades sliced through the air above, side, and in front of her. Lena could see Ren watching intently from her periphery. She thought that he looked with contentment as she moved. The dance continued slowly and gracefully as Lena progressed to the middle of the floor.

"May I join you?"

"At your own risk," Lena replied, winking at Ren. "Although now that I think about it, you've probably been practicing longer than I've been alive."

Ren winked at her as he clutched the staff. He began to spin it above and in front of him. The reverberation of whirring accompanied his advance with the bo staff. She could tell that he was not a stranger to the weapon. They began to dance around the dojo. Metal hitting wood, wood hitting metal, the bracing of each weapon on it self and against the other. Sound of whirring and clacking accompanied those of a whoosh and chime. He tried to catch her off guard several times; Lena countered all but one. She scowled as he tapped her bottom with the staff. He tried to sweep the bo under her feet to trip her, but Lena flipped backward, landing on her feet, both swords held in front.

"Nice bow and arrow stance coming out of that flip."

Lena rolled her eyes. He was good, but she was better. Clashing of blades and the staff, clinking and whistling again. This time, Lena turned away from a strike, and smacked Ren on the butt with the flat of her blade before she swept him off his feet. Lena grinned and winked at him before she flipped away. After the subsequent impact between the blades and the staff, the staff was cut into three pieces. The two of them were now evenly matched. Ren manipulated two parts to combat her swords. Around and around, they went. Lena was enjoying their little dance. She had often dreamed of being with a man she could spar with. Here she was, and they would fight for eternity. But right now, Lena figured she would end it. She was within his space with a slip and twist of her sword. The blade rested on his skin; Lena could see the smoke from his burning flesh float through the air like a dancing ribbon as the scent of charred flesh entered her nose.

"You win," Ren said as he relaxed his arms. "I've never had a teacher for any extensive period, so I look forward to practicing with you."

Yalena lowered the sword and gaped at the red and black burnt flesh heal instantly. "Did I hurt you?"

"That was nothing. But I am thirsty, and seeing you in this form has made me want you even more than me being away from you all day."

"You say the sweetest things. But this is a secret." Lena paused to catch her breath. "The only people that know are my mom, dad, and Theo. Let's keep it that way. At least until the children are old enough to be trained. No need to alert the council." That was all she needed, for the council to learn that she was more dangerous than they thought.

"As you decide," Ren replied.

Lena rested the steel back into their box as Ren picked it up. Lena jumped on his back and held on tight. "Just want to be close to you."

"I don't have a problem with that." He carried them both up to the bedroom. Lena leaped onto the bed, and Ren put the box back into the closet floor. Then within a flash, he was by her side. And their sunrise passions took over. As usual, Lena enjoyed every moment. "I am going to miss your blood when you are a vampire."

"At least you'll still have me, all of me."

"I am truly satiated by that fact," Ren paused for a moment just to watch his beautiful wife. "Lena, I have so much to tell you. We haven't taken any time to talk about our new life. Do you have any questions about vampires?"

"Well, actually, I wanted to know the basics first. I'm not cognizant of much. My mom stopped talking to me about them after about seven or eight. So I only know what I've seen on TV."

"Unbelievable, a lot of that isn't real. As you've seen, I can walk in the sun. It isn't dangerous for me. Although, my eyes are a bit sensitive to brightness. Of course, sunglasses take care of that. We are not immortal but live very long lives. People think that living a long time makes one indestructible, but we can be killed; it's just more difficult. Our women are barren, but not the men. A bit odd. I guess it does maintain the population. Of course, because we love for life, we stay with our love or never mate again.

"Another thing that humans don't comprehend is that we are not as effortlessly killed as they seem to think. Garlic doesn't work other than maybe changing the fragrance of your blood. Some vampires don't like the smell. Unfortunately, it is part of the tonic drink we feed to our feeders at Zoe's. It helps the body stay healthy. Garlic is not an issue in New York. The only way to dispatch a vampire is with silver. The only thing you can do with a stake is enrage a vampire. Of course, a silver stake would be substantial if you can get close enough and not put yourself at risk."

"Okay. So would garlic in one's system deter a vampire from feeding? And that dagger you used on Seth?"

"Not, really. Particularly, if he's really thirsty. And it has a mahogany handle and a silver blade."

"Good to know. "

"Vampires, like each human, have their own distinct talents. And when a human transforms into a vampire, that talent is amplified. I haven't discovered where the originals are, except one. Well Yalena, those are some things I needed to tell you. But there is something else I want to say."

"Is this about you or me?"

"Me. Actually, I should show you."

He sat utterly still on the bed. Lena was very curious about what else she would be acquainted with as his Queen. It was weird, actually. Lena wasn't sure what was going on; she just kept watching him. And when she didn't look up, he called her name. Lena looked up, and there Ren stood. Lena looked back at his body, sitting on the bed, and then at the ghostly image standing before her. The ghostly image smiled at her. And Lena could have sworn that a chuckle escaped his pale lips. She was speechless. Her life had taken an unfathomable turn into science fiction this evening. She was the wife of a vampire and the and descendant of an immortal vampire. She found out that she had a bodyguard who was not only a vampire but could become invisible, then there was something else about him she didn't know and couldn't quite put her finger on. Of all things, Ren could project his spirit out of his body. What else would she see?

"Speechless, Lena?"

"Starting to think I'm losing my mind. You can project yourself."

"Yes."

"How far can you project yourself?"

"Not sure, really. I haven't done more than a few miles. From here to my room in the club."

"This is all too much now. It's like some kind of sci-fi movie." Lena put distance between herself and Ren. He crawled over to her and put his head in her lap. Lena couldn't help but run her fingers through his curls. Well, Lena was glad that he wasn't a shapeshifter; no offense to them. It was overwhelming to absorb so much in so little time. For now, Ren seemed content. He purred as Lena stroked his thick hair. That made her giggle, and Lena seemed to relax. Then he did it again. Lena looked down at her love. She stroked his cheeks and nose and ran her fingers across his lips. He had chiseled features and olive tone skin with her blood coursing through him. Ren moved to lay on the bed. "Come lay down; you need your rest."

Lena didn't say anything but turned to lie down next to him. Ren phased between next to her and above her. Finally, Lena fell asleep, enveloped in his arms and looking into his brown eyes.

As it had been for the last few weeks, Lena awoke wrapped in his arms. "Good afternoon, my love."

"Mmmm, Good afternoon Ren. Did I see what I thought I saw yesterday?" Without responding, he phased himself into the bathroom this time. When his spirit returned to his body, Lena lowered her head to kiss him. He smiled as his lips met hers.

"Lena, did you finally finish the book?"

"Yes, and I messengered my novel early afternoon, yesterday."

"Great. So my phasing doesn't bother you."

"I wouldn't say that. It's growing on me. I'm sure it's a grand ability to have."

"Yes, it can be useful."

"Ren, we still needed to talk about what you are and what you will transform me into."

"You're right. I hope you understand, there isn't much to refashion. Your body has been assimilating each time you feed from me. I was actually hoping we could slowly work through what you need to know. There is so much to tell you."

"Well, we don't have to talk about everything. How about my body assimilation?"

"Okay, well, since your body has vampire DNA within it, my blood will help your body slowly transition from mostly human to mostly vampire, unlike most new vampires whose bodies go through a monumental metamorphosis in a short time. Your body will slowly transform. One example is that you won't need to feed regularly. Your body still makes its own blood and will continue to do so until the final stage." Ren paused for a few minutes.

"So, my body is slowly becoming more and more like yours."

"To some degree. Because of who you are, your body is actually becoming what you were always; a true vampire. For some reason, your body was always more vampire than human. My blood has just awakened a catalyst that revealed what was dormant in you."

"I see. And as for the basics, what's real and what's a myth."

"Okay, there is a lot to dispute, actually. Like all natural creatures, each vampire is different, unique in its own way. We each have gifts and/or talents, some more than others. We are stronger than our human counterparts. We are partly mammal, the organic makeup. We can climb walls and move at tre speeds. Some of us shapeshift, not all. And when I say shapeshift, I mean into almost anything, animal. Still, that's within reason. I can't transform into a squirrel or something, so minute from my composition. We are not truly allergic to garlic; it gives the blood an odor and flavor that some of us don't like, actually hate."

Lena couldn't help but laugh when she thought about the garlic he had been putting in her food lately.

"If you're thinking about the amount of garlic I've put in your food, it's for a good reason. Seth actually hates garlic. I hope it would keep him from feeding on you should he get his hands on you. It would give me time to find you." She shuddered at the thought of another man touching her or feeding from her. The idea of that man being Seth was even more extremely revolting.

"It is best not to invite strangers into your home because that tale is true. Vampires can't enter the home of a human without an invitation. However, that invitation can be revoked. The only challenge is if you can revoke that invitation before they feed on you? A vampire feeding from a human will give that vampire some control over that human. I say some, because nothing is absolute. And of course, I do have a reflection; I can walk into a church, place my hand on the cross or in holy water. Last but not least, the sun has little to no effect on vampires. Of course, the more evil hearted the vampire, the more adverse the sun's effect on him. It can be unpleasant. To some degree, the sun may even be painful but in no way life-threatening. Daylight could aid in slowing down one, though."

"But vampires are allergic to silver?"

"Now, that is true. If you can decapitate a vampire with a silver blade, he's dead. Otherwise, it's just excruciatingly painful. Silver burns the skin and the body."

"The true nature and powers of a vampire are scarier than most humans believe."

"Yes, Lena, they are. I guess I should say we are deadly creatures. That is why we must control what they do or can do. It is imperative for our survival and that of humans."

"Babe, what time is it."

"It's about four o'clock in the afternoon."

"Have you been up long?"

"No, I just did not want to wake you. Are you coming to the Halloween party? You haven't been there for a few weeks. Come celebrate, you can show off your fangs."

"I don't know."

"It will be fun. Come on, everyone and everything comes to the Halloween soiree. Besides, I want to show you off. You have everyone at the club thinking I keep you prisoner."

"Guess it is more of a demand than a request." Lena paused to read Ren's reaction to what she had said. But couldn't detect any change in his face or body. "Fine, I'll come."

"Fetching, now come help us set up. We were open last night, so we did not decorate. And your clothes are already there."

"What kind of gala is it anyway?"

"Costume." Lena knew she would go with him, but she thought she would make him ask. Finally, Both of them got showered and dressed, then were off to Zoe's.

The club was actually a mess. There were cups everywhere and plates on the tables still. There was blood on the leather chase for some strange reason and in the middle of the dance floor. It appeared that everyone had just begun to clean up the room. Lena had not seen Zoe's after. There was glass and trash everywhere. Lena spun in a circle to look at the whole club. She would be surrounded by this club for an extensive time. That wasn't a good feeling. Good thing it wasn't hers. Lena was not a club person, and it wasn't the highlight of her weekends until Ren. Now Lena would have to hear about it and be part of it for how long? She took a deep breath before she turned to the person who had been vastly approaching her.

"If you're going to be here, you're going to help clean." Lena was so lost in her thoughts, and she hadn't discerned that it was actually Cell who approached her. Cell's long hair was up in a floppy bun on top of his head. He wore jeans and a t-shirt. The t-shirt hugged his athletically muscled chest. Lena eyed him, with an eyebrow raised. Was that how he spoke to their rulers? He stopped right in front of her and gave a curt nod. "We need someone to help with the glasses at the bar. Just don't overload the washer back there, or we'll be in trouble."

"Sure, Cell. No problem. That's why I'm here early. So what happened to the floor?"

"One of our clients got a little happy with their feed. We had to eliminate him."

"Does that often happen here?"

"Maybe twice a year. We get some vamps who are not accustomed to how we do things here. It's different in other states. Newcomers to New York don't understand that we don't kill our food. We tried to tell that guy, but he wouldn't listen. You should have seen the terror in that girl's eyes."

"Did you save her?"

"You know Ren did. She's fine."

"Good thing."

Everyone was busy as bees for the rest of the afternoon. It was demanded that Lena rest before the night's festivities began. So she didn't get to see how the club was decorated. Lena had to admit, however, that she was tired. She stayed up late to finish that last chapter in the book. When Ren returned home for the last week or two, Lena was still wrestling with it. Then she went to bed with him, only for him to feed before she would go to sleep. And now she could be expecting. It was an understatement to say that her body needed rest. Lena woke refreshed and ready to celebrate. She had just opened her eyes when Theo walked into her room.

"Hey, sleepyhead. Time to glamorize for the party. Your debut is getting nigh."

Lena peered up at him. "What debut?"

"You can't seriously be asking me that question. You are the Queen of this clan and family. The Halloween party is your introduction to everyone. Let me guess you thought that you only had to greet the council?"

"I didn't really think about meeting anyone."

"Start thinking of your decisions, Lena." She ignored him and decided to look at the dress hanging over the closet door. "Seriously, Lena, your decisions affect your whole vampire family."

"Yes, of course. You can leave me now; I'll get dressed and wait for Ren here."

"Sure, I'll tell Ren. Your fangs become you, by the way." He walked out and slammed the door. Lena knew she hurt him, and she was sorry now. But who was he to tell her how to act? She took a deep breath. A friend, she answered herself. Lena would make a point to say sorry to him before she went to the gala. Her biggest problem was going to be hiding her swords in this outfit. Ren had taken the two she wore in their sheath when she arrived. She had not been carrying any of them until then, but it seemed like she should start. After all, Lena was totally capable of taking care of herself. And if she had to tonight, she would.

There was nowhere to hide the blade, so Lena decided she would wear one. The dress was an eggshell color, form-fitting, and flowing. It clung to her curves, rolled over her slight bulge, and draped the floor. It was beautiful. Lena put on the thin sword belt she had made for her; it hung slanted over her waist, her rapier sat on her hip as it should. Lena looked as though she was royalty from the Middle Ages. As she looked in the mirror, Ren appeared behind her. He smiled and wrapped his arms around her. Lena closed her eyes and relaxed into him.

"I see we are Maryann and Robin Hood."

"You are correct. Are you ready to meet your subjects, my Queen?"

"I guess so. Yes, your majesty." He turned her to him and gently kissed her lips. "I also see you managed to fit a blade to your side."

"Yes, I feel naked without them. Especially in such an environment."

"It fits very well with your dress. I never noticed what a beautiful scabbard it had."

"Thank you, I have a thing for dragons and roses. Well, guess now or never. I am ready." His arm circled her waist, guiding her through the door and down the hall. Lena knew where she was, but she had not been down this side of the building before. He opened the door, and a balcony stood above the club. They stood watching the crowd, which to her seemed reasonable enough for a bunch of vampires. She couldn't distinguish who was human or vampire. Lena wondered what else was in the room that may have been disguised. Everyone seemed to be having a good time. She really liked the view from here. Lena could see all the way to the door. No wonder Ren often stood and watched from the DJ booth, which she could see was next to this balcony; he had a great view of everyone entering the club.

After a few minutes, the music volume began to go down, and Lena discerned the wireless microphone in Ren's other hand.

"I hope everyone is enjoying the festivities here at Club Zoe's." There was a cheer from the masses in response. "Well, I just need a minute of your time. This is a cherished All Hallows Eve for me. Unlike many others that have passed, I have finally found my mate. I would like to introduce my Queen and yours, Yalena." Lena was pleased he didn't hand her the microphone. She just smiled and waved like the next Miss America. The crowd under her feet cheered and whistled after his announcement. Lena wondered if they would feel so happy about her being Queen if they knew her lineage and how the rules applied to New York vampires would soon be implemented in other cities and states. "Enjoy the rest of your night here at Club Zoe's." The spotlight went out, and they quickly moved behind a sealed door. "Now that wasn't that bad, was it?"

"No, not at all."

"Well, let's go celebrate." With his arm lightly pressing against the small of her back, Ren led Lena to the stairs. They walked down them and went through the doors that led to the club. It seemed as though they were surrounded instantly upon entering. Ren was not taking any chances with her here. With Ren and Lena at the center of the unit, they moved to the dance floor through the crowd. Once they reached the midpoint of the dance floor, the music slowed down. Lena felt like she was at her cotillion all over again. She was being introduced to the world as a young woman; well, in this case, a vampire queen. Lena smiled at the moment. The memory seemed to ease the tautness that was building in her. She had been apprehensive walking into Zoe's. If Ren felt the need to encompass them in a circle of their guards, he expected something to transpire.

As they danced, Lena saw that the floor had cleared, and all eyes were on them. This was their first dance as King and Queen, she thought. It was not at their wedding but at the Halloween party. How apropos Lena guessed; after all, she was now Queen to a strangely freakish tale. She thought she would have to write this down for a fictional book someday. No one would believe it was true. Well, at least no one that lives outside of this world. While they danced, Lena lost sight of where the bodyguards had disappeared until they began to move the circle back in as they had upon entering the club. Outside of their protective ring, people began to dance on the dance floor, and the music's tempo increased.

"Relax, my love. Think of all the times we danced here, and it felt like we were the only two in the room." Lena nodded and looked into his eyes, and once again, they were there. Even though the club was now packed and under heavy surveillance, it felt akin to them being the only two on the floor, and the prying eyes melted away. "That's my lady," he whispered before kissing her cheek.

As the song ended, the music tempo shifted to one of a faster nature. Time to have a little fun, Lena thought. Possibly, she could indulge amongst this crowd. But unfortunately, the music was deafening, a little too loud for her liking, and her now sensitive ears. Lena didn't know how vampires could stand it.

She finally started to let her guard down and not keep tabs on how her sword felt at her side. But she shouldn't have begun to relax. It all happened way too suddenly. Even with her keen senses, Lena was uninformed of why Ren and Patrick were suddenly whisking her away. Before Lena could catch herself, she was put in the DJ booth with Cell, and Ren was gone. Lena walked over to the glass and looked at the dance floor. There was no trace of any disturbance.

"Happened a little too quickly for you?"

"Yes, I don't even know what happened. I just know I was rushed out of the club before I could catch my breath."

"I am sure your senses picked it up; your brain has to process. Just sit for a minute. You will know before Ren returns to you." Lena did as he advised. She sat on the couch opposite the window that looked into the club. Then Lena closed her eyes because that usually helped her visualize things. Lena saw herself dancing in the middle of their soldiers, who she now realized were also dancing with whom Lena would guess would be their counterparts. Then Lena saw it. A shiny object sailed through the air. Patrick caught it before it could pass his head, and three guards headed in a beeline to the person who threw it while Patrick and Ren rushed her out of place.

"Did you see it as it happened?"

"Yes, Cell, that was amazing. Completely clear."

"Just think in about a year or so, you'll have seen the action while it took place instead of after."

"Yes, I suppose that is true. I would like to see the one who threw the knife. I would like to talk to him."

"Don't worry, your pretty little head. I'm sure Ren has rid us of the traitor."

"Hmmm, I shall have to talk to him about that." As the last syllable escaped her lips, in Ren walked. This time she wasn't surprised; he seemed to have a knack for appearing when she wanted him. Lena smiled and walked toward him, reaching to brush his face with her hand.

"Come, I believe you wanted to speak with the gentleman."

"Yes. Is the vampire one of our tribe or an outsider?"

"We're not sure. We haven't questioned him, just holding him downstairs. I figured you would want in on the interrogation since he was aiming at you."

"Of course." For the first time since Lena had been to the club, they took an elevator down into the basement. Lena knew there was an entrance from the club, but she presumed this would lead to a different part of the basement. Once off the elevator, Lena noticed a sentinel at the door. They walked straight towards him. He didn't say anything but opened the door for them to enter. The room looked like a medieval prison. And as such, the prisoner was chained to the wall. This seemed to amuse Lena and disturb her at the same time. When she stepped closer to him, she recognized him. He looked the same even though it had been a decade since she had seen him. He was the carpenter, the exact same one who carved the box that now held her swords.

"Mr. Johnson, I was unaware that you were a vampire."

"There are a lot of things you don't know."

"Lena, how do you know this man?"

"He carved that box for me that I showed you last night. But I don't understand; why try to kill me now and not before."

"I didn't know exactly who you were. I was just told to make the box you asked for and not to harm you. I was told that you were off limits. I didn't know who you would become, or I would have gladly died to end your existence." How odd Lena thought that this man just told her he wanted to end her life. That he would have ended it long ago if he knew who she was. Yet she felt nothing, numb, actually. Lena unsheathed her sword and put it to his throat. He didn't react, but Lena could see he was in pain as the silver began to melt into his skin like a hot knife through butter.

"Why, who sent you here?"

"We don't want to hide. We don't want to live harmoniously with our food."

"Don't be ridiculous; humans don't live harmonious with anything. Who dispatched you?" He refused to answer, so Lena sliced into his torso with her blade. Lena cut on an angle from the base of his throat down to his left side. She could see that he wanted to scream but didn't want to give her the satisfaction. She watched him closely. This pleased her, but why? This was not a movie; this was real. Still, she felt nothing.

The other guards in the room were silent as well as Ren. Her violent and vindictive behavior caught them off guard. When she glanced at them, Lena could tell that this was not quite what they were predicting.

"Who sent you?" Again he said nothing, and Lena began to slice slowly from his left side to his right. The cuts were shallow, but that didn't matter; the silver burned his skin. Lena could smell the burnt flesh in the air.

"Just because you carry his seed means nothing. We will not obey." Now, his reaction caught her off guard, and Lena lowered her blade. Carrying his seed. How was he aware that she could be expecting? Even after a day to digest, Lena wavered back and forth between tangible and impossible. "I will say this, we are going to put an end to your reign Arias." Finally, Lena had enough; he was useless. Before anyone could gather themselves to react, Lena had raised her sword and beheaded their new friend. His body fell still as his head hit the ground, splattering blood; Lena smirked. He deserved to die, she thought. She stared as his body began to smolder and turn to ash. How dare he speak to them that way. While she praised herself, Ren came up behind her and embraced her tightly.

"You didn't have to dispose of him."

"Why, he was useless. He would have told us nothing, and sending him back to report that he had failed would have given him another chance to try to eliminate me. This way, they'll know when he doesn't come back; we have ended it. And they are short a man. Too bad, though, he was a marvelous carpenter."

Ren gestured for the men to take care of the mess before speaking to Lena. "That is not what I mean. We have people who execute for you. Specifically, since you're pregnant with our children; they pick up everything you do or think about." Ren walked her out of the room quickly and onto the elevator.

"You act like killing is all I have been doing. I have been working on my book and completing research, and sparing with you. Our babies have had varied experiences, thank you." She couldn't believe he was reprimanding her. Unbelievable, she thought. That man had just tried to terminate her. Should she not return the favor? Why was she so angry and confused. Lena tried to calm down, gather her composure as they rode up in the elevator.

"I think we should go home," Ren said. Lena began to clean her sword with the handkerchief she put in her bosom when he grabbed her and turned her to face him.

"The night is young. I want to fete. Tonight was the first in a long time since we've danced." Ren looked at her in disbelief. He couldn't believe that Lena was so nonchalant about what had just happened.

"Yalena, are you puerile? Have you no concept as to what just happened here?"

"I fully comprehend, thank you. Mr. Johnson tried to murder me; I killed him. What's your point?" They had just gotten off of the elevator. Ren didn't say another word. Lena turned to look in the direction that Ren was looking, and there he was, Seth.

"Is this your first lovers' spat?" He asked grinning.

"Can I help you, Seth," Ren asked.

"My Lady, excellent to see you looking so well. I was just looking for the bathroom."

"Seth, how did you get in here?"

"I have my ways."

"Well, since you are obviously lost, let me escort you back to the club."

"Oh, I am sure I can find my way. Besides, you wouldn't want to leave your love all alone. Especially after what just happened." Then her reflexes kicked in. After he said that, he moved toward her quickly. As soon as he shifted, Lena pulled her sword from its sheath, and it met with his chest just as Ren snagged him by the neck and threw him to the ground.

"Taking chances, aren't we?" As Seth hit the ground, Patrick materialized from behind Lena.

"Escort Mister Mysterious out of my club. Tell the bouncers; he's banned, no access to the club at all. Thanks." Once Patrick had disappeared down the hall, Ren lifted Lena up and took her out a back exit where a cab was waiting. "You're going home."

"Ren, baby." He didn't want to hear anymore about it. After everything, he wanted her home, where Lena would be safer than her being at the club. Lena knew he was upset. Ren didn't say a word for the entire ride as he held her tightly and looked out of the window. Lena didn't want to break his train of thought. So she didn't say anything until they were in their bathroom getting ready for bed.

"Ren, you were so quiet in the car. What's going through your mind?"

"I should have known that you had conceived. How could I have not known?"

"You really haven't been home much. I have spent much of the last month working on my book. While you have been at Zoe's and the restaurant. We make love, you feed, and we pass out and do repeat all over again the next day."

"Can you forgive me, Lena?"

"Nothing to forgive; we have been functioning just fine. I didn't even fathom I was pregnant until yesterday after talking with Theo." He stood in front of her looking into her eyes. He kissed her lips gingerly. Then he walked into the bathroom to run a bath for her.

"I will no longer make that mistake. I will stay with you longer now. This could be arduous for you. Our babies will grow rapidly."

"Babies?"

"Yes, there are two, from what I could tell. I did not pay attention until the assassin said something. How could I not hear our children's heartbeats? Their heartbeats are not as fast as human babies, but it is strong enough to hear. They sound healthy. You may start to crave blood by the time they have grown to half their size."

"How do you know so much?"

"I helped Madeline with her pregnancy."

Wow, Lena thought. How things have changed? She never imagined from Madeline's hostility that Ren had helped her give birth to Seth. "Will the pregnancy be ten months like a human?"

"No, you will not be gestational for more than five months. The problem will be the delivery. If the babies survive. Some have killed their mothers in childbirth, trying to get out. They are mostly larger than their counterparts. They also mentally develop faster. Enough talk, bath time for you."

"Only if you join me."

"Ok, I will try to control myself."

"Ren, when was the last time you fed?"

"I believe early yesterday morning with you. I did not feed at the club as usual, and then the events took my mind off the hunger. You climb in the tub; I will grab a glass before I join you."

"Okay." Lena got in and slowly lowered herself into the tub. The water was hotter than she would usually run it. When she relaxed, she looked around the room. It was a beautiful bathroom. She loved the claw foot tub she now sat in. The water spout looked like a waterfall. She was grateful that the knobs were on the side instead of at the tub's head or foot. She stretched out fully, relaxing as she waited for her love's return.

He took out a glass and poured some of the liquid before returning it to the fridge. He would keep some in the kitchen from now on, in case Lena craved it. He paused thinking about it. In case she needed it? He questioned himself out loud. "Needed blood?" She was carrying his children. Ren couldn't believe the turn of events. It had taken his wife several intimate moments to conceive. He had been home for many months before it happened. But Yalena was expecting after their first night. How did he not know?

Gliding in behind his beloved, Ren was cautious. Lena had not begun to show, but he knew that his children had to be kept safe and calm. He was in such shock that she was pregnant. He wrapped one arm around her waist and kissed her cheek and neck before sipping his drink. How did he not notice? Lena wasn't upset with him, but he was upset with himself. He would guard her more now. She would need a soldier whenever she left the house. Two would be better. It would be important that one of them could actually touch her. But the thought of another man touching his pregnant wife, even to protect her, made him angry. He paused for a moment, collecting himself. It would be important for Kiyoshi to be there for her. But would Kiyoshi keep their deal? It was imperative for all the children to be his. But his sire had never explained why.

As much as Ren could assess, he was sired by her grandfather. While he was not the only one, his process was different. He went through a similar process as the soldiers. He was told that he had to be the one for Yalena, but he remembered little of the process. Of what he did recall, he was bitten and drained over several days. During one of his wakings he was soaking in a barrel. He only had a slight idea as to what it was and at the time he rather ignored it. He was forced to remain there for what he thought were days. Ren had no sense of time, he went in and out of consciousness. He was amazed he was alive at the time.

Lena leaned further into him. "Do not go to sleep here." Lena didn't so much as reply as she murmured and waved her hand back and forth. He could tell she was drifting off. "Yalena." He paused to see if she would answer, but she made no reply. "Lena, if you're sleepy, shower and get ready for bed."

"Fine," she replied as she got out of the tub and headed for the shower.

Ren watched her as she lazily lathered her body with a loofah and rinsed off. She oiled her skin without drying off and stood in the doorway of the shower for several minutes. Guess that was her toweling tonight, Ren thought as a smirk slowly spread across his face. "Bed," Ren said after several minutes. Lena turned to look at him before dragging herself toward the bed. She crawled half way up and dropped herself on the bed. Ren was about to yell don't when she did. He would have to remember to speak to her about not jerking the twins.

Ren sighed before draining his glass. He pulled the plug on the tub before getting out and heading for the shower. Once he was done, he turned off all of the lights and walked toward the bed. He stood close to it and watched his beloved. He listened carefully for her heart beat and then the children. Yes, indeed, he said to himself and smiled before finishing the contents of his glass and climbing into bed with Lena. He was gentle as not to wake her. As he slid close to her, she turned to him. Ren smiled as he wrapped his arms around her. She smiled. His final thoughts before closing his eyes was that he needed to make sure that she and her offspring, their offspring were safe, always.

Chapter 11

After that warm bath, Lena lay in Ren's arms and fell asleep. The next day was serene. She made sure to practice her sword form, but Lena was tired and spent more than half the day sleeping, the rest of the day eating and watching TV. She was delighted when Ren came home. He greeted her with a hug and kissed her longingly, and unlike most nights, they spent it talking about the nanny/feeder they would need to hire for the babies.

Lena had awakened early enough in the morning to enjoy the sunrise. She appreciated it without even getting up out of bed. Now Lena lay awake thinking of what led up to that moment. Sometimes she deemed it all happened in a blur. But it didn't take her long to remember. She fell for his charm way before she had any idea what or who he was. He was warm and kind to her, paying attention to her needs at the club even without asking. She smiled, thinking of her first time meeting him, the first time they danced.

Ren claimed he never used his powers to win her heart, and Lena believed him because she remembered when she fell for him. Now, more than six months had passed. Yet it seemed like only yesterday their eyes met above the crowd at his club. She realized that the glimpse above the crowded club wasn't just attraction; it was recognition. Her soul had recognized Ren. Lena turned to regard him as he lay next to her. He was beautiful, his thick brown curls in perfect cascade along his face and down his neck. Lena discerned that he wasn't sleeping, but his stillness and even breathing gave that appearance.

"Are you going to awake every morning or afternoon and stare at me?"

"Probably. You're beautiful to gaze upon."

"So are you. Gorgeous, in fact," he replied as he opened his eyes to stare at her.

"You're just saying that because my scent is intoxicating to you."

"So, because your redolence drives me insane, I can not appreciate your beauty."

"You got it."

"Still think you're beautiful. And I'm hungry."

"For my body or my blood."

"Both." He smiled at her as he rolled over to hover over her body."

"Have they healed yet?"

"Which one?"

"You will just have to wear a scarf when you go out today."

"I was just starting to enjoy not having to wear one."

"You do not have to, just did not think you wanted to advertise being food."

"Please, as if your employees aren't aware, and others can't smell me on you."

"You talk too much." He stared at her for a second with a slight smile across his full lips. Then he began to kiss her. His fingers plunged into her and began to caress the soft point of tissue above her depths. He mastered how to caress her when he wanted to feed. For Lena, the two went together; sex and feeding. Somehow it made it easier to take the pain if he was inside her. It seemed to make no difference to him. He could feed without making love. But making love or sex did not exist without feeding.

There was a quick exchange between his fingers and his long hard length. Then, without fail, Lena gasped for air when he entered her, and he used that moment to sink his fangs into her neck. His thrusting into her and sucking blood from her throat seemed to be a rhythm. The pain and the pleasure together always made her hold her breath and clench her eyes shut until he stopped feeding.

"I hate when you do that. When you do not breathe, you change the flavor of your blood."

"I can't help it. It's not something I think about. Please tell me you're not going to feed the whole time we fuck."

"So, vulgar, my lady."

"I can't take that. It leaves me so weak. I don't think that would be good for the babies, and I wanted to party tonight."

"I want you in bed tonight." Lena turned her face from him. He usually fed longer when he wanted to keep her from going to his club. This happened at least every few weeks when a particular group of vampires came to feed. He never seemed to trust other vampires around her, but this group he mistrusted more. Plus, Lena was sure he was still running the events of a few nights ago through his mind.

"Why are you so conniving when you don't want me out? Why not just ask me to stay home."

"Would you listen?

"Probably not. But I would take Patrick with me."

"Then this is the only solution that we can both enjoy. So moan loudly and enjoy me pounding into you.'

Besides, I made your drink. Your body will be making blood in no time."

Lena couldn't help but stick her tongue at him. Ren snapped at it with his fangs bared and pushed a little deeper into her. Lena closed her eyes, deciding to enjoy their lovemaking. After the two climaxed together, Ren licked the blood that streamed down her neck and kissed her. They kissed for a while before he began to feed again.

Ren usually fed once a day, at sunrise, a few hours after returning home from his club for the night. And each time they made love or had sex or well, it was needless to say, but Lena was delighted with him. She just wished he would change her. But he wouldn't be able to feed if he turned her, and they probably wouldn't be able to have children.

After reaching orgasm once again, Lena just lay in his arms. She was where she was most cozy. They stayed up late at night and talked for hours just like that. She had adjusted to her new life and her fangs, no longer putting holes in her lip.

It was a peculiar afternoon, or she presumed it might be. Lena wasn't sure what would happen today. But she anticipated that it was one of those days where one would prefer to stay in bed. Still, she had done that yesterday. This time she wanted company, so she figured she would tempt Ren to stay with her. Lena climbed on top of him and enveloped his length inside her. Lena began to glide back and forth. The sensation made her body quiver, and she moaned as he took a nipple into his mouth. Lena was unaware of what most people's sex life was like, but the two were intimate at least once every day. Then there were days when Lena just couldn't gratify her desire for him.

"You are insatiable, and I relish it." They enjoyed each other most of the afternoon before Ren got out of bed to start his day. Lena didn't have any plans for the day. She thought she would take it easy. She wasn't in the mood for much of anything. She just rolled over onto her side after Ren got up, propped her head on her hand, and began to sip her smoothie.

"Ohh, strawberries, This one is better than the one at the club."

Ren smiled. "Yalena, when are you going to call back your mother. She has left ten messages over the last week."

"Wasn't planning on doing that today. I'm tired. I just want to rest, Ren. Please don't start."

"Yalena, you two were so close. You told me yourself that even when we were dating, you spent Saturday with your Mom. She's probably worried."

"And how am I supposed to explain the fangs and the pregnancy?" The intercom buzzed before he replied, and Ren left the room to answer it.

When he returned he said, "think of something quickly because she is on her way up. A soldier just let her in our private elevator."

"Ren, how does she know where I live."

"Give you one guess."

"Theo." Lena got up and hurried into the bathroom to put on clothes. She grabbed her shorts and a shelf-bra tank-top. The house was always too warm for winter clothes, even though it was below thirty degrees outside. She didn't wear many clothes at home. No one was allowed to come to the penthouse since she lived there except Theo. By the time Lena finished dressing, Ren had greeted her Mom at the elevator door.

"Lorenzo Arias, I should have known," said Carol.

"Nice to see you too, Carol. Still as beautiful as you were when I met you." Ren glanced down at the feisty middle age lady who didn't look a day over thirty-five except for the few gray strands in her hair. "You can have a seat to remove your shoes. Slippers are next to you.

"Don't nice-to-see-you-Carol-me, and save the sweet talk. Where is my daughter? And why didn't you have her return my phone calls?"

"Now, Carol, you're familiar with your daughter. She wasn't willing to call you back. You don't fathom what it took for her to call you in the first place. She was afraid you wouldn't understand."

"You didn't tell her. How could you not tell her? Why wouldn't you tell her you've waited for her. That you came for her on her sixteenth birthday? Don't answer that," Carol held up her hand and took a deep breath. "You thought she would turn from you before you made her yours."

"Mom, you know Ren?" Lena wasn't trying to listen, but she discerned everything they said from the hallway. She slowed her pace. She could see that Ren was more than a foot taller than her mom. Still, her mom stood tall; her dark dreadlocks pulled back from her face. They now stretched the length of her back. He smiled down at Carol.

"Baby girl, how are you?" Her mom walked over to her, taking her hands in hers.

"Hi, mom," Lena smiled slightly.

"Lena, your fangs grew in." Carol embraced her daughter in a bear hug. "Oh, baby, you should have called me."

After embracing her mom, Lena pulled back a little, still looking from her mom to Ren. "Mom, you've met Ren? You're not surprised by my fangs? He came to my sixteenth birthday party looking for me?" Ren didn't maintain eye contact with her.

"Okay, so, Carol, I will see you later. Lena, I will be at the club."

"Oh, no, you don't. Ren, you promised you'd tell her. Lena, is there a place we can speak?"

"Sure, mom, this way." Ren tried to take her hand, but Lena pulled away from him. He had been around her family. Why didn't he just tell her? It had been more than six months, and Ren bound her to him for three of those six. Lena led her Mom to her favorite room and plopped down on the futon by the window. Her Mom sat next to her, and Ren grabbed a pillow and sat in front of Lena. Lena didn't look at him at first. She sat staring at the plush lavender carpet and running her hand over the soft and fluffy futon cover.

Then Lena took a deep breath and glared at her mate. "Alright, Ren, spill it. What have you been keeping from me? And why? I'm sure you perceive that all secrets come to light."

"I just couldn't find the words," he replied softly. "Lena, I should have told you from the beginning, but I was afraid you would take off. And I wanted you so badly." Ren paused, taking her hands in his. "Yalena, I've been in love with you from the moment I glanced your way. That is the truth. What I didn't tell you was that the moment I beheld you was on your sixteenth birthday." Lena pulled her hands from Ren's and folded her arms across her chest.

Ren sighed, "I came to your house looking for the first line. I had met your mom and grandma over the years. Seeing you awakened in me something no other woman had. But your Mom wouldn't let me take you. She made me promise that I would let you have a life before I brought you into my world."

"What? Okay, mom, explain, please. What is going on? What knowledge do you have of the legend?"

"Yes, Lena, I've known. It was a story that my mother told me when I was a little girl that we were the descendants of Sekhmet's first line, the Khemetic goddess. The goddess who came here to rid the earth of the unrighteous. But she became bloodthirsty. Eventually became, Het Heru, the goddess of love and beauty. She told me that the fictional stories about vampires weren't all fake. Vampires did exist. The first line was a line of the goddess that became full fledged vampires, and we were part of that line.

"She told me that she was a dhampir. She was born to a human mother and a vampire father. That the vampire that found her mom was in search of the first line. She also told me that what vampires know is only part of the story. Only one person can wield the power of the first line. She said that the vampire who was her father was angry when his presence didn't bring about the legend. He left your great grandmother with a child she didn't understand and had no clue how to take care of. It's a miracle they both survived."

"Did grandma ever meet her dad?"

"Oh, yes. He came to see her on several occasions. He said he wanted to make up for leaving her. And she kept a relationship with him until her funeral. He attended her funeral and many of your birthday parties. You used to look forward to seeing him when he came around, but as you got older, he said his presence would endanger you and your sisters. So his visits became less and less.

"Senor Arias here showed up when your grandmother was a young woman. He told her she had already given her heart to someone. And indeed she had; my father. He recognized it before she had. He came around when I was born and later for birthdays. My mom explained his presence. I had no intention of living that life, and I told Ren, so he left. Actually, what happened to you? I was expecting to encounter you when Lena was born, and you weren't there."

"I thought that I had followed the wrong family and began to investigate other lineages. It was one of the council members that pointed me back to your family. Your great grandfather, Lena."

"Well, of course, Mr. Lockington. He's the only one on the council that would fit Khemetic ancestry. And even though I hadn't seen him in years, I would recognize that face anywhere."

Ren smiled and nodded."But you mustn't tell anyone. Your future and that of our children could depend on him later."

"He promised that he would stay nearby, and he kept his promise."

"Yes, Carol, he kept his promise. He waited sixteen years to tell me. And he knew I was looking for the first line. He was the one who told me the legend and told me to search for you. He sent me on a wild goose chase and then said he had to be sure I was who I portrayed. Yet he's my sire. He told me he would rather I be Lena's mate than anyone else. Lena, you have to promise me; you can't tell anyone. Not even Cell or Theo know."

"I promise. When can I see grandfather?"

"Soon."

"Let's focus on the story. Ren came by for your sixteenth birthday, and you were so smitten. Do you remember me telling you he was too old for you to even entertain any fantasy with him?

"Yes, I remember. And Ren gave me this diamond heart pendant with the necklace." Lena remembers the first time she and Ren mated. He tried to hide it, but he was surprised to see it. It was like the pendant triggered something for him. But he said nothing.

"I never imagined that you would still be wearing it."

"Why didn't I remember all of that until now?"

"I made you forget about the memory of me the day I met you. I didn't want you looking for me before you had some time to mature. And I just helped your memory return."

"I remember mom trying to beguile me to give the necklace back."

"And you refused to return it. That is why I let Ren bury those memories. It was best that way."

"Now, ladies, I need to go. Lena, see you in the morning. Mom, see you next time you come. Please visit whenever you want to see her."

"I sure will." And with that, he left them. Carol turned to her daughter. "You couldn't have left him alone? Out of all the men in Manhattan, you had to pick the head of the New York City Vampires." Lena chuckled. There was the familiar voice she had missed so much. "Now, I have to grow used to you with these fangs."

"Mom, is it that bad?"

"No, just different. You got to remember I have been looking at this face since you were born. But you're still beautiful."

"Thanks, mom. I have missed you." Lena reached over and hugged her mom. "I didn't call because I didn't grasp it all myself. How could I explain it? What would you say or think. I didn't think you would accept the decision I've made."

"Baby girl, I recognized that from the way you looked at him when he came to your party that you wouldn't let him pass you by if he wanted you. And I saw it in his eyes. He wanted you something awful. I'm surprised he waited this long."

"I lost track of her for a few years. But I found her again a couple of years ago, and I have kept my eye on Lena ever since. Just waiting for her to come to me, Lena where were you?" he called as he headed to the door.

"I went to Shanghai for a little over a year to train in the temple." When Ren didn't reply she continued speaking with her mom. "I love him, mom; I love him so much."

"Love you, too, Lena."

"Go to the club, Ren," Lena replied. She could hear him laughing as he went out the door.

"I see that, baby. I see that you both revere each other very much. It was quiet for several moments. Lena thought about what she had just learned. Knowing that he had chosen her over ten years ago makes their courtship seem so much longer than the six months they had been together.

Her mom broke the silence. "Theo says your life is in danger."

"Yes, the council wants me dead because of who I am. I am the first, and they don't want Ren to have that power. I'm not sure there is any power."

"It'll be subtle at first. You will be a lot stronger when you turn. Probably stronger than other vampires. Right now, I see you two are starting a family."

"Ren already has a family, mom."

"That's not what I'm talking about," she replied as she ran her hand across Lena's belly. As she did so, Lena noticed her stomach was a little more round than just yesterday. And it had begun to stick out even further. Lena wondered how far along she was. Human pregnancies didn't show so early. But of course, her children were not fully human.

"Oh, yes. Twins, he says."

"He would know. Baby girl, he can sense every change that goes on in your body. Ren understands. Your body won't be able to feed all of you soon." She pointed to the bite marks on Lena's thigh and her neck. "Are you aware of how far along you are?"

"No, I wasn't aware that I was pregnant three days ago. Mom, how many children am I suppose to have? Ren said three total. Two now, one the second pregnancy. He was unsure if there will be any more after that."

"Not sure. I have heard at least three children. There isn't much evidence either way. There may be more. How are you going to nurse two children?"

"I have no clue. Maybe one won't want to. You think we're going to have three children."

"Well, regardless, each child will have their special gift to maintain order in his realm."

"I don't understand."

"Dhampirs historically are usually used to track and eliminate vampires. Your children will probably be used to maintain order for Ren. They will be the ones to help Ren find the vampires who are not following the laws. And they will be the ones to carry out sentencing; possibly trial."

Lena was quiet for a while, thinking about the morning and what her mom had just said. "I was unaware that my children would hold such a significant position in this." Theo had been right, she thought. She needed to think about the decisions she made. Everything relied on what she said and did. "Mom, if vampires live forever unless killed; why did grandma grow old and die?"

"Who said she grew old and died?"

"Mom, stop playing. I saw grandma, and all of us went to her funeral."

"Well, it would be strange if she didn't grow old and die; after all, we live in the human world."

Her grandma was alive? She should feel shocked, but her world had been crazy lately. She turned to look at her mom. "Mom, why did you let me believe that she was dead? Oh, my God! I have missed her so much, mom. Where is she?" Lena was fuming. All this time her mom had lied to her and kept secrets. She folded her arms under her bosom.

"Up until a little while ago, you didn't believe in vampires." Carol turned to look at her baby girl again. "She's fine. Yazmine and I made her up every morning to make her seem her age. Because she is part vampire, she will live long, but her human side means she will eventually die." Lena was surprised to learn that she was still alive. She never died. She had cried so much for her when she thought her grandma was gone. Yazmine knew all that time and never said her word.

"So, where is she?" Lena sighed to keep her anger out of her voice.

"Funny thing, she's in Argentina right now. Some years after your grandpa died, she found a vampire to love. They are traveling the world right now. I guess they have been for some time."

"Will he turn her to keep her with him? It would be awesome to have Gram with me."

"We've talked about it. But Gram doesn't think she wants to live forever, at least a few hundred years. We're not sure how long she will live. We're unfamiliar with any other dhampirs, and no vampire seems to know any who weren't hunted down in their youth. The only reason they didn't threaten your grandmother's life was that vampires weren't aware of her. She led a typical human life.

"Your grandmother is the only one your great grandfather has encountered, and he is only a few centuries older than Ren. Well, or so he says. Unfortunately, he's not always forthcoming. He has a long habit of telling half-truths."

"I can't wait to see her." Lena rested her head on the pillow behind her. She was getting tired. Lena popped up from the pillow. "Wasn't great grandma home? How did he meet her in Barbados?"

"Well, back in dem days, the world was connected. So you just had to walk."

"Mom, seriously."

"According to Gram, he was on the island for a while. Lockington was left alone. Most people were scared of him because of the rumors. She didn't even talk about it. But there were so many tales passed from one generation to another. Anyway, he was a loner, didn't leave his property often. Lockington met your great grandmother by accident, at least that's what she thinks. Back in the early nineteen hundreds, life was different. I'm not even sure how he convinced my grandfather that he should marry your great grandmother, Caroline. Of course, being the island is small, she couldn't take the gossip when he left her. She was devastated and left home to come here. Her father abandoned her and made sure the rest of the family wouldn't help. I don't know how she had the strength to sail, pregnant as she was. But here we are." Carol sighed and took a breath.

"What a world Caroline coaxed us into with the decision to be with Lockington." She sighed again. "Have you eaten this morning?"

"I had a smoothie. We were locked in the throes of passion just before you arrived, so I haven't eaten."

"You look haggard. You have to take care of yourself. Having these two children will take the life right out of you. It would be easier if it were just one. You go lie down, and I will make you something to nosh; point me to the kitchen and show me your bedroom."

Lena did as her mother said. She showed her Mom the kitchen, which was on the way to the master bedroom. Lena was indeed tired. All that sex and feeding took its toll, exacerbated by the fact that she was pregnant with two, not one dhampir. When Lena reached the bed and crawled halfway to the head, she fell flat on her face. That was a massive mistake because Lena felt sharp strikes to her side and back; she let out a piercing scream. Who would have thought that tiny beings would pack such a punch, or slice, she thought. Who knew? Her mom came running, and so did Patrick. By the time they got there, she had managed to turn herself on her side, but Lena lay curled in pain, her eyes squeezed shut.

"Yalena, are you alright."

"It's okay, Patrick. No one attacked me, well, the children."

"Would you like me to call Mr. Arias for you?"

"No, he needs to work. I'll be okay."

"What happened?" Her mom asked as she pushed her way past Patrick, standing in the doorway.

"I forgot I was so developed for this pregnancy and fell flat on my face after I climbed into bed." She managed to say through staggered breaths. "I probably scared the babies, and they struck or sliced me in the side and back. The pain is beyond excruciating."

"Oh, dear. Lena, you must be careful. Patrick, is that your name?" Patrick nodded. "Please, pick her up and lay her at the top of the bed, propped up by the pillows." Patrick didn't move. He seemed unsure of whether or not that was a reasonable request. "What's wrong? You are here to help her, aren't you?"

"Ma'am, I'm her bodyguard. I don't touch her unless she's in harm's way. Mrs. Arias, I can call Ren for you."

"It's okay. I am just going to lay here until I can move."

"This is ridiculous. Just gently lift Lena and place her sitting up at the head of the bed."

"Sorry, Ma'am, I am not allowed to touch her unless she is in danger. And she's in no trouble. I was on the phone with Ren when you screamed; he was at the restaurant and said he would be right over. I will make sure that Kiyoshi is home when Ren is out from now on."

Lena's eyes popped open. "If he knows, then why did you ask if I wanted you to?"

"It would be better if you wanted me to call. Ren instructed me to call if you hurt yourself or if I believed he should be here." Lena nodded but said no more. She laid her head on the bed and tried to get comfy. However, the pain she endured was searing her from the inside out. Tears rolled down her cheeks. Lena tried to turn onto her back, but that was uncomfortable for both the babies and herself, and they lashed out, causing more excruciating pain. Lena whimpered a bit. Finally, Lena decided to lie still until Ren could move her.

Carol seemed beside herself. She just stood there watching Lena in horror with the fork in one hand and the spatula in the other. She took a deep breath and once again pushed past Patrick standing in the doorway. Lena knew her mom would finish cooking. When her Mom was upset and couldn't help, she would cook. When Lena broke up with her first boyfriend and locked herself in her room for the weekend, her mom prepared everything she could to make her feel better.

Lena couldn't move anymore. Her children seemed content for her to be on her side, so they rested. Lena was happy about that, and she couldn't take another blow. Her body felt like she was shredded and aflame from within. From the agony she endured, she surmised her children had shredded her inside. But wasn't she supposed to be stronger than her female counterparts? At the same time, Ren was potent. The most powerful of the vampires she had seen so far. His children would be somewhat like him. Lena guessed that her being the first line was the only reason she was still breathing. And her breathing was getting a little easier. She could talk now.

"Patrick, you can go back to wherever or whatever you were doing. I'll be fine."

"Yes, Mrs. Arias, Mr. Arias should be here any minute." Lena tried to smile, but it came out as a grimace. Patrick just disappeared.

Lena tried to move a little, to work her way to the pillow at the top of the bed, but she couldn't. Her movement had stirred her children, and Lena suffered through their movement, which caused her agonizing pain after they butchered her insides. Her eyes welled with tears, and Lena stopped moving and closed her eyes. Again she thought she should lay still until Ren got home. She wasn't comfortable, yet she made do, propped on her arm. She imagined Ren in a cab trying to return to her. He probably wished that he had run instead because of the late afternoon traffic. Ren might be moving slower than he would have been on foot.

Thoughts of him calmed her down, which in turn, seemed to calm her little ones. At last, she could rest a little. She could hear her Mom's footsteps and the aroma of the food she was bringing for her. She had been cooking up a storm. The aroma of the callaloo and codfish came into the room. Her being an island girl, she loved the food of her culture. This dish was her favorite. Lena wondered where her Mom had found the ingredients for it. How did Ren know? Then Lena remembered he had been around her family for at least a century, probably more. He would have learned something about her culture and, of course, her favorite food.

When her mom had finished cooking and brought her a plate, Lena managed to sit up a little. She ate every last drop of the callaloo and codfish, along with the pumpkin and dumpling her

Mom had made. Lena was finishing when Ren came into the room. She had finally stopped crying, and her Mom had just gotten through telling her that she looked a lot better with something in her stomach.

"Patrick told me what happened. Yalena, you must be careful. You scared me half to death. You must be gentle and steady, don't upset the babies. They could kill you, and I'm speaking literally."

"Ren, what are you not telling me about our children?"

"Well, let's just say I'm pleased you're still alive."

"Come again."

"You are not the first human I've gotten pregnant. Sometime after I became a vampire, I returned home to my wife. She accepted me for what I had become. Like you, she let me feed. We made love, and she got pregnant. But at the end of the second month, the children shredded her from the inside out. The children didn't mean to hurt her. She fell off of the step stool, and they got scared. They ripped through her womb, killing themselves and their mother in the process. They still needed their mother to survive. Just please try not to shake them up too much."

"It wasn't on purpose. I was tired; I climbed halfway up the bed and fell on my face; they reacted by what I think was kicking and scratching me in the side and back. Then I tried to lay on my back, which wasn't genial for the twins either." He gently picked her up, laid her down at the top of the bed, and propped her up on pillows. "Thank you, that's better."

"How do you feel?"

"Honestly, tired and a little queasy." He grabbed the garbage can and put it under Lena's chin just in time for her to throw up most of what Lena had just eaten. "I hate throwing up."

"I want you to try something without asking any questions."

"Will it make me better?"

"I said no questions, Yalena."

"Fine, Lorenzo."

"Carol, do you have any more food left?

"Yes, Ren."

"Bring another bowl. Lena will consume more in a little while. I want you to drink." He used his nail to cut his wrist and put it up to her mouth. Lena stared up at him, and he nodded. So she drank. His blood was as tantalizing as she remembered it. It soothed her stomach. Like the first time, he pulled his wrist away from her before Lena finished. "Enough. Give it a few minutes, and then I want you to eat. We will see what they prefer to eat or how they prefer to eat." Lena leaned into the pillows and rested. She was waiting to see her body's reaction. The pain seemed to subside, and Lena could adjust herself to what was most cozy.

"I'm a bit better. How did you know?"

"I have been around for a few pregnancies. Each is different. But most dhampir infants don't drink blood in the womb until they are almost ready to be born. Ours wouldn't be like most. By the third month of a friend's wife's pregnancy, she craved blood, which is all she drank. For Madeline, it was raw meat. After the fourth month, she ate fresh raw meat. Good thing they lived on a farm. I figured ours would be unusual. Now, are you hungry?"

"Yes, very." Lena's Mom was waiting with a bowl of food. Lena was all too happy. She ate slowly this time. Ren's twist had done the trick, it seems. Lena felt better, and the babies seemed calm. She sank further into the pillows. Ren laid next to her and rubbed her stomach.

"Now you two in there have to behave. I love your mom, and you are inside of her. Treat her well, and you will be born when it is time. She is my Queen, and I am your father." Lena was surprised by their reaction. She could sense them moving but gentle and light. It must have been his tone of voice, she thought.

"They're calm now. I didn't think the twins would have understood you."

"Not sure, but I figured it was worth a try. You sleep; I will be in the office. I won't leave. I will work from home for a few days." Lena didn't want to sleep, but her body said otherwise. Her eyes grew heavy, and the sheets and pillows engulfed her. Oh yeah, having one vampire baby was too much, but twins are damn near deadly.

Chapter 12

Lena relaxed for the rest of the day. She watched some tv, but mostly it stared at her. Opening her eyes for the third time that day, she looked around, seeing Patrick walking by the bedroom door.

"Patrick."

"Yes, my Queen."

"Where is my mom?"

"She's trying to get Mr. Arias to speak with her, and he's trying to concentrate on business. He's trying to ignore her, but she hasn't moved."

"Of course not; she knows he's aware of her presence."

"Indeed, my Queen. I'm sure he cannot ignore her much longer. It is Carol, after all." Lena nodded and closed her eyes once again.

Then her mom's voice was discernible from the office down the hall. "Ren, you can't ignore me much longer. I am worried about her. You should have seen her after. She appeared so fragile and ashen, not the virile woman we revere and adore. Maybe, the first line isn't as strong as we think."

"No, she is who we believe she is. If you had seen my wife once the babies had finished with her, you would comprehend how potent your daughter's body is. Besides, I have been keeping her healthy. I have been feeding her well."

"How were you not aware of her pregnancy until two days ago"I didn't hear the heartbeat before someone brought it to my attention. The heartbeats aren't human and even softer than a dhampir. It's similar to a vampire's heartbeat. I fear that she may be further along than I originally figured. I thought a few weeks the other night, but I was wrong, probably about six to eight weeks with their strength. She will begin to crave more and more blood each day. I am trying to find a feeder for her and the babies. The blood they consume in her womb should be the one they drink once their teeth grow. Lena won't like it, but she can't keep drinking my blood."

"Is there any way to be sure how far along she is?"

"Only if I can purchase or rent an ultrasound machine. It is probably best not to do that. We wouldn't want to startle Yalena. But, I will not make that mistake again to leave her without someone who can help. I will make sure that she and the children will be cared for."

"Patrick mentioned a Key someone. And why couldn't her bodyguard pick her up and put her in the bed?"

"Kiyoshi, he is the only one who can touch her without consequence. No other vampire is allowed to touch her, and her bodyguard cannot touch her without me there. It's for her safety. Her blood tends to call most male vampires. It would be difficult to resist feeding if they were close. They could lose control and drain her dry. Either way, I would have to dispatch them and I'd be without my mate."

The room was still for a while. Lena could hear nothing. She closed her eyes again and drifted between sleep and wake. She awoke again to the motion of the bed and Ren picked her up and cradled her.

"What," she asked, looking up at Ren. He smiled, but Lena could see the worry in his eyes. She understood that he was concerned for her health and safety.

"Your restlessness was quite audible, so I came to check on you. When I walked in, your limbs were moving all over the place. Like you knew you shouldn't roll over, but you weren't comfortable. Better?" Lena gazed into his eyes and smiled at him as she relaxed into his body. Ren was her haven. As her mom entered the room, Lena began to shiver.

"You just could not make this easy, could you." He whispered to Lena as she shivered in his arms.

"Ren, why is she shivering," asked Carol.

"I am cold now because I have not been feeding from a human body as much as before. Most of the blood in my system is from the reserve over the last forty-eight hours. As a result of using blood from my reserve, my body is cold. Can you reach into the chest at the end of the bed and get me a blanket?" Carol did as requested, and Ren wrapped Lena in the blanket to keep her warm. "Carole, how much callaloo is left?"

"Enough for her to feast for the rest of today and tomorrow. You will have to cook after that."

"Thank you. Cell should be here soon with our feeders."

"So, she will feed like a vampire?"

"Yes, she is carrying vampires, after all, well they're mostly anyway. They will probably always drink blood. After they are born, she will not want it, and then her feeder can help feed the children. At least until her next pregnancy."

"Next pregnancy! Let's survive this one. Please, take care of her. I beg you, Ren. I leave the life of my daughter in your hands. I hope to come back in a few days and find her still human."

"You will find her alive, in a matter of speaking, one way or the other."

"I will be back in a few days. Tell Lena I love her."

"I love you too, mom." Lena woke up to the end of the conversation. She was delighted to see that she was cocooned in her husband's arms. Lena smiled up at Ren before she struggled to unwrap herself and get up to give her mom a hug and a kiss goodbye. Finally, she had her vigor back. Lena had been sleeping and resting for two days now. She was hoping that the babies would let her. Ren helped her out of the blanket and off of his lap. Lena looked down at her stomach, which seemed a little more swollen with her twins. She smiled and helped her mom into her jacket and then hugged her.

"Take care of yourself, Lena. And, of course, be good to my grand babies. Half vampire or not, I think they are going to give you a run for your money."

Lena smiled as she walked her mom to the entrance of the private elevator door. It was amazing what a little food and blood could do. After the door closed, Lena took a deep breath before walking back to the bedroom. Thank goodness she had just passed the front door when she heard a knock. The person called her name, and Lena recognized the voice. It was Cell. Lena opened the door, and there he stood with two other people. Cell was in his usual attire. A thick gold tone chair went from his belt to his jean pocket. The two people with him were of an athletic build, but average height. They were average looking but had the most startling blue eyes.

"How did you know it was me? I could have been someone else."

"Ren would have sensed it and came to protect me. Not to mention, Patrick wouldn't have let you get this far." Lena was about to call Ren when he appeared at her side.

"Hey Cell, Thanks for coming. I appreciate it."

"No problem. Lena looks fine, though. You sure you need two feeders."

"Yeah, I'm sure. We'll both need to feed soon. And I definitely can not feed on Lena right now."

"Okay. Lena, aren't you going to invite me in?"

"Oh, I'm sorry. I thought you would be able to come in since you've been here before."

"No. This is your home now; I cannot enter without an invitation. So please keep that in mind if other people show up here."

"Sure, thanks. You may come in. Please take your shoes off," she stated pointing to the bench. "There are slippers in the basket."

Ren hugged her from behind and kissed her cheek. "Lena, love, go back to the bedroom. I need to speak with Cell and our guests."

"Sure. I'm just going to stop by the kitchen to munch."

"I prefer that you wait until you've fed, please. You may eat after."

"Okay, but please hurry. I am famished." He nodded, and Lena turned to walk back to the room. She was starving and wondered if she could talk him into going out for Chinese food. The thought of getting out of the house put a smile on her face. This time Lena was careful getting into the bed and slowly crawling up before turning to lay on her side. She rested her head on her pillow and took a deep breath. The children were quiet; that was wonderful.

Meanwhile, Ren spoke with the new feeders in the other room. Lena didn't understand why he didn't want her there. After all, she could hear them.

"Ren, this is Michael and Fern. They are married and are willing to be the feeders for you and your wife for five years or until you move. The only thing that would hinder them is if Fern became pregnant. They have already accepted your generous offer."

"Yes, Mr. Arias. Cell told us that you were looking for feeders for your family. We thought it would be an experience of a lifetime. We didn't know that your wife was pregnant."

"Yes, she is. That is the main reason I am requesting feeders. I used to feed from my wife alone, but that would be detrimental to her and the children."

"Children?"

"Yes, my wife is pregnant with twins, and I am afraid that requires more attention than just one baby. Now we have a guest room for you next to the master suite. I usually feed once a day. Fern, you will be my feeder, and Michael will be Lena's. She is not a vampire, but the children she carries are, and they require blood.

I will provide meals as well as protection when you leave the penthouse. You can live here if you want, but it is not required. I just ask that you be here during scheduled feeding times."

The couple nodded in agreement. And Ren paused to listen for her before continuing. "Cell, I assume you have had them tested, and they are healthy."

"Yes, we got the results this morning before you called."

"I do have a question, Mr. Arias."

"Please call me Ren. You may ask Fern."

Fern smiled shyly. "Will we be required to be intimate also?"

"Not for me. That would be deadly for you, Fern." Fern seemed a bit disappointed but smiled and nodded.

"Michael, if she wishes, you may. That is totally up to her. Cell, if you don't mind, I made some of the juice this morning; please pour three glasses and leave them on the counter before you leave. Michael and Fern this way."

When he walked to the bedroom, Lena was sitting up because she was not feeling well. It seems she only had a few hours of well being for all the queasiness she suffered. And it was most unfortunate that it came in spurts of minutes at a time.

Lena stared at Ren as he entered the room. He seemed uneasy to her. She knew that he was worried. But his worry made her worry. Would her body withstand the pregnancy? He just stood at the entrance of their room, staring at her. As he looked her over, he smiled, making Lena smile. Lena could tell that the people Cell brought with him were behind Ren. She drew in a deep breath; what a sweet aroma, she thought. Lena took a deep breath and chuckled to herself. Wow, this is what she chose. That notion or question in her mind didn't last long once their eyes met again. She smiled and suddenly had the urge to reach for him and be embraced close to him. But the aggressive squirming in her stomach reminded her of why that wasn't possible.

"Guess you're not the only one who is hungry," teased Ren. Lena put her hand on her stomach and rubbed in a circle. The warmth seemed to help, and the wriggling slowed down. Strangely, their shifting reminded her of a frenzy when sharks smell blood. "Lena, I would like you to meet our feeders, Michael and Fern." As he introduced them, they all walked over to the bed. Michael sat on her left; Fern sat at the end of the bed, and Ren on her right side. He leaned in to kiss her lips. Lena wanted so much to make love to him right then and there.

Lena took no notice of the two strangers in her room. She was shocked by that thought. As they stopped kissing, his beautiful browns met hers. His expression was one Lena hadn't seen before; questioning. He ran his hand down her side as he watched her. Lena guessed he missed her too, which she thought strange. They were together no more than a few hours ago.

Even though they locked eyes, Lena could sense the movement as Michael moved closer to her. Ren's touch aroused Lena, which seemed to awaken a raging hunger. The bouquet of Michael's blood assailed her nostrils. She broke her gaze with Ren and looked at Michael, who had loosened his shirt collar and rolled up his sleeves. Lena guessed he didn't perceive where she would prefer to bite. She looked at his face and into his deep blue eyes; he appeared as frightened as he seemed curious. Lena tried not to alarm him with her movement as she took his arm and put it to her mouth. His body tensed in pain as Lena bit into his wrist.

This was the first time she had fed from anyone other than her love, the first time anyone else's blood had touched her lips. As Lena fed, she looked up for Ren, and there he was at Fern's throat, feeding. She had not seen him feed on anyone else. Yet there he was, seemingly savoring Fern's blood as Lena did Michael's. Lena stopped feeding. She slowly got to her knees and crawled to the bottom of the bed, where he sat with Fern. Ren regarded her motion without turning to look at her. Then reached for Lena's hand but didn't stop feeding until she touched his.

"What's the matter? Don't you like the way Michael tastes?" Lena didn't answer. Her only response was to stare into his eyes, then Lena kissed him longingly. He gently moved Fern off of his lap in one move and took Lena in his arms. His palm on her cheek.

"You are jealous. I haven't fed on anyone since we have mated." Lena said nothing, but she lowered her gaze from his. "I am not upset." He took her head in his hands once again and kissed her lips. Mixing the feeders' blood in their mouths allowed her to understand why Cell had brought them. Lena couldn't describe the taste, she could only say it fueled their passion, and they began to kiss more furiously. Then he stopped suddenly.

"I don't think this is a good idea after today's scare. I cannot make love to you now. In a few months." There was a long silence as Lena and Ren tried to control the desire that consumed them both. "You have not finished feeding; finish. I had Patrick buy you some Chinese food."

"Okay, you have got to be physic. How did you know?"

"I have been watching you for over five years. I have studied each movement and each expression on your face. I know you, and soon you will know me as well. I will finish, and so will you." Lena fed longer than Ren. He had to stop her from feeding. After the first bite of him, she just couldn't sate her hunger. Michael's blood was delicious.

After Ren took Michael away from her, Lena sat back on a pillow, very full and satisfied. The tang of his blood still on her lips, Lena licked them. The twins in her belly seemed genuinely content, and each picked a side of her body to curl up. She was finally relieved and tried to make herself as comfortable as possible. Then she found the remote and turned on the tv. Lena liked the noise. She wasn't watching it, but it kept her company. It allowed her to think. And that's all Lena wanted to do now.

Ren didn't bother her with details and planning, so Lena had no idea of her responsibility. But, at the same time, her hands were full at the moment.

Wow, Lena thought she was pregnant. Pregnant with twins. She was carrying two dhampirs. If anyone had told her a year ago that she would have children with a man she had only known for six months, Lena would have said to them that they were crazy, but here she was. She had pledged herself and her life to him. And now she was carrying his children who were growing twice the rate of a healthy human child, possibly even faster.

Then Lena thought about her great-grandfather. Her mom's grandfather was a vampire. Did vampires even acknowledge such a connection? They didn't appear to do so in the movies she had seen. What mattered to them most was their love, their partner. Maybe he figured that he would be rewarded if he played his role. That made more sense. After all, he wasn't only a vampire but a man. Men always have an agenda. Even Ren kept watching over her all this time because he wanted her as his mate. Otherwise, what would it matter if Seth wanted her? But then Seth wouldn't want her if Ren didn't. Lena began to rub her protruding belly as she ran those thoughts repeatedly in her mind.

Thinking about Seth made her want to practice again. Lena wanted to regard the silver in her hands, the blades flowing as extensions of herself. Lena wondered how her babies would react to her walking through her form. Lena decided to give it a try. She walked over to the spot where they were hidden, got on her hands and knees, and opened the floor. Lena didn't take the trunk out of the floor. She just removed the two Jian swords. Lena used them to help her stand. Holding the swords felt right. She could feel her babies change their position. As if they went from lying down to sitting straight up. That was odd. Were they paying attention? Did they perceive what was going on or what Lena was about to do? Maybe it is just the way her body reacted right then; that made them pay attention. She thought she would see how it went. Lena took both swords and headed for the private elevator. She didn't even enter before Ren appeared in front of her when the elevator doors opened up.

"And what do you think you're going to do with two swords?"

"I am going to practice. I need to practice. I miss the steel and silver in my hands."

"You should not be doing anything strenuous in your condition."

"This isn't strenuous. Even the children are curious." That didn't seem to convince him. Ren stood in front of her with his arms folded over his chest as he leaned on the wall. "Please, Ren. Just for a short while."

"Okay, if you insist, but only for a little while. Your food is here, and I want you to eat. I will go with you in case you need me; you might."

"Fine. Where are Michael and Fern?"

"They are in the guest room resting." That caught her attention, and her head popped up to glare into his eyes with a question. "Patrick is keeping a watchful eye." Lena nodded, and they got into the elevator. Lena thought about her reaction to them being in their home. Lena had always been suspicious, but she guessed her new life would make her more so.

Lena was elated she had gotten up out of bed to practice. She was elated to wield her swords again. She made sure to take her time and slowly move across the floor and through the form. Lena could feel the children the whole time pushing on her stomach. Then, as if they were reaching for the swords, she swung in her hands. Lena put both swords in one hand and patted her hand to where theirs were.

"You will wield them soon, little ones."

"To whom are you talking? As if I could not fathom."

"The children, of course. They are pushing against my stomach as I move." He smiled at her statement. It was as if he was hoping for such longing from her children. Lena scoffed and returned to repeating the form she had just completed. Lena enjoyed the way the swords glided through the air. She moved slowly at first. It was thrilling to hold them again. Then she advanced quickly across the floor, swords twirling around her. Too soon, Lena slowed, sensing her energy waning. She continued for a bit longer. As slowly as Lena moved, the blades grew heavy, and her breathing quickened, so she decided to stop. Her body began to feel as if all the ardor and strength had drained. She tried to lean on her swords to keep her balance, but Lena didn't have enough energy left. As Lena began to collapse to the floor, Ren scooped her up in his arms, swords and all.

"I told you not to push it. You do not have the strength right now to work out for hours."Lena said nothing. What could she say? He was right, but she needed to work out. Lena didn't want to lose the fluidity that she had gained over the years, and if she didn't practice regularly, it would slowly go. Now, Lena was beginning to experience the laboring weight of the children she carried in her womb. Admittedly, the entire form would be too much as she got closer to their birth.

"Let's get you some food. I had Patrick order your favorite. Hopefully, you'll feel better."

"Okay. How did you find Michael and Fern?"

"Cell found them, I think. Not sure. Usually, Cell finds safe feeders for me, so I leave it up to him. Why?"

"I don't know. It just seems too easy, and their blood, too enticing."

"Well, I guess it was quite speedy that he found them. We've been looking for a while. I didn't think we would need them so soon. If you don't want them in the house, they can come just for feedings."

"No, them being here is fine. Let's just let it play out. I could be wrong." They sat in the kitchen as Lena ate, but she couldn't shake the notion that something was afoot. She sensed something was coming. Lena perceived that they were going to try again. She just wasn't sure how. Now Lena was getting tired of staying in the house. It had been more than a month. She wanted to encounter the wind of winter on her face and blowing through her thick curls.

"Is my beautiful caramel princess feeling better?"

"Yes. I think I am ready to lay down again. Can I go out tomorrow?"

"Where would you like to go? I can arrange a car for you."

"Not sure, perhaps to lunch and a boutique."

"Lunch sounds okay, but shopping? I don't think that's a good idea. You couldn't even go through your full workout. So shopping is out of the question. You can dine at the restaurant. Have brunch with one of your sisters."

"Do you think they know? And is that safe for any of us?

"Well, love, the only other option is to lock yourself in this penthouse and don't come out until after the babies are born."

"I don't think I could stay in this house another day. I need to get out, even if it's just an hour or two."

"Wonderful. The matter is settled."

"And after we have lunch?"

"You can return to the penthouse or come to the club."

"I guess I could visit the club for a few hours and take a nap before the party. After that, I would probably just sit in the booth for a little while."

Lena called her sister, whom she hadn't spoken to in a few months. Lena was surprised that Yazmine picked up the phone. Her sister was surprised but said that mom had filled her in on her condition and told her that Lena would probably call. They made arrangements for the next day, and Lena even invited her to come to the club with her. Yazmine was the middle sister. She had heard about the club and wanted to take a tour without being dinner. Lena was looking forward to seeing her. It had been a long time since she had spent time with Yazmine or Yolanda. Yolanda had been in England ever since she went to college. She was bent on going to the same college as their great grandfather.

The next day began quite peacefully. The children woke her, and Lena fed before Ren brought her favorite fruit-filled crepes. Lena fathomed it would take her a while to dress, so she started early. Her belly had grown so fast Lena hadn't had time to shop. She immediately sat on the bench in the bathroom, feeling beaten. What would she wear? Lena hadn't ever purchased big roomy clothes. Hers were all well fitted, if not tight. When she didn't come out of the bathroom after some time, Ren came looking for her.

"My love, are you alright?"

"Yes, fine. It's just that I have nothing to wear. I haven't bought any maternity clothes. I've spent the last few weeks in my t-shirts and your sweats."

"Have you searched in the closet lately? There are a few things for you in the corner of the closet." When Lena looked, there they were. Ren had not ceased to amaze her. Lena perused through the small selection of clothing and picked out an outfit. Out of the corner of her eye, she saw the smile on his face before he left the room, and it filled her. She was excited to see her sister, and now she would appear the part.

Lena and Patrick took a cab from the penthouse to the restaurant, which was uptown. Lena would meet her sister there, and then they would go to the club. It was late afternoon when they arrived at Angelo's. She didn't have to wait; her table was set in the reserved section at the back of the restaurant. She was ready to eat and ordered the same bloody drink that Ren had when they dined there. She sat and took a deep breath. Patrick was nowhere to be seen, just like him, making himself scarce. Lena wasn't waiting long before Yazmine showed up. It took Lena a minute, but she managed to rise from the chair to greet her sister.

"Yazzi, so glad you could make it." They greeted each other with a hug and then stepped back to check each other out. "You look wonderful." Of course she did, thought Lena. Yazmine was their glamour girl. Her make up was perfect. Her aqua eyeshadow matched her blouse, which neatly tucked into her low rise jeans.

"Thanks, Lena. You're beautiful. A lot bigger than I thought you would be."

"Twins, they are giving me a run for my money." Lena smoothed out her sweater dress. It was a muted copper, and she wore her favorite pair of cream boots.

As they sat down Yazmine asked, "What are you drinking?"

"Bloody Mary."

"You're not supposed to drink while you're pregnant."

"Not that kind of bloody mary."

"Gross. I thought you were still, you know."

"I am, but the kids are part."

"Mom said you scared the crap out of her the other day."

"Scared me too. I wasn't sure I would make it, but Ren figured it out, and we've been cool since, of course, that could change at any time."

"Yeah, any minute, I'm told." There was silence for a few moments as they perused the menu. Then she grabbed Lena's glass and examined it. "You haven't touched it."

"Yeah, don't appreciate the smell. Not sure how the others stand it. I guess Ren has been babying me. I fed on him the first time, and then he arranged for feeders. I haven't had to use blood from any other source."

"And I see that you have fangs."

"Yeah, a product of the bond between Ren and I. He's taking fabulous care of me. Maybe you can come over to the penthouse someday soon." Lena thought she saw Yazmine's eye twitch before her sister managed to plaster a smile on her face.

Yazmine nodded. "Of course I will, just waiting for an invitation."

Finally, the waiter came over and took their orders. He seemed a little nervous, and that worried Lena. After all, he worked in a restaurant frequented by vampires. Why else would they be concerned?

"Does the waiter's behavior seem a little off to you?"

"Yes, Yazzie, it does." Lena looked up above Yazzie's head and distinguished a brief shimmer. She was pleased that Patrick was going to investigate. His gift came in handy in this circle. A few minutes passed before Lena saw the shimmer heading to the door. Something must be very wrong in the kitchen.

"I don't think we'll be eating here today. Do you feel like Indian? I know this sublime place."

"That bad?"

"We'll see in a minute; here comes Patrick and Ren."

"Who's Patrick?"

"He's my bodyguard. Ren is the one with the ponytail."

"He's hot, sis."

"For sure," she replied as she gave a short giggle. "Ren didn't mention anything about coming here today. Patrick must have called him. Guess we were right. The question is, how accurate? We're going to have to go somewhere else."

"So tell me about your husband? He seems to have a commanding presence."

"Yazzi, that is an understatement. He is the owner of both the club and this restaurant." Lena moved in near to her sister before continuing. "He is the leader of his clan and his family. He is the King of the New York vamps."

"You sure know how to pick them, don't you, Lena." Lena nodded, and they continued to dish about her new husband and her sister's boyfriend, whom Lena had yet to meet. While they were passing the time, Ren and Patrick were in the kitchen. Lena was having a hard time listening to both.

"Where is Vincent?"

"He called in sick. This guy Richard came in and said that Vincent sent him."

"And no one called me."

"Vincent called this morning and said he would handle it." Lena looked over in time to see an exchange of looks between Ren and Patrick; Patrick walked away with the phone to his ear.

"Any complaints from the customers?"

"No, sir."

"How was the food cooked?"

"Same as before. However, when I insisted that I cook for Mrs. Arias since Vincent wasn't here, he flew into a rage, so we let him."

"Did she eat any of it?"

"It hasn't been taken to the table. He had insisted on taking it to the table himself."

"Where is he?"

"Patrick locked him in the storage about half an hour ago and told us not to serve anything he cooked." Ren nodded and walked over to the storage closet. When he unlocked and opened the door, the chef tried to lunge at Ren with a knife. Ren heartily laughed as he stepped out of the way. "Humans," Ren muttered. He grabbed the knife as Patrick grabbed him from behind.

"Who sent you?"

"I don't know."

"I'm sure you have some idea of who would want you to poison a pregnant woman. Or is that something you do regularly?"

"No, sir. I am a chef at a restaurant across town."

"How did you come to be here today?"

"Some men met me in front of my building today. They said they needed me to do something for them. At first, I refused, but then my wife and little girl came out of the building while the men talked to me. They grabbed them and put them in this black car. They said that if I didn't do as they asked, they would kill my wife and child. Then they put me in the car also and drove us here. They gave me a vial of something and told me to put it in her food. Please, you gotta help me save my wife and child."

Patrick stopped holding the chef and let him sink to the floor. Ren shook his head.

"It begins," Lena whispered.

"What," asked Yazmine.

"Oh nothing," Lena replied. She couldn't believe that it was beginning. How did they know she was going to be here today? At least Patrick came with her today.

Lena was sure Ren would help the young chef get his wife back. She was also confident that the consequences would be dire for anyone involved. At least that would send a message. People would be less willing to help the council eliminate her, she hoped.

Lena knew that Ren was watching her. He always kept a watchful eye when she was around. She smiled as she rubbed her stomach. Sure didn't seem like she was going to eat here today. Lena was hungry. She hadn't drunk the blood in her glass yet. Lena figured she'd give it a try. Before she brought the drink to her lips, Ren caught her hand. Without putting the glass down, he leaned over to kiss her. There was blood in his mouth, his blood. Lena began to understand. Lena drank from him as they kissed. There wasn't much, but it seemed enough to calm her sickness. He smiled at her and took the glass from her hand, before returning to the kitchen. As Lena shifted her scrutiny from Ren to Yazmine, she noted the sour appearance on her sister's face. She would ask her after she eavesdropped on what was happening in the kitchen.

"Patrick, any word from Vincent."

"Ren, he was sick. Something he ate yesterday. He answered the door of his apartment. The guys said he seemed off, though. He wouldn't let them into his apartment. So far, I'm the only one that he'll let in. So after we wrap this up, I will go there."

"You asked two of the men to come here?"

"Should be coming in through the back any minute. Don't want to alarm anyone in the black car sitting out front."

"I'm surprised they weren't forced to move. When our soldiers arrive, I want this to go down rapidly. I don't want them to know that we're coming."

"They won't notice me."

"Mack, they have been here for a while. Throw out this food and whip up something quick for Lena and her sister to eat. You, Chef, stay here. Don't move; anything happens to my wife or her sister before we return, and no one will leave this place alive." All one could hear was the clinking of pots and pans and knives against the cutting board while Ren left the kitchen and walked past Lena.

It all seemed to happen rather quickly. In a shorter time than Lena conceived, a guard brought in a small girl and a woman. She assumed they belonged to the man who was sitting on the floor. He had not moved since Ren went outside. He appeared so relieved when he spied the woman and child. He was helped up off the floor and taken out the back of the restaurant. Neither Ren nor Patrick had returned. Lena didn't have a favorable impression.

For the first time since Lena had been with Ren, she was terrified. Someone had tried to poison her. Had Patrick not come with her. This was not going to end unless they were dead or all council members, except her grandfather, were killed. Lena didn't want to live like that. How horrible that she could not even go to her husband's restaurant without someone trying to kill her. It was too much, Lena thought to herself. And who had known she would be here? They hadn't made arrangements until late this morning to ensure no one would have time to try anything. The only one who knew last night was her... Lena sighed; she wouldn't finish that thought. There was absolutely no way.

Lena hadn't touched the plate placed in front of her. Instead, her glare remained on the door for a long time. She was waiting for Ren to break that gaze. And while she waited, her mind began to wonder if she would ever be safe. For the first time, Lena marveled at why she was so vulnerable. Lena hated it; she wanted to be able to fight back.

"Lena, you should try some. They're actually pretty good." Her sister's voice broke her trance. Her voice didn't seem to belong in her world. How odd, Lena thought. Lena looked at her sister, then her plate. Her sister had at least enjoyed the appetizers. Lena smiled. "Lena, are you okay? You look a little peaked."

"The spice smell of the food is making me sick. I think I will have Ren fix me something at the club. I need to eat, and I need to feed." Lena paused to take a deep breath, trying to calm herself. "Do you mind going to the house with me?"

"Not at all. We can go to the club another day."

"I still want you to go to the club today. I just really need to eat, and the restaurant is not working for me." Lena wanted to get up and head to the door, but she felt fragile, not to mention severely queasy. Then both babies stretched, and Lena thought she would die from the pain. She didn't want to scream in the crowded restaurant, but a whimper escaped her lips. Between the sound and the look on Lena's face, her sister seemed beside herself.

"Yalena, what happened?"

Lena couldn't answer. The tears had finally made it to her eyes. Lena hadn't discerned what to do. She couldn't leave or call a cab without Patrick or Ren. It just wouldn't be a good idea. Lena was in no condition to fend off an attack from one of their disgruntled clan members. Lena wanted to double over, but the twins' position made her sit up so straight her back began to bow. She tried to take a deep breath, which made her wince. She guessed that she wouldn't be going out again for the remainder of this pregnancy. There was no way to tell when they would do something that would cause her agony.

"Lena, I really think we should leave here. Can you stand?" Lena shook her head no. Yazzi huffed and crossed her arms in front of her. She often did that when she was thinking about what to do. "Where is that husband of yours? I thought they were right outside."

Lena had also wondered what was taking so long. She was pretty sure he heard her whimper. Where was he? Since Lena had known him, he has always appeared by her side when needed. Where was he now?

"Should I go look out of the window to see if the black car is still there?"

Lena was finally able to find her voice. "No, that would probably put you in danger. We will just wait. Ren knows I am here and in need of him. He will come."

"Does that usually happen?" Lena nodded in response. "I wonder what happened this time?"

Lena felt a draft come through the restaurant, but she didn't hear footsteps. There he was. He seemed relieved until he saw her face. Lena guessed that even though there was some relief, her face did not display that. He rushed to her side, wrapped her in her coat and swept her up in his arms.

"I need to get you home." He turned to Yazmine and invited her to come along. Lena was delighted. She didn't want their day together to end, but she couldn't stay at the restaurant any longer.

Chapter 13

Lena was rushed out of the restaurant and into the cab that waited outside. For the first time, she spent the taxi ride in Ren's lap. He had refused to let her sit beside him. Lena had not discerned how much Ren cherished and cared for her until then. As he held her snug to him, she started to think of how dangerous this was getting. She had never thought she would be in such danger with Ren as her mate. She must admit that she didn't think there was anything dangerous about being his mate when she decided to give him her heart. Lena should have re-thought staying with him after she discovered who he was. Still, even after finding that out, Lena didn't know that people, well vampires, would be after her with such fervor. Lena probably would have had a more peaceful time if she hadn't gotten pregnant early. Her head was whirling with the thoughts of what ifs and her safety. Soon, she fell asleep in Ren's arms and didn't wake up until he put her on their bed.

"Yalena, babe, how are you feeling."

"Better, I guess." Lena looked around the room. She saw her sister sitting on the couch in the corner and Patrick at the bedroom door, watching her. Lena was glad Yazmine came with them. They hadn't talked a whole lot at the restaurant. Lena got up and excused herself to the bathroom. Ren followed and decided that a warm bath would help her feel better. Anything sounded appealing to her at the moment. So Lena undressed and got into the tub. She sat for a moment and closed her eyes. It was so soothing and warm. The sound of the water filling up the bathtub was peaceful. But Lena was still a little dizzy, and her stomach was turning. That is when she remembered that she hadn't eaten. Lena had only had a small amount of blood that she got from Ren's kiss.

"Ren, I need to eat. I didn't eat anything at Angelo's. The odor of the food made me queasy. There was an acridness to the dish."

"I am going to have to spend a lot of time at the restaurant getting things right. I may end up shutting it down for a while. I'll get Michael." Ren went to the guest bedroom, but it was empty. He walked down to the kitchen, but they weren't there. "Patrick, have you seen the feeders?"

"No. I've been with Lena. But they should be here anyway." Ren came back to the bathroom with a bag of blood. Lena didn't say anything, but she was certain she would not drink it. Lena had been feeding on Ren when she needed to and after Michael. Lena wasn't used to anything other than warm blood running down her throat. What a thing to be used to, she thought before turning her attention to Ren once again. Since Ren didn't seem to pay any attention to the look on her face as he poured the blood into a glass, she figured she'd voice her disgust.

"I'm not drinking that, Ren."

"Michael isn't here. Probably because we told them you would be with me. You need to feed, Yalena."

"Couldn't you just feed me?"

"Are you going to make this difficult?"

"I like the flavor of your blood." She couldn't help but think that was a horrible thing to like.

"What happens when we don't have feeders, and you have to drink from the reserve."

"You can drink twice as much of it, and I will feed on you."

"Just take a drop. It happens to be from the personal stash. Besides, it takes my body a while to process the blood."

"Come join me in the tub. I feed, you feed."

Ren closed his eyes and shook his head. "Fine, just this once." He undressed, and Lena enjoyed watching his naturally muscular form emerging from his tailored clothes. He finished pouring the blood into a glass and then got into the tub and sat behind her. Their initial contact made her shiver. If the water weren't hot, Lena would be cold sitting in front of him.

"You're still mostly feeding on the reserve, aren't you."

"Guilty. I still miss the savoriness of my wife." As he finished, he kissed her neck. "If you have a bit of the blood in the glass, I will let you feed from me. Just know we're not making it a habit."

"Fine, I'll take a sip." Of course, it was cold. This blood was kept in a large refrigerator. He was right, though; it wasn't bad, just a bit thicker than warm blood. "I don't like it. It's too cold."

"You'll acclimate." She got on her knees and turned to face Ren. Lena looked into his eyes and kissed his lips slowly. Being that close to him was arousing. She so wanted to make love to him right now. As the sexual energy built up inside her, Lena leaned in and bit into his neck. The blood gushed into her mouth and down her throat. It was chilled and sweet. Ren held her as close as he could while she fed. When he began to rub her back, Lena knew he was ready for her to stop, even though she didn't want to. She pulled away and sat on his legs. Lena looked up at him as she licked her lips. Ren just sat back and sipped from his glass. His neck was still dripping blood as the wound began to close. Lena leaned forward and licked his neck, and he laughed out loud.

"Like it that much, do you?"

"Hmm. I love the taste of your blood as much as you love mine. I am going to need something to eat when we get out of the tub. Any chance of getting some Indian food?"

"Too spicy."

"Babe, I am craving some naan, jasmine rice, and something spicy."

"No," Ren replied firmly. "How about Italian or Afghani food?"

"Afghani. Make sure you order some okras for me, please."

"No doubt. Patrick.."

"I heard. I'm on it. Think you'll be able to handle both ladies?"

"I got it."

They got out of the tub, and Ren helped her dry off, and he creamed her body for her. Lena loved his touch, gentle even though he was capable of such violent force. Lena was enjoying the attention from him. It was nice he cared enough to do it. However, she was a little disheartened when he left her to finish some work in his office. Granted, Lena wanted to spend time with her sister, but Ren and Lena had spent less time together, and Lena craved his attention. He kissed her and told her that he would be in the office.

She huffed, watching him coyly as he walked away. Oh, well, Lena thought as she walked toward Yazmine, tugging her sister from the couch and dragging her to her favorite room. Lena was tired of sitting in bed all the time and figured a change of scenery would be a good idea. So they sat on the futon and grabbed the matching fuzzy pink pillow. She and Yazmine watched some of their favorite shows from when they were growing up.

"Let's watch Remington Steele."

"Only if you view tonight's episode of my favorite show."

"You still watch that? Absolutely not."

"Fine, the medical show."

"Is it on tonight?"

"You're killing me, Lena."

"Okay, fine." They sat and ate the food Patrick had brought them; they talked about the guy Yazmine had seen for over a year.

Lena was a little upset that Yazmine knew more about vampires and their families than she did. Yazmine told Lena that mom always thought Ren would come for her, so she was prepared. Lena guessed her mom didn't believe Ren would choose her, especially since he didn't come until Yalena's sixteenth birthday. Well, Lena had no idea what was running through her mom's mind. Even after he came for her, her mom said nothing of vampires. She just knew that she hadn't conceived that this part of the world existed until several months ago.

Even after talking about her boyfriend, Lena didn't remember hearing his name. She found that a little odd for her sister. Usually, Yazzi shared stories with Lena that everyone would want private. Lena was happy for her sister, but something kept bugging her. She said he was a bit possessive, but he had never hurt her. It was beautiful that he cared, but something kept gnawing at Lena about the guy. Lena couldn't figure out what was bothering her.She said they had been dating for almost a year, but they still lived in separate apartments. She said they saw each other several times a week. Finally, she let it slip that he was also a vampire. They shared that they both have allowed their vampire mates to feed upon them.

They had been sitting and talking for hours. Lena thought that it was enchanting to spend time with her sister. She was starting to get hungry again, and Lena wondered if Michael had made it back to the penthouse.

"Yazzie, help me up." So she did, and Lena walked back to the master bedroom and laid down.

"Do you mind if I call him?"

"Call who? What's his name, Yazmine?"

"Seth Pierre." Lena tried not to show the shock and repulsion on her face when the name she had been dreading escaped her sister's lips.

"Sure, you can call. Just don't invite him in, please. Ren and Patrick have to okay all visitors to the penthouse, and so far, Ren's partner is the only other vampire allowed here besides Patrick." She had hoped that her last-minute excuse would ward off any apprehension Yazmine had picked up from her.

"I understand," Yazmine replied. Lena thought that they were lucky that he didn't answer the phone. Yazmine left him a message that she was spending a few days with her sister. Lena hoped he wasn't aware of who she was, but she was sure he knew. It would be too easy; otherwise. So, unfortunately, Lena would have to face Seth sooner rather than later. She hoped Ren had been paying enough attention and that he heard what had transpired. And when he came into the bedroom and looked into her eyes, Lena deciphered that he had been listening. Lena wondered how long Seth had been watching their family. She knew that Ren had been waiting for several generations, but how long had Seth been around watching her and her sisters?

"Ren, it's late; has Michael made it anywhere near the penthouse?"

"He should be here soon, Lena. Patrick said he called just a little while ago."

"I hope they don't take too long."

The rest of the evening proved uneventful. Lena spent the evening with her sister but in her room. Michael and Fern finally arrived but were of little help to them. Lena was fuming. They had been gone all day and hadn't eaten enough to support Lena's feeding. She needed to feed, and at this point, Michael barely sustained her growing appetite for blood. His need for food and rest didn't make him a suitable feeder. While Ren had fed today, Lena fed on him as well. Ren needed to feed to circulate warm blood through his body, or Lena would be unable to be close to him. Since he had not been able to feed or be intimate with her, their closeness was essential. Lena didn't like anything between them.

"Fern and Michael, you must remember your job is to be healthy enough for us to feed. You can't run around all day and not eat. That doesn't leave your body with enough nutrients to replenish the blood that we take from you. I have noticed you two are producing less and less blood each day. You are starting to look drawn and sickly. If you don't take care of yourselves, you won't be any use to yourselves or us."

"We're sorry. We were having so much fun we didn't think of food until we headed back to the penthouse."

"You have to think. You must remember that what you feed your body nourishes your blood, and your blood nourishes the children Lena carries. It is of the utmost importance that you take care of yourselves."

She couldn't believe what was going on. Lena understood that this life was new for Michael and Fern. Still, they would have to be more responsible. Lena was beside herself. Her children seemed quite agitated and were stretching and moving around a lot. Lena knew what that meant, they were hungry, and now that would be delayed. Lena had mastered keeping them calm and soothing them. Feeding on a schedule certainly did that. As Lena thought of this, she folded her arms on top of her stomach and pouted.

"Fern, Michael, please eat something. I will need both of you to feed Lena."

"What? Ren that means you won't feed and..." Lena became hysterical, and tears started to stream down her face. It didn't take her long to catch herself and realize that her hormones were raging. Ren came back over to the bed and held her in his arms.

"I'm sure you can stand one night without me at your side." Lena refused to speak but instead shook her head no. She had no desire to sleep without him. They hadn't been living together that long, but the few months of sleeping in his arms were heaven, and Lena didn't want to be without it. As it was now, he sat with a blanket between them, and Lena hated it. She longed to feel his skin against hers again.

"I believe you could, but I'll figure something out this time." When her sister appeared at the bedroom door, both Ren and Lena looked at each other. There was another person in the house that could act as a feeder. Even though that was the first thought in her mind, it wasn't the only thought. Lena wondered who her sister had met within the last week and whether they had any grudge against them. Or if Seth could put something in Yazmine's blood. It had been a bizarre week, and her sister being part of the plot to terminate her was not so far fetched. Lena would hope that it would never come to that, but one never knows these days.

"Yazmine, I wonder if you could do me a favor?"

"Why do I have a feeling that I am going to regret this?"

"I don't think it's that bad," Lena explained to her sister the problem and what it meant to herself and the children. She didn't seem the least bit taken aback, and she agreed to help them. It was remarkable that Lena needed to feed at least four to five times a day, whereas Ren fed only once. The two children in her womb grew rapidly, consuming twice as much blood and food as adults. Lena sat in awe as her sister raved on and on about her boyfriend. Fortunately or unfortunately, Lena didn't have the heart to tell her why he was dating her or that he was trying to kill Lena and eventually kill her. Lena became increasingly worried about Yazmine and she aspired for her to spend more time with Ren and herself.

Things calmed down for a while after that day. Her sister, Yazmine, spent the night with them and then returned to her apartment. Even after spending all that time with her, Lena couldn't tell her who Seth was. Lena wondered how he reacted to her not being home that night, and she hoped he wouldn't hurt her. Lena wouldn't stand for that. Pregnant or not, Lena didn't want anyone to hurt her family.

After the restaurant incident, Lena didn't leave the house, and Ren made most of her meals if not all. He even made sure to make all her favorites. Still, Lena was getting restless. She was tired of being in the house day in and day out. Cabin fever had struck, and

Lena wasn't sure she could stand it anymore. She wanted to get out of the penthouse. Not even her family visits helped after a couple of weeks. Lena woke up the next day, determined to go out.

"Ren."

"Good morning, my love. And good morning, children." Every morning since he realized that the children responded to his voice, Ren said, 'good morning' to them. Then he rubbed her huge stomach and kissed her lips.

"Ren, love."

"Don't start, Lena. This is no picnic for either of us."

"Easy for you to say. You can leave the penthouse."

"Lena, it isn't safe for you to leave the penthouse in your condition. I shouldn't have to go through this often. You will deliver it soon."

"Unless it's any day now, it's not soon enough." Lena would have been totally miserable if not for the visits from her mom, Yazmine, and Theo. Even having Ren, there was a comfort except when he denied her what she wanted.

The feeders were no fun and provided no companionship. After Lena fed, they returned to their room or left for their morning jog. Lena got the impression that they wished they hadn't committed to so many years. Lena was unsure what they expected, but based on their behavior, she was sure they weren't getting it. Lena thought they were supposed to be companions for them. That didn't happen.

"Now, you know that there is no way to tell when it is time. It should be soon. I may have to go in and drag them out if they grow any bigger. You are drinking enough blood for three full-grown vampires."

"At least it has decreased a little. The babies do allow me to eat something."

"Are you ready for our walk?"

"Sure, just help me get up and change my clothes." Every morning before Ren made his check-in at the club and the restaurant, they walked around the inside of the building to make sure Lena was getting enough exercise. Without her morning walks, Lena spent most of the day in bed. The weight of the twins was becoming more and more unbearable. So each week, it was getting significantly more difficult to walk. Lena had now been showing for almost three months. Ren was pretty sure Lena would give birth to them quite soon.

Ren helped Lena up, but she was unable to move much further. Lena whimpered as a stream of blood began to run down her leg. Lena looked at Ren, surprised, and he seemed to be also. Lena heard Ren say soon, but she didn't think it would be any minute.

"Today it is," he stated. The fact that he was surprised bothered Lena just a little. He sat her back down on the bed and gently propped her up on a few pillows.

"Don't I have to squat or push?"

"No, I just need to give them a way out. Between your vaginal muscles and the children's strength, it won't be necessary." He was gentle as he sat on the bed and parted her legs. Lena relaxed as his hands slowly massaged her legs. Then he ripped her panties, and Lena felt his fingers enter her, and he began to search her womb. "Lena, I know you're in pain and uncomfortable, but I need you to be motionless. I need to cut the sac so they can come out." Then a sharp pain made her cry out. "I'm sorry, my love. Just continue to hold still."

Ren moved to sit behind her, which was a slight distraction. "Shouldn't we call my mom," Lena asked as she panted. She didn't know what would happen, and she was afraid of what was happening. He held her in his arms, and Lena could feel the blood rushing from her body. The pain of childbirth is only half of a description of the pain that emanated from between her legs. Excruciating only covers about half of it. Ren held her tight enough to make sure that Lena was still. She was unsure she would have been immobile otherwise, and motion worsened the feeling.

"No time. Once you're settled with the children I will call."

Lena felt a little hand grab her leg as if bracing itself. "What just grabbed my leg?"

Ren lifted her nightdress a little higher so that they could watch what was happening. "Remember dhampirs are more advanced than human babies," Ren replied. One baby seemed to crawl out of her. The baby turned around and sat down right between her legs. Then held on to her leg and reached as if to help its sibling. Lena was amazed as they both sat and regarded her. Lena wanted to extend her hand to them, but she was still in intense pain. Her birthing them was like her vagina being ripped open.

Once the second child was sitting in front of them, Ren put his wrist to her mouth. "You must feed to heal, my love," Ren whispered to her and Lena fed greedily. This time he didn't stop her. As Lena fed, she felt her body contract to squeeze the excess blood and the placenta out of her. Then her muscles tightened as if pulling at her to seal the wound or tear.

Lena wondered why Ren had been feeding from Fern twice as much and using the reserve over the last week. It would appear that he was preparing to feed her after his children's birth. Lena fed until the hunger subsided. Then Lena looked at them. They had been watching her the entire time. Lena opened her arms, and they came to her and nestled in her bosom. One was a girl. She wasn't sure what color their hair was with all the blood plastering it to the children's heads. Both of their eyes were a deep blue, and they had a kind of caramel mocha skin color. Their eyes were like looking into the ocean. They were both gorgeous.

Ren began to press gently at the top of her stomach and then push. "Ren, what about the placenta? We're not cutting the umbilical cord, right? Will it take long for them to absorb the nutrients?"

"No, we just have to wait. It should fall off soon. It doesn't take days unless cut like human counterparts. Just relax. I am going to run a warm bath. While you bathe Lena, I will clean up the twins."

"Okay. I wish more women knew not to cut the umbilical cord. After it dried out my grandmother's was buried by a tree on the property. She used to say that it gave a bountiful harvest of mangoes for years after." Lena was quiet for a time, watching her children and they watched her. She wondered what was going through their little minds. She could only think how precious they were. "What shall we call our children?"

"That's up to you. You endured the pain to bring them into this world."

"Really?" Lena asked rhetorically. "How about Kissa Amenet for our beautiful girl and Kamau Her Wer for our handsome boy?"

"What does Amenet, Kamau, and Her Wer mean?"

"Amenet is Khemetic for the hidden female. Kamau is African; possibly from Kenya means 'quiet warrior.' And Her Wer is

Khemetic for Great Heru or Heru, the elder. He is, after all, our eldest boy."

"You've been studying. I see there is a Khemetic theme here. And are all of our children going to have names that start with 'K?"

"It's possible." Lena looked at her beautiful children, who were still quite bloody. They were gorgeous. Ren took Kamau from her and helped her up from the bed with his other hand. He guided her slowly to the bathtub. Even though her body had healed because of Ren's blood, there was still an echo of pain and fatigue. They sat the children on the bathroom rug. Then Ren helped her remove the bloody nightshirt and helped her get into the tub. Lena reached for Kissa, but Ren had taken both of them.

"Ren, give me my children."

"Soon, Yalena. Wash up; they will need to feed soon. Right now, the water is too hot." It's so strange, Lena thought as she looked longingly at her two while Ren washed them off in the sink, and they were watching her. This was the first time they had been without her womb's embrace. Lena submerged herself in the water and held her breath for a while. Tranquility washed over her as she submerged, and the hot water embraced her. Lena wouldn't have come up soon, but she began to hear muffled sounds through the water. The babies started to cry, and Lena could make out Ren trying to calm them.

"Lena, come up. You've scared them." Lena immediately sat up, wiping water from her face and pushing back her thick curls as she looked at them. Ren wrapped them both in towels and brought them over to the bathtub to see that Lena was well.

"I am fine, my little ones. Your mom likes to be under the water." They seem to calm down after seeing nothing wrong with their mother and hearing her voice. Kissa reached for her, and Lena did the same, but Ren got up and took them with him.

"Ren!"

"Hurry and wash up. I will dress them." Oh yeah, Lena muttered. She had almost forgotten that she was in labor with two dhampirs just an hour ago. They didn't look like newborns. They were about the size of a three month old baby. No wonder her stomach was so engorged. Ren called her name again, and she came out of the daydream and washed off. Lena got dressed in the fresh clothes Ren had left in the bathroom for her. As Lena walked out of the bathroom, she looked up, and their bright smiles greeted her from the sofa. All three of them. In just five months, Lena had become a mom. Crazy, isn't it? She thought to herself. Still, Lena couldn't help but smile back.

"I'd like to go into my room. After all, you'll need to clean this up." Ren changed his shirt and then scooped both babies up. He followed Lena to her room. Lena sat on the futon propped up by a few pillows, and he put one on each leg. "Will we need a wet nurse?"

"That depends on them." Lena took out both of her breasts, and Ren punctured a small hole slightly above each of her nipples. They both suckled, one on each breast. Lena wondered how much food she would have to consume to feed her babies and Ren. She also asked whether she would still crave blood. Ren now sat at her feet, watching them. It must have been a sight to see. He smiled at her and gently passed his hand over each child.

"Now, it would be okay for you to go out."

"And who would watch the children?"

"I don't think they will want to leave your side for a while."

"I don't want them to. Our children are beautiful." They sat for a while, just enjoying the moment. Words scarcely expressed how Lena felt. They were healthy, with all the right appendages in the right place. Life had taught her to enjoy each moment because one might not always have them. Lena gazed at each child as they suckled at her breast, and each child looked up at her. Lena couldn't help but be grateful for this blessing. "Ren, when did you get clothes for them?"

"I have been ordering baby items for over a month. The nursery is next to ours. I believe we are outgrowing our penthouse. As it is, the feeders will be on this side of the house." Lena smiled.

She was happy, and it was a beautiful moment. Lena was in love with her life and didn't want the moment to end.

It was quiet and just a regular day after that. Ren fixed her an appetizing lunch, and they just sat on the futon wrapped in each other. The only other thing besides the children's birth was the reaction of Fern and Michael. They came in late that afternoon. For the first time in a long time, they came looking for Ren and Lena. The look on their faces when they saw Lena's children was a mix of fascination and horror.

"We didn't see you on the way to our room. And our room now has cribs in it." Michael's eyes grew wide when he saw the children. "Wow, they are born already."

"Yeah, Wow. You were barely showing when we came here, and now boom, babies. They're not the size of most newborns."

"Nor do they act like newborns. They seem old. The way they look at you like they are sizing you up."

"Lena just wanted a change of scenery, so we came in here," replied Ren. " I have moved your things to the room next to this one. Sorry for the inconvenience. And yes, the babies are sizing you up. They have never seen you, only heard your voices and tasted your blood."

"Yes, Ren, that is true. I guess you'll need us more than ever now. We understand about the room change."

"Well, I will need you, not Lena. And of course, if the children decide to feed. Please relax, get something to eat. I will need both of you sooner than later. Lena was quite greedy today." Lena bashfully grinned at his statement. Lena was so hungry. After all of the blood that flowed out of her body today, it's miraculous that she was still alive.

The rest of the day was pretty serene. Ren and Lena spent time with Kissa and Kamau. They were playful and sweet. Both of them nestled in her neck when they were tired. As soon as they fell asleep, Ren demanded that Lena take a nap. Lena rested the children on the futon and surrounded it with pillows before lying next to Ren on the carpet. The fluffy, soft carpet tickled her skin when she moved to draw closer to Ren. He was right; she needed to sleep; she was exhausted.

After a couple of days, her family came to see her. Lena guessed Ren had called them and told them that she had given birth. Lena was happy to see them, but her children hid from them. Lena thought that it was pretty funny. She was sitting in her favorite room, where she seemed to spend a lot of time since the children were born when her parents and sister came to visit. As soon as they heard their voices, Kissa and Kamau hid behind their mother. When Lena tried to get up to hug her mom and dad, the children held on for dear life. So Lena remained seated.

"Hi, mom and dad, Yazmine."

"How's my baby girl?"

"Fine, daddy."

"You know you don't look like you just gave birth a few days ago."

"That's mainly thanks to Ren, Yazzi."

"I see little hands, but where are my grandchildren?" Her mom chided as she walked toward Lena. "Are you hiding from grandma"? As her mom got closer and closer to them, the children's grip got tighter as they peeked out from behind Lena. It always amazed her what a grip most babies had; now multiply that by two, and that was how tight they held her.

"Kissa, Kamau, it's okay. It's my mom, my dad, and my older sister." They didn't let go but inched around, sat next to Lena, and each child rested a head on each arm.

"Wow, they don't look like newborns."

"And their eyes are so intense."

"Yes," Lena agreed. "Their eyes are very intense." Lena had noticed that the first time she watched them as they nursed. It felt like they were hypnotizing you in the deep pools of blue. Everyone sat in silence for a few minutes. It appeared that the children were watching their family, and their family was watching them. And in those few minutes, Kamau and Kissa relaxed their hold on Lena, but they didn't move.

"They just have to get used to you. The children are very attached to their mother, as it should be. They only seem to tolerate me because of Lena's fondness and love for me."

"Nonsense Ren. You're their father. They have heard your voice since conception."

"Humph, Kissa, and Kamau, let's go. I have food for you in the kitchen."

"They're eating food already."

"Not sure; we're testing. Both of the twins took a nibble of Lena's food yesterday."

Kissa smiled up at Ren. She let go of her mother and crawled towards her dad, but Kamau wasn't the least interested. Ren had to call him again, and even then, Kamau hesitated before moving. Finally, Ren picked them up and left the room, heading for the kitchen.

"Lena, how are you, really?"

"I'm fine, mom, excellent."

"How do you feed them?"

"I nurse them as you would any other child. The only difference is they feed as they nurse."

"You mean they drink your blood with your milk?"

"Yes, dad. They are vampires, after all, or part. Ren finds them quite interesting. They were not at all what he was expecting. That probably has something to do with our lineage."

"I never really bought those stories your grandmother used to tell you all. I guess I should have paid more attention." Lena smiled at her dad. She could see he was having a hard time with all of this. She remembered him telling her grandmother to stop filling their heads with such nonsense.

"Was their birth painful?"

"That is an understatement. It was more than excruciating Yazzi. But thanks to Ren, I am well. It didn't last long at all. They seemed eager to leave the womb." They spent a while talking about her experience. Lena tried not to give too many gory details. She was trying to convince her dad that all was well.

Then Ren came back into the room with the children. It appeared that he was wearing lunch instead of the children eating it, his shirt covered in splashes of food. Lena couldn't help but laugh, and his stern stare turned into a smile when he saw her face. "It would appear that Kamau isn't ready to eat food or doesn't want to. Kissa, on the other hand, ate more than she spat out."

"They spat out the food," Lena asked, pretending she was surprised.

"Yes. At first, Kissa and Kamau didn't seem to know what to make of it until I showed them me eating. You should have seen the look on their faces. It was as if they comprehended that I don't eat."

"You should have let me feed them. The children have seen me eat; all they've seen you do is feed."

"You feed in front of the children?"

"Yes, Carol. In fact, at night, we all feed on mother." Lena could tell by the look on her face that her mom was horrified and quite surprised. Lena wished he wouldn't taunt her like that.

"Are you trying to kill her?"

"Mom, I'm fine. Ren doesn't drink a lot from me. He has a feeder. It's just that he likes the taste of my bl...." Her words trailed off at the end. Lena realized that she had probably said too much at that point. She didn't think her dad thought about the relationship that she had with Ren. He choked and began coughing. Lena wasn't sure how much her dad knew about their family history and kindred to vampires. This was something he was going to have to get used to. She never thought that she would be having this conversation with her family. Her dad didn't say much, he just watched everything. They didn't stay long but vowed to visit soon. Lena made sure to ask her dad to come over more often and told him that she missed him. He nodded and gave her a polite smile. She was aware that her father disagreed with the life she had chosen, but Lena contemplated whether having grandchildren would change his mind.

Another month passed before Lena even left the house. When the weather was beautiful, she would stand on the balcony with one of the twins in her arms and one strapped to her back, just enjoying the view and getting some air and sun. Now assured of Lena's safety, Ren would leave the house for more extended periods. Still, he would check in during the day.

Chapter 14

By the time Ren let Lena go back to the club with the children, they were about six months old. They were walking by then and had mastered speaking but chose to say as little as possible. Lena had been working with them on the alphabet and numbers. She wanted their minds to be as advanced, if not more than they appeared. They also spent at least two hours a day in the dojo. Lena would set down a comforter to sit on and spread out their toys. Of course, Kamau and Kissa spent most of the time watching her workout and practicing her form. Once they started walking, Lena decided to show them the first form she'd learned. Lena wanted to make sure her children were prepared for the life they led, even if she hadn't been.

Lena finally did go to the club. It was a Friday, and there was a council meeting that night. Lena wasn't excited. After all, they had tried to kill her twice so far. She had never imagined they would try to poison a pregnant lady. Lucky for her, Patrick caught the knife the night she was introduced to the clan. Now that they were proving the prophecy by having children, Lena was well aware that she was becoming more of a threat.

They arrived early in the evening. The sun was still bright in the New York sky. Spring had come and gone. The humidity pressed against them. Finally, the leaves rustled and flowers waved in the summer heat. Ren had rented a car to drive them there. As she stood in front of the club, Lena thought about how Cell had not visited them at the penthouse since the children were born. Lena thought it was a little odd, but eventually, she dismissed the thought. Cell was indeed surprised at how they had grown. He said he didn't expect them to be that big. Kissa and Kama were born six months ago but they were almost the size of a three year old. Not to mention they were walking and practicing martial arts with Lena, but he was unaware of that.

Lorenzo and Yalena carried them. Ren introduced them to the guards at the door. The children had seen them at their home before and reached to place their hands in the palm of each to greet them. As they walked through the long hall, the children looked every which way before shaking their heads and pointing.

"It's fine, children," Ren replied. "They are my staff and most are amicable. Kiyoshi and Patrick are also here," The children responded by putting their heads down on their parents' chest.

Once they walked through the glass door at the end of the long hall they were greeted by many of the staff who gathered around to behold them. Lena was flattered at first and then annoyed. Her children were not freaks to be gawked at. Despite the rising agitation, Lena smiled and thanked everyone for their compliments. Lena could tell by the way the children responded that they also didn't appreciate being the center of attention. It took them several visits to become used to her parents and sister. They didn't like the feeders and refused to feed from Michael or Fern. They would eat. Kissa always ate more than Kamau, which meant he nursed and fed more from his mom.

The clan gathering to see them startled the children so much that they dug their tiny nails into their parents. Even though there were only seven or eight people, the children had never encountered them before. It appeared they could detect vampires at an early age. Lena was not prepared for that. She had hoped they would have some time for total innocence.

Lena was tired now more than before, so when they finally got upstairs to Ren's room, both the children and Lena took a nap. Lena was awakened by her husband climbing into the king size bed next to her. Lena stretched as he wrapped his arms around her, and she turned to look into his eyes.

"My love," He said as he gazed into her eyes. Lena kissed his lips in response. Many months had passed since she felt his touch and kissed him longingly. Even though he sampled her blood every night, they did not make love for fear that Lena would end up pregnant too soon after the twins.

"Lena, I don't think I can stay away from you much longer."

"It wasn't my idea. I have missed your touch and our intimacy." As they kissed again, the children stirred, and one hand touched her arm. "Guess it won't happen right now," Lena said with a smile as she sat up and turned to see the children. They were sitting up, their blue eyes on their mom. Lena had grown accustomed to their stare now.

"I had originally come up to ask you if you wanted to eat."

"I am hungry. I'm not sure about Kissa or Kamau." Kissa nodded, and Kamau, as usual, stared at the wall, disinterested. His parents knew that he preferred to feed instead of eat. "I'm sure he will eat some with me." Ren was motionless before the food was brought to the room. It was set on a tray and placed in front of Lena.

"I oversaw all of the cooking while you three were up here." Lena and the children hadn't quite finished eating when someone knocked at the door and then entered.

"Sorry to disturb you, but your sister Yazmine is downstairs."

"Cell, why didn't you bring her upstairs?"

"There's a problem with who her date is."

"What?" Cell didn't reply. "Fine, I'll go down." Lena was hoping that she didn't bring her present boyfriend with her. "Mommy will be right back," she said to the children before looking at Ren. His glance reminded Lena to be cautious. Lena didn't think anything of it as she walked out of the door.

"I'll accompany her, Ren; no need to worry." They took the elevator down to the ground floor and walked the long hall from the back of the club to the front door. The long hall ran the club's length and let out right next to the club entrance. Lena saw her sister through the crowd as she opened the door and ran to hug her.

They started talking about how excited she was to be here and that Lena was thrilled she had come. Lena was so wrapped up in her sister being there that she had not taken the time to observe her environment. Lena had no idea who was standing around her or next to her. She hadn't realized that Cell had not followed her outdoors.

"Lena, I want you to meet someone. This is Seth. Seth, this is my sister Yalena." Lena hadn't moved to shake his hand. "Lena, what's wrong? Remember, I told you about him." Finally, Lena began to take stock of her surroundings. She should have done that when she first came outside. She discerned that lack of vigilance may cost her. Lena looked around. At least the lights made it seem as though the sun never set. Then she became cognizant of Cell's presence or the lack thereof. She was standing encircled by patrons in the middle of the block. The line creeped forward as the crowd snaked forward and back.

"Yazzi, I should have told you that I objected before. I didn't think you would bring him here. You made it sound like he didn't like the place."

"He came here because I told him I wanted you to meet him. But you're being so rude."

Lena rolled her eyes before saying, "Yazzi, Seth isn't allowed at the club."

"Why?"

"Yes, Yalena, tell your sister why I have been banned from the club."

"For disrespecting Ren and threatening him." Her sister appeared so bewildered by all of this new information.

"You forgot for killing you."

"What?" Seth caught Lena off guard. He hadn't made any attempt to kill her. But while she hesitated, he moved stealthily behind her. He was holding a knife to her throat before Lena could unsheathe her blade.

"Too bad Cell didn't come out with you, and you appear to be without a bodyguard." Why hadn't Lena seemed to notice the bodyguard part? Lena had been so sheltered and pampered she neglected to think for herself. She felt she should have paid more attention to the whereabouts of Cell before she came outside the safety of the club. She was trying to calm down, which was difficult for a moment or two. Seth was at her back and she stood with a knife to her throat. He was taller than her, so Lena was on her toes. Any move to escape or to ground herself would lead to him cutting her throat. Lena glared at Yazzi who went still, except for her hands, twisting and turning in front of her. Only seconds had passed.

"Seth, what the hell are you doing," Yazmine asked.

"You know Lena, I found your sister before you bedded that deluded ruler we have in there, but of course, she doesn't have the power you have. At most, she didn't get sick when she fed from me. That was it. Not to mention she's sterile."

Lena didn't reply to his ranting. She couldn't figure out why no one was paying attention to them. She couldn't help but wonder why no one regarded them. Lena was trying to find Cell among the other vampires. She mentally retraced her steps, or so she thought. It was hard to locate him. Eventually, Lena found him talking to Marcia in the back hallway. Lena guessed he had followed her but was detained by Marcia. Surely it was nothing, but Lena would mention this to Ren. He was walking away now. If she could just figure out how to shift out of this position.

Lena decided to go for it. If she got cut, Ren could help her heal. Seth was still rambling on to Yazzi, so she decided to make her move when Cell walked outside. As soon as the door opened and Cell called her name, Seth let up slightly on the knife and turned to look. Lena rammed her blade into his side and cut up. His reflexes made him cut the left side of her throat before he doubled over and flashed himself across the street. As the blood dripped down her neck, she wondered if he was able to flash before. Cell caught her in his arms as she fell, and her sister rushed to her side. Cell picked her up and carried her inside. Marcia was still waiting.

"Cell, what happened?"

"We'll talk later." Lena could swear she saw the left side of Marcia's lips tick up, which quickly changed when Yazzi turned to look at her. Cell gave Yazzi instructions to find them and race upstairs to Ren, who was feeding when they got to the room.

"Cell, what the fuck happened?" Ren immediately let go of Fern, took his beloved Yalena, and laid her on the bed while Cell explained.

"Marcia stopped me on the way out. When I got to her, Seth had Lena by the throat. She stabbed him to get away, and he cut her." Ren gently turned her head to see the wound on her neck.

"Doesn't look deep. Can you talk, my love?"

Lena was in such a daze and didn't understand why. She hadn't lost that much blood. Had she? Lena whispered that she could talk.

But that hadn't changed the look on Ren's face. "Cell, I believe she's been poisoned. I'm going to need the special reserve."

"Ren, I hate cold blood."

"Be quiet," Ren said his voice pushed from between his clenched teeth. "This is a life and death matter, Yalena. Of course, I could wait for it to slowly kill you and let you feed from me so that you turn, or you could drink the reserve and let it fight for you."

Cell hadn't waited to hear her objection. He had gone and returned by the time Ren had lifted her into his arms and dismissed their feeder. He also told Kissa that she couldn't feed from her mom right then. Lena saw her eyes become glassy, and the tears rolled down her cheeks. Her distress disturbed Kamau's sleep, and he sat up. Kissa had never been denied her mother's solace or her blood. Ren tried to tell the children that Lena was hurt and that feeding from her now would kill them. They sat quietly at her side, and Lena's heart sank a little as the tears flowed. They didn't really cry. As she thought about it, her children had been communicating with them for a while, there was no need to cry. Granted they hadn't spoken at first, but they would point and tap to get attention and to let her know what they wanted.

Ren's reserve was cold and made her shiver. Ren covered her with a soft blanket, and they sat in silence, waiting. Lena had finished the entire pouch of blood by the time Yazzi showed up.

"Ren, I am so sorry. I had no idea."

"You mean to tell me Seth was the guy you brought to the club." Yazzi didn't reply. She shook her head as she knelt by her sister.

"Will she be alright?"

"Yes, I have taken care of that. But I'm definitely going to have to turn Lena soon. It is too dangerous for her to be human here. And I can't keep her in the penthouse forever."

Lena wasn't sure how long she had been asleep, but she had been asleep shortly after her sister got to the room. Lena awoke to Kissa's touch. Her beautiful baby girl sat very close to her. Lena looked over to see where Kamau was. His back to them. She hoped he was asleep.

"Mom."

"Yes, Kissa."

"How do you feel?"

"Better love."

"Your cut healed," Kissa whispered, pointing to her mom's throat.

Lena's fingers traced where the wound had been. Indeed it had, although her clothes were still bloody. Lena sat up slowly and surveyed the room. If Ren hadn't brought her here every time, she wouldn't have recognized it was his room. Lena couldn't help but think the room was bare. The only thing that stood out was the carvings on the bed. There were beautiful flowers carved on the headboard.

As she examined the room for the first time, Lena could hear him coming down the hall. He opened the door, and Lena smiled. "I'm so glad you're feeling better."

"Yes, and very hot, actually."

"Just my blood running through your body energizing your cells."

"Your blood? But it came from a pouch." He smiled and sat at the edge of the bed.

"Each of us here has a reserve of our own blood. It's taken once a month after we gorge ourselves with blood. It makes us stronger when we need, or if a loved one or we are hurt. You'll be required to do it soon enough." Lena nodded.

"Where is Yazzi?"

"With Cell. He has taken a fancy to your sister."

"That sounds dangerous. If Marcia finds out. But I thought vampires have only one true mate."

"Marcellus is a sensuous creature. He doesn't do well without a plaything. Marcia has been his for centuries, but they are not mates. And yes, that could be deadly."

"Speaking of Marcia. She stopped Cell from following behind me to talk to him. And I could've sworn she was smiling when he carried me back in. Not a full smile, but all the same."

"How do you know it was she who stopped him?"

"I could see it in my mind."

"Has it ever happened before?"

"No, I just started retracing my steps, and there they were." It was silent for a moment before he responded to her. He smiled.

"What is so amusing?"

"I was wondering when your gifts would begin to manifest themselves and what they were. I am hoping the children will get at least one."

"At least one. How many will I have."

"Let's just see what happens." Their eyes were locked as Lena crawled over to him and kissed his lips. She truly desired her beloved now. Lena wanted to feel their bodies intertwined. She didn't care if she got pregnant again. At least not at that moment. The more children Lena had soon, the quicker Ren could turn her. They were so engrossed in each other that they forgot that the children were next to them. When Lena turned her head as Ren kissed her neck, Kissa smiled as she gazed at her parents.

"Maybe we should take this into the bathroom."

"Sure."

"Did Kissa feed, Ren?"

"No, she didn't want anyone but her mom."

"Did you heat up the bottles?"

"I completely forgot. Glad we made them last night." Ren took a bottle out of the small fridge, ran it under the hot water, and vigorously shook it. Yes, indeed, it was a good idea that Lena had pumped milk while the twins were asleep last night. She wasn't sure why she needed to bring the bottles with her, but in the end, Lena was glad that she had followed her sixth sense.

Kissa hesitated to take the bottle. Once she did, she peered at it in her hand. Lena put it to her lips. Once a few drops flowed into her mouth, she was content. Ren helped her prop Kissa up on a pillow to make sure she was comfortable. Lena watched her child as she continued to drink from the bottle. She seemed content. Ren locked the bedroom door, and they disappeared into the bathroom.

Ren and Lena stood several feet from each other, their gaze locked. Lena wanted to take him in. As she stood facing Ren, and for the first time, she began to see more of what he was. Lena would not delude herself into thinking that she knew all of him. But she learned a lot. He was more than what he appeared to be. On the outside, he was debonaire and handsome. His dark brown hair pulled back from his face. Allowing one to see his chiseled tan features. His lips were full, and his eyes large almonds. Lena now discerned an air about him to be power. He wore it like a cape that shrouded him. His muscles rippled through his silk shirt that was opened to the middle of his chest, giving her a glimpse of his muscular golden mocha chest. She never really paid much attention to people's color, but she found that she considered it now. Maybe because she and Ren were different. Lena was black or African Caribbean American, and Ren was Spaniard and Moor. Lena had never put much stock in the color lines. She dated whom she chose, but now Lena took note of the difference as she stared into the mirror behind Ren. She surveyed the contrast between them. Beautiful as it was. They are brilliant together--their differences combined to create their gorgeous children with their distinctions.

Lena smiled at him now and wondered what had crossed his mind while they stood there. Tension was building between them. They had not been intimate for six months for fear that Lena would bear children before it was healthy for her to do so. Although, with any pregnancy, each child's birth can be overshadowed by her death. In this case, her transformation.

Ren began to unbutton his shirt and moved closer to her. Lena copied him, removing her silk knit sweater and stretching before undoing her bra. Her breasts, sprung free from their bondage, now plump with milk, and her nipples erect. Lena removed her skirt and panties as he watched her. His trousers were unbuttoned and unzipped but sat on his hips. They seemed tight now, stretched by his excitement. Seeing that aroused her, Lena felt the blood rushing between her thighs.

Ren smiled as he reached for her. He took her face gently in his hands and lightly brushed his lips over hers. Lena began to slip down his pants and boxers to allow him room to be fully aroused. His kisses lit a trail of fire down her body as he lowered himself to his knees. He kissed her thigh as he gently parted her legs. Lena could feel his fingers pet between her lips, pressing more firmly each time. She began to moan, and he smiled at her. His smile said everything just as his deliberate actions spoke to her. Lena knew he would torment her now, not allowing her to be filled by him until she could no longer stand.

His fingers opened her lips, and his tongue tasted her. Blood hastened through her flesh. Having his blood coursing through her body seemed to intensify all of her senses. He continued to gently stroke her, every once in a while plunging his tongue into her depths. Lena drew air between her clenched teeth and parted lips. Ren looked up and smiled at her as his fingers teased her. He plunged his fingers into her, and his tongue began to stroke. Moans escaped her lips. She was sensitive to his every touch, kiss, and caress. As his strokes became more and more furious. Her body revealed her pleasure as her wetness dripped down her legs. Her body trembled slightly.

Ren stopped and stood in front of her. His hands grabbed her full breasts, his thumbs brushing lightly over her already sensitive and erect nipples. Her milk streamed from them. Ren squeezed one nipple as he put the other in his mouth. He suckled at each breast, alleviating the pain of their fullness. Piercing them to feed as he drained their milk. Her body shook at his touch, and his length pressed against her. Finally, he filled her, and Lena gasped at his intrusion into her body. Her eyes locked with his, and he smiled. Her body had betrayed her and reacted to each touch. He filled her, and Lena didn't think she could take any more. Yet, he pushed and pounded into her. Lena sucked in the air and moaned for him. So hot and aroused, her body shuddered with each movement. She could not control herself. Yet, he was focused and showed no sign of pleasure or displeasure. Lena heard no sounds from him.

When she couldn't take any more, she began to whimper and call his name. Lena looked at his face, and he gave a slight smile. From his throat came a sound that had not been audible before. It sounded as if it came deep from within him. It radiated through her, and Lena could no longer control her body. Her climax sent waves through her body that seemed to go through Ren. They rested against the shower glass, and Lena unwrapped her legs.

"Have I satisfied you, my love?" Lena couldn't answer him, she peeked up at him through her lashes, and a smile lit up her face. He lifted her chin and kissed her lips. If it hadn't been for the fact that they had a council meeting soon and an awake child in the other room, Ren and Lena would have probably made love all night long.

"Well, now was time to dress and put on a show for the others."

"Are you alright, my love?"

"Yeah, just need a minute to gather myself. My senses seem so intense right now."

"Those are some of the side effects of the extra blood coursing through your body. My blood. Part of the reason we do it. This reserve blood makes us faster and more attuned."

"Is that what makes you able to flash?"

"Yes, well, it makes us faster and stronger, so the movement looks like a flash."

"Well, Seth can do it now."

"When did you see this?"

"After I cut him. He flashed across the street."

"That would explain how he was able to get behind you. We'll talk at home. And I believe in a couple of weeks we'll be able to hear the sound of three hearts beating."

"No way. That is totally unexpected. You said twins and then one child." He simply smiled at her, kissed her cheek, and walked out of the bathroom to check on the twins. She guessed that was why he had been avoiding her. No doubt, his blood helped. That also meant that he'd turn her within the next year, or they'd have too many kids to feed. There was no way their feeders would be able to supply all four of them. Now they're adding three more to the mix. They're going to have to extend their feeding time as it is.

When Ren called for her, Lena looked at herself in the bathroom mirror. She was flawless for a woman having had twins six months ago; still, she was starting to look tired. She loses too much blood daily now. Lena was going to have to help that along. Now three more. Lena finished dressing and came out of the bathroom to find Ren carrying Kamau and Kissa. A slightly strange sight for her. Odd, Lena thought. But it was nothing new. Still, she hadn't noticed how much darker her children were compared to their father.

Lena smiled at them before reaching to take Kamau, who stretched for her. They walked to the elevator and took it to the first floor. Lena could hear the music boom in the club and remembered hearing it before her first council meeting. She had missed one conference because of her pregnancy. Ren said they all thought he was up to something. They didn't believe she had just delivered the twins. Ren wanted to make sure that Lena made this one.

"Mom, vampire like dad all around us."

"Yes Kamau, this is your dad's club. Is that why you two were scared when we first got here?"

"Yes, Kissa and I didn't know what to make of them. We only know dad and Patrick."

"But, he stands outside of our home." Ren stopped in his tracks and spoke to Kissa.

"Kissa, you and Kamau have sensed Patrick? Your mom didn't."

"Mom would not, dad."

"Of course, Kissa." Wow, Lena thought. Only out of her womb, six months, and already so attuned to things. They were gifted children. They continued toward the door. "Kissa, Kamau, what do you sense beyond that door?"

"More like Patrick and Dad. Well, not quite but vampires."

"Dad, why are we going in there?"

"Well, Kamau, your mother and I are the rulers of this city. Beyond that door is our council. You must meet with them." Ren turned the knob, and heads turned to see who was entering. The room stayed silent. "Goodnight, everyone. Glad we're all here."

All council members nodded their heads as Ren and Lena seated themselves at the head of the table. After they were seated, Ren introduced the twins to the council. While they clung to their parents, they regarded each face as Ren called out the council members' names. It was as if they were making a mental note of who each member was

"Your children have such striking eyes, Yalena."

"Thank you, Madeline."

"Yes, they are beautiful and strong. Quite unusual for dhampirs."

"We see you are hell-bent on proving that she is the legitimate line to Sekhmet. Will you take her to find and meet the first line?"

"We are still searching for her, Lockington." That certainly brought everyone to focus on Lena. She and Ren had not discussed a trip to Africa. She was as shocked as they were, but Lena held her composure. She smiled, but unfortunately, her human heart was a telltale sign when it changed its rhythm for a fraction of a second. But no one let on. Lena wondered why Lockington would bring that up. She thought he was supposed to be on their side.

"Madeline, we are getting complaints from other vampires besides Ren. They are complaining of Seth's behavior."

"Mohammed, what drivel are you talking?"

"Yes, Madeline, I too am getting complaints about your son," replied Lockington. "Missing persons and the dead body count is increasing. It isn't just the mayor who is complaining."

"I must admit I have heard, but surely it isn't that bad."

"If Ren isn't the only one addressing the situation, surely it is that bad," said Jon. "Ren usually hears before it gets to be serious. Now it is. So what are you going to do about it?"

"Oh, now I'm the problem. Certainly you need to protect your territories better." Ren and Lena stared as the council seemed to turn on each other. Lena wondered if this was real or performance for their benefit.

"Enough! Madeline, you need to control your son and whatever he is getting into. It is starting to affect too many territories. And tonight, he had the nerve to attack my Queen."

"We heard about it, but we weren't sure," Jon murmured.

"She looks fine, must not have been that bad."

"Nothing I couldn't handle, Madeline. If I catch him, I assure you it will be his last day."

"Well," Madeline huffed. "It seems like gang up on Madeline day." There was silence in the room as everyone waited for her to respond. "I will deal with Seth," she replied grudgingly.

The meeting continued for at least another hour. Lena was surprised that the children didn't fuss. Each sat with a parent and either sat straight and looked at the people speaking or took a nap. Lena was shocked. She never saw any child behave in such a manner.

During that meeting, the council talked about the visiting vampires and their reaction to the rules here in New York. And how another ruling family from a southern state enjoyed the way they lived. The council wanted to expand its territories outside of the Tri-State area. Which was the goal, but there would be some challenges to that. Many of the places they wanted to take over were already ruled. Some rulers would cooperate with them, but the merciless ones would be a problem. Ren tried to persuade them to wait before beginning to expand. They seemed suspicious, but all agreed. Before the end of the meeting, they decided that every council member had to develop a plan over the next three months, which they would discuss at the next meeting.

Lena didn't grasp why they would have to leave the club for the airport after Ren spoke with Cell. Fern and Michael were already in the limo with Patrick parked outside the club. When Lena got into the car, their presence threw her off. Lena expected to see Patrick after being sent on some errand instead of watching her that night. She had not expected to see the feeders.

Chapter 15

"Patrick, did you bring what we needed?"

"Everything, sir." Patrick handed Ren a briefcase. "I've been told that we found what we were looking for."

"So we're off. Just relax, my love. I will explain soon enough."

Lena was unsure of what was going on. It was a big secret, and apparently, Ren didn't want anyone to know. This life had many unexpected events. She had no idea what to expect from this life. Her son touched her fangs and pointed to the driver. Lena understood that the driver was a vampire but wasn't that expected? Well, she did, but the little ones wouldn't. They had no idea what to make of their world. Lena had surrounded them with the closest family and little of Ren's actual world. She figured they would be part of it soon enough; no need to immediately push them into it.

The driver dropped them off at JFK and asked when to return to get them. He was told they would take a cab, and then he was paid. Lena understood why. There was no need to alert anyone as to the length of their trip. Lena was sure that the council would be alerted to their absence. Ren ushered them to the counter, and from the leather case came all of their passports, documents, and tickets. They had at least two hours before the flight left for Britain.

"Ren."

"I will explain it soon." Patrick left them at the gate. Ren instructed him to take a taxi back to the penthouse and keep an eye on things.

Patrick needed to remain hidden. No one should be aware of his presence unless necessary. Except for his mate, of course. That's when it dawned on her that Patrick wasn't just her bodyguard. He was also Ren's eyes and ears because of his gift. If everyone thought he had gone with Ren and his family, they would be more relaxed. When the cats are away and all. Lena now had genuine admiration for Ren. Her husband and ruler of their clan. He was carrying quite a burden on his shoulders, and Lena wondered how she could ease that. She would have a part to play, but she wasn't sure what it was. She did figure her full role wouldn't be revealed until she transformed. Lena wasn't sure how she felt about that. He only told her what she needed to know and no more. If it wasn't that she had the children to take care of, she would be more upset.

They walked a short way to one of the private lounges in the airport. Ren unlocked one. Lena was unaware that he flew enough to be a member of one. She had indeed married a puissant man. She smiled. Up until now, Lena only had glimpses of Ren.

Ren checked them in at the desk, and then they walked to the farthest corner to sit in the lounge chairs. Other than the young lady at the desk, it was empty.

"Sorry to be so mysterious about the whole thing." Ren began after they settled and got comfortable in the room."

"Ren, love, what is going on?"

"We are going to meet the daughter of Sekhmet."

"You've found Sekhmet?"

"Yes. I was told that she has been awaiting our arrival for some time. I didn't want anyone to know we were going or when we were going. Patrick will send word if there is any problem."

"I need to make a phone call," stated Fern a little anxiously.

"I'm afraid that isn't going to happen right now, Fern. I have made the necessary arrangements. No one must perceive where we are or that we have gone. Just relax."

"Ren, we have no clothes or toiletries."

"We will purchase what is necessary when we get to London. Others will be provided when we arrive in Cairo. We'll be fine."

Lena used the baby bag's blankets to make a place for the children to lie down on the couch before she went to curl up with Ren. Lena put her legs over his and rested her head against his arm. "You're going to change me soon, aren't you?"

"Thinking about one more pregnancy."

"Really! How will we feed our brood."

"Cell has been working on replacing Fern and Michael. They don't seem to be happy with us. There is no bond between them and us as it should be."

"Maybe because we don't make love to them?"

"No, the relationship Theo has with Cell and Marcia is rare. I have heard of a few like theirs. I wish our feeders to be just that, feeders. Of course, a lifelong friendship is usually built within it. You come to count on each other. As our children get older and grow, they will find their own feeders."

"Of course." Lena reached up to kiss his lips, and he took her face in his hands.

"I love you, Yalena."

"I love you, Lorenzo." Even though Ren's life was dangerous, Lena knew he'd do everything to keep her safe. Lena was unaware of how the children would fit in. But she had a feeling they would be the ones who kept peace in their kingdom one day.

Lena fell asleep in Ren's arms. Later, he gently woke her up, telling her it was time to go. Ren then woke Fern and Michael before picking up both children as Lena got their things. Then, they were off on a new adventure. Lena had never been on the Concord before; she was excited. Lena was glad it wasn't a long flight. Nothing beats cutting the time in half. When they got off the plane, they were greeted by a chauffeur from the hotel.

"Mr. Arias, it has been years."

"Yes, it has. This is my wife, Yalena, and our two children, Kissa and Kamau."

"What a beautiful family. And you have friends also." Ren smiled and introduced Fern and Michael before the van pulled off.

The hotel was beautiful, old but beautiful. The artwork was exquisite. Lena had never been out of the United States before, and now she wondered how much travel this life would afford her. The room was a two-bedroom suite with the bedrooms on either side of the living room. It must have been remodeled in recent years.Lena sat down on the sofa with a child on each side. They had slept for quite some time, and we're now very much awake and curious. After all, their surroundings were entirely unfamiliar, but they didn't wander far from their mother. The suite was comfortably furnished with Victorian style furniture. Beautiful balloon back chairs sat opposite each other on either side of the sofa.

Lena made herself comfortable and prepared to nurse them. Upon seeing her undoing the top buttons of her shirt, the two were at her side. While they fed, Ren was silent. He sat next to her, staring into space, one arm around her shoulder, the other on her leg. It was evident that Ren was making decisions as they progressed.

They ate dinner in the suite and rested before shopping in London the next day. They needed clothes for themselves and the children. The stay was short, only a few days--just enough time to get what they needed for their trip to Egypt. Lena was nervous, of course. She wasn't sure what to expect. After checking out the London sights, she put the children on the couch for a nap. Ren had spent a few decades in London during the nineteenth century. He had given them a personal tour. One can easily forget how old he was by his looks, but the stories he told them gave details no one could have known unless they had been there.

Lena was lying on the bed just relaxing, reading the latest book from her favorite author when Ren came and lay next to her. He wrapped his arms around her and kissed her neck.

"So, have you been enjoying yourself?"

"Absolutely," Lena replied. "How can I not. You told such juicy stories on our tour. And of course, I love to shop." Lena turned towards him and stared into his dark eyes. He unbuttoned her blouse and raised her breast from her bra. Ren began to feed and nurse.

"I see you have found another way to feed."

"I understand why our children love it. Between your blood and your milk, how could they want anything else."

"I suppose. It's a good thing you know how to take great care of me. Plus, I take my vitamins and eat well enough to feed a horse." He kissed her lips lightly. Running his tongue over her lower lip. "Didn't you feed, Ren?"

"Only partially." He put a finger to her lips and his lips to her ear. "Their blood doesn't appeal to me anymore. It's not as enticing."

"Really? Are we feeding them well enough?"

"I feed them what I feed you. Or what they choose."

"Could it be because they don't want to be with us anymore?"

"Wouldn't alter it that much." He motioned for her to be quiet and walked to the door of the room. Lena wasn't sure what was happening, but she followed behind him. "What exactly do you two think you're doing," Ren asked. When Lena looked around her husband, she could see Fern and Michael heading to the door with her sleeping children in their arms.

"We thought we would take the children for a walk."

"We just came in," Lena replied sternly. Everyone stood for moments in silence, watching each other. Fern and Michael stared coldly at them. Lena thought of how Fern and Michael had become indifferent. They had seemed so sweet and friendly for the first couple of months. Now, they seemed so distant, especially since the children were born. Not that they ever were close to them. Lena was unsure what they were expecting from life with them, but they were not happy.

"Fern and Michael, please; please put my children down," Lena pleaded with them. She wasn't sure they knew it, but Ren could end their lives without even waking or harming the children.

"I don't think so. You won't let us leave here without the children."

"You're not leaving with them," Lena replied.

"Please, Ren, let us go. We aren't happy with you. Your abominations will ruin our world."

"What? Our children are the farthest thing from abominations. You comprehend nothing of what is truly going on."

"Please, Lena, we know you and your husband are planning to rule the world with these children and enslave mankind."

"Rule the world?" Ren began to chuckle. It was apparent someone had been filling their heads with convoluted stories. But who?

"What is so funny?" Michael seemed quite annoyed and confused when Ren began to laugh. Ren reached the door in the blink of an eye to block them from leaving. Lena reached out to Fern so that she could hand her Kamau. Ren didn't care about spooking them and quietly took Kissa before Michael could react. While Ren stayed to make sure they didn't leave, Lena took her children and placed them in their bedroom to rest. Then Lena closed the door.

"Please sit."

"You're not going to let us leave?"

"I'm afraid that we cannot let you leave. We've only been gone a few days. No one can find out what is going on."

"We won't tell anyone."

"People will think it strange if they notice you're around and they haven't seen me. This way, they are not sure."

"Michael, Fern; we are not trying to control the human world. We are trying to keep the vampire world in order; or under control."

"The vampire world? We were told you wanted to control everyone and everything. They said that we would be just like cattle to you."

"Fern," Ren replied. "That is what I am trying to prevent. In New York, we're trying to maintain our way of life by having feeders. People who agree to let us feed. Some in exchange for a better lifestyle. The people who told you that are ignorant of what is going on or are trying to prevent me from gaining complete control.

"Some vampires believe that since we are stronger, we should run the human world and that humans are no more than cattle. Actually, it would be much the way humans treat their livestock, with little respect for the life they are taking. If we can't control the states, it could get even more dangerous for humans. Most of those stories about missing people and murders are vampires that we want to keep under control. It would be best for all if we maintained our secrecy and seclusion. A fight between the two would not be beneficial for either side."

"We didn't know. They said you wanted all humans as your food and slaves. Why else would you keep having children?"

"Our children will be the ones to keep the peace. Who are they?"

Fern and Michael exchanged a look. "We're so sorry.Can we leave now?"

"No, who are they," asked Ren.

"We don't know," replied Michael.

"So you trusted people you don't know who told you to take our children?"

"Lena, they told us your children would be your muscle. She said they would be killing machines. You even teach them martial arts. We've seen it."

"How are they supposed to protect themselves and others if they don't know how to fight?" Lena was pacing the floor. She couldn't believe what was happening. "You fuckin' idiots, we let you into our home to help, not to steal my children."

"Yalena."

"Don't Yalena me, Lorenzo." She took a breath. "If you," she pointed at the couple, "Michael or Fern ever touch my children again for any reason not approved by me, I will rip your heart out and feed it to you." Lena began to breathe heavily as she held onto Kamau and Kissa.

"Kissa, Kamau, take your mom in the room with you. She needs to calm down." The children didn't reply but grabbed each of Lena's hands and toddled with her back to the room." He turned back to the couple. " You said she. Do you know who she is?"

"She said she works at the club with you. She described you as being very evil."

"I appear evil to you?"

"She said it was an act," replied Fern. Can we go now?"

"I'm afraid not. You can possibly stay here until we return from Egypt, and then you can go."

Lena conceived that Ren was trying to be compassionate. Still, she was more concerned about their safety and that of her children. Lena believed if they left Fern and Micheal in London, they would leave as soon as she and Ren were gone. So when Ren entered the room, Lena suggested that Fern and Michael continue the journey. He said he would think about it, but if they tried to escape before they left for Egypt, he would have no control over what they found outside. Lena didn't understand. She was just hoping Fern and

Micheal would think about it and make a wise decision. After all, Ren could have just killed them.

She had set up a comfortable bed on the lush carpet on the floor of their room for the children, and she and Ren got back into bed. Lena had missed being near Ren over the last few months. Lena wanted to make love to him again; he had the same idea.

Early the following day, they were off to Egypt to find Sekhmet's daughter, Sekhmet. They took Michael and Fern with them on the private jet. Thankfully, they had not refused Ren. Once Lena got the children settled and in their seats with toys, she went to talk to Ren about their trip.

"So, where are we going?"

"Small village in Cairo."

"Is that where we will meet her?"

"I believe so. That is where our guide will be, at least. We will go from there. She has been waiting to meet you."

"She knows of me?"

"It is more likely because I have asked for a meeting and her blessing, I presume. At least, I believe that is how she knows of you. Of course, I could be wrong."

"Her blessing?"

"Yes, she must bless our union before I turn you."

"And if she doesn't?"

"There will be no power to harness from our union, and we will lose the war between myself and the council or barely escape. She can either release your power or bind it forever. We'll just be another vampire couple."

"So, this meeting is of the utmost importance, to say the least."

"Yes."

Lena didn't give their union much thought. Still, it wasn't like she knew much about this life before Ren. In addition to her being from a vampire line, control of their world rested on her shoulders. Soon it would rest on her children's shoulders also. She reminded herself that Ren was no one to be trifled with. Therefore, their children would definitely be extraordinary. Since the children slept the whole way, Lena sat next to her husband, wrapped in his arms. She wondered if there was no power to harness from their union, would he still want her? What would happen to her and her children? Lena sighed before putting the questions out of her mind. She would have to just wait and see.

When they landed in Cairo, they were greeted by a gentleman her children believed was a vampire; as a result, they clung to her and Ren. The driver drove them to an area with many villas and apartments. Lena wasn't sure if this was what Ren had planned. They didn't speak the whole time from the airport to the house. They only heard the few words spoken between Ren and the driver. When they finally stopped, Ren got out of the car. Lena wasn't sure if she should have followed, so she sat in the limo until she saw Ren embrace the man who met him at the house's threshold.

"Ahmed, it is great to see you after so many centuries." The man Ren called Ahmed smiled and nodded his head. "This is my wife Yalena and our children, Kissa and Kamau. And, of course, our companions, Fern and Michael."

"Of course. Welcome to my home, well, one of many. Come in, eat, relax; you have traveled a long way. Your guide will be here in the morning." They followed him into his home as the driver unloaded the few bags they had and brought them in.

A table was laid with food for all of them. It was a considerable welcome. Ren seemed to be at ease, and, in turn, that made Lena relax. Lena spent the rest of the time with the children and their companions. They ate and retired to the room that was set up for them. Kamau and Kissa sampled the food but preferred to nurse and feed from their mother. It wasn't long before everyone was asleep. Lena awoke briefly when Ren came in but soon fell back to sleep.

Ren didn't sleep well or at all that night or early morning. When Lena awoke, he was watching her. Lena smiled at him before he softly kissed her and then fed. He didn't feed long before calling Fern to him to finish.

When he was finished, he dismissed Fern and turned to Lena. "We will go find her. It may take a few days. They are not sure."

"How long have you known Ahmed?"

"A few centuries."

"You trust him?"

"Yes, with my life."

"Was he the one who found her?"

"No, someone who worked for him."

"Does he grasp what's at stake?"

"Yes, He thinks you're going to be a grand ruler."

"Really?"

"He's a good judge of character," Ren smiled and kissed her cheek.

The next morning, after a substantial breakfast, they began to get themselves together. Their guide Muhammed came for them and put everything in the van. They weren't expecting to return to this house. As the day progressed, Lena was grateful for the warm spring weather. She couldn't imagine searching for the village in the hot desert heat. Unfortunately, Lena wasn't prepared for the desert heat. Ren tried to get her to regulate her body, but it was still too much. Eventually, the children got the hang of it and managed to adjust their bodies to the weather.

After searching for several temples, they decided to rest at a small hotel in Asyut. They believed that they were about halfway to their destination. They would start again in the morning. The temperature was much cooler than when they arrived. It took a few tries the next day before they found the temple that fit the description they were looking for. They weren't sure they had found the right one, but something pulled at Lena. The energy of the old temple was intense. The temple was in ruins Lena thought she recognized the neter or gods. Then it came to her, Lena recognized it from a picture of a temple where many statues of Mut were located. They had reached the Temple Precinct of Mut at Karnak.

Lena didn't understand the energy that she felt radiate from the temple or what called to her. This was a tourist site. People were regularly around this place. How could there be a hidden village? Lena climbed out of the van and began to walk through the temple with Kamau in her arms. It was a beautiful place. She had read that it took over fifteen hundred years to build this wondrous place. That would have taken more than fifty pharaohs.

Lena had no idea where she was going, but she followed her instincts. There were many statues, carvings, and a wall full of prayers in metu neter, the ancient language often referred to as hieroglyphs. The words metu neter translates as the language of god. How beautiful she thought. Lena didn't walk far before her family got out of the van and followed her. It was early evening, and the sun was low in the sky. Lena walked through the temple building until she came to an end. The small village was on the side of the temple that looked out onto Luxor. The town was quiet.

Could it be a town, she wondered. It looked so deserted. She didn't remember reading of buildings or huts behind the temple. Lena was tired and needed to rest regardless of finding the right place.

"I believe we have finally found it," Ren said.

"Yes, we have, sir," Ahmed's employee replied.

They all began to descend the steep slope into the village. They walked a few feet from the bottom of the hill before they were greeted by a group of men and women. Lena looked at their faces, seeing every shade of brown she could think of and more. Well, they weren't actually greeted. They surrounded Ren's family. Lena wasn't even sure where they came from. She hadn't discerned any movement in the village before they descended the hill. She was scared at first, wondering what they had disturbed by their presence. That didn't last for long; the energy began to change. Lena could feel them say that they meant no harm, even though Lena couldn't understand what they were saying. Did they speak the ancient language? Either way, she held Kamau closer to her.

Then Muhammed spoke to them in a language Lena vaguely remembered. There wasn't much to go on because Lena had heard many different languages. He talked with a man who then left the circle and ran toward the houses behind them, but he didn't go in. Instead, he was greeted at the door by someone. Lena couldn't make out more than a tiny brown figure with long white hair that fell more than halfway down her form. She didn't move any further but gestured for Ren and his family to come to her. The circle of what Lena believed were vampires opened to pass through. They walked with purpose towards the old woman. As they did, the crowd that had quietly gathered began to chatter. Lena couldn't understand, but she sensed they were talking about her.

When she got to the house, a woman stood in front of her. She appeared rather frail. Yet there was something in her eyes that said she was preeminent; an apparent contradiction to her present appearance.

"Hotepu, Sem ntr da chin."

"Hotep. Anedge herack Sent Sekhmet," Ren replied as he bowed before her. After he greeted her, Ren and Lena were allowed to enter the dwelling. Michael and Fern were instructed to wait outside.

"Ren, what is being said?"

"You should have prepared her, Ren." Her heavily accented English startled Lena. Sekhmet laughed to herself.

"In over five hundred thousand years, you did not think I would learn many languages?"

"I really didn't think about it."

"You keep staring at me. Do I look familiar? Or does this form bother you? Should I change it." In front of her eyes, Sekhmet's form became what Lena believed was the younger form of the goddess. It was much like looking into a mirror. "Dumbfounded."

A smirk came across Sekhmet's face as she turned to Ren. "You have not shown her your gifts?"

"Gifts,?" Lena asked, confused.

"Yes, your mate can project himself as well as shape shift." Before her eyes, two replicas of Lena appeared. As quickly as Ren changed into his wife, he returned to his natural form.

"Why didn't you tell me, Ren?"

"I thought it would be too much for you. You've accepted so much already."

"I am not a porcelain doll. Can anyone shape shift?"

"I know you're not a porcelain doll," he replied with a smile before embracing her. "And no, it seems we all have our own gifts for the most part. Some of us have the same gifts, but not many."

"Sent Sekhmet, will I have the same gifts as you do?"

"Possible. I have yet to decide. What do you have so far?"

"I am agile and fast with a blade. I can search for people I'm acquainted with if they are not with me, and I can see what they are doing. However, that has only happened once."

"When?"

"Last week. I was in danger and needed to find Marcellus. He's Ren's partner."

"Find him now."

"I'll try. I haven't done it from such a long distance." Lena closed her eyes and retraced her steps to the home they had stayed just a day or so ago. The house now sat empty, and she was surprised by that. When she opened her eyes to tell Ren, she jumped because Sekhmet was far less than an arm's length away from her.

"Tell him later. Focus!" Lena closed her eyes again. In her mind, she went from the house to the airport, then to the hotel in London. It was amazing how much she saw and with such detail. She could see the room they had stayed in at the hotel. People were moving about there. Strangely, their images were not clear at all; their faces were a blur. She made a mental note to ask Sekhmet about that. Then continued her trace, from the hotel to the airport in London, then to JFK and the club. Her mind searched the club but didn't find Cell. She never thought he ever left the club. Lena took a deep breath and exhaled slowly to relax. She let her mind or inner self guide her. Oddly enough, it led her back to the penthouse, up the stairs instead of in the elevator. She moved through the doorway to an apartment on the first floor and into the bedroom. Cell was with someone, but it wasn't Theo or Marcia. The skin of the person was too bronze for that. Then she discerned the face of the woman and gasped. That seemed to break her connection.

"Ren, we got a problem."

"Later, tell me what you saw."

"Everything had such detail."

"Where was this Marcellus as you called him?"

"He's with my sister. In his bed at his apartment. That image I didn't need." Sekhmet chuckled. "I didn't know he lived at the penthouse."

"You already have one of my gifts," Sekhmet whispered as she backed away. Lena wasn't sure if she was talking to them or herself. "It doesn't allow you to see into the future, but you can find anyone at any time if you know who you are looking for. That, of course, is the drawback. You need a name and a face. But, as you get better with practice, a name will suffice. Only the person you seek will have a clear image and kin to you."

"That would explain why the people at the hotel were so blurry." There was a moment of silence as Lena absorbed all that had taken place so far. "Can I ask why you were named after your mother?"

"I was born with all of her knowledge and power. She felt it was befitting to name me as she was named. I am tired. You can go now. Come back tomorrow morning, and we'll talk. Heru will find you a place to stay in one of the huts."

Lena thought that the time had been short. She wondered what would be in store for tomorrow and wished she had been more prepared today. Of course, if she knew that they would meet her someday, she would have done more research about the myths and the history of Egypt and its gods. Her mom and grandma had taught her parts of its history, but she was much younger then and didn't remember much.

"Ren, why didn't you tell me I was going to meet her? I feel like such a fool. I didn't even think more about you having to prove my lineage."

"I apologize, my love. I wasn't planning this visit so soon. I just didn't want to lose the opportunity if something happened. I knew once you were into your second pregnancy, we would need to come to pay our respects to her."

"So, I am definitely into my second pregnancy?"

"Yalena, I told you after we made love at the club. All three babies are developing well. I'm also glad to see that your body is adapting better than the first time." Lena nodded but said nothing.

They were staying in a simple hut. There were mats on the floor where they would sleep. They had brought a few things with them that proved to be somewhat more comfortable. Lena had gotten the children ready to sleep before laying a quilt over the mats. Then she proceeded to remove her clothes and wrap herself in her lappa. A lappa is a wide piece of material wrapped around your body to make a skirt or dress. Hers was made from a beautiful blue batik. Lena brought both ends to the front, overlapped them, and tied it around her neck.

"Getting into the culture?"

"I have always appreciated my heritage."

"You look very sexy that way."

"Thank you." Lena smiled as she opened the front of her wrap briefly. Ren motioned for her to join him on their quilt. He took her hand and gently pulled her towards him. Her body shuddered. Lena sat next to Ren, looking down upon him. She was happy with him. She noted that she kept saying that to herself, but it was true, even with the danger and the stress of the pregnancies. She was happy.

Ren reached up and pulled her face to his. His kiss was loving. As he kissed Lena, he untied her wrap, giving his hands unhindered access to her body. They made love that night under the protection of their hut amid the African desert village. They didn't worry about what their feeders were doing or thinking. Their passion was as fiery as the day they walked through. When their ardor had burned like fire and finally left them, they just kissed and wrapped themselves in each other, and there they slept.

When Lena awoke the following day, Ren, the children, and the feeders were already dressed. "Ren, why didn't you wake me?"

"I was going to as soon as we were going out of the door." He knelt over her and kissed her eyes before walking towards the hut entrance. "We're going to breakfast. There is water next to you. Sekhmet will be in for you soon."

"But, I haven't fed the children."

"You will later."

Ren left her alone in the hut. She was bewildered. She didn't understand why she was left there. She began to wash up and get dressed. Shortly after she had dressed, there were footsteps outside her hut. Sekhmet had come to greet her.

"Hotep, Anedge herak Sent Sekhmet."

"Hotepu," she replied as she sat down. "Anedge herak meri djt. And how did you sleep?"

"Well, Sent Sekhmet."

"I'm glad. We have much work to do."

"Work to do? Forgive me. I am unaware of what is to happen here."

"Of course you are. Don't worry. You will be in full knowing soon. By the way, how is my no-good son?"

"I'm not sure of whom you speak."

"Of course you know. How is your great-grandfather, Mr. Lockington? I believe that is what he calls himself these days."

"Lockington, is your son?" Lena's eyes opened wide. "He must be an ancient vampire."

"Mmmmm, not too old. Just over a few thousand years. He is the youngest of my sons."

"There are others? Will we meet them?"

"No, they have left this world."

"I'm sorry."

"Don't be. I shouldn't have had them. A foolish woman yearned to bear children. I had three, but you must fathom we are not all meant to have children."

"May I ask what happened."

"Yes. My sons tried to outsmart me and put an end to my rule here. Both expired as a result. Lockington wasn't as power-hungry as his brothers. So, I let him live. He has limited strength and power. He no longer has the power to stand against me."

Wow, Lena thought. It sounded so much like the dramas she watched on TV. "That must be an interesting tale. It must be the reason grandfather was looking to sire a powerful vampire."

"He is a manipulative son of a bitch." Lena chuckled at Sekhmet's comment as she got to her feet. She couldn't help but think of how indifferent he seemed to her. He tended to play the devil's advocate at their meetings. Lena was never sure if he was doing it to keep the others off his track or because he wanted to be on whichever side wins. Probably the latter. "How far are you with child?"

"Not sure. Can't really be more than a week. Well, I guess that would mean they are as developed as a baby who is about two weeks because of who they are."

"Indeed. I bet it's hard to keep yourself from someone you love so much?"

"It is."

"You will try even harder next time."

"I don't understand. We weren't planning on the next time. We already have more than I wanted. Ren is ready to change me."

"Well, he can't change you until after this birth. You must have one more pregnancy."

"Grandmother, they already take such a toll on me. Another pregnancy you wish for me. We will have five after this. Of course, we are more concerned with feeding our brood."

"You will have another. This brood will not be as bloodthirsty as the first. The last two will lead."

"The youngest."

"You heard me. The last two will be painful to bear, like the first, strong vampires. The three you carry now will serve as council; they will be impartial and fair. They will serve as your court. You'll see that I speak the truth as you watch them grow. Four will be warriors and three will council."

"The prophecy says nothing of seven," Yalena replied as they continued their walk towards Sekhmet's home and temple.

"And where did you think it came from? I gave it, I shall change it. The first prophecy has been fulfilled. My eldest created the line. I met her, and I refused to fulfill my end of it. We weren't in such dire straits at that time. Anyway, I kept it to myself. You will have seven children. Of the seven, only four will regularly drink blood. You may take some of my people to serve. Ren will find suitable feeders for you and the children. After your third pregnancy, he can change you. You will hold on until then."

"What do you mean to hold on?"

"I have been waiting for you. I am tired of humanity now and wish to join my family, who have left this world."

"I thought gods lived forever."

"I will not die, you fool. It's Khepera."

"Transformation."

"So, your grandmother has taught you something."

"You knew my grandmother?"

"She has visited. Anyway, enough talk. We work." Lena's face looked a bit bewildered. They had just reached Sekhmet's temple. Lena had no idea what kind of work she was referring to. "Yes, work! Sit. I have seen you practice martial arts. Now be still. I bet you they haven't taught you to still your mind. I don't want you to think of anything or anyone. Don't even think of what you have learned. Be still totally."

"I recognized you from my dreams."

Sekhmet chuckled. "No talking either."

Lena had been taught to be still. She had been taught to move so slowly that her movement was not easily detected, and she had to keep it flowing, but she had never stilled her mind before. "Let go of all attachment to this world. Forget about me, your father and mother, your sisters, Ren, and your children. Forget all. Let it go."

As she said it, an image of each person appeared before Lena. She wanted to find each one as their vivid image came before her. "Do not look for them. Just let go. When an image or thought comes to mind, don't focus on it. Just let the thoughts float and let go."

Lena wasn't allowed to take a break until Ren brought her something to eat. As she ate, Sekhmet was still. She sat across from her about five feet away, just unmoving. One could hardly detect that she was breathing, and her heartbeat was very slight. After some time had passed, Ren asked Sekhmet if he could bring the children in to feed. A suitable nurse for the children had been refused. And they never really desired the feeders they had. Sekhmet appeared irritated, but she allowed it.

Lena had truly missed holding her two that morning. Her breasts were so full that her milk had leaked through the pads and her shirt. Ren no longer needed to puncture her skin for the twins. Their little fangs were the first set of teeth to come in. The children didn't speak to their mother. Their need to nurse seemed to take precedence over anything they might want to communicate to her. Lena held them in her arms as they fed. Each child had put one of their small arms around their mother.

As Lena looked into Kamau's eyes, they connected, and many images flooded Lena's brain. Apparently, Ren had taken them through the village searching for feeders and a nurse that morning. Unfortunately, those he had handpicked for Kissa and Kamau were rejected by them. As Kamau conveyed images to his mother, she also tried to emit that she was expecting their siblings. And then she bounced back to him the pictures of the four feeders that Ren had found for them. Kamau then broke his gaze with Lena and connected with Kissa. They both rested their tiny hands on their mother's stomach. They understood that soon they would have to choose a feeder because they wouldn't be able to nurse from Lena.

"Enough! You'll be able to nurse them just fine during your pregnancy, but soon they will require feeders. After all, children the size of a three-year-old don't need to be nursed."

They all looked up in surprise. Sekhmet knew what they were discussing, even though no words were exchanged. It also caught Ren off guard. After all, he had no idea what was communicated between Lena and her children. That was a bond only they shared. They all looked directly at Sekhmet, but she hadn't even opened her eyes. That puzzled them even more.

"Ren, how much research have you done about the prophecy?"

"Only a little; there wasn't much left about it after so many centuries."

"Of course, there is little because that prophecy has been fulfilled." Her eyes flew open as soon as she said the last few words. She regarded Ren with such intent. It was as if her whole body, mind, and spirit were tuned in to him, waiting for his response. When she couldn't read one, she decided to taunt him some more. "Really, Ren, not the least bit disappointed? Even though she is mine, there is nothing to fulfill."

"Sent Sekhmet, there has been a link between Yalena and me from the moment we saw each other over a decade ago. I have waited for her. She is my mate. So prophecy or no prophecy, my need and want for her will not change."

"Mhmm." She said nothing more to either of them. She didn't even look at the twins, who had not returned to nursing after she spoke. She closed her eyes and returned to her meditation. It was as if that gave the rest of them permission to resume whatever they were doing. Lena connected with her children once again, who had returned to nursing. Neither of them understood what had happened. She only replied that she would answer their questions later. Lena couldn't think of an image to convey what happened. While she returned to nursing her children, Ren decided to sit behind her and encircle them in his strong arms. Lena leaned into Ren's embrace. He felt warm to her, which meant that he had recently fed adequately. Lena guessed he had found a suitable feeder.

"Ren, you feed too often."

"I know, Sent Sekhmet. We began to feed daily to keep up our strength in these times."

"You will have to slow down. Maybe you can do so while you are here. You are safe here. No one will harm you. Slow down.

Feeding too often will eventually wear you down. And all that you rely on will fail when you need it most. Also, you don't sleep enough. You constantly run, doing too many things. So your body requires more blood. Rest when your wife rests as much as possible. I understand your plight. Trust me, rest will help."

"Dua, Sent Sekhmet."

"Feeding once or twice a week is plenty. It will give you enough to keep up your strength and fuel your gifts."

Ren nodded and rested his chin on Lena's shoulder. "I love you, and nothing will change that, Yalena."

"I know, babe. I love you also." He kissed her cheek and neck before taking the babies and walking out of the hut. As Lena buttoned her shirt, she watched, wishing for nothing more than to lay in his arms.

"You have centuries, if not an eternity, to be close to him. Now we focus."

"But how did you even know that?" Lena had not truly understood Sekhmet or her vast knowledge. She stared at her, puzzled. Sekhmet had yet to even look at her.

"How did I know what you were thinking?" Lena nodded yes in response to her question. "Please, you two are such lovesick puppies. It is not hard to guess how you feel at times. Now, let's focus--still your mind. Oh, and let's not tell him about the prophecy still existing. I want him to sweat a little. Just testing." Sekhmet smiled, and for a moment, Lena thought that her great-great-grandmother looked like a predator spotting prey within leaping distance. "Now, focus!"

For three days straight, that's all Yalena did. Sekhmet wanted Yalena to be able to still her mind. Nothing was to break that focus. Each day at noon, Ren brought her lunch and the children in to nurse. Once the sun began to set, she was allowed to stop and get something to eat before returning to her mate. Each night Ren ravaged his beloved bride. Yalena was sure that had she not been pregnant, there would be no doubt she would be before they left the African desert.

Chapter 16

On the fourth day in the village, Lena enjoyed sitting and talking with Sekhmet after meditating for a while. "Well, Yalena, you have done well."

"How can you tell?"

"The rhythm of your heart changed, and so did your breathing. You were almost perfectly still. Tomorrow you need to slow down your heart rate and breathing even more. This will help you bear your children. Especially the next set."

"You make it seem like the next set will be savages."

"No, they will be warriors. They will be endearing to you, their mother. Fortunately, or unfortunately, you will die giving birth to them. But of course, that is eventually what has to happen for you to completely change. After all, I can't imagine the world between vampire and human is all that fun."

"It has its benefits, but I am vulnerable, making it dangerous for me to be with Ren. Although, I can't imagine him being any less protective once I have fully turned. Wait a minute. If I am to change directly after their birth, I won't be able to nurse them."

"I'm unsure. Nursing may be possible, but it is more likely that you won't be able to. They will be as much vampire as their father. Your body will make sure of that. By the time they are born, your body would have taken on most of a vampire's characteristics. I am positive that your body will almost be completely drained of your own blood by the time the babies are ready to be born. Anyway, the last brood will drink blood immediately after birth. They will be a match to Kamau and Kissa." The two women were silent for several moments. They could hear all the sounds filtering in from the village.

"But if my body will almost be completely drained of my blood before they are born, why wouldn't my body have made the final change?"

"Well, even now, your body produces blood. There hasn't been much change in your DNA, only slight variations. Each time your children feed and Ren feeds, they take that blood. Each time Ren feeds you his blood, your body changes ever so slightly. The more this reciprocation happens, the more your body changes. Once all of your blood is gone and replaced by Ren, as it will have to be before you give birth, your body will cease to produce blood.

Vampires' bodies don't make blood; that is the genetic flaw in exchange for everything they are capable of.

"Okay, that kind of makes sense, I guess. What happens if my body doesn't stop making blood?"

"Never had that problem before. Then, of course, no dhampir has ever lived and reproduced. You're a new breed."

"Oh."

"I am worried about you, Yalena Merit. You are so drawn and in love with this life, or maybe I should say Ren. I almost wish you weren't. I'd gladly remain on earth if it means I can spear you this."

"Sent Sekhmet, I would not have chosen this life had I loved another. What Ren said is true. From the first time we met, it was kismet. Even though he had wiped my memories of him, I never stopped wearing the necklace he gave me, and I finally found him. I was so drawn to him. I know life will be dangerous at times. But, I am also sure we will have a life filled with love." Sekhmet smiled and watched her great-great gran for a moment before she replied.

"You should have been drawn to him. You two were created for each other. He has searched his entire vampire life for you. Your great grandfather sired Ren. Ren was created hundreds of years before your conception. He has walked his life without a mate. I have always meant for you to be his, his love. You should feel no other way.

"I have watched you meri djt, as you have grown. You are astute and tenderhearted. I have seen your practice. I saw you the day you were presented with your swords by your grandfather. I am afraid I have fallen in love with who you have become. Would you damn your daughter to an eternity as I have you?"

"Have I not done so by conceiving them for my love?" Sekhmet didn't answer immediately.

"You are right. You and your children and your mate shall spend an eternity together. I have not made Kissa barren as I have made your sisters. Your daughters will bear children should they choose to. Like you, they will be more vampire than human, and your boys can give their seed regardless of them being a full vampires or not. But your daughters will be like you.

"One day, you will decide who to bestow your powers to as you leave this world and join me on the next plane." Yalena didn't speak. She didn't know what to say to what she was being told. She nodded to acknowledge that she had heard Sekhmet. "This village shall be yours one day, should you chose to claim it. Once I have gone, all you will need to do to bring life to this land is walk the streets."

"Yes, Sent Sekhmet, but how will I find it again?"

"No need to worry. When it's time, it will beckon. You are not to tell Lorenzo anything until you have left here. And you will soon." She paused once again as if she was listening to someone whisper in her ear. "I believe your children have found playmates."

"Playmates? How is that possible? There are no children here."

"Oh, aren't they? I have already told you; you bring life to this place."

They were quiet for a moment. Lena thought of all the questions she wanted to ask. She thought she'd start with the easiest one. "Was there really a Scorpion King?"

"Yes, but I don't know much of him. I went to meditate in seclusion. Ask your grandfather. He had his hand in the king's fate. I was so angry with him for meddling."

"Oh. I will when I remember again. What was life like when gods walked the earth?"

"Would you believe that Khemet was a savannah for centuries?"

"No. I thought it was always a desert."

"No, Khemet was a grassland. The earth is in constant change."

"Does man have anything to do with that?"

"More than most know. Man and the earth are connected. As man changes and becomes more greedy or more peaceful, the earth changes. Many believe the fight between Heru and Set scorched this land. Dried the savannah so much, it became a desert."

"Is that true?"

"I'll never tell." Sekhmet smiled at her and winked. "Now enough talk. Go and be with your family." Lena did what she was told and left Sekhmet with what seemed to be tears in her eyes. Lena reached to embrace her, but she stopped her. Sekhmet's servant appeared to take Lena from her to where Ren was waiting. Both Kissa and Kamau were playing with children who seemed to be their age. She would have to ask Sekhmet to explain that tomorrow. The rest of today belonged to her family.

Even though Lena came ready with questions the next day, they were left unasked. After leaving her family, Sekhmet put her to work as soon as she arrived at the hut. She said she wanted to make sure Lena could still her mind.

For several more days, at least by Lena's calculations, she worked on the same meditation. She was ecstatic when she had finally mastered the technique, and Sekhmet allowed her to spend the rest of the day with Ren.

Ren and Lena walked the Nile village together, arm and arm. It was as if the town was taken from ancient Thebes and placed in modern times. As they walked, she could tell by looking at the people who were vampires and who she believed were other supernatural beings she had no knowledge of and didn't care to ask. Still, the village appeared to be filled with more life than the day they first arrived. Ren seemed to notice it also. It intrigued him, but he said nothing.

Their children brought their playmates to meet their parents. Their names were Adayo and Yero. They were the size of children, but there was something ancient in their eyes.

"Mom," Kissa called. "Can we take Adayo and Yero home with us?"

"I do not know. I will have to ask Sekhmet. She said nothing about taking children with us."

Ren and Lena walked for a while through the village, and life seemed to spring up at their feet. Their children and their mates walked behind them, playing and giggling. Their laughter filled Lena's heart with joy.

Ren brought Lena to a small house that looked like it was made from the soil at their feet. A woman met them at the entrance and invited them in. She smiled at Lena before showing them where they could sit. The children that Kissa and Kamau were playing with appeared to belong to her.

"Yalena, this is Kai. She will be my feeder, and I was hoping that her husband would be yours." Lena smiled and nodded as she was introduced. Right after which, a man entered the hut. He was tall and handsome. Both the woman and man had a regal air to them.

Kai introduced her husband, Nomar, before asking the couple to sit. Both of the children sat next to Kai and rested their heads in her lap. Kamau and Kissa came to nurse.

"I see they still nurse," stated Kai.

"I have not the strength or heart to stop them, but I must admit it has decreased quite a bit."

"Ren tells us that you are with child again."

Lena looked up. The woman had the knack of restating what was said, thought Lena. "Yes, triplets, I believe."

"Yes, triplets. I will need help caring for Yalena and the children. I am unable to devote all of my time to her, my business and clan matters. She may also begin to feed again soon. Our present feeders wish to be released from their duty to us. "

"I understand," replied Nomar, Kai's husband. "I do not think that will be a problem. We are here to serve you."

"Nomar, I am glad to hear this. We only have to find suitable feeders for our children. Would you be able to assist us?"

"I do believe so. My niece, my brother's daughter, stays with us since her mother and father have been called to serve Sekhmet."

"Are you speaking of Heru, Sekhmet's servant and priest? He's your brother?"

"Yes, yes. Candace is their daughter. She is quite shy but devoted. I believe the twins have already met her."

"Okay. If the children have already accepted her, that sounds fine."

"Just so you understand, neither her father nor I would wish her to be a feeder for the rest of her life. We wish her to choose. We want a better life for her."

"That sounds like a reasonable request, Nomar. We will let it be her choice."

"Do you know when we all leave? We have no documents."

"I will take care of everything. Everything will be ready when we are."

"Sekhmet says that we will leave shortly. I am not sure what that means."

Ren and Lena didn't stay much longer. Lena wanted to spend some time with Ren and the children. So they went back to the hut. Lena finished nursing the children and put them down for a nap.

"Ren, this has been quite a journey."

"Yes, my love. I hope you have at least appreciated and enjoyed it.

"This journey has been quite exciting and challenging. It does have value to me. Much of it was so unexpected that I'm still adjusting."

"I'm more concerned about what is happening at home."

"I was wondering if time passes the same here as it does outside the village. Honestly, I am not sure. I suspect so. Mohamed said he would check back with us in a week. I have not heard a word that he has come back."

"How would you know? Maybe he can't find it."

"They would know. I have asked for someone to fetch me if he comes back." Lena nodded and then smiled at him as he untied her wrap. "Lena, I've missed you. You've been so preoccupied since we've arrived. I thought this would be our journey, but it seems to be yours alone."

"Oh, Ren. I know there is so much at stake. We don't talk about what will be required of me. It's almost like you don't want me to be the one you were looking for."

"That is probably true. Things would be easier if I had just taken any mate. You are not going to be just any old vampire. To them, you will be a goddess with powers and abilities none can fathom. I was sired for you. But I don't know that I am strong enough for you."

Wow, Lena thought. She never thought Ren would doubt himself. She smiled at him and kissed his lips. "Never doubt it. There could be no other."

"Not for me either, my love." Lena smiled down at him as Ren lowered her to the mat next to him. Lena's fingers furiously worked at the buttons on his shirt. His chest glistened from the heat of the noonday sun. Her hands opened his shirt and ran over his smooth chest as she slipped the shirt off.

Ren cradled her in his arms as they gazed into each other's eyes. The acknowledgment of the love they had reflected and seemed to ignite the flames between them. Ren began to kiss every inch of her he could find. First, he kissed her forehead, then her eyelids and cheeks. Then Ren kissed his way down Lena's neck to the valley between her full breasts before cupping each in his hands. His thumbs rubbed and brushed over each nipple, her milk leaking down the sides. Ren took his time, fanning the flames that ran over her skin. Finally, he slowly took each nipple into his mouth, caressing her with his tongue and lips. As his mouth aroused her, so did his fingers as they dove deeper inside of her.

Lena's moans were soft at first. Her body was in sync with each caress of his tongue and the push of his fingers. Each movement was deliberate and slow, ensuring that he felt each motion inside her before removing his pants. His length thick with need. He knelt over her and gently parted her legs with his knee. Lena peered down at his hard length as Ren rubbed his tip against her peak and then slowly plunged deep into her. His lips almost immediately found hers. Each push surged deeper into her wetness, sending fire through her veins. Lena pushed up against Ren matching each stroke and propelling him into her depths. Her body began to shudder each time he pushed into her. Each moment that passed was filled with his love for her, and she bathed in it.

When they had pushed each other over the brink, they relaxed in each other's arms. Never feeling safer than at that moment. They didn't speak but stayed in silence, listening to the ease of their breathing and the steady beat of each other's hearts. There in Ren's arms, Lena fell asleep.

Later, Yalena woke up to Ren's voice talking to the children. She looked around to see him with Kissa and Kamau. It took Lena a minute to come out of the fog she was in from sleeping. Lena didn't think much time had passed, but as she looked around the hut, she noticed the lantern burning in the corner, and the darkness peeked in from beyond the opening of their shelter. Then she observed that Fern and Michael were nowhere to be seen.

"Glad you are awake. There is supposed to be a ceremony tonight in the temple. You are to attend. Are you hungry?"

"Yes, extremely."

"Beside you. It is probably cold now, but it will suffice."

"I can't wait for you to cook me something when we get home. I miss that now." Ren looked down at her with a smile and pointed to the food next to her. Lena ate but truly hungered for food that she couldn't have at the moment.

When she was finished, she dressed and walked with Ren and the children to the temple. Lanterns lit the path, and candles illuminated the temple, bringing the mtu ntr to life. It was surprising to behold the colors that embellished the pictures and carvings on the temple walls. The pigments were as vibrant as they might have been thousands of years before.

"This is quite an illusion."

"Maybe, but I don't believe it is an illusion. It's beautiful anyway." One of Sekhmet's priests met and guided them to sit with her.

She could have never imagined anything like it. The small village of what seemed like twenty people was now more than fifty with elders and children. Sekhmet wasn't joking when she said they brought life to this place. As she looked across the crowd, they all seemed to be happy and content. The children were all teeth, and even some adults were smiling. Kai's family sat directly across from them; her husband, the two little ones, and a young lady Lena presumed was Candace.

The priest performed a ritual she barely understood. Summer solstice had passed and it wasn't time for any other major ceremonies that Lena knew. The priest spoke in mtu ntr. It was beautiful. It reminded her a lot of the church ceremonies with prayer and incense burning. Several people played drums, flute, and shekere, while another priest sang songs that honored the creator and different deities.

Before they left the temple, Sekhmet got up to speak. As she spoke, Ren translated for Lena. She thanked everyone for coming. Then she explained why Lena had come to find the village. She told them that she counted the days she would walk with them and that her son would soon be there to fill her place. Many started to cry. And a child ran to her and hugged her leg while asking her to stay with them. She hugged the small girl, which seemed to take everyone by surprise. Then she made Lena promise to return to them one day after becoming tired of the world. Ren pledged that they would return, and that ended the ceremony. She said goodnight to everyone and many left. She had mentioned that she needed to speak with Lena and her family and Kai's family, so they remained as requested.

When most had left the temple and they were mostly alone, Sekhmet addressed them. "Ren, I made Yalena promise not to tell you about the return to this place. Someone must keep it going. Yalena will be able to keep an eye on things from here when you two are ready to turn things over to your grandchildren. I suspect it will be quite sometime before that happens."

"Our grandchildren," Ren asked.

"Yes, my love. Our children will be able to give life. One that will hopefully bring a promise of peace to our world."

"You and Yalena will have seven children. All of which will be in three pregnancies. This pregnancy will give you three children, and one more pregnancy will give you your last two. This pregnancy will yield your council. Kissa, Kamau, and the two from her last pregnancy will be your warriors. They will carry out the sentence of the council. They will keep the law."

"So, our children will keep vampires under control?"

"We were children of the creator, each from a different culture but one and the same. We were sent to rid the world of the unrighteous. But we know that nothing is as it is created. We strayed; well, many of us did. We didn't want to destroy what we created. Then we figured out a way to maintain it. That is Yalena and her family.

"Kai, I am afraid once your family leaves this place, you will begin to age. You will be as you should have been before you stumbled onto this place. You now have children that you have wished for. Once you leave you can not return, and I will not see you again on this plane."

"We understand, and thank you so much for all you have done for us, dua."

"You're welcome. You will leave in three days. Before I say goodnight, Ren, your guide, left an envelope for you. It has been left in your hut. Yalena, I will see you in the morning. Gr nfr."

"Gr nfr," we replied as she left us in front of the temple.

The following day was much like the others before. Lena awoke after her children and Ren were ready to leave. She washed up, dressed, and walked to the small temple across from where they slept. There she sat, waiting for Sekhmet.

"Hotepu, Yalena."

"Anedge herak, Sent Sekhmet."

"Did you enjoy your time with your family? And I take it Kai's family is to your liking?"

"Yes, yes. I enjoyed the time we had. This trip hasn't been what we expected."

"Is anything?"

"No, actually."

"Tomorrow, you and Ren will sit with me."

"Okay." The two meditated for most of the morning. Sekhmet wanted to make sure Lena could find her center, her place of peace. Sekhmet said she would need it. She said that her emotions and powers were linked and that if she didn't learn to control her abilities under stress, she would be destructive--that made sense. Sekhmet, after all, was a potent and deadly force.

That morning was difficult for Lena. Sekhmet kept creating illusions that she knew would anger and frustrate Lena. She expected her to remain calm and find her center. By the time Ren came to retrieve Lena that night, she was mentally and physically tired. She didn't think that remaining calm and controlling herself would have taken so much energy. During the day, she had started a lightning storm and burnt down a hut. Lena was so grateful that it was unoccupied.

Chapter 17

After Lena ate that night, she fell straight to sleep. She was so tired. The very next morning, she awoke to find Ren and Kai packing up what little they had. She looked around for the children, and to her surprise they were feeding from Candace's wrist. As soon as they saw that Lena was up, they stopped and came to nurse.

The time they had spent in the village had gone by so fast. Lena wasn't genuinely sure she was ready to go. They were at peace there. Ren didn't have to worry about attacks; they were safe. Lena knew they couldn't stay until the triplets were born, but she wished they could.

She was lost in thought when Ren came and sat by her. She had not even noticed his presence. Ren kissed her cheek, and she immediately felt his warmth. His hand lightly brushed her cheek, and she looked up and smiled at him.

"Are you ready to go home?"

Lena smiled and nodded. She was ready to return to the luxury to which she had grown accustomed. "Ren, how long ago did you let Fern and Michael leave."

"I was wondering when you would ask. A few days ago. I didn't want to send them back until we were almost ready to leave."

"Ren, you know they are going to be ready to try again."

"Yes, but we will be ready for them. You're going to have to keep tabs on Seth daily."

"I figured that you would say something along those lines." It had been on Lena's mind while they stayed in the village. If they did succeed, Ren would be next. But, of course, she had no intention of leaving her children without a mother or father.

The newly formed family left that evening at sunset. Lena had mixed feelings about leaving the village. She loathed the idea that she would not see Sekhmet again in this life. She wanted to learn more from her. Lena understood that even though she was far away, she could contact Sekhmet at any time. Yet that knowledge did little to comfort her.

Their guide would pick them up on the other side of the temple at sunset. As Lena and her family walked up the steep hill, she recognized that things would never be the same again; arriving home would be different this time. Of course, she wasn't looking forward to that, yet she understood that it was time to take her rightful place by Lorenzo's side. After her children were born, she would no longer have to hide in their penthouse.

When she reached the hill's top, Lena turned around to view the small village she had just left. She would not espy it again for centuries. But, to Yalena's surprise, there was nothing to see, even in the sunlit area. No visible life betrayed the village's existence. She couldn't tell that there had been a village there, but she knew that over fifty people gathered in the village street to say goodbye.

"That is how it is." Lena nodded in reply to Kai's comment and proceeded to walk the temple ruins' long halls once again. She guessed once you step out, they don't want you to change your mind.

Everything went smoothly from that point on. A different driver picked them up and took them to one of Ahmed's houses to freshen up and rest before heading for the Cairo airport the next morning. No problems arose with the passports or tickets. Lena thought that was unusual. Surely, they found it odd that she and Ren left with people going one way.

It was the first time Kai and their family saw a plane, much less flew on one. And they had never left their country. It was quite an experience for them. Kai and Nomar were nervous at first. Candace was a little anxious, but the little ones were fine, probably because they were sitting with Kissa and Kamau, who seemed content.

Instead of returning to England, like when they were going to Egypt, they landed in Paris. It is a beautiful city. The family enjoyed the few days that they spent there. Yalena even made sure that she went to see the Eiffel Tower and, of course, the Gardens at the Palace of Versailles. Kai and her family were amazed by it all. They thanked Ren profusely for choosing to bring them. It wasn't until that moment that Lena wondered whether Kai and her family were even from this century. Odd that it had never occurred to her that the village existed without time. It was as if time passed around it. Sekhmet even said that they would begin to age outside of it and that now they had children. Had they had no children before, Ren and Lena chose them?

Lena wished that they could have stayed in Paris a little longer. A few days were not enough, but she was glad they spent some time in the city. She vowed to make Ren bring her back once they were relatively safe again. When they arrived at John F. Kennedy Airport, also known as JFK, the whole family was ushered through quickly by someone Ren knew. When they reached the baggage claim area, it was pretty desolate. Patrick had already taken their bags off the belt. He was standing by their suitcases, waiting for them.

"Glad I got a limo instead of bringing the car. It seems we have grown over our little trip."

"Yes, Patrick." Ren had a handler grab their bags, and Patrick showed them to the limo waiting outside the glass doors.

"Ren, there is much to discuss." Ren nodded in response as he glided into the car after the rest of the group.Ren settled across from Lena, who glanced at the driver and then back at Ren, as she shook her head no. After, Patrick gave the driver instructions, and the car pulled off. It was utterly silent in the car, except for a few pleasantries and the introduction of our family's newest members.

Lena perceived it would take some time to get home from the airport, so she closed her eyes and rested her head on the headrest. She was tired, and the driver's presence made her weary. He seemed perplexed and frustrated by his befuddlement. Lena wasn't sure why, but it felt like trouble had been brewing while they were gone. They wanted a heads up from the time they came back into town. She wondered if the driver was an associate of Patrick's because she hated the idea of telling him he was for the other team. He wasn't a vampire. Lena knew that. He was human, and she could smell the compulsion on him. She tried to retrace his steps but couldn't. It was useless. She would just have to make sure he wouldn't enter their home.

They pulled up in front of their Park Avenue home, and Lena was relieved. But unfortunately, she didn't get the much-needed nap in the car. Something kept gnawing at her. At some point during the ride, she tried to read the driver. She wanted to have an idea of his intentions. Sekhmet had told her that she would eventually read people, but reading the driver just gave her a headache. All she experienced was vexation pouring out of him. Like he couldn't figure out why he was thinking or feeling a certain way.

Patrick helped Yalena out of the car with the twins in her arms. Ren had already gotten out of the car and proceeded to collect the bags from the trunk.

"Please, sir, allow me to help you with the bags," the driver said. Ren nodded, and the two of them began unloading the car. The family didn't leave with much, but they returned with a lot. They had done some shopping in Paris, mainly for Kai's family.

After setting the bags on the curb, Ren reached to pay the driver. He thanked him before gesturing for Lena and the rest of them to go in with Patrick.

"Thank you, sir. Would you like some help inside?" Yalena shook her head no. But they ignored her. There was a moment of silence as Ren examined the driver for the first time. The driver was now nervous and agitated. Yalena began to wonder what was at stake for him.

"Sure, you can help us inside." Ren couldn't be serious, Lena thought. Was he going to let this guy into their home? Yalena hadn't gone inside with Kai; she had stood in the vestibule. Kai and Candace had taken the children into the elevator. Lena wanted to be aware of exactly what was going to happen. When she turned to see where Kai was with Kissa and Kamau, she saw her sister and Cell.

"Cell, can you help Ren and Patrick with the bags? Yazzie and I will catch the elevator with everyone." Lena had only turned and walked a short distance to the elevator Kai had held for her when they heard a scream. Lena turned just in time to see Cell and Patrick step into the building, followed by Ren. Before she blinked, Cell had seized the driver.

"Lena, go upstairs, now." Lena wanted to disagree with him. She wanted to be fully aware of what was going on, but she saw the look on his face. It was the same expression he had after she killed the vampire in the club's basement. Lena was as pregnant now as she was then. So she got onto the elevator, which opened up onto the penthouse floor.

Lena put the children to sleep in the nursery. She was surprised that instead of cribs, the room had four loft beds, each secured into the far wall--two on either side and a few feet from each other. A separate ladder led to each bed. All four children could sleep in the same room. She and Kai were sure it was going to be trouble. After putting the children to bed, Lena showed Kai and her family to their rooms on the other side of the house. Kai and Nomar complained that they didn't want to be so far from the children. Yes, there were two bedrooms next to Lena and Ren's, but the rooms would soon be needed for the children in her womb. Kai, Nomar, and Candace conceded to the two large bedrooms past Lena's favorite room. After Kai's family and the children were settled, Lena decided to sit and relax in her bed's comfort.

"So, where have you been," asked Yazmine.

"Africa, Yazzi. The continent is so beautiful, and so were Paris and London."

"That doesn't sound like the secretive trip Cell has made it out to be."

"This trip was an important one. I cannot discuss it now. You'll eventually learn about it. I just wish to rest now. I have missed my bed. We were in a hut for over a month."

"Oh yeah, I want to learn about this trip when you're ready to tell me. So how are you? I mean, how do you feel?"

"Like I said, tired. I am expecting again. Ren believes they're three this time."

"Triplets?"

"Yes, triplets." They sat in silence for a while before Lena turned on the TV. Lena was not expecting Ren to take so long. She and Yazzi fell asleep side by side after watching television for an hour or so. Their partner's kiss awakened each.

"Ren, you're back. Took long enough."

"Yes, we needed to take care of the situation immediately."

"Why was he here?"

"They wanted to learn how to get to you in the penthouse. The driver was supposed to get in and tell them how to find us inside."

"Cell, what did you two do?"

"Nothing we haven't done before."

"That doesn't say much, does it, Yazzi?"

"We had to make sure the two of you were safe. Not to mention the children."

"Fine, Ren."

"Goodnight, Lena, good to have you home."

"Thanks, Marcellus. Goodnight, Yazmine".

"Goodnight."

Lena was glad to be home again. Nothing within the walls had changed except in the children's room. Lena lay in Ren's arms for a while, listening to the sounds of their home. The children were sleeping in the next room. Kai and Nomar discussed how exciting their trip had been so far on the other side of the penthouse. They liked the couple and we're glad that they could help them. Lena didn't want to eavesdrop, but she was glad they loved it. She hoped that they would become close friends.

"You are content, my love."

"Yes, I am. I love you, Lorenzo. I am happy to be with you."

"Things are about to get very dangerous. They need to make sure you don't become a vampire. They would have no control then, and they wouldn't be able to stop us."

"Ren, you have yet to tell me what is truly going on. Why did you wait so long to take me as your mate? And what is my place here?"

"I guess it's about time that I told you. Aren't you tired?"

"Nope, I took a nap. Now storytime," Lena replied and smiled up at him.

Chapter 18

Ren proceeded to tell his story from when he and Cell had arrived in New York. He reached the U.S. shore in the eighteenth century, the year 1750. He was in the city for the yellow fever outbreaks and the Great New York fire which destroyed the Trinity church.

Ren described the city so vividly that Lena visualized the city as though the memories were her own. He hadn't started the club for at least thirty years after he had arrived. The thought of wooden buildings instead of the stone ones they saw now was monumental. His first club wasn't even in the city but in present day Brooklyn. He said he wanted to familiarize himself with the city and how it would develop and change. So he started a bar with a brothel next door. He described it as if he had missed the place. He said it was something about its beginnings that touched him.

Lena couldn't help but wonder if Ren had seen himself dating or marrying a Black woman. She was curious if he owned slaves. She was pretty sure if he did, but knew that he wouldn't tell her. She cocked her head as she continued to listen.

There weren't many vampires in New York at that time. So he had to be very careful. Their presence needed to remain hidden. It was difficult because they couldn't heal the wounds they inflicted on their human counterparts. Ren noted that it was easier to feed from the prostitutes. No one cared about whether or not they were safe. In return, he sheltered them. That was how the bordello began. They were comfortable for quite a while. They remained in the same location for almost half a century, but it became difficult because they didn't age. For a time, they added makeup to their faces and powdered their hair. Some of their lodgers helped them in exchange for life eternal.

Ren admitted that the decision was a mistake. The women were new at controlling their urges. Then, one night, a woman fed from an unwilling client, and the disguise was up. Ren said he hated to, but he closed down the bordello and told the women who wanted to stay that they had to abide by his rules. Many stayed, and a few left to wreak havoc on another town.

Later during the Industrial Revolution, around 1818, he and Cell started Zoe's in its exact location. He said that the neighborhood at the time was nowhere near what it is today. They thought about resurrecting the brothel but decided against it. Angelo's didn't begin until the nineteen seventies. He said they realized as the vampire population grew, they would need another place to take their companions and feeders. Lena asked how long Marcia had been with them. Ren figured a little over a century or so, give or take a decade.

He didn't believe she was a threat but wasn't willing to swear to it.

Zoe's had been up and running for a while before Prohibition took effect. They called it a noble experiment. Wow, what a law it was, considering it influenced people to do just the opposite. Luckily, Ren's influence kept Zoe's going during that time. He managed to keep it running despite the increase in unemployment. And his little bar, which was by no means half the club's size today, was the place to be. Even the mayor and other council members visited at least once a month.

After her attack by Seth, Lena kept getting the feeling Marcia couldn't be trusted. Ren wasn't aware of her background or history. Cell had known her back in Argentina. Cell said the two of them were passing acquaintances. The club in New York brought them together. Marcia became a trusted member of the family. Still, she wasn't privy to everything. With almost a thousand years of walking the earth, Ren had taught himself to trust no one totally and completely. Cell was the closest to knowing nearly everything about him.

During the few minutes of silence, Lena took the opportunity to find Marcia. She wanted to prove to herself and Ren that her intuition was accurate, but she wasn't doing anything suspicious. At least not at that moment. Lena focused on Marcia's surroundings. She wasn't at the club. She figured Cell closed the club for the night because he would be there if Zoe's were open. The place was quiet. The bar looked like it was in Manhattan. She was sipping a drink. Yalena was about to stop watching when she saw Jon walk up to Marcia. Jon was one of the council members Lena didn't trust. He had agreed with the council members to kill her.

There had not been sound before when she retraced her steps. This time Lena heard the exchange between them. As if she was sitting right next to Marcia. "Wasn't expecting you to show."

"Of course. I wanted the update."

"Not much of one."

"Are they back?"

"Yes, they're back. Our driver was unsuccessful at getting into the penthouse. For some reason, she suspected him."

"How is that possible? She couldn't know he was a threat."

"Well, she did and warned Ren. He got past the front door, but that was all."

"Did you have a chance to talk to him?"

"Not before they got to him. He doesn't remember the little he did espy."

"How come you can't give us a layout?"

"Never been to the building, much less inside. Cell mostly stayed at the club, and he's extremely protective about his home."

"So in over a century, you haven't been to the man's real home? Fucking grand! Now what?"

Lena opened her eyes and searched the room. Ren was lost in thought, and she had sat up and away from him.

"Ren, I'm sorry, but I have to say. For whatever reason, Marcia is on the opposite side."

"Why would you say that?"

"I just saw her talking to Jon at a bar. He wanted to discern if we arrived yet and if she deciphered anything. She marked the driver. Maybe it's nothing, but still, this adds to my suspicions."

"We'll examine what happens. I'll deal with it. You'll have your hands full with the children. You're starting to show a little."

"A little? Seems more to me."

It was true. Lena had been away from New York for over a month. So, of course, since she was carrying triplets, her stomach showed more like she was about twenty weeks. This pregnancy had been more comfortable. Well, at first, anyway. After all, this was only the beginning. She was surprised it had not been worse. Then Ren touched her stomach, and the children pressed against his hand. She had felt them moving about before, but they had not responded to Ren's touch until then. Now they had connected with their father. As he spoke to them, they moved in response.

"Get some rest, Yalena. You will need it," Ren chided.

Yalena was already exhausted. All the traveling and training had taken its toll, and soon the three inside of her would require more than she felt she had. She closed her eyes as she turned on her side.

Ren stroked her hair and watched her fall asleep before getting up and going to his office. After being away from his business for over a month, he had a lot to catch up on.

He had asked Cell to check in on the restaurant. He sat in his chair and closed his eyes. He was tired, but he wanted to check his messages and video cameras before he rested. Ren hoped that Lockington and Akbar had left him some information. They seem to be the only two council members on his side. He didn't like being away from his businesses, but it was necessary if he and Lena were going to rule. Yalena's potency and strength increased since she returned. She would be the driving force that united the vampires all across the world.

He pressed play on the machine and listened to the few messages there were. Since Cell took over while he was gone, he was not bombarded with calls. Patrick called and told him to watch the video footage. Cell wanted him to know the council members frequented the club and the restaurant. Cell felt that was unusual. They did patronize both establishments but not often. It would appear they were trying to familiarize themselves with everything. Ren only guessed, but it seemed as though they were optimistic about their chances of ruling. If they did succeed, they would be in for a rude awakening. He knew all council members well enough to be cognizant of the fact that they wouldn't want to rule together. Therefore, their coup d'etat would put his realm in further turmoil by subjecting his people to a civil war.

Wow, Ren thought. He had never really considered what would happen if they succeeded. He was sure now that he and Yalena had to survive. The future of vampires and humans depended on him keeping his wife and children safe. He was sure that Yalena wasn't going to like it, but he would confine her to the penthouse after the next council meeting. He wasn't sure she would even make it. It was apparent that she would begin to feel the effects of the three growing in her womb. He didn't want to risk another pregnancy, but he figured that Sekhmet knew best.

Chapter 19

The following day, Ren made sure Yalena and their companions were comfortable and had all they desired, he left the penthouse. He was headed for the restaurant and the club. Ren complained to Lena that the council members had been snooping around the restaurant while he was gone. He disliked council members familiarizing themselves with his businesses. They both were worried that it would make things more dangerous. He said that even Cell didn't grasp the ramifications of the details he had given.

Lena had little interest in listening to Ren explain how the club and restaurant schedule went. It was even more difficult to focus as she sat with the twins. Knowing the council's intentions, Ren told her that he thought it was better to set up programs for the restaurant and the club that rotated. He didn't have to keep a program in either place. Each employee memorized their work schedule and where they worked. And on his personal computer in the penthouse was the rotating schedule and all the employees' names.

Lena nodded as he talked. Then, as if he knew she had only half listened, Ren kissed her cheek, picked up his jacket, and walked out of the door.

It was a good thing he had decided to come. He wasn't sure how long she had been there, but Madeline Pierre tried to convince Missy that it was okay to tell her about the schedule and the employees. She kept asking how many people worked at Angelo's.

"Missy, it's okay. I am here to help you in Ren's absence."

"Look, Mrs. Pierre, I got instructions, and I am not to discuss the schedule with anyone. We have been running quite well, thank you. I'm sure Mr. Arias will be back soon."

"Yes, I've been told so. I just wanted to know your chef's schedule. Do you have two or three different chefs here?" Ren thought the council was alerted to his return after the cab driver's performance the night before. Still, he marveled at Madeline's response to his entrance.

"Now, Madeline, why are you harassing my staff? This is my restaurant. Shouldn't you be running yours?"

"Y- yes," she stammered. "Well, I was trying to be helpful. You were gone so long; your staff seemed bewildered. I came here a couple of times a week, and I never had the same server."Ren had to hold back a smile. He decided not to acknowledge her observation. "Missy, was everything okay while I was gone?"

"Yes, sir. Everything ran smoothly as if you were here."

"Madeline, everything was fine. Thank you for wanting to help. I am sure we will be back on schedule soon." He smiled at Madeline, but Ren's face still appeared cold. It made him seem more predacious. "Will you be joining us for dinner later?"

"No, I have things to tend to, but if you're short staffed, I have someone who needs a job."

"I am remorseful, no present openings; thank you for all your help." After Madeline left, Ren locked the door and put the closed sign in the window. He asked Missy to turn on the music and called everyone to the back of the restaurant for a meeting. Then he closed all the blinds as everyone assembled in the back of Angelo's. As Ren walked toward them, he looked at the faces of his staff. Everyone was there except one. And instead of the beautiful blonde girl, there was a dark haired young man.

"Missy, where is Stacey?"

"She's been late and absent a lot while you were gone."

"And who is the newcomer?"

"Stefano Arias, Cell brought him a few weeks ago to cover for Stacey."

"I see."

"Well, look, here comes Ms. Stacey," one of the staff called out.

At first, Ren didn't recognize the blonde bombshell. She didn't seem like herself. She was paler than her usual tone, and her eyes were dull and glazed over. "Stacey, I'm going to ask you to stay in the front. I will be with you in a few. No one move. We have yet to begin." With that, Ren walked briskly toward her to get a better read of Stacey. Ren wanted to know if he was right about his suspicions. "Stacey, look at me."

She did as asked and stared into Ren's eyes. He could tell that someone compelled her, he could only guess why. She had bite marks on her neck and one on her arm. Both were poorly hidden behind makeup. Stacey sat quietly as Ren examined her. Then her hands began to tremble, and she pulled a knife from her boot. Ren pretended not to notice. He wanted to ruminate on her next move. He had been squatting in front of her. Ren stood upright before she struck. She had not adjusted her aim and stabbed him in the leg.

When she noticed where she had stabbed him, she began to scream that they would kill her. She became hysterical, and Ren wanted to comfort her and heal her wounds. He felt sorry for what had happened to Stacey. But, before he closed in, someone was standing between them. It caught him off guard, and he took several steps back. He hadn't seen anyone moving in the restaurant, furthermore moving toward him.

"Please, Ren, don't. You cannot save her now. She is already dead, I'm afraid. Please back away."

"Yalena, since when could you project yourself? And what do you mean she is already dead."

"I've been practicing with Sekhmet. I have been watching for almost an hour on and off. When you called your meeting and noticed she wasn't there, I looked for her. Someone I didn't recognize dropped her here with the promise that they would stop hurting her and give her the antidote for the poison if she succeeds. I guess they figured she could stab you, and it would slow you down. I have already asked Patrick to send Kiyoshi and a few guards. They should be picking the vamps up as I speak. I had Kai call 911, but I am unsure if they can help her. I don't believe she should become one of us either." With that, Lena disappeared. It wasn't long after Lena vanished that Stacey collapsed on the floor. Her body began to convulse. The ambulance had just arrived, and medics were on their way through the unlocked door Stacey had opened.

The paramedics asked a few questions as they worked on her. It didn't seem as though she would survive. Ren stood near, calculating for a moment. He perceived who had tried this. The person probably thought that Ren would be injured and weak. If Seth could kill him, he would try to force Lena to be his queen. He didn't believe the council knew about this strike.

As the paramedics whisked Stacey into the ambulance, one of his soldiers walked through the restaurant door. "Patrick said I should be with you at every turn he isn't there for."

"You believe you're up to it?"

"Absolutely. Kiyoshi and the rest are doing rounds." Ren nodded. Yes, he is, Ren thought to himself. One of the strongest of his soldiers after Kiyoshi.

"The others are resting. I believe they will soon be active."

"Thank you, John."

Ren turned toward his employees in the back of the restaurant and began his walk to them. He could tell they were in shock; no one said a word. "Okay, this is a perilous time. I am unsure how much you know or have heard about what's going on. Whatever schedule you are on should be known by two people; myself and you. No one needs to know what schedule you're on. No one who is looking out for your best interest will ever ask. Anyone does, I need you to tell me. Does everyone here have my number?" All of the staff nodded except for Stefano.

"If I'm not there, you can speak with Patrick. Stefano, I will give the number to you before I leave. Any questions or problems about your shift no longer goes through Stacey or Missy. Please call me directly." Ren paused to observe the faces of each of his crew. No one responded or reacted. There were a few nodes.

"So, does everyone know why all of this is happening?" Despite the question, Ren didn't wait for a response. "Vampires have threatened my wife, and I guess myself now. So we all need to be careful. Anyone who wants to take a leave of absence will be allowed to do so. You can take your leave of us now, call me, and we'll discuss how it will work." Ren paused to see if anyone volunteered to leave. "Fine, be careful. If the situation becomes more dangerous, I'll close down Angelo's until it's over. I don't want anyone else hurt."

"We hear the talk from our customers here and at the club," stated an employee.

"Yeah, my lover tells me everything. We'll be fine. The only reason they got to Stacey was because they lured her in with the promise of being a vampire," stated another.

"Anyone else want to be one? We can arrange it, but **it** will not change the danger. I'm afraid I can't have you work until you've learned to control the urge once you've changed." No one spoke but instead looked around at each other. "Fine, get back to work. I'll be back tomorrow. Oh, Arias, come here." Ren gave his new employee his number and then left. He had to check in at the club.

When he reached Zoe's, things ran almost as smoothly as if he were there. He didn't find any new employees or council members snooping. He would remember to check with Cell about Stefano.

"Now darlings, where were we before daddy started to complain?" Kissa pointed to a picture in a book Lena had been reading to them. After reading to them for a while, Lena called Kai to feed the children and put them down for a nap. She wanted to check in with Ren. She figured he had arrived at the restaurant by then.

It was as if she was a bird on his shoulder. She saw everything he did. As he walked towards Angelo's, he focused on what was going on inside. Lena looked toward the restaurant, but it was fuzzy until Ren entered.

"Yalena, Yalena."

"Yes?"

"Are you alright?"

"Yes, thank you, Kai. I'm just tired."

"Well, rest. You have been through a lot. I hope you're not further exhausting yourself."

"I'm afraid I was. But with good cause."

"Watching out for the Mister."

"How did you know?"

"Oh please, you came to train from the goddess herself. I'm well aware of what Sekhmet is capable of, and you soon will wheel most of that power. Still, you're most like me. So I know you're exhausted."

"Will you keep an eye on the children?" Kai nodded. "Thank you, Kai."

"Sure. I will ask Nomar to take them for a walk."

"NO!" Kai's eyes grew wide with surprise. Lena knew she had never yelled before. She calmed herself. "No, they cannot; we cannot leave the building. It isn't safe. They will hurt my babies."

"Okay, not outside. Maybe in the new playroom." Lena smiled and gave a slight nod. She was tired, and the weight of her eyelids was too much to bear. She fell asleep.

While at the club, Ren decided to take inventory of the central refrigerators. He needed to discern any missing reserves. Seth had been a sickly child and young adult. Ren had heard that the young Joel had drunk his dying father's blood, completely changing him. He became more potent, but he had not matched the strength of any of the counsel. Ren thought about it a little longer. There was a notable difference between vampires and dhampirs. Even if their parents chose to make them full vampires by drinking the blood of one, they were never as strong.

Yalena's family brought another variable to the equation. Her grandmother had never been like other dhampirs; still, she was born and grew most human looking. He was told that her mother's pregnancy with her had passed the normal gestation for dhampirs. Based on his knowledge and experiences, dhampirs usually had five months gestation, possibly six, but Marguerite was born almost three months later than she should have been. Yalena's pregnancy was a little shorter than five months. Kissa and Kamau were nothing like dhampirs in appearance, behavior, or anything else for that matter. His children were beautiful. Everything about them leads one to believe that they were full fledged vampires. Even though dhampirs are very intelligent, their appearances usually left something more to be desired. Even his first children were strange looking. More animal than human. Maybe a trait in the bloodlines.

Now back to his original question. What was making Seth so strong? Someone had to be giving him part of their private stock. But who? And which supply was he feeding? He headed for the basement cold room.

As Ren walked through the rows of refrigerators, he noted that they were short by more than fifty blood bags. It wasn't just one person's reserve missing. Several of Cell's, Marcia's, and more than half of his stock were gone.How was that possible? He had not used that much of his stock before. How did he not notice? But, of course, he had not used the club refrigerators other than to move some of his stock. He fed her more than usual but still. He would need to check the scan log. Every family member's fingerprints were a part of the database. That was how he set up their system. No need for keys, each person had a code they would input after their fingers pressed against the scanning pad. He decided to check the log from his office. On his walk to the stairs that lead to his office on the top floor, he came across Marcia.

"Hey Ren, you're back. From where might I ask?"

"Yes, we're all back. Couldn't stay away too long."

"Yes, you are much needed here."

"I realize that. If you see Cell, tell him I'm in my office."

"Of course."

As Ren walked up the next flight of stairs, he wondered if his beloved Yalena was on to something about Marcia. After Cell, she had the most access to everything in the Club. She had been looking out for the club whenever Ren was away. He would have to check the rest of the reserves in his office and for their family.As he checked his databases for all reserve storage areas, he noticed something quite interesting. Yalena had been right about Marcia. She had been removing much of the blood bags from all three areas. Funny how he never thought to check the reserve before now. They had used some blood for their soldiers, but more blood was missing than they regularly allotted.

It appeared that other than Cell the day that Seth poisoned Yalena, none of the family members had used the reserve in more than a month. He would shut down the access panel. Anyone needing blood would require his permission to access refrigerators. Why had it never occurred to him before to check the reserve? Did he need to do everything for them to be safe? That would be draining. At least for now, he would make a mental note to keep an eye on it. He would wait until Yalena could assume some of the responsibility for the family. It would make his life easier.

If Seth were using the reserve, he would soon run low. Since the reserve loss had only been happening a little over a month, he wondered what Seth had done with the blood. He would need over two hundred bags to create soldiers. And if he were drinking it all himself, he would do more damage to himself than he seemed to be aware.Marcia was going to be surprised when she tried to get into the reserve. How was he going to stop Seth? He would have to make sure all of his soldiers were up and ready. They would need the soldiers to protect his family and his club.

"Kai... Kai."

"Yes, Yalena. Are you alright?"

"I don't feel well at all. I thought I was hungry, but the thought of food is making my stomach heave."

"Oh, dear. Nomar and Candace are in the basement. Ren said not to leave you alone. Perhaps my blood would help."

"Don't mean to be obnoxious, but the smell of your blood does little to help."

"Not at all?" Lena slowly shook her head no. "Does your penthouse have an intercom, perhaps?"

"I'm not sure, actually, but if you call Patrick, he can help. He can go to Nomar or perhaps stay with me."

"Silly of me. Of course. I don't see him, so I forget he is here. Do I just call him?"

"Yes, he is probably in the office." It would appear that Patrick had been listening because he was there before Kai called for him.

"My Queen, how can I help?"

"Patrick, who is watching the Penthouse."

"No need to worry. Soldiers will always guard you. As the soldiers finish their training, they start work. Now how can I help you?"

"I believe I need to feed. Nomar has gone to the playroom downstairs with Candace and the children. Can you stay with me while Kai goes to get them?"

"Of course. No need to ask. Kai, I am always with Yalena unless Lorenzo is home. If you need to run out, just let me know. And if you ever want to leave the building, please tell me so that I may arrange a guard for you as well."

"Yes, of course. Wow, there's even a guard for me."

"Of course. You and your husband are companions and feeders for our sovereign and his queen. Your safety is important." Kai nodded and left to retrieve Nomar.

"Too bad, we don't have a courtyard."

"Yes, of course, Yalena. However, the two buildings would share the courtyard. So unless Ren owned that as well, you still would be unable to use it."

"I want to go out, Patrick."

"I am afraid that is not possible. It's imperative that I keep you safe. Things will ease soon. Well, within a couple of years."

"A couple of years isn't soon."

"In comparison to how long Lorenzo has waited for you, two years is a blink of an eye."

"When you put it like that, I wish I could be more useful."

"You are fulfilling the most important of jobs right now. You are creating the council that will protect our way of life for thousands of years to come."

Lena took a deep breath. "I wish I could spend more time with my children. Since they don't nurse anymore, they hardly come to see me."

"Ren has instructed all of us to keep the children occupied. They should keep their distance. Their presence can trigger the early birth of those you carry. I assure you they miss you very much. The playroom seems to be the only thing to keep them content."

Wow, she thought. Could the connection between the children be so strong as to trigger premature birth? She still had about two and a half months to go.

Chapter 20

The following two months were uneventful. One would guess they would be grateful for the grace period, but it made Arias's clan more anxious. Lena had expressed to Ren that she was also stunned. Without any danger, his beloved had spent most of her time, either asleep or sketching out her reading ancient texts. Since the children inside his wife were growing so quickly, Ren moved the meeting date up so that she could attend. At a little over three months, her stomach was huge. Carrying two babies was more than uncomfortable, so three children growing at a tremendous rate was unbearable.

Ren brought her to the club early to rest. Plus, he didn't want her to deal with the crowds. He wasn't sure what their clan would think. Knowing that recently, she had given birth, and here she was again, ventricose with child.

"Babe, are you okay?"

"Sure. Ren, please tell me the council meeting is soon. I don't want to be here, and I don't want to wait here by myself while you run around and take care of business."

"You won't be alone. I am here."

"Really?" Ren nodded. "I've missed you. You've been so busy. And we haven't done more than sleep together over the last few weeks."

"It was necessary, babe. There has been quite a bit to take care of, and I didn't want to have to leave your side during your last month." There was silence for a while. Finally, Lena lay on her side, and Ren curled his body protectively around hers. He rubbed her round protruding belly. Lena took a deep breath and let it out slowly as she relaxed into him.

"I am not sure I can stay away from you for six months after the children are born."

"Maybe you should change me after the triplets are born."

"That isn't what Sekhmet told us."

"I'm not sure my body can take any more pregnancies. I am so tired all the time. And I feel so weak. Instead of my face being round and full because I am pregnant, it appears thin and drawn."

"I know they are taking their toll, my love. You seem to eat and drink constantly. Your feeding is back to that of three vampires. I have already had to bring in blood for our home reserve. Nomar can't keep up. I may allow these three to come early."

"What will happen to them if they're early?"

"I am unsure, my love. I will not lose you to this or ever. We'll be fine. Is it okay if I leave you to bring you something to eat?"

"Yes, I am tired. Please lock the door."

"Kiyoshi is right outside." Lena smiled but didn't answer. It had been a while since she had seen Patrick's lieutenant. She was already too tired to reply. She fell asleep before Ren left her side.

"Any unusual activity tonight?"

"No, Ren. Everything is quiet and peaceful. Of course, the council has not arrived. Patrick said to let you know he's making rounds." Ren nodded as he proceeded to the elevator. Patrick had started walking the club in his invisible form since Ren and Lena were in Africa. He thought it was a good idea to continue doing so with things how they were. Ren had no clue how he managed to walk around a crowded club, but it had proven helpful in gathering pertinent information about the clans. With his soldiers taking care of their safety and the clubs running smoothly, it meant he had more time to be with his beloved wife. He had spent the last month working on his business. He was getting rid of any person or process that would put himself or his family in harm's way. He wanted everything to run so smoothly that it would become apparent when something was amiss.

Unfortunately, that meant less time at home with Lena. She had not complained at all. She opened her eyes to greet him when he got into the bed to lay beside her, and she hugged him before he left for the restaurant. Despite all she was going through, Lena had been outstanding. He was genuinely grateful for Kai and her family. Without them, Lena would be alone often. Ren worried about his wife. She was beginning to look gaunt and sickly. Her pregnancy was not as painful as the first. She remembered to move with ease to avoid jarring the triplets, but they drained every ounce of life from her. Even his blood made little difference when she fed from him. Her mom cooked for her every day. Between her regular feedings with Nomar and the blood she drank from the reserve, she should have had enough nutrients in her system to support herself and the babies.

Lena had told Ren about Sekhmet's concerns. The two link almost every day. Well, in reality, Sekhmet connected with Lena. Lena didn't have enough energy to link with Sekhmet, but there wasn't much she was able to do other than send her healing energy. Ren could always tell when the two linked. Lena would look like a reflection of her former self. So radiant and healthy with such a glow, but they took that from her within less than a day.

Maybe, Ren thought, he should allow their children to interact with their siblings. A premature birth may not be so horrible. Lena would be four months soon. The constant interaction between Lena and her twins may entice the triplets to become part of this world sooner than expected. But, of course, he longed for his wife so much he understood that he would not be able to stay away from her loving comfort, possibly if he didn't come home. He could leave Kai and Nomar to care for her for a time, but his Yalena would not stand for such distance between the two of them. She could endure a day or two, at the most a week. But he could not stay away. He loved her and longed to savor and explore her again, yet he would have to restrain himself. Even a month or two would help. If she got pregnant right away, her body would not support the life that grew within her, that is to say the least. If her body couldn't support itself, it would be of little help to the children.

He stopped outside the kitchen door. He hadn't paid attention as he walked the halls, yet here he stood. He stopped and took a deep breath before entering the kitchen to supervise the cooking of her food. He would feed again before allowing her to feed directly from him; at least, he would have that closeness--his blood running through her expecting body.

"You are friggin' huge!"
"Not in the least bit funny, Theolonius."

"Seriously, Lena, you have got to stop popping out these little vamps."

"Soon. Very soon. I have not seen you in a while. Where have you been?"

"Yes, I'm sorry. I did stop by, honestly. I met Kai and Nomar and their brood. Honestly, honey, your family keeps growing; actually expanding is a better word. Anyway, you were sound asleep, and I didn't want to wake you. Ren told me they are draining you."

"You have no idea. They absorb my essence and strength." Yalena gave a slight smile. "But they're sweet. They are not as active as they used to be. The children are quiet. Their touch is gentle. It will be over soon."

"I hope so. I miss my friend. I have no one to party with." Theo smiled as he walked around to the other side of the bed to glance at his friend's face. He paused before he spoke, his smile gone. Yalena was all eyes looking up at him. Her face was drawn and hard. She didn't have the sweet round face and smiling cheeks as before. It took him a few moments before he spoke again. Lena knew she barely resembled her former self. Her triplets had taken it all. She was all stomach now, like the emaciated children the organizations show you to make you pity them and give them money. The difference was that Lena was pregnant, not starving. Her stomach lay there, heavy and oblong in front of her. Who would have thought a woman's abdomen would stretch to such an extent in any pregnancy?

"Speak to me, Theo. I know it's scary. I have mirrors at home. No matter how Kai and Ren try to distract me, I see it, even in their eyes."

"Lena, I am sorry. I wasn't expecting them to have drained you so. I don't think you should have anymore. The first two were a piece of cake in comparison."

"I am not in pain. The first two were painful. I am at peace; they are at peace. I am just tired a lot." Theo sat gently on the bed in front of her. He took her hand just as gently, afraid that she would break if he held her hand too hard. "Guess I look like I will break, but I am strong. I will be fine."

"You see, if you had just listened to me and stayed away from him, you'd be fine."

"I don't regret anything. We all have our developmental burdens." Lena closed her eyes again. She hadn't moved or raised any of her appendages. She hadn't walked, but she was tired. When Ren came back to the room, Theo was still there.

Ren glared as Theo brushed a curl out of her face.

"Why couldn't you have left her alone?"

"Let it go, Theo. She will be well again soon."

"Her countenance appears worse than when they poisoned her."

"She will be fine. And she can hear you. Now leave us. She needs to feed." Theo didn't reply. He just kissed Lena's forehead and hesitated before getting up to leave. "She'll be fine, Theo. Leave."

Ren placed the food tray on the table before carefully crawling into bed beside her. He gazed at her with such passion in his eyes, watched and worried. She will be fine, he repeatedly told himself. She will be back to her beautiful self after their birth. The triplets would exude all of the beauty and energy they had imbibed from their mother. Then Ren would have his Yalena back, even if it was just a few months before she was pregnant again. Ren didn't understand why Sekhmet would want to push her like this. Force her human body past its limitations.

He sighed as he stroked her hair. The children were moving slowly inside of her. She had given so much of herself to be with him. He only hoped that he would be the mate she deserved. Once this was over, she would be her brilliant self again. He decided to move her. He cradled her neck and legs in the crook of each arm and brought her body against his. She was warm. Even in her delicate state, her body radiated warmth. That, of course, brought a smile to his face. He cradled her in his lap.

She was his. He had searched the world for her for more than half of his vampire life. Over seven centuries he traveled looking for the mate Lockington promised him after he was sired. The memory of his change and the events thereafter were still clear to him. As though it were just yesterday, instead of nine hundred years. He didn't believe it at first. After his transformation, Serna explained it to him. She said that he was created to rule the vampire world. He laughed at her at first. He thought she had damned him for her perverse pleasure. Why else would a person change him? Almost a year before she let him return home to his wife. She told him he had to gain his full strength first. She wanted him to meet others like himself and her sire, Heru Khuti Seker. Ren thought that was an odd name. Still, he figured he didn't have much choice, so he stayed and met him. He listened to Heru Khuti before he returned to his beloved Marisol. Less than six months after he returned to Serna, begging for her guidance after Marisol's death.

Lena stirred in his lap and brought Ren back from his memories. "Lena, are you alright?"

"Yes, Ren. I just need to stretch a little." He gently laid her on her side in the bed before she uncurled her legs and stretched her arms above her head. She moved slowly so as not to startle her children. Yet, as tired and voluminous as she was, he noticed that she still exuded grace and a hint of seduction in her movement.

"Would you like to feed now," Ren asked.

"Yes, I would." Ren kneeled beside her swollen abdomen and bent over her. Lena laced her fingers together around his neck. He slid his arms under her to lift her once again onto his lap. Their eyes met as he lifted her, and a sly smile crossed his lips. "What are you thinking about that you look like a predator hunting prey?"

"That you are mine."

"And," she asked.

"That together, we produce powerful offspring." He stared as a slight smile reached her full lips and briefly touched her eyes. "We have brought beautiful children into a dangerous world. We must keep them safe."

"Who is keeping them safe now?"

"Our family is well taken care of, Lena. They are safe."

"But Patrick is...." Ren placed his finger lightly against her lips.

"Our family is safe. Now you said you wish to feed." Yalena nodded as she curled into him ever so slightly. It had been a while since she had fed from Ren. She more than enjoyed the flavor of his blood on her tongue. Ren cradled her head to the hollow of his neck. She licked at the skin over the vein that held the beating pulse in his neck. The savoriness of him awakened her body. It had been too long since her body caressed her husband. She longed for their bodies to join. As she sank her teeth into him, his body jerked. She could only imagine how her feeding made his body react. She was sure that it awakened a hunger he couldn't quench. She held him closer as his body hardened against her. She drank from him until her blood lust was satiated.

"You seem so much better, my love."

"Yes, now that your blood flows through me. But now you are pale."

"I will rectify that soon. I just want you to feel better."

"I do. You've fed from the reserve tonight."

"I fed from someone who fed from the reserve. A private blood bank if you will."

"Do you do this often?"

"No, it is not safe to practice it often, but Theo was more than willing to help. Now eat my love."Lena obliged. He had propped her up on pillows so that she could rest against them and sit up. She was surprised by how hungry she was. The blood only increased her appetite. By the time she finished, she was content, and it was time for the council meeting. Neither Ren nor Lena were looking forward to the forum, but it was necessary.

Ren picked her up and carried her to the council room. He didn't want them to think she was weak, so he put her down right before opening the door. His blood had done the trick. She walked steadily with just his hand lightly pressed on the small of her back. Everyone stood up when they entered. It was apparent by their gasps and shocked faces that they didn't have a clue that she was pregnant again.

"All may be seated," Ren stated as he pulled out Lena's chair for her to sit.

"Well, that explains why you've moved up the meeting by a couple of weeks. She looks like she will be ready to pop any second now," said Jon.

"My goodness. You didn't have to put her through all of this. You should have had her conference call in," commented Muhammed.

"Would you have believed me if you did not see her for yourself," asked Ren.

"He's got a point," replied Jon.

Smoothing her raven hair, Madeline asked, "We take it the Prince and Princess of our clan are well?"

"Indeed," Lena replied

Lockington smiled as he asked. "So Ren, how many do we have the pleasure of welcoming into the world this time?"

"Three."

"Triplets, how delightful. So Yalena of Sekhmet's noble line; will you claim what is rightfully yours?" Lena had become better at keeping her composure, but once again, she was surprised. Ren neglected to tell her no more than what was necessary for her survival. Claiming her place as ruler of vampires was never really discussed. Sekhmet jested about it. It would seem today's vampires made a joke also. She always assumed that Ren would rule. She knew that none of them genuinely wanted such a thing. Anyone who tried to claim it became a target for assassination.

"I believe that isn't my utmost concern at this moment. Healthy children have been my concern for almost a year with you. Maybe at a later date or century. I haven't gotten the impression that vampires are willing to come under noble rule. Ren has been ruling well enough. Although, he is more lenient with his subjects. If I were to take my rightful place, Seth would have been hunted and beheaded for his behavior and lack of regard for the rules, not to mention his assassination attempts on my life. And anyone who helps him would receive the same sentence," Lena paused looking into the eyes of her grandfather who sat on the other side of the table.

"Of course, Madeline. Ren knows what it is like to lose a child. So he has allowed your indigent offspring's life." Lena watched each face as she spoke. She saw a flicker of fear in their eyes. Even Mohammed and Lockington were a little uneasy. "So, to answer your question again, no. My concern right now is healthy children. I leave ruling to my more than capable and caring sovereign. Now you must excuse me; I have little energy these days. You don't need me to discuss expansion. Also, I discourage creating any new vampires, at least until we can control what we have. Ren, please."

Ren stood up and helped Yalena to the door. Once they were outside, the guard closed the door behind them, and Ren picked her up and carried her to the third floor room.

"Ren, why is it that you neglect to tell me the next step at every turn?"

"I am truly sorry, my love. We still spend so little time together. I forget anything else that doesn't have to do with your safety, but you handled that well. Except now, they are going to be wary of you. You called me lenient."

"Maybe I pushed a little too hard. I wanted them to grasp that I am not going to be bullied." There was silence for a moment between them. Then, finally, Ren placed Lena gently on the sofa and sat beside her. His hand spanned over her huge belly as he turned her face toward him to kiss her. "Mhmm, do you understand how much I miss you?"

"It is mutual, my love."

"What's going on in the room, Ren?"

"They have only murmured a few exclamations here and there. Let's turn on the surveillance, shall we." Lena nodded at his suggestion. Indeed the room was quiet. Muhammed was the first to speak.

"This is ridiculous. Is everyone scared? She can do nothing if she is dead." Lena gazed at Ren. She knew he was supposed to be on their side, but did he have to be so convincing?

"Do you think she knows what we plan?"

"That is not possible."

"Isn't it. She is from the line of Sekhmet."

"Okay, let's not get ahead of ourselves. We have all reviewed what there is to find Sekhmet. She doesn't have the power of reading minds or seeing into the future."

"But we don't know all of it. There is no definitive account."

"I wish Seth would let me put a sniper on her, but he wants to get close and personal. After today, there is no way Ren's bringing her back out of the penthouse."

"For sure, and she has to be strong. You observed how steadily she carried her three. As huge as her stomach is, she didn't even falter at all. I suspect they will be born soon."

"Yes, and that puts them closer to what we don't want."

"I heard something from Marcia that may give us a little more time."

Yalena quickly glimpsed at Ren; she wondered what secret Lockington would betray. She wondered where his true allegiance lay.

"Well, Lockington, spit it out."

"Jon, keep your knickers on. I heard they are going to try for a third pregnancy."

"That is preposterous. There was nothing in the legend about five, furthermore six or seven."

"Muhammed, I am just relaying what I heard."

Madeline folded her pale hands and placed them on the table. "Well, that means the game has changed, gentlemen. The only way to stop it is to kill her."

"Unless you can arrange that sniper," replied Jon. "I say hail and long live the Queen."

Before the conversation continued any further, Ren entered the conference room once again. It took all of his self control not to execute everyone in the room immediately for treason, but that would result in a war he didn't want, and he wasn't sure it would be beneficial. Both sides would be decimated in a battle. The family heads acting alone was one thing. If he eliminated them immediately, the families would be angry. As far as they were concerned, there would be no just cause. He framed a smile on his face and sat once again before the council.

"Sorry about the interruption. Yalena needs her rest. The little tykes are taking their toll."

"Does that mean you'll turn her soon?" Ah, he thought, now they are trying to confirm Lockington's rumor.

"We haven't decided. We'll see how her body does in birth."

"A little bird told us you were going to try one last time." Ren deliberately shot Lockington with a look of contempt. He wanted to make them feel that Lockington was a reliable source, his confidant if you will. Madeline's face wore a smile, and she steepled her hands in front of her. Now they would fall for anything Lockington told them. Ren looked around at the council members.

"As I said, we'll see how the birth goes." There was a moment of silence, finally broken by Cell's entrance into the meeting. "I managed to compile a list of all ruling clans and families worldwide. "Cell is handing out the ten most influential. Once they are on our side, the others will follow."

"And the list of the others?"

"I have it on my trusty database." Ren waited for that to register. All heads turned to him, and Madeline's eyebrows shot up. Yes, Ren thought, take the bait. "Each of you takes one. Visit them. We will reconvene in two months, and you can tell me what you find. Then we go to the other list. Over a hundred and fifty ruling families all together. And we will control it all."

"Yes," everyone murmured and smiled. Ren was pretty sure they were smiling at the prospect of ruling, not bringing their world together. Either way, he would let it play out. Each of the people on the list was a friend from before he controlled New York. He'd spoken to each one, and they had pledged their allegiance to him and their Queen, the First Line of Sekhmet. He was curious to learn how each of the ten would deal with the treason of the council. Already Jon and Madeline were volunteering to split the list so that Lockington and Muhammed wouldn't have to leave the state. Each, in turn, promised to oversee the property of Jon and or Madeline.

Everyone filed out of the conference room except Mohammed. He was the last to stand, taking his time to smooth his shirt over his portly belly. Ren was on his way out of the door, hoping Lockington would eventually find his way to his office. However, before he could leave the room, Muhammed cleared his throat.

"Muhammed, can I be of assistance?"

"I offer my last piece of information to you. They are going to hire a sniper or an assassin."

"Well, thank you very much, Muhammed, but you say this is your last."

"Yes, I am going out of the country. Back home, actually. I will be safe there. When they think they've got the upper hand, they will put an end to myself and my family. I cannot allow that to happen. So please keep an eye out for my small area. I would appreciate it. And I am in your debt."

"No, Muhammed, I am in yours. Thank you for your help. Would you like an escort to make sure you and your family are safe?"

"I don't want to draw attention to myself."

"They won't. Patrick is right outside. Tell him to send a friend with a car. They will take you anywhere you want to go."

"Thank you." Sure enough, Patrick was outside and helped Muhammed safely arrive at the airport, where his family was waiting for him. Ren wondered how Madeline and Jon would view Muhammed's extended vacation if they returned. The only person he would have to worry about would be Seth, with them out of the way. Well, and the assassin.

Once Ren left the conference room, he headed for his office, where Lockington was waiting. He was sitting behind Ren's desk with his feet crossed on top of it, one of Ren's cigars hanging from his mouth.

"Nice to see you have made yourself comfortable."

"Of course. I figured my grandson-in-law wouldn't mind me getting comfortable. I guess Muhammed told you about the assassin?"

"Yes."

"Jolly good."

"Drop the English accent."

"Sorry, can't do that, old boy. I've been speaking like this for over three centuries. That makes it a habit."

"Sure, Heru Khuti. We have a message from your mom." Ren saw that he had struck a nerve.

"Refrain from using that name. How is dear old mum?"

"Ready to move on."

"Oh, let me guess. She is ready for me to take her place."

"Yes."

"Ha! Not going to happen. Do you know once I go, I can never leave except to move on?"

"Well, it is your duty. Yalena and I will have to follow one day."

"You've got each other. I would be alone."

"Oh, please, spare me. I'm sure you can take someone, or someone would be willing to serve you."

"Yeah, yeah. Perhaps in a few centuries, after I become tired of this tedious life. Serving under a man less than ten times my junior."

"We were wondering how old you were."

"How long do you expect my granddaughter to last if you keep getting her pregnant so soon after her first pregnancy? Her body can't take anymore."

"I am worried that we're pushing it. But you know how things are."

"Yes, I do. That is still no bloody excuse to rush her into death. Are you truly going to try for one more?"

"Yes, your mom said one more, but she is worried about Yalena. None of us expected them to take such a toll. The twins in the last pregnancy are supposed to be like the first. She won't survive that if she doesn't give birth soon."

"Well, you've got to change her soon. She needs all of her powers."

"You're going to have to go home for that to happen."

"Is that what my wonderful mum told you? Oh no. The only reason she's alive is that she has Sekhmet's powers."

"Really?"

"Oh, your children are going to be fierce, and I want to be around to train my grands. Well, I've stayed long enough. I'll be around more after this is all over. Ta-tah."

"Yeah, yeah." Ren sat in his leather chair behind his desk. The weight on his shoulders threatened to crush him beneath it. So much for a peaceful time. He was sure they would come after him with all they had before they left to visit clan leaders in other states. He perceived that in the end, Seth would be his most formidable opponent. He wasn't as strong as Ren but he was strategically sneaky, he would catch them totally off guard like when Lena was poisoned. Ren knew that he needed to prepare for anything. They at least have an idea of what the council is coming with, but Seth would make this close and personal before he even attempted to go after them.

He took a deep breath to try and shake off the dread he felt to his bones. He recognized that it was going to be close and dangerous. Even after Jon and Madeline are contained, their family would be a challenge. Yalena would need to be ready. He would tell her everything. After all, it was long overdue. He shut down his computer and locked up his office. If anyone tried to break in, he would know, and they would be in for a surprise. He didn't keep any vital information on his work system, and his home and office computers weren't linked.

He walked from his office to the room where he left Yalena. When he entered the room, she was asleep on the couch. She had curled up into a ball with one arm draped over her extended belly. Ren paused in the doorway and gazed at her. For a moment, he allowed himself to wonder if she would have been safe if he had not desired her. Suppose he had allowed her to come and go from the club without meeting and his decree. Would she have been safe? He shook off the doubt as one would shake the snow off of a jacket. She was his now, and he would keep her safe.

He needed to speak with Cell before he left the club. He wanted to spend a few days at home with his family. He had missed them. The twins' growth had slowed down considerably, yet according to Kai, their abilities and mental capacity were startling. They were brilliant. Still, he didn't want to rush them into his world. They would be a part of it for a very long time.

When he reached the DJ booth, he glanced at his watch. Hours had passed while he sat in his office. It was now a quarter after one. The club would still be pumping. So, of course, Cell was standing over his equipment, looking from his booth at the club below.

"You've been closed off for a while. I was wondering if I would see you."

"I know. So much on my mind. Things are getting intense."

"Yeah, I know. People sense it. I've heard rumors. People think you're keeping her prisoner. Some are beginning to wonder if you are so wonderful, after all. They haven't seen her since Halloween. When they ask, I tell them the truth. She's expecting and that you are worried about her safety. People know of the threat. But."

"But they still need to lay eyes on her. Do you think now would be a good time?"

"No, she looks too sickly."

"Where is Marcia?"

"Around, I guess. We haven't been hanging out lately. She was miffed about not being able to access the reserve. What was that about?"

"There is a substantial amount of the reserve missing. So anyone wanting to enter has to go through me.

"Whoa, I didn't know. That's not good at all. She asked me if I could talk to you so that she could enter. But I said no, she's mad at me."

"I see. Well, keep your eyes and ears open. I want to know who took it and who's using it."

"Got ya."

"I'm going to be spending some time at home. Keep an eye on things. Let me know what's going on. And don't let in any strays, please."

"Got you. I don't think you'll have to worry about Jon or Madeline. They seemed quite excited about that list."

"Alright. Good night, then."

"Good night." Ren wanted to leave his club and make it home to his children. He knew Lena would be happy to have him home, even if it was only for a couple of days.

He walked into the view room just in time to witness Marcia trying to get Lena to eat something, but Lena refused.

"Ren, I'm glad you're here. Surely you can get her to eat this."

"I brought her food earlier. If she is hungry, I will arrange something." Ren regarded Marcia's reaction. If he hadn't known her, he wouldn't have noted the very subtle change in her facial expression before her face resumed her concerned look.

"Ren, she is wasting away. She must eat. Why put yourself through the trouble of getting something ready when I have a delectable bowl of soup."

"Nothing is given to Lena unless I witness the cook sample it, but since the cook isn't here, perhaps you would like to try it for her."

"But I'm not hungry. I fed before I came up to check on her. Besides, I hate human food."

Ren took a deep breath. Did she think she was going to fool him with this ridiculous charade? "Tell the cook, thank you, but no thank you. Of course, I will see you tomorrow."

"Of course." Ren was sure that Marcia didn't think Lena sensed anything wrong. But, Lena and Ren hoped that she would do something more obvious to tip her hand.

Ren walked over to the couch and knelt in front of Lena, still half asleep. He took her hand in his and kissed it as she opened her eyes and gazed up at him.

"I told her I didn't want it. It just smelled all wrong."

Ren shook his head. "We have a lot to talk about. Let's go home," Ren replied. Lena sat up on the couch and smiled at Ren. Then, for the first time in weeks, she stood up by herself as she gazed into Ren's eyes.

"You're looking stronger, and your face looks better. Feel up to seeing your subjects? They are anxious about you and are starting to think I am up to no good with you."

"I believe that an appearance on the balcony is fine." So Ren carried her to the second floor balcony, where he opened the door and set her down on her feet. She saw Patrick's shimmer slightly to her left, and Ren was standing on her right. It seemed that Cell knew they were there because the spotlight came on, and people began to look up. A gasp followed the silence.

"Ren, do I look okay?"

"Radiant, my love," Ren replied as he handed her the microphone. She looked at Ren, puzzled, before taking it.

"Just wanted to greet my clan and family. Ren and I have heard some disheartening tales. I want you to know I am well. Our children are well. I am in good hands. I haven't been out much since I am expecting again." Lena paused due to the cheer that went through the crowd. Then someone yelled over the murmuring that followed.

"Is it true, there have been attempts on your life."

Lena looked at Ren. She didn't know what else she should say. Ren nodded, so she figured she could tell the truth. "Yes, unfortunately, there have been attempts. As you can see, our king is doing a fabulous job of keeping me safe. No need to worry. Well, good night. Until next time." The crowd cheered as the light went out. Lena took a step through the door before Ren picked her up. They were followed by Patrick.

Chapter 21

They returned home to a sleeping family. Ren told Patrick to go home, and Kiyoshi took his place. Ren didn't want to take any chances now. The guards would rotate. Someone would always be on watch, and because of the new threat, he would have the glass in the building changed to bulletproof glass.

Lena hadn't stirred much since she had fallen asleep in the cab. When Ren placed her on the bed, she opened her eyes and stretched. "My love."

"Yes, Ren. I feel as though I have my energy back?"

"I'm happy you're feeling better. How are the children?

"At peace."

"Tomorrow, you can spend some time with Kissa and Kamau. They have missed you."'

"Of course, they've missed me. You've kept them from me."

"I thought it better that way. I didn't want you overexerting yourself or jeopardizing your pregnancy."

"I know, but I have missed them. They don't even feed anymore."

"Not from you but Candace. A few times a week. And they eat as well. Their feeding is mostly for routine. They don't have a real desire for it as it seems."

"I have missed my husband also."

"Oh?" Her words brought a smile to Ren's face. He had missed her and wondered if she felt the same.

"I was wondering if you preferred your work to me."

"No, I missed you, my love, dearly, but I needed to set some things in place to make sure that we are safe."

"Are you going to tell me what is going on? Or are they going to keep catching me off guard?"

"There's so much to tell you. I've been waiting to discuss things with you, but between Africa and our return, then you being so out of it; I didn't think it was that dire a need."

"And now?"

"Now, we need to work together."

"So, my place?"

"We are matriarchal. It is only natural we be ruled by my Queen."

"When were you planning on telling me that you were keeping my throne warm."

"Definitely before your last pregnancy."

"Oh, of course. At least by then."

Ren's lips twisted into a crooked smile. "Yes, I wasn't sure how you would react to the thought of someone else raising our children."

"Why would that be necessary?"

"It would depend on your duties. Whatever was necessary. It may change from time to time. The most important thing right now is our children."

"What exactly happened at the restaurant?"

"When?"

"You know when."

"I had a new employee I never met or heard of, and I had come in to find Madeline trying to get the schedule."

"And?"

"Someone had control of one of my employees. They wanted her to kill me or catch me off guard. There was even a bit of poison on the blade."

"Lorenzo Arias, why did you keep that from me?"

"I didn't want you to worry. You couldn't help. I dealt with the poison before it was a problem."

"I see. Anything else?"

"In the morning, we are replacing the windows with bulletproof glass, and no going out on the balcony. They are going to hire an assassin or have already. While we replace the windows, you can go into the playroom."

"Think they'll gas us?"

"That will only affect Kai's family."

"They could get in while it knocked us out."

"The building would go into emergency mode, and everything would be locked down, and all soldiers would be on alert."

"Yes, soldiers. What are they? Are they different from normal vamps?"

"Somewhat, I guess."

"That doesn't explain anything."

"Hard to explain."

"Try."

"It is an ancient technique. Your grandfather helped me. I take the best and the strongest vampires or humans, and make them a special breed, mine, more than the others. That's all you need to know. Most are not even on duty yet."

"Okay. And what happened after I left the meeting?"

"I gave them the list of clan leaders to visit. We're going to unite all vampires in the United States."

"Let me guess; we're already united?" Ren smiled as he sat beside her and removed her slippers and pants before wrapping her in a robe. "Have you decided if I can spend time with our children?"

"Yes, we're going to spend the day together. You must rest."

"I'm not tired now. Help me up so I can peer in on them."

"Sure." Ren helped her up, and they walked to the children's room next door. Yalena was so glad to gaze upon their little sleeping faces. She had missed holding them. As she stared at Kissa and Kamau, the triplets began to stir inside her. It was like they were in sync. The twins opened their eyes as soon as the triplets began to move. Lena was surprised at the reaction; she hadn't realized their bond was so strong. Kamau and Kissa stood up in their beds and reached for their mom. Ren picked up both children, and they returned to the master bedroom. There Ren sat the children on the bed and then helped Lena sit and get herself comfortable. Kamau and Kissa crawled toward their mother and laid against each side of her, resting a hand on her predominately swollen abdomen. The triplets responded by what seemed to Lena as reaching for their siblings.

Lena laid back on the pillows and closed her eyes. She took a deep breath and reached for Sekhmet. Instantly she heard Sekhmet's laughter in her head, and she smiled. Ren just regarded her in awe as his beloved Queen and his children connected. He could only guess how beautiful it was to be that close to them.

"Ren, come here." He gently sat next to his beautiful family, placing his arm on Lena's shoulders and his other around Kissa. He instantly felt touched by a blanket of tranquility in the energy that they created. He had sat encircling Lena many times while she fed their children, yet he had not experienced anything like this. "You are feeling Sekhmet's energy. She is with us now." Ren wanted to be closer to Lena. So he placed Kissa on his lap and moved over to his wife. All without breaking the connection Kissa had established. Lena felt refreshed by Sekhmet's energy and the link between them. Then Sekhmet inquired after her son.

"Why has Lockington not returned?"

"He wishes to train his grans after the war ends. He wants to build a bond with them."

"And I don't? Duty is more important."

"I have tried to speak to him, but to no avail. Could you not bring the village here?"

"Away from the healing energy of this sacred place?"

"Is not everywhere sacred? What difference would the longitude and latitude make? Are you not everywhere?"

Sekhmet replies in metu neter, and neither Ren nor Lena understands. "I'm not the creator; I'm only his child. I'm where he wishes me to be. If I am to be in New York or England or France, that is where I will be; no other. Do you think I wish not to be with you and my grans? Not being able to be there teaching you all I know. You wheel a power not given to humans or vampires before, despite the blood that runs in your veins. Ahh, we'll talk later. Ren, you don't have to suffer and be apart from your mate. Your intimacy will not affect your children." As soon as she said that, Ren withdrew from his family. He could only guess that his need for Yalena was so great it exuded from touching her.

"My love."

"Yes, Yalena." He turned to look at her. Her eyes brushed over him before locking his gaze. "I will take the children back to bed." Lena only nodded.

It didn't take him long before he was back by her side. Lena refused to meet his gaze again. She had seen the need for her in his eyes. It had only been a couple of months since he had joined with her in bliss. Too many, that might not seem like a long time, but a day without his touch was torture. The longer they were together, the more torture it was to be without him. She didn't remember it being that agonizing after having the twins, but him standing above her made her desire all the more painful.

He lifted her from the bed and walked from their bedroom down the hall. She didn't have to guess where he was taking her. She knew. When he first brought her to his home, he brought her to that room. There, in all of its brilliant colored pillows, he had lavished her with his affection.

Ren had not jostled her as a man would carrying one as he walked. Instead, he glided through the halls to her favorite room. The candles lit the room, and pillows covered the floor by the futon. He gently laid her down on the futon and surveyed her as she sat before him. He couldn't help but be thankful that she was his in all her resplendent beauty and grace. She was the woman he had walked the earth in search of. Until just a few hundred years ago, he hadn't dreamed that the woman he would love, irrevocably, would be from the line of Sekhmet. Yalena Arias was the most beautiful he had ever seen. She was curvaceous. The curve of her hips made a man want to give her children. Her bosom was full even before he had given her their twins. Her body was full and feminine. To him, she was sheer perfection.

Now she sat on the futon before him. Her stomach stretched with his children. He could not have seen her more beautiful and sexy. He wished he could think her clothes away. As he thought it, she pulled her shirt over her head. Before seeing the children, he had already removed her pants. Now all that stood in the way was her lace bra and panties. Lena stared as his eyes took her in from head to pointed toes. She saw the hunger in his eyes. She smiled as she extended her hand out to him. Ren removed his shirt and unzipped his pants and removed them and his boxers before reaching for her hand. He kneeled before her and kissed the palm of her hand and sucked on each of her fingers.

Lena used her other hand to lift his shirt and caress every rippling muscle beneath it, feeling the line of hair that went from his abdomen and expanded lightly over his chest. Ren felt the heat building within his body. He had to have her. He had worried that his aggressive lovemaking would cause the children to hurt Lena. Even with Sekhmet's encouragement, he wondered. Seeing her before him with such need and desire in her eyes had undone him. He couldn't deny her his touch. He removed his shirt as both of her hands wandered over his body. She continued to lightly run her hand over his chest and then his legs. Finally, her hand reached between his thighs and under him. Her fingers lightly brushed his sac. They tightened and she felt him tense slightly as his length slightly bounced tapping her. She gripped him firmly in her hand and began stroking him gently.

Her touch momentarily froze him. Ren closed his eyes, savoring her warmth. Her grasp was gentle at first. As each moment passed, her stroke became tighter, and more aggressive, and she made sure to squeeze his tip gently. When an overwhelming surge of heat ran through him, he threw his head back and stifled a growl, rumbling in his chest. Lena slowly sucked him in and out of her mouth. She enjoyed pleasing him so much that she throbbed. She wanted him but wasn't ready to relinquish control over him. Lena's arms encircled him, bringing him closer to her and pushing him deeper into her mouth, lightly pressing his head between the root of her tongue and her soft palate. Each time pushing him a little further. The rumble in his chest grew louder. Her hands rubbed his buttocks and lightly squeezed, pushing him deeper.

Ren's brain had been hazy while he was in her mouth. Lena knew that each time his eyes were closed, but behind his lids, he witnessed her full lips encircling his length and her tongue circling his tip every time she pulled away. Her jaws suck like a vacuum. The further he went into her mouth, the tighter his muscles tensed, the thicker the haze. His body was in such ecstasy. His length throbbed and hardened with every stroke in and out of her mouth. As his tip hit the back of her throat, he could no longer be silent. The first time, he tried to muffle his groan. His chest rumbled again. Lena didn't stop, but she appreciated that he was lost in her actions. She continued to push a little further each time. Finally, a growl escaped his lips. He could no longer contain it. He had to have her. He pulled entirely away from her and just stood and gaped at her. Her breasts hung free from their bondage. His eyes moved over her possessively, caressing even.

"Lay down on your side," he demanded softly. Lena had been watching him the whole time. Her gaze seared with need. She was silent as she slowly turned her body and lay on her side. Her head rested on a large soft pillow. She fathomed that he would want to stare into her eyes as he took her, but her stomach would make it uncomfortable for her to lay on her back and take him pounding into her.

As he lay next to her, he curled his body around her. She felt that he wanted to delight in her warmth, and he wanted her sensitive to his pulsing length against her. From his touch, she knew that he utterly desired to lick the folds of her lips between her thick thighs. But from the way his throbbing rock hard length felt against her, she knew that he would take her. After making her body shudder and explode, he would take her to the precipice with his tongue. He eased away from her to ease his length inside. As he moved away, she parted her legs, allowing him entrance into her, but he couldn't go slowly. She had pushed him hard. He pressed into her, and she released a moan he had yet to hear from her. He pulled away again until his tip threatened to slip out, and then he pushed into her. Her cry became deeper.

He had not touched her before that moment, yet she was wet for him. Lena knew that arousing and pleasing her beloved made her body ready for him. She was warm and slick. He eased himself as close as he could be. He felt her heat against him and enclosed her in his arms. His hand moved around her, finding her nipples and fondling them as he pushed into her. Lena began to rock back against him. That brought the haze that had encased him before.

From her nipples to between her thighs, his hands roamed her body. His fingers twirled and rubbed her secret places as her body shuddered against his. The rumble in his chest returned as he glided against her; sweat began to bead across her back. He licked at the droplets before he pulled her closer and held her tighter as his teeth sunk into her shoulder. The piercing of his teeth was not painful; it brought her satisfaction and pleasure. She knew she pleased him. Her moans and trembling of her body made him aware that she was more than satisfied.

When they reached the peak and dived into the ocean together, they were too tired to separate. And there, in her favorite room, Yalena lay in his arms, and he was wrapped in her. When morning came, Yalena awoke to the touch of her husband. His tongue stroked her lightly yet aggressively. She opened her eyes and peered down at him.

"What? We fell asleep before I finished worshiping you." Lena chuckled silently before she was spirited away by the caress of her body. Wrapped in his love, he brought her to ecstasy. "My love, how do you feel?' She couldn't help but moan and stretch before she answered him.

"We're well, Ren. I am but pleasingly sore." Ren smiled and gently drew her closer to him. Lena and Ren lay in each other's arms, enjoying the languor created by their passion and the peace they shared. Not a word was uttered between them. Even if for a moment. There was no place either of them would rather be.

Chapter 22

Lorenzo sat up and looked down at his beautiful wife, naked and glistening. His eyes lingered on the changes the pregnancy had made to her body. He had never seen a human woman strong enough to carry one of his kind. Yet, she was not fully human, was she? She was a descendant of the line of Sekhmet.

He couldn't help but feel blessed that he had found her. He was happy that he had waited for her. Taking her at sixteen from her home and into his world would have been too much for her. He remembered the day he saw her for the first time. It was on her birthday. He had spoken with Lockington that morning. Lockington wanted to know why Ren wasn't around his family anymore. Ren thought that was an odd question, but he told him that it was because he didn't think that they would ever produce who he was looking for. Lockington laughed. Ren would never forget what he said after that.

'Patience, my boy. I do believe an heir was born that will be to your liking. Today should be a good day to visit them.'

Of course, he would not go when asked. Instead, he would research the family again. After several hours of researching the Count family's latest arrival, he decided to show up on her birthday. He would never forget that day. When he walked into the backyard where they were having a party, he saw Yalena. Her presence stole his heart. As if his journey had finally connected to hers. She was dancing on a raised dance floor that covered the lawn. She was beautiful. She didn't notice him at first because she was in the arms of some boy--possibly her boyfriend, who could be no more than eighteen.

Finally, her head turned his way and their eyes locked. She smiled before looking away from him. He couldn't imagine what she was thinking, but it was as though they shared a secret in that one glance. Then he was distracted for a while by her mom. She had been surprised and upset that he returned. She had no desire for any of her girls to fulfill the prophecy her grandmother told her. She would have taken the gift from him and more than likely thrown it away had he not insisted that he give it to her. Carol frowned at him but didn't waste any more energy.

He wouldn't stay long. He felt out of place, and there were no other adults at the party but her parents. He decided to give her the gift the first chance he got, then leave. He didn't have to wait long to meet her. When the song finished, she excused herself from her dance partner and walked right over to him.

"Hello. Are you a friend of my parents?"

"Your grandfather."

"Really? I wouldn't have pegged you for his friend. Apprentice, maybe."

"That too. Happy Birthday!" he exclaimed as he handed her the silver box.

"Thank you. I'll put it with the others."

"I would prefer you opened it now. I want to see if you like it."

"I'm sure I'll love it. My mom would be upset if I opened the gift right now."

"Tell Carol, I insisted. I'm sure she'll let you slide."

"You know my mom?"

"We've met a few times."

There was silence as she stood with the box in her hand. She stood for a long minute, looking from the box to him over and over before she decided. Ren sensed her nervousness. He could tell that he aroused her. And her smell whispered to him. Before he caught himself, he closed the distance between them. "Please open it. I must be going soon."

Lena smiled and nodded before opening the box to find a beautiful diamond heart pendant on a gold chain.

"It's beautiful, ah, I don't know your name."

"Lorenzo."

"It's beautiful, Lorenzo, but I can't accept this. It's too expensive."

"Please, Yalena." Hearing her name pass his lips made her stop looking at his feet and peer into his eyes.

"It's clear that you like it. Please keep it. It would make me very happy if you kept it."

"Thank you," she replied and lightly kissed his cheek. Her fragrance encircled him briefly and then was gone as she was. Before he could escape her notice, Carol caught up with him and made him promise to wait before taking her. He had agreed. She was still so young, but how long could he go on without her by his side?He looked down at her now. She still wore the pendant he had given her. He never saw her take it off. Ren sat beside her and passed a finger over it before his hand glided down the side of her body. Her eyelids fluttered before she gazed up at him.

"Buenos Dias, Ren."

"Buenos Dias, mi amor. Glad you're well." Lena stretched before pushing herself into a sitting position. He rubbed her stomach before gently touching her cheek and kissing her lips.

"It was a beautiful night, Ren."

"Yes, it was. Can I hope for another?" Lena smiled before responding.

"I believe so. Unless your children decide to come tonight, they are restless. And speaking of children, when can I spend time with mine?"

"Soon, they are probably in the playroom. Let's get ourselves dressed, and we'll go down." As they passed the door, there was a knock. Ren sent Lena to their bedroom while he dealt with whatever the problem was. "Hey, Patrick."

"Good evening Mr. Arias. I just wanted you to know the men are here to begin working from the outside. I have men stationed throughout the house, and the children and your human family are on the second floor in the sanctum. The men will start on the first floor. So please, escort Yalena down there soon, and you stay with them."

"Giving orders, Patrick?"

"Only when it comes to your safety, sir. Please, there is something off with one of the men." Ren smiled at Patrick's response. He had given Patrick permission to make final decisions without consulting him in cases of safety, but until now, it hadn't been necessary.

"We will be dressed and in the private elevator as quickly as possible."

"I will escort you. Please make haste, sir." By the time Ren got to Lena, she was partially dressed.

"You're quick," Ren said walking into the bedroom. "Just give me a second to put on some pants and a t-shirt and grab a few items. There is a shower on the second floor."

"We are at risk even when we take precautions," Lena asked. She was still amazed at being able to hear all the conversations that took place in her home and the building.

"It appears so," Ren called from the closet. He came back into the bathroom in fresh clothes and clothes wrapped in one of his T-shirts. "Let's go, Lena. Patrick is waiting. The men are still setting up to begin downstairs."

Patrick was waiting at the elevator door when they got out on the second floor. Candace would take the children down to the second floor sanctum for the last couple of months of the pregnancy. If they were in the apartment, they would search for their mother, and Lena would look for them.

Each afternoon after she awoke, Lena would listen for her children, her son or daughter's voice, breath, or heartbeat. And each afternoon, they wouldn't be there. She had no idea what time they awoke or what they required on a day to day basis. She was not allowed to provide anything for them. That was painful for her. It broke her heart not to see them and be with them. She had nursed their tiny bodies to the healthy toddlers they were then. Both Kamau and Kissa, her children, had connected with her and Sekhmet.

As she stood before the door, she was anxious. She could hear both playing with Candace and the other two children. They were happy. The door opened to Lena's fingerprints, and before she could step into the room, both Kissa and Kamau stood at the threshold and looked up at her with excitement in their eyes. They rushed to her and hugged her legs before Ren could catch them. They took her hand and tried to pull her into the room.

Lena had never been in the sanctum before. It was like another apartment, although it had almost no walls. Instead, it was like a large loft with partitions. The kitchen was to her right and about a hundred feet in front of her was a play area. Lena nodded her head in greeting toward Kai and Candace as she looked around the room.

The children played before they led their mother toward their toys and motioned to sit on the floor. With Ren's help, she was able to.

"Ren, I will return to you when they are finished. But, for the time being, you have everything you need." Ren nodded to Patrick before he sealed the door and disappeared behind the only wall.

"Lena, it is good to see you out of that room. I see you and Ren are back to your regular selves." Lena just blushed and nodded. She knew the last comment referred to them being in her favorite room without cover or closed doors.

"It is good to be out of the room, indeed. And I will remember to be more cautious next time."

"Your children found you first. I found both Kissa and Kamau curled up beside you."

"Thank you, Kai, for taking them and closing the door. They awoke to me watching them early this morning. When they fell back to sleep, Ren placed them in their beds." As Lena spoke with Kai, Kissa, and Kamau came to sit beside her. The two slowly began to rub Lena's protruding belly. What had barely caught her attention before had become painfully obvious. The children inside of her became restless and moved around more than usual.

"Kissa and Kamau, leave your siblings; they are hurting your mother," Ren called as he walked from behind the wall.

"But Dad, they are ready to come out." There was silence in the room after Kamau spoke.

"Kamau, please, you're hurting your mother. Just stop for a little while, please. Come here, both of you". Lena hadn't heard them speak so clearly before. How did Kamau know that his siblings were ready to be born? Ren told her that the twins had not spoken since they had been apart from their mother. They clung to him before he left the house. He fed them every morning, but they didn't say a word.

"Ren, there is a problem in our penthouse room."

"Sure, that's not residue from the pain of the triplets?"

"No, I have searched every inch of the building. Most of the men are working on the windows. One has stopped. A guard found him in our room."

"They will handle it."

"Ren."

"Yes, Lena."

"I am bleeding." Ren put Kamau down and went over to Yalena. "You should not have been bleeding. I was hoping to get you as close to their due time as possible. The children had barely made eighteen weeks." Ren sighed. "I was afraid this would happen."

"Maybe it's just time."

"I couldn't stop it now even if I thought I wanted to." Ren picked up Yalena from the floor. "You can rest on one of the futons while I prepare. Kai, will you come and stay with her until I return?" Kai nodded.

"Ren, we can't leave the sanctum."

"I am not. I have what I need here. I may have erred in not letting you spend time with your children. Remember, do not push.

Lena clung to Ren for relief as the pain ripped through her womb. She could feel the blood flow out of her and down her thigh. While human babies were surrounded by the water, children of vampires were surrounded by a sac of blood, Ren had explained during her first delivery. As the pain increased, so did the blood flow. Her grip on Ren tightened. The walk to the back seemed as if it had taken hours rather than a few seconds.

Ren had to walk calmly and at human speed, fearing the triplets would tear through their mother in a panic if he moved more quickly. It had been easier with the first two. They had not left the sanctuary of their room before the pain started. He was well aware of what was happening inside her, and he wanted to give the triplets a way out before they created one. There would be no chance of a third pregnancy if they tore their way out.

As he walked through the partition of the bedroom, he felt Yalena's grip tighten. "Relax, love," as he said that, he gently laid her on the mattress. Yalena curled around her abdomen. Ren grabbed a few pillows and positioned them before moving her up to the top. The blood continued to run, now more freely, almost like a small stream. Ren was glad that he had prepared the room in the sanctum for her delivery.

"Who knew that we would need the room," Lena asked breathlessly.

"I want to make sure we will always be safe. I had hoped not to use it." Ren raced around to gather the rest of what he needed while Kai sat with Yalena. When he finished, he excused Kai.

"Okay, just like the last time. I am going to make sure the children can exit safely. I believe one of them has started to rip their way out."

Ren removed Yalena's pants and undergarments and then placed them in the plastic bag on the floor. Upon arrival, when he had slipped away, he gathered the things needed for the children's early arrival. He was sure that they would arrive soon, but he had hoped that another day would pass before they decided to leave the womb.How had Kamau known that his siblings were ready to leave their mom? Ren had believed he would be the only one who could sense it. Yet Kamau's ability had shown at such an early age. He would be a powerful vampire once he was grown. He would be ready to take his place as one of the council's warriors in a century or before.

As Ren felt around inside Yalena, he grazed the rip in the thick sac that encased his children. Whichever child had begun to tear, they had a good sense of where to go. Ren used his sharp extended fingernail to lengthen the tear at the top and the bottom. He had tried to be gentle, but he was sure it didn't help. Yalena was in excruciating pain and would be for a while longer. After Ren extended the opening, he parted Yalena's legs a little more before sitting behind her.

"Alright, Lena, brace yourself. These children are smarter. One of them had already ripped open the sac on the same side as your vaginal opening. I just had to extend it a little."

Ren always thought of how amazing their birth was. He could never imagined how painful the delivery was, as it was wondrous. Having Kamau and Kissa was pretty much the same. Lena's body's natural contractions help push the children as they make their way through her birth canal and out of her body. He hoped that his help had made it easier for Lena. Ren sat right behind her with his arms wrapped around her and lightly pushing on her stomach. He whispered beautiful things in her ear and reminded her to breathe and try to relax every muscle in her body. He wanted her to remember that her body and their children would do the work of giving birth.

They watched all three of their children and the afterbirth slowly slide out of Lena's body. The order was very much the same as their first set. The boy, the first of the triplets, came out and then turned around to help his siblings. And when the pain was over the three sat before them, two girls and a boy.

"Well, I hope you have been filling up because I have lost a lot of blood."

"I think you'll be fine." He lifted his arm and placed his wrist in front of her lips as he replied. Lena kissed and then wrapped her lips around his wrist and sank her teeth into his arm. Immediately, Ren felt his connection to her. He knew that Lena thought his blood was sweet and it would keep his beloved healthy as she healed. As it slid down her throat, he could see her body slowly regain its strength. Her skin's golden brown returned and her face filled out a little. He saw her scrunch her face and knew that her womb began to contract and close.

As she drank from Ren, their children watched with such volition. Ren knew that soon she would have to feed them. Thanks to Kai's quick thinking, Lena had been pumping milk from the time the twins were removed from her care. They were drinking at least half of what she was producing. So whichever triplet wouldn't suckle would have enough milk even if she had to pump continually.

Once Lena had enough blood, Ren removed his wrist. He moved from behind her and picked up two of the triplets. Lena grabbed the youngest girl and followed Ren into the bathroom, where Kai had drawn a bath for her. She gave Ren the baby and removed her clothing to step into the warm bath."And how are you going to bathe three babies?" Ren didn't respond but moved aside so that Lena could see the three babies each in their bath seat lined up against the mirrored wall on the long counter. "I see you're well prepared."

"As much as vampirely possible." Lena couldn't help but laugh as she sank lower into the tub. "Lena," Ren called sternly. "No underwater bathing, please. Remember the twins?"

"Yeah, yeah. I need to be under, just... Babies, mommy is fine." Lena immediately submerged herself after her last words. Even though the water muffled the sound, Lena could still hear the water running in the sink and Ren talking to the triplets. She didn't hear any crying, and neither did Ren appear with all three babies in his arms, telling her to come up. So, Lena stayed a little longer with her eyes closed. She found that her body didn't miss the air as much as she thought. She noticed that she could hold her breath longer each time over the last few months. She pondered what changes her body had undergone over the previous year. She was not sure how she sensed the changes. She hadn't paid any attention to it until that point, but she knew there was a difference. Earlier in the year, it was her hearing and speed that changed. Since then, she has had many blood exchanges between herself and Ren since the first one. Yet there was no difference between her heart rhythm and Ren's or the children's.That was something she guessed, Lena listened to her heartbeat; it was slower still. She listened to all of the heartbeats in the room. She could tell Ren's immediately. The triplets' heartbeat was the same pattern. It was as if they were in sync. Yet theirs were a little bit faster than their father's. As much as her heartbeat had slowed, it was still quicker than her new babies.

"Yalena." she could hear Ren calling her, but she ignored him. "Yalena, come up. Your lips are turning blue." Yalena came up and wiped the water from her face.

"I'm fine."

"Don't push yourself too far too fast. It's unnecessary."

"I didn't mean to. I was taking stock of the changes in my body. I always thought the transformation from human to a vampire would be faster."

"Usually it is, but only because the body has lost almost all of its blood. Your body has never lost that much. I would say I have replaced at least half of your body's blood volume, but your body keeps making it. Each time there is a slight genetic difference. Your body is beginning to reproduce blood with part of the vampire trait as well. As a result, your body changes slowly. I imagine that has to do with who you are."

"How sure are you of that?"

"About 99.8% sure. Cell has drained a few women in the bar about halfway and given them even less blood than you drank today. Within twenty-four hours, their bodies had changed. They became vampires. Run your tongue across your teeth. Notice anything?"

As Lena did what Ren suggested, she realized that her eye teeth no longer extended past her bottom teeth. Instead, they were pretty much back to normal. Just slightly longer.

"Want my arm again?" The thought of blood immediately caused her body to react, her incisors lengthened, and her mouth watered. She guessed the change was almost complete.

By the time Lena had washed up and gotten dressed, Ren had dressed the children and taken them out to the playroom. Everyone looked at her and smiled as she walked out of the bedroom area. Ren had placed each of the triplets in a bouncer. All three children had dirty blonde hair and violet eyes. While the boy was the image of Lena, with a mocha complexion, her girls looked like their father with Lena's caramel complexion. Yalena couldn't imagine how their eyes became such a brilliant violet, but she had become accustomed to Kissa and Kamau's eyes and figured the triplets would be the same.

Yalena sat in front of them and opened her arms wide. Each child responded by reaching for her. Then, one by one, she took them out and placed them leaning between her legs. The triplets were smaller than the twins, but of course, the triplets had less room to develop and less time.

"What will we name them, Yalena?"

"The boy will be Tehuti Zahir."

"So is 'T' the letter for this birth?"

"Yes."

"Khemetic names to suit."

"The girl with the deeper violet eyes will be Tendai Anuket, and the lovely girl with my curls and brilliant violet eyes will be Tahira Auset."

"That's beautiful, mi amor." Lena looked at the three of her newly born children. They were going to be a handful. She could sense it. She couldn't even feed them all at the same time. "So Tahira, Tehuti, and Tendai meet your beautiful siblings Kamau and Kissa." Both Kamau and Kissa had been standing near, wanting to get close to their siblings. As soon as Lena called, they were both at their mother's side, touching each head of their siblings.

"Well, Ren, congratulations are in order."

"Thank you, Nomar."

"Beautiful offspring, Yalena, and Lorenzo. They are striking."

"Thank you, Kai. Do we have any of the milk I pumped down here?"

"Yes, this is where we've been keeping it."

"Well, good. Let's see who wants to nurse." Tehuti was in his mother's arms and had tried to latch on before Lena had opened her shirt. So she opened it and used her nail to puncture a spot above her nipple. Tehuti smelled the blood and latched on. But neither Tendai nor Tahira were interested.

"Four bottles are coming up."

"Candace, I don't believe the girls will drink it with blood."

"They're not stored that way. I only add it after I heat the bottles."

Chapter 23

"Ren, I believe we can go back to our penthouse."

"Maybe. Let's wait for Patrick. You relax. You should be resting; all of the children are asleep."

"I guess I'm tired." Ren took her hand and guided her to the back bedroom. Fresh linen replaced the blood soaked sheets.

Lena laid down. She had not realized how exhausted she was until her head hit the pillow. She was only half conscious when he climbed in next to her and gently wrapped his body around hers.

During the night, Ren moved Lena and the children back to their apartment. Yalena Arias had given him five beautiful children in two births. He propped his head upon his hand and looked at her. She looked so peaceful and angelic, just lying next to him. One would not conceive that she had given birth to twins and triplets in a little over a year. His blood had rejuvenated her to her prior glory. Not that she wasn't beautiful pregnant, but the pregnancies had taken so much from her.

Ren ran his finger down her arm ever so gently, barely touching her soft skin. When he reached her fingers, he laced his through hers. He was so grateful to have her.

After resting, Lena awoke to brilliant sunlight streaming through the bedroom window. She threw on her robe and walked over to welcome the day.

"Glad to see you up after such a trying day."

"Of course. You didn't tell me what happened with the worker who didn't feel right to me."

"You had other things to tend to. Still, as I told you, Patrick managed. He found the man in our room. Luckily, because he had knocked out a soldier and was trying to push him out the window."

"How's the soldier?

"He was injected with something so we have him downstairs. He'll be looked after. I was glad it was an unsuccessful try." Lena turned to see Ren place the food tray on the coffee table in the sitting area and walk over to her. She turned back to the window and leaned into his embrace.

"Do we know what's going on with Madeline and Jonathan?"

"I receive calls when they arrive at a new territory. They've covered a few."

"I take it they aren't happy with the response they're getting?"

Ren smiled. "The last call said Jon was down right boiling, to quote the lady."

"Interesting."

"How long will they be gone?"

"Not sure."

While Jon was away, Ren and Lena were enjoying their family time. Seth's threats and attempts had failed. The family had been quite content with the way things were happening. The oldest of Yalena's children had grown in size to that of a ten year old. Lena was glad their growth had finally slowed down. She was amazed by how her children had grown. Ren tried to explain that a vampire was a child for at least a century and a half, unlike their human counterparts. So while their bodies grew fast so they wouldn't be defenseless, they would take time to mature.

It had been almost a month since their birth, and the triplets were crawling behind their older siblings. Yalena had already begun to train Kissa and Kamau in martial arts. They were living in a dangerous time. Ren and Lena decided to wait before they had the last set of children. Yalena had a feeling that everything would come to a head all too soon.

Chapter 24

"Lorenzo, things have been so quiet."

"No assassination attempts, and you're bored."

"A bit anxious. We're literally waiting for the other shoe to drop."

"Lena, I truly love this time with you, the children, and Kai's family."

"I love spending time with the children, and having you here is great. I just want this war over."

"Soon, my love. Jonathan has reached New Orleans, and Jean Pierre is dealing with him. Incidentally, you're going to have to keep an eye on him. He has a taste for horrendous deeds."

"Who is that and should I track them now?"

"No, this is his freebie. He's an old friend. Don't think you want to learn how he disposes of his enemies. Have you done your training with Kissa today?"

"This afternoon all the children are with Candace. I believe they're in the sanctuary."

"So, if I wanted to make love to my sexy wife?" Lena smiled up at her husband. They were spending the evening in her favorite room. Lena lay on the futon rubbing her hands over the fuzzy lavender cover, staring up at Ren, who stared down at her. His hands twirling and pulling at her thick curly hair. "Have I told you how beautiful you look? Especially after having twins and triplets."

"Really! Flattery will beguile me."

"Mhmm." Ren held Lena's face in his hands and gently kissed her lips. "When was the last time you fed?"

"I don't remember. Maybe a week or so ago."

"We cannot have that. You must feed." Ren removed his shirt before lying down next to his wife. "Come closer and feed my love."

Lena snuggled closer to Ren. Her breath whirled over the hollow of his throat. The minute and slow rhythm of his blood flowing through his body whispered to her. Lena's mouth filled with saliva, and her incisors lengthened. Lena bit into Ren's neck, and his blood streamed over her tongue and down her throat. She relaxed as it flowed into every one of her cells. She hadn't realized how much her body had needed the blood.

"I've forgotten how fabulous I feel after feeding. I have been living on human food." As soon as Lena stopped feeding and withdrew her fangs, the two holes in Ren's neck closed completely.

"How long have we waited?"

"Almost three months now."

"After this pregnancy, we won't have to restrain ourselves."

"I will enjoy that, Ren, but I don't want to be pregnant when this war erupts."

"It's getting harder and harder for me to control myself."

"Then don't, my love. Madeline has been away for too long. She'll be back soon." Ren lightly ran his fingers down the middle of Lena's body. He gazed at her to surveil her reaction. She inhaled quickly as his finger ran along the inside of her thigh, teasing her. He made sure that his finger lightly brushed her innermost tip. She gasped and exhaled.

Yalena had missed her husband's touch. She recognized it was essential to wait in between each pregnancy so that her body could recover. At least partially there was no way she was at her prime after her body had taken such a beating. Each pregnancy wore her down.

"Perhaps, we should just wait a little longer. We have no idea how this pregnancy will affect you."

Lena took a deep breath. "I'm disappointed, but I agree. I lose a piece of myself each time. I miss you, my love, your touch, your stroke is heaven to me." Ren slid his arm under Yalena and pulled her closer to him. His only reply was to draw her closer to him, so close that their noses touched. His tongue protruded from his mouth, and he flicked his tongue over her lips. Lena couldn't help but smile. He kissed her slow and soft at first; then, his kisses became more urgent and arduous. His arms encircled her waist and held her tightly.

He had missed his beautiful wife. His body reacted instantly to her proximity. He wanted her; there was no doubt that he needed to indulge in her innermost warmth. Her body was so welcoming to his. If he remained close to her any longer, he wouldn't be able to stop. He slowly pulled his tongue from her mouth, and with one quick peck on her chest, he gave them distance.

"I love you, Ren."

"Oh, Yalena, my love for you knows no bounds. Just bare with this a little longer. I will ravage you soon."Yalena gave a soft chuckle. "I can sense your resolve dissipating, my love."

"Had you not told me of Sekhmet's new prophecy, I would have changed you after your second pregnancy. You lost so much blood. I was tempted. You won't survive another pregnancy."

"That's the idea, isn't it?"

"Even after almost living a thousand years, the transformation still shakes me, and you are my life." Lena smiled and gently touched her hand to the side of Ren's face.

"We will be fine. I am going to be fine. I'll probably catch up on some much needed rest during the transformation."

"Sekhmet has told you about it?"

"Yes, she has. She's also concerned about my change. She's amazed at the fact that I haven't changed as of yet. She says she notices the subtle differences each time I take your blood." Lena took a moment before she continued. "Are you okay with the roll our children will take?"

"Who would be, Lena? Kamau and Kissa, as well as the last two hunting down vampires. They will always be in danger."

"Only if they forget to cover each other. We will make sure they are safe in their city. Out of town will be dangerous."

"Will we survive the half a century they will need to be fully prepared?"

"No." The shortness of Lena's answer shocked Ren, and he turned toward her. "They will have to hunt as early as I have killed.

"They'll be just babies. Even in a century, a vampire is still just a teenager."

"They grow at an accelerated rate but are teenagers at a hundred?" Lena smiled. "They'll be fine. A little overconfident until the first time they're caught off guard. They're strong and have each developed their own powers. Kamau is becoming as fierce as Heru Khuti, and Kissa has developed Nebhtet's gifts. They are learning to work together. They'll be fine."

"And how are you so calm about it?"

"Honestly," she paused for a moment. "Because it hasn't happened yet."

The two of them sat curled into each other for a while, each lost in their thoughts. Yalena had been training her twins and nursing the triplets. She was enjoying the reprieve from continually being on the defensive. Still, it made her a bit uneasy. It could be nerve racking when you're aware of what is coming but not when.

"I wish we had a few centuries just to enjoy being a family."

"Me too Ren, but once this is over, we'll have at least two decades give or take."

"That isn't long at all."

"But so much can happen."

Chapter 25

A few more weeks went by, with things going peacefully. Ren had resumed his routine. He left his growing brood to check on the restaurant and the club, leaving Lena and the family home to train and grow. Periodically, Lena frequented the club so that the clan saw that she was safe and healthy. Then, for the first time, Lockington visited the penthouse to regard his expanding family.

"Grandpa?"

"Wow, I haven't heard that name leave your mouth in a few years. I was afraid you had forgotten who I was."

"Not at all. You can come in. I was wondering when you would visit."

"I've been laying low. Even after Madeline and Jon left town, vamps were still looking for me. Of course, no one knows where I live or what I own." Lockington walked in and looked around as soon as he entered the threshold. "Nice place you're living in."

"Thanks, shoes you've never been here?"

"I thought it best not to show sides too early. At this time, it would appear that they're familiar with my allegiance. So here I am. I want to get to know my great great grandchildren, and years have past since I've spent any time with you."

"That's so true. I've missed you, grandpa." Lena gave him a big hug and pulled Lockington towards the personal elevator on the other side of the penthouse. "They're in the sanctuary. You've got to give them time to adjust to you. It may take a couple of visits."

"Once they see me and realize I'm like them, they will warm up just fine."

"Possibly." Lena took her grandfather in the elevator to the second floor. She could discern the children playing inside the room even with the door closed.

"Closed doors everywhere I turn. You don't take any chances with security here, do you?"

"Nope. Even though no one can enter into the building, we leave the doors closed, and you need to have security clearance to enter into any of the rooms. Why all the questions?"

"Just want to make sure you're all secure. I've known Ren for centuries. I was sure that he would keep you safe, just checking. But, before we go in, I must warn you, let very few people into your circle Yalena. This is for your safety and theirs. Even family can be treacherous."

"Grandfather, why would you say that? Who do you think will betray me? It's not like people surround me. Very few keep my company."

"You'll see soon enough. Even those who are close can become viperous."

"Grandfather, I think your years here on earth have made you paranoid."

"Possibly, but you'll understand soon enough. Now let me enjoy the children."

"You can't just spring that on a person and not give them any information."

"Enough! It is as I say it is." Just then, he put his hand on the door, and it opened to the children waiting on the other side. They discerned their mother's voice and were waiting anxiously for her to enter. When they saw Lockington, they slowly backed away from the door. Both of Kai's children went to hide behind Candace.

The room was large enough for a small apartment. There was an area with short tables and a board to the right of the door. But it appeared unused. There were notebooks, coloring books as well as crayons littering the middle of the floor. There was only one piece of furniture in the left corner with a throw over it and a small table at the head.

"Children, this is your.."

"We're aware of who he is, mom."

"Then why are you all backing away, Kissa?"

"We don't trust him entirely."

"Well, you shouldn't trust anyone entirely," Lockington replied. "Now let me see if I can guess the names right. And you come, give me a hug."

Both Lena and Lockington had walked into the sanctuary room as they spoke. Lena had gone to the children, and they clung to her side as they stared at their grandfather.

"Let's see. The young lady who spoke first is Kissa." Kissa nodded but wouldn't walk towards Lockington.

"You'll get used to me being with you once the danger has subsided."

"Subsided. Grandfather, seriously?"

"The danger is never truly over, Yalena. You will have periods of peace, but the danger will not be over until you resign to the healing grounds where my mother resides. Now let's see, Kamau had the deep blue eyes like his twin, so you must be Kamau."

"Hello, grandfather," Kamau replied as he left his mother's side to shake Lockington's hand.

"Well, at least one of the two likes me." Kamau smiled but said nothing. Lena had already begun to teach her eldest the 'Art of War' by Sun Tzu. Kamau had trusted no one who came into the penthouse other than his mother, father, and siblings. "Smart boy. Okay, the violet eyed boy is Tehuti. So that leaves me with Tahira and Tendai, and I definitely can't tell you two apart."

"It's tricky, but Tahira has a birthmark shaped like Auset's symbol on the back of her neck. And she's also the one dressed in pink. It makes it easier to tell them apart."

"And, of course, Tendai has my dimples."

"So nice of you to come home and be with your family."

"Don't start, Gordon." Ren walked around the children's mess and over to Lena and kissed her. Then he whispered in her ear, "how long has he been here."

"I can hear you, Lorenzo."

"Of course, Gordon." Ren turned towards Gordon. "So, what brings you here?"

"Just visiting. I figured it was overdue. And to bring you some news. Not in front of the children."

"Grandfather, you'd have to go into Ren's office. Otherwise, we can all hear you."

"Guess it doesn't matter. Jonathan Dunne is deceased." Gordon waited for a reaction. When no one reacted, he continued, "and Madeline is back."

"Any word on any movement?"

"No, Yalena. Everything is quiet right now. Too quiet for my liking."

"See Ren; I'm not the only one. She's plotting something big."

"Well, All Hallow's Eve is around the corner?"

"Bite your tongue, Gordon." Ren replied as he looked at Yalena with raised eyebrows. "Yes, that would be a perfect time, yet we have no idea how they'll attack."

"So, on a more positive note. Are you pregnant with the last set or what?"

"Grandfather!" When he didn't recant, "no. We're holding on until after this is over. I guess it won't be long now. All Hallows Eve is in a couple of days. We're not ready for an attack."

"I would prefer that our yearly celebration didn't turn into a war, but I've been planning for the upheaval Yalena, since you were pregnant with the triplets."

"And why do I keep finding out about these things right before it happens?"

"Sorry, love, I honestly didn't want to burden you. On the night of the party, we will greet our clan, including the children. After, your grandfather will go with Patrick, taking the children and Kai's family to a safe place. You and I will stay to take care of whatever happens."

"I promise, the children will be guarded with my life, Yalena."

"Thank you, granddad. I appreciate that." Ren embraced Lena from behind and kissed her neck.

"I'm going back to work, love. Keeping things regular. Wouldn't want them to suspect anything."

"Are we sure when they returned to New York," asked Lockington.

"I believe they came in last night. And they weren't accompanied by anyone in particular, but I've gotten a report that we have an influx of visitors. Something tells me they're with Madeline and her new beau, Carlos," stated Ren.

"Well, I guess we'll be ready for anything."

"We will, Lena, we will."

"Later, Gordon. See you in the morning, Lena."

Lena smiled and regarded Ren as he left. Then she turned to the children and walked them over to the sitting area. The children had been working on their latest lessons.

"Not wasting any time with them, Yalena?"

"No, I'm not. They have got to be ready when the time comes. Candace and Kai teach them about Khemetic Spirituality, practices, and history. I cover basic math and reading, as well as our history. After all, I want my children to be aware the people they deal with in Ren's world and the human world."

"Mind if I give them a lesson of my own? I'm sure their powers have started to manifest. I would like to help them use and control them."

"That's fine, but don't destroy the sanctuary, please, or the building for that matter."

"Fine, fine. You have them sitting on the floor for class? Do you use the classroom area?"

"We kind of like it. And yes, Kissa and Kamau when they have class. But the children prefer the center of the room for some reason." Even though Lena allowed her grandfather to teach the children, she preferred not to leave them alone. So she remained on the chaise lounge across from where they were all gathered.

She sat comfortably, watching and listening. The children seemed to be veritably fascinated by Lockington. The tales he wove seem to materialize right in front of them. She remembered when she was young; she, too, had been fascinated by his stories. Her father would continuously say, 'Gordon, stop filling my daughters' heads with nonsense,' but it wasn't nonsense after all. Now, she reveled in that world and brought children into it, whose purpose was to tame it.

She was just getting comfortable in the chair. Lena had settled into work on her next book. She knew she no longer needed to write, but she loved it, and she wanted to have the first draft done before the week was up. That's when her sister came into the room.

Lena was a little shocked. She had no idea her sister was familiar with the penthouse or that she was there. Then it crossed Lena's mind, how did her sister gain access to the room? The last time she asked Cell for her, he said she hadn't been around and had been acting peculiarly.

"Yazzi, are you okay?"

"Fine." Lena realized that everything was not okay. Yazmine was not herself. "Hi, Kamau, Kissa. Granddaddy, I haven't seen you in a while." None of the children answered Yazmine, and as she walked toward them, they backed away.

"Yazz, you're scaring the children."

"Oh, please. They're not scared of me, are you Kamau? You recognize me, your aunt Yazzi." Kamau didn't answer but looked at Lena, who shook her head no. She discerned that Kamau would go to Yazmine just to appease her, but Lena was leery of her sister now. She had often wondered what the outcome would be of her sister's relationship with Seth and whether Yazmine would be able to break it. Not to mention, her grandfather had just mentioned not trusting family.

It was apparent now that she couldn't trust her sister. Lena was waiting for something, she anticipated Seth would try again, and Sekhmet had warned her that he would use her sister against her. Lena didn't want to believe it, but she had a feeling when Cell said she had been acting strangely and she hadn't visited. Still, Yazzi had seemed so into Cell. Maybe that had been part of the plan all the time. Lena didn't want to believe that, but it made sense. Yazmine had been allowed to go where Seth would never be allowed. The only question in Lena's mind now was whether or not Yazmine was genuinely involved. Had she been forced to, compelled by Seth, or was she doing this of her own free will? Lena couldn't tell. Ren told her that compulsion couldn't make someone act against their intrinsic beliefs.

Yazmine's mind seemed shrouded in a haze of anger. She wasn't sure what that meant. When the driver was compelled, his mind was different.

"Yazzi, come here." Yalena tried her soft angelic voice. Ren had been training her as he noticed her powers develop. Yazmine turned but didn't respond. It was as if her body and mind were fighting. Then Yazmine shook her head and turned back to the children. That must have been a strong compulsion. Even Ren had succumbed to Lena's voice. "Yazzi," Lena called her sister even more softly. There was a firm push at the end. "Yazzi, come here. I only want to hug you. I have missed you."

"Lies! You haven't even called. Your brood keeps growing, and I cannot even bear a child."

"I am sorry, Yazzi, but I didn't create that. That decision was out of my hands."

"Please, I know you're the favorite, but why have I been punished for it. I have done nothing to warrant such a life sentence. Perhaps you can give me one of yours. I would take Tahira." The whole time Yazmine and Lena spoke, Yazmine moved closer and closer to the children, and hiding behind Lockington seemed to make little difference. He seemed unwilling to aid her. Lena didn't want to scare Yazmine with any sudden movements. Yet, she perceived no other way to move Yazmine away from her children.

"I'm sorry, Yazzi, but my children don't go anywhere with anyone. Even Kai's family has escorts."

"Don't pretend it is because you don't trust them. All of you are protected because Ren has enemies and many of them."

"Enough with the dance. Yazmine, come here!" Lena had pushed a little extra against Yazmine's compulsion, and the scream that came from her sister frightened everyone except Lena. She had known that pushing against the compulsion already placed in her sister's mind would cause some pain. Yet, she had not expected such a reaction. It was evidence that Seth was torturing Yazmine. She knew who was responsible and guessed that this was his attempt. He had waited until his mother returned, and they were probably going to make a joint effort. Yet, she had no idea what the objective was. Was Yazmine supposed to kidnap the children or herself?

"Don't do that, Yalena!" She shouted.

"Why are you here, Yazmine? We haven't seen you in a few weeks. Where have you been?" Yazmine's countenance changed ever so slightly as she tried to remember. Lena witnessed the change again as Yazmine got angry at not remembering.

"I'm just going to take one of the children with me."

"Now that's not going to happen, Yazmine. The children don't leave my home without Kai or me, and Patrick will not allow it."

"I believe you don't have a choice." Before Lena reacted, Yazmine picked up Tahira, who had been walking toward her aunt. "Now, I just have to bring back one of you. Either Tahira or you go, but one of you is going."

Lena didn't reply immediately. Instead, she decided to take a moment and weigh her options. Kai and her family were on their lunch break and wouldn't be back to the house for an hour or so. Patrick was just beyond the door, waiting for an opportunity. She was sure that her grandfather was weighing all the options. In actuality, there weren't many that would result in Tahira being safe. If she tried to take Tahira away from Yazmine, she would be hurt or killed. They were still researching the strength and longevity of her children. They had no idea what they were dealing with. It was almost as though her children were the first of their kind--the first children born of a vampire and a human who were more vampire than human.

"Yazmine, I'm going to need you to put Tahira down. Granddad, I need you to take the other children upstairs, please." Lockington nodded, picked up the other two triplets, and called Kissa and Kamau to follow him. He guided them around Yazmine and ensured they were out of reach before stopping and waiting for Tahira.

"I'm sorry I can't do that. If I put Tahira down, you won't go willingly. I'm well aware that you are powerful enough to stop me. I am not stupid, Yalena. I see that you have calculated your options. I would like to return to my love in one piece."

"You know that if you take me to Seth, he will kill you anyway. He's using you. He doesn't love you at all."

"Please; how would you understand? You know nothing of him. You disregarded him because he is not as eminent or handsome as you think Ren is. The truth is he is more prominent and handsome, and he loves me."

"You're fooling yourself, Yazmine. He had every intention of making me his from the moment I set foot in the club."

"While that may be true, it was the power he was after, not you. Sorry, Granddad, I'm not giving Tahira back until I'm sure that I am safely away from here. So do as Yelena says." Lena nodded, and Lockington continued his trek with the children up to their apartment. All except Tahira, who was calm but started to get restless in her aunt's arms and began to squirm.

"Alright, Yazmine. What do I have to do for you to put Tahira down?"

"Walk with me out of the door. Don't call Patrick or any other guard. I will release Tahira when we get to the door."

"Patrick has been standing outside the sanctuary door for a while now. I didn't call him. Can you please give him Tahira when we approach the main door?"

"That is fine with me as long as he doesn't try anything to save you. Let's go. You first." Lena walked to the door and opened it. Of course, there was Patrick, as expected.

"Patrick, please let us pass."

"I heard everything. Are you sure this is the right thing? Mr. Arias will be quite distraught."

"Yes, he will be, but it will all work out for the best. Now Yazmine, I need you to give Patrick Tahira. Patrick, take her straight upstairs and tell my grandfather he needs to stay until Kai and her family get back."

Yazmine hesitated. "Yazmine, it's okay. I will go with you, but I will tell you now that you have chosen to side against me. That's unfortunate for you and it will not end well once we step out of this door. Seth can't be trusted, darling. He will not keep his word. You are collateral damage, I'm afraid. However, this could stop here, and I promise to help you. I promise I will do everything in my power to keep you safe. I understand that he has control over you.

Let this stop, Yazmine." As Lena spoke, she witnessed the ray of emotions pass through her sister's face, but in the end, her anger seemed to return.

"We have been here too long already. Let's go." Lena was disappointed that Yazmine didn't change her mind, but wasn't surprised.

They walked out of the front door, followed by several soldiers who kept their distance. Yalena had motioned for them not to respond. She conceived that they would want to monitor as much as possible. It was essential to observe which direction she was going or the type of vehicle.

As soon as they stepped out of the building, a car pulled up. There was nothing that stood out about the vehicle. She was sure if there was anything significant to see, her soldiers would find out. She stepped into the car and greeted blackness.

Chapter 26

"I returned as soon as I felt something was wrong. Patrick, how could you let her walk out of the door?"

"You told me to follow her orders no matter what. You didn't say that I should take over in a matter of security. I was following orders. And Yazmine was under his control. We discerned it, and I could hear it through the door. She was not herself. Seth had gotten to her."

"We perceived that would happen if it hadn't already. I let her into our sanctum to appease Lena. I shouldn't have. Now, all we can do is wait. The family will be under 24-hour guard. It is clear that our home is no longer safe."

"I understand, Ren."

"Has Kai and her family returned?"

"Yes. We are preparing them to leave."

"Yes. Our plan stays. You stay with me, Kai and her family will take the children to our compound. Of course, a soldier will accompany them. Tell them only to take the necessities. Have we moved any of our stock?"

"Yes, all except a few bags in each storage facility. There's enough here to get you through. The staff has been advised. Everything will run as it should, Ren."

"Now, we wait for Lena."

"Are you sure she will be okay? Will she try to make contact?"

"Yes, she is developing as we expected. They have no clue what they have unleashed. And I like it that way. But, I must say, I'm curious if he'll figure it out in time to save himself."

When Lena's unconscious body arrived at the warehouse, Seth was occupied. They lay her on a cot in a back room. It took a while before she awoke. She had gathered herself before opening her eyes. She listened intently to her surroundings. She sensed that there were less than ten people in the building and made a point to identify each of them. She smelled Seth close to her, and that made her skin crawl. Yet she kept her composure. When she did, she looked up into the face of Seth, who was smiling down at her.

Before she opened her eyes, the last thing she did was try to contact Sekhmet. Sekhmet had assured her she could escape, but she had to find a way to do it. She sensed a guard was outside of her door, and Seth would make sure she stayed with him at all costs. She hadn't even had enough time to identify the area or contact Ren. She would need an empty room to do that. Finally, she opened her eyes.

"Not so high and mighty now, are you?"

"Nothing has changed, Seth."

"Of course it has. I have you, so I rule." Yalena laughed before answering. Seth stroked her cheek, and Lena jerked up and away to give herself room.

"You are not my mate! So nothing has changed." Yalena hissed. Seth didn't reply but surveyed her. She could tell he was trying to figure out whether she was telling the truth or lying.

"You being here changes everything. After tomorrow, he'll be dead, and you will be mine. Your children will be hunted and killed." He stopped after he noticed her immediate reaction. A reaction she couldn't help no matter how she tried to control her body. "Yes, I'm sorry, but I will not be raising Ren's brood. We will start our own. After a while, you will come to love me as all victims love their captors. Once I'm bound to you, I will have the power to rule." He had slowly sat on the bed and began to run his hand up her leg. Yalena removed his hand as he squeezed her knee.

"Once you kill my mate, my power dies with him. Only my true mate can manifest the powers within me. Only my true mate can control me. If I had fallen in love with a human, my powers would never have come."

"You lie!" Seth jumped up. Lena backed away from Seth, lay back on the bed, crossed her arms over her chest, and looked up at the ceiling. It didn't matter whether he believed her or not. She was more than satisfied to get a rise from him. "You smug little bitch. You lie. There is no way that the power is connected to that man. You lie."

"It's not connected to him; it is a direct link to the love we share. It began when we became committed." She realized she had said too much. If he were smart, he would imprison Ren and make her obey his every command. Somehow she had to escape and make it to the party tomorrow. When she would no longer respond to him, he left. She twisted the knob to make sure Seth had locked the door. The guard on the other side of the door laughed, mistaking it for her trying to escape. She put the chair under the doorknob and lay back on the bed.

By the time she had calmed herself enough to project, Ren was asleep in their bed with the children stretched out next to him. She had been gone for only a few hours, and she missed them immensely. She called to him softly. She wanted him awake but didn't want to disturb the children. They would wonder where she was, and she wasn't sure what he told them.

"Ren, my love." She didn't have to call him more than once.

"Yalena, are you well, my love?"

"Yes, I'm fine. Little grossed out, perhaps."

"He touched you?"

"Listen, I have to make this quick. They're planning some coup at the All Hallows Eve party tomorrow. I believe my disappearance has something to do with it. They plan on killing you, my love."

"They won't succeed. My love, I need you by my side. Do you know where you are? Kiyoshi and a few others followed the car but lost track of it near the docks."

"No, I was knocked out when I got into the car. I have no clue how far we are. But I'm sure Seth wouldn't want to be far from the club. So probably somewhere in the city. I will be by your side. I'll be okay. Just make sure my babies are well and out of harm's way tomorrow, and I will see you at the party." Now she made the promise, how was she going to keep it? If she had suspected right, they were planning on keeping her from the party. So she would be locked up here. The question is whether Seth would support his mother's attempt. Would he leave her alone? She only had certain powers now; she may require some assistance. She would hope to manipulate Yazmine, but only if Seth had released her from the compulsion would she be of any use. She would need all of her energy for tomorrow. Tonight she would try to sleep. She went again to Ren's side. He had laid back down amidst the children. How she longed to be by his side and hold her children. Now she would sleep alone--something she had not done all night in over a year.

She lay utterly still, phasing between her penthouse home and sleep. While she slept, Sekhmet filled her with all the energy Lena's body could manage. When Lena awoke the following day, she felt a surge of strength she had not felt before.

When Seth couldn't drag any more information from her, he decided to use his ace, Lena's sister Yazmine. Lena refused to rise or even open her eyes when the door opened. She wasn't sure who it was, but as soon as Yazmine stepped through, she knew. She thought that she could feel the compulsion coming off her in waves. What exactly had Seth sent her sister to do that needed so much compulsion? Now she wondered how to prevent Kai's family from falling prey. She would have to research it as soon as possible to protect Kai's family and hers. She still hadn't opened her eyes when Yazmine sat on the bed. She wanted to ease her sister's pain. Seth could have eased her suffering but let her suffer instead. She had warned her. Why did she go back to him? Maybe it wasn't her choice. Since Seth had taken her blood, he could control her. Her bond with Cell didn't negate her bond with Seth.

"I know you're awake, and you recognized that I'm here. So you might as well sit up and talk to me. I fathom what you must be thinking."

"How could you possibly grasp what I must be thinking," Yalena sputtered. "I don't know what to think. I comprehend that my sister has betrayed me to my enemy. To a man, she thinks loves her. Honestly, Yazmine, men who love us don't force us to kill our family."

"What would make you think I'm here to kill you?"

"Seriously? The knife in your hand."

"Well, I just need to drain some of your blood. Seth seems to think that your blood will heal me, and by sucking your blood, the poison that runs through my body will run through yours." There was silence for several moments before Lena replied.

"Sorry, sis, but I'm not letting you anywhere near me. I will not attempt to save anyone who is deliberately out to harm me."

"Oh, please, you'll be fine by tomorrow."

"Yazzi, he's going to kill my children and the love of my life. You can't honestly think I would help him or you at this point?"

"But I am your sister, your flesh and blood. You would think of your love before me?"

"My children are also my flesh and blood. They are growing fast but are in no way ready to defend themselves."

"Okay, if I make him promise to keep the children alive, will you help me."

"I will not make a deal with the devil. I cannot trust you as I once thought I could. For him, life and death are not important unless we're talking about his life."

"You know, he said you wouldn't help me because I betrayed you, but I told him you would always help your own. Guess I forgot about the blood of your womb."

"Yazmine, please don't push me. I beg of you. I will defend myself, and I will punish him for making me have to." Yazmine smiled, and then an awful sound escaped her lips as she crashed to the floor.

"I would not let anyone hurt you, Yalena." Seth had entered without Lena's knowledge. She was so focused on her sister that she didn't notice. How careless of her not to be vigilant under all circumstances. Seth had stabbed Yazmine. Yalena was in shock. That, she was not expecting. The wound didn't appear fatal; Lena could see that her sister was still breathing. The pain Yazmine felt shook Lena. She had not realized how connected she was to her sister.

Lena closed her eyes and centered herself. She would have to have a clear head. This had to be some sort of trick. Either he wanted to make sure she knew he would protect her. Fat chance, she thought. He believed Lena would let down her guard. Or he figured if Lena saw her sister suffering, she would let her feed to save her life. She would not let him manipulate her that easily. But Yazmine wasn't a vampire, she thought to herself. Then she opened her eyes and stared at both of them.

"Are you going to forgive your sister and heal her. Or should I put her out of her misery? It's not like she'll live long. She doesn't have the blood of an ancient flowing through her, nor does she have Ren to save her. I'd rather let her die than let Cell anywhere near her. She thought she was rid of me. Can you imagine the betrayal? I was hurt, Yazmine. I thought we had something cherished."

As Seth spoke, Lena stared at her sister as she lay on the floor. It took every ounce of her to maintain her composer. She would not let him see how he had shaken her. Had it all been a ruse? it dawned on her that from the moment Yazmine grabbed Tahira she would have to kill her sister, but she had hoped it wouldn't go that far. Had Yazmine feigned the haze and anger? They were sisters; they loved each other, or so she had thought. How long had Yazmine hated her?

"Yazmine, how long have you hated me?" Lena asked before she could catch herself. Seth smiled but didn't look at Lena, and she made sure not to glance in his direction. She conceived that they wanted her to respond and wonder where it would lead.

At first, Yazmine didn't respond. She didn't even move. Then, after moments of deadly silence, Yazmine slowly moved to sit up. She was smiling. Lena had only seen a smile once when they were in high school together. Yazmine had hated this Barbie doll looking ninth grader, and when she finally got the chance to fight her, she smiled that smile.

"From the moment you were born," seemed to hiss from her sister's mouth.

"How sad," Lena replied softly. "From the moment I could, I have loved you." There was an uneasy silence for a while before Lena spoke again. "I will not help you. Please leave me." Seth bent to pick Yazmine from the floor.

"Well, Yazmine, I guess your sister has made her decision. She is willing to let you die. Not the most compassionate, my Queen." Lena didn't answer but turned to face the wall, showing them her back.

Lena waited for them to close the door before she started to cry. There were no words to express the pain. Her heart broke into pieces. She had always admired Yazmine as a child. She utterly adored her and wanted to be like her. How could her sister possibly hate her enough to want to see everything in her life destroyed? She brought her knees up to her chest and wrapped her arms around them before putting her head down to cry. They had wanted to break her, and for the moment, she felt broken.

"Did you have to stab me? I mean, you could have thought of something else."

"Well, your idea was moving too slow, and we still don't have a way to control her. You taking her blood was key."

"She can hear us, can't she?"

"Yes, I believe so."

The conversation stopped, and Yalena believed the footsteps were them walking away. What Yalena heard was more than enough to still her tears. If they were trying to fake her out, they would be surprised when they came into the room. She sat quietly and began to build an energy field around her. She didn't want to use all of her energy, so she created a small one. Just enough to cover her body.

They didn't enter, and Yalena didn't move. There was no window so Lena couldn't gauge the time of day. As time passed, she knew she had to escape the building. She listened carefully, but the building was full of life before and was now deathly silent. She closed her eyes and centered her body. She needed to find Yazmine or Seth. With minimal effort, she found them sitting at a coffee shop not far from the club. They were sitting and chatting like they didn't have a care in the world.

Lena took a deep breath before getting off the cot and trying the door. To her surprise, the knob turned. As soon as she opened it and saw the man standing on the other side, she closed it. She could hear the explosion of laughter to her reaction.

"My Queen, won't you grace us with your presence. You didn't actually think they would leave you alone, did you?" There was more laughter.

Lena didn't respond. She had not heard anyone in the building. Or maybe they hadn't been there when she scanned.

"She's confused. Let me help you; we've been outside for a while. That's where Seth instructed us to kill you, but you took so long, we brought the fight inside to you."

Lena took a deep breath once more before she opened the door. "I do apologize for being rude. I was not expecting anyone other than the usual guard." She lied. She didn't want them to know that they were right. She wanted to close her eyes and scan them, but she grasped that there would be no time for that. Before going to the club, she would have to face them immediately to flee the warehouse. She wondered where she was when the sound of movement brought her back to the actual situation.

"Don't daydream. We wouldn't want to catch you off guard. We want to play with you a little."

By the time she came back to her senses, the man, if he was that, was grabbing her hand, but not for long. His paramount response was to pull back, but he only held on tighter. What happened next was unexpected. As he was about to turn to the men in the room, his hand and arm caught on fire. He pulled away and waved his arm, trying to put out the fire. But, of course, we all know that fanning a flame does nothing more than create a more significant fire.

Lena was amazed. She didn't know that she had that ability, but Sekhmet is sometimes depicted surrounded by fire after all. She held back a smirk as she eased her way to the staircase while everyone watched as the fire grew. Unfortunately, she only made it from the door to the middle of the room, which meant she was surrounded. She had no weapon and was unaware of what she was fighting. Still, a wounded animal doesn't take long to show its colors. They began to transform before her eyes. She wondered how Seth had managed to get werewolves working for him.

"Fire won't help you if you're dead," One of the wolves yelled as the other lay quivering on the floor.

"You have to do more than touch me to kill me." Yalena couldn't help but smirk. Still, she knew that channeling the fire would make her exhausted. She would be of no use to Ren when she made it to the club. She had to think of a way to escape them.

As they moved in on her, her back was toward the staircase. It had been a long time since she fought more than one person. She sensed that the werewolves wouldn't be as polite or fair as her fellow students at the martial arts school.

The first attack was way too easy. Even though it clawed her as she threw it to the other side of the room, they wanted to gauge her prowess and her abilities. One lunged at her from behind. The leap was so high that she only had to raise her hand to connect with him in mid-strike and throw him over her head as she made sure to begin burning his chest as she did so. The whimper that came from it was disconcerting, but it opened up a hole for her to at least put her back against the wall. Now, none of them were behind her. She would have a better chance. She changed her strategy. She began to execute the final form she learned with her master. It was perfect for a situation like this. Not the werewolf issue, but surrounded by your enemy. She began to circle and eye each wolf that surrounded her. She had disabled two, she only had four to go and quite a few openings to escape. She just wanted to make sure that she had no pursuers.

While Yalena was fighting for her life, Ren ensured that everything was going smoothly. He couldn't afford to have one thing go wrong. The children were on their way to a house in South Hampton. He had rented a mansion for the year. He hoped that the owner would eventually let him buy it. It was big enough to hold his expanding family as well as a few of his closest clan members and the soldiers.

Ren was glad to have the assistance and counsel of Lockington. He had served as a great friend over the centuries, and now he seemed to be vested in Ren's children. Ren was relieved when Lockington volunteered to take Kai, her family, and the children to the Hamptons with the soldier. He trusted the soldiers with his life, but he trusted very few with the lives of his children. He knew Kai would look after the children until he arrived with Lena. He took a deep breath hoping that she was well and on her way. He wished she was by his side and prayed for her safe return. He had several soldiers looking for her, but he would have preferred Patrick to be the one looking. Patrick didn't think it was a good idea to leave Ren. They both suspected something as a result of the negative energy circulating the city, as though something was brewing. It was tense and dark; it didn't feel right.

"Cell, anything from anyone?"

"Kiyoshi called in, and there was no sign of her. They did, however, pick up the scent of werewolves in the city."

"Werewolves, of course. We have several that are coming here tonight. They're trusted allies."

"Kiyoshi said this was a different clan. Our allies are still where we left them. They're following the scent."

"Keep me abreast. It's getting late. I wish she were here already."

"She'll be here, Ren. You know she'll fight her way out, and our soldiers are looking for her."

"I know she'll be here, but when?"

While Ren was organizing, Lena was still fighting her way out of the building. They had closed in the circle with the four. They tried to pounce on her, but she kept jumping out of the way. They were trying to push her into the center to surround her. Lena held her position but was tired and needed to eliminate them. But how? The room was empty of a chair or any furniture. Maybe she should just make a run for it. Before she could bound for the stairs, two lunged at her. Lena ducked and dived between its legs, but not before she got a long gash on her side as they crashed into each other. Just two left. She bound for the stairs. She barely made it before one jumped on her and sent her sailing down the last few steps. She thought of flames, and he caught on fire and rolled off of her while it lashed out. The blow caught the side of her face leaving a gash from her ear to her lip.

Lena got up before the other came down the final stair. He had pulled back because of what happened to his partner. Yalena didn't want to go straight for the door because she would get caught between the door and the wolf. She was slowly losing energy due to going around and around, trying to avoid the wolves and then burning them. She could hear Sekhmet's voice as she tried to figure out what to do.

"I told you that the flames would drain you."

If he was a regular man, she would fight him in hand to hand combat, but she hadn't learned how to fight a wolf, much less without her sword. She wondered if she would have to walk with it all the time now.

"Listen, I don't want to end up like my friend here, but if I let you go, Seth will kill me."

"If you don't let me go, I'll kill you."

"Should I rip your throat out? It'll be quick."

"If anything happens to me, my husband will kill you."

"Please, your husband's probably already dead." His words enraged her so much that she decided to take him on, no matter what. As she raised her hands, fire shot from her palms and engulfed the wolf in mid-leap. It shocked Lena; she thought she would have to fight her way out. Then, before she could even open the door to leave, she passed out.

Lena awoke to banging on the door. The noise was making her head hurt. She sat for a moment and tried putting the pieces of what had happened together. She knew that the use of fire would drain her, but she had no idea how much. Finally, she collected herself and got up off the floor.

"Queen Yalena? Queen Yalena, are you okay?"

"Kiyoshi? Kiyoshi, is that you?"

"Yes, are you alright?"

"More or less in one piece. I don't have the energy to break the door or open it." As she said this, she leaned against the wall and slid down to the floor. She was barely awake at this point. The only thing she wanted to do was sleep.

"Your majesty, please stand away from the door."

"I'm not standing at all. I'm sitting on the side of the door.""Damien, if you please," she heard Kiyoshi say. Damien verbally confirmed before breaking down the door. He then stood aside as Kiyoshi rushed in and immediately lifted her, cradling Lena in his arms. As soon as she was close, her smell entangled itself around him, and he turned his head.

"John, how do we return her if we can't be close to her. I can restrain myself, but I don't want to have to fight you all off as we drive." He moved his arm from under her knee, and her feet hit the floor, waking her up.

"Wrap her in this blanket."

"John, that thing smells god awful," Lena said groggily.

"It's either god awful, or we kill Kiyoshi in the van, then ravage you and get killed by Ren when he finds out."

"As if you all could take me," Kiyoshi replied with a wry smile.

"Fine, the blanket."

"Let me dress your wounds; we don't want them to fester, they'll leave a scar as it is, but the faster I tend to them the better," said Kiyoshi. He asked Damon to put the blanket on the floor, and Lena lay down. Kiyoshi raised her torn shirt to take a look at her wound. The slash down her side was deep and almost cut to the bone.

"I need to wash out the wound. I have everything I need. Just brace yourself, it's deep." Lena grunted as Kiyoshi poured a clear liquid over the wounds and then gently began to cover it with a green salve before wrapping it with gauze. "Your face isn't too bad, but it requires more than I have here. I'll wash it at least and spread as much of the salve as I have before wrapping it.'"

"Kiyoshi, what time is it?"

"Thirty minutes before midnight, your majesty. We must take you back to the club."

"How far away are we?"

"Honestly, a few blocks away. This warehouse is one of the many warehouses that Ren keeps. You've been under our nose the whole time. We were on a wild goose chase following the scent of those wolves."

"Take me to Ren; immediately!" They nodded in response as Kiyoshi lifted her and carried her to the van. She was so exhausted that she fell back to sleep before they pulled off.

"Kiyoshi, did you see the wolves in there?'"

"No, I believe I was tending to her wounds while you and the others searched the place. I hope you put them out of their misery."

"What was left of them. At least three of the six wolves were burnt to a crisp. We killed the two unconscious ones."

"We'll come back after we drop her off and clean up, but we need to take her back."

It wasn't long before the guards reunited Lena with Ren. Although she was out of it, she could hear the constant footsteps that didn't match those who carried her. It was nearly twelve and she was sure that Ren was beside himself with worry.

"Dua ntr, Patrick, what happened to her?"

"She fought her way out. Good thing, Kiyoshi got there when he did. She was exhausted and passed out. Apparently, she burned them. Some to a crisp."

"Bring me two bags from the stock."'

"Already on it." By the time he finished his sentence, Cell was at the door with several bags of blood.

"Leave us. We should be ready for the midnight welcome." Both nodded and left, closing the door behind them.

Ren unwrapped the blanket. "Man, that is a god awful smell, but I guess it helped you come back in one piece." He paused for a second to examine her. She was bloody, and her lip swollen. He removed the dressing from her wounds. "Kiyoshi had done an excellent job, but as it is with wolf bites or scratches, they fester quickly no matter what." There was a ghastly gash from the side of her right bosom down to her hip. "I will have to tend to them carefully to minimize scarring, but they will always be there, a reminder to both of us. My love." She had a grueling fight to free herself; werewolves are a fierce bunch. One is a handful, but six. Thankfully, she survived, even though her wounds looked terrible. "Yalena, you must wake and drink to heal. I need you cleaned and dressed shortly."

"Okay, but you know I hate that stuff cold. Can you drink it? Please."

"Yalena, this is our special stock. You must drink it."

"Ren."

"Yalena, drink it," he growled between his teeth. Her eyes shot open after his last response, and she stared up at him. "I'm sorry. I was racked with worry. My heart aches to see you this way. Why did you go with her? You didn't have to get into the car once you left the building. You could have gotten away."

"I thought she was under compulsion. I thought he would have killed her if she didn't return with me, but she was really on his side. She betrayed me. They wanted control of me. I was surprised by the whole thing. Then when I thought that they were gone, I found six werewolves, and they were there to kill me."

"We will deal with your sister and Seth. Drink my love. We will show them that you are stronger than ever."Lena put her mouth to the pouch and greedily gulped its contents as Ren stared at her. He had been so worried while she was gone. He had no clue what to do. He sent the soldiers to look for her as soon as he perceived, but he continued his routine. He didn't want anyone aware that she was gone. He told the children that she had to go away but would be back.

Ren cleaned her wounds and watched her body recover from her ordeal as she drank the blood.

Chapter 27

It would take time for her body to heal itself. As it began, Yalena opened her eyes and smiled at Ren.

"I told you nothing to worry about; I came back as I said I would."

"Yes, but you took too long, and you came back all beaten and bloody." They smiled at each other, and Ren lowered his head to kiss her. His beloved came back to him.

Lena gazed up at Ren with a sparkle in her eyes. "I've missed you so much."

"I will enjoy pleasing you when this is over. Right now, wash and dress quickly. I will greet our clan while you do. It is after midnight. Patrick will wait for you."

Lena slowly got up off the bed with Ren's help. Her body was racked with pain as her wounds healed. Lena stood transfixed at the bathroom door after Ren left. She stood watching as Ren's blood disappeared and her muscles knitted back together. She was horrified at how nasty her wounds were. Her sister had set her up to be killed. Lena never thought that Yazmine would betray her. She had not known that her sister hated her so much that she would want her dead. Lena stared at her face for a few moments.

She came out of her stillness, knowing Ren would be waiting on her. Ren had cleaned each gash and rubbed his blood into her wounds, but they still looked swollen and jagged. She watched, transfixed as the cuts slowly closed. She thought that vampire blood held no healing properties but there was something about his blood that she didn't know. Each time she was hurt his blood had been used to heal her.

Lena made sure it didn't take long to get herself together. After a short time, she couldn't bear to look at herself in the mirror. As soon as she opened the door to the room, Patrick materialized in front of her.

"It would be faster if you carried me, Patrick. I can't move very fast right now."

"That shouldn't be a problem." Immediately Patrick put a scarf around his nose and mouth and picked up Yalena. He tried to move gingerly in order not to jostle her too much. Yalena found it interesting that the soldiers didn't have Ren's gracefulness. They were fast like other vampires, but there was something awkward and mechanical about them.

As Lena was getting herself together, Ren observed the crowd from the balcony. It appeared to be the regular Halloween crowd, but the vibe he felt was quite the opposite. He perceived the vision beneath him would change as soon as he mentioned his Queen. He signaled Cell to turn the balcony light on and waited for the crowd to quiet down. The music volume slowly disappeared, and everyone looked up. Ren smiled, looking down upon his subjects.

"Happy Hallows Eve." The crowd roared a reply, and everyone clapped. Ren remembered the celebration of the year before as he stood on the balcony. Last year he introduced his Queen to them. It was a happy occasion. Now, the threat of war hung in the balance. When the crowd had quieted again, he started once more.

"Glad to see everyone tonight. It is indeed a blessed occasion. We've had the pleasure of welcoming our twins and triplets into the world this year." As he said this, a screen came down from the ceiling. Images of the children flashed across. Gasps and ahhs escaped from the club floor. The photos showed how each child had grown over the years. At the end of the slides, the screen returned to the ceiling.

"As you have seen, the children are growing at a rapid rate. My Queen and I are pleased with their progress." Ren paused, not wanting to continue. "At present, my beloved is recovering from being kidnapped and fighting her way out of a den of wolves." Horror escaped the crowd, and the clan members began to bicker animatedly beneath Ren. Then someone yelled amidst the crowd.

"How do we know she's alive?"

"Rumors say that you kidnapped her." Ren laughed at their response. It was more than expected. He was certain his enemies were in the crowd. Even Seth and Lena's sister were present.

"It was stupid for someone to say that I had her kidnapped. It would serve no purpose other than to keep her safe from my enemies, and I definitely would not put her in harm's way for any reason."

"Prove it," yelled Yazmine. "'We want to see her. We were told that she's dead."

At that moment, Patrick arrived with Lena at the balcony door. She heard her sister's voice and cringed. Her heart was scarred by her sister's betrayal. Rage and pain seeping to the top at the thought of what her sister did. Patrick put her gently on her feet, and she opened the door to the balcony. Ren turned towards her, moving the mic from his mouth.

"Yalena, are you feeling better." She smiled as she took the few pain-filled steps forward into the spotlight. The crowd gasped. The screen came down again, and Yalena's image appeared larger than life before them. The slash on her cheek was still open and slowly healing before their eyes. Yalena grabbed the mic.

"I stand before you, scarred but whole. I have only returned to my husband quite recently, and as you see, the injuries have yet to heal." As she spoke, she raised the fitted shirt to her a bit above her waist and turned to the side, so they could see the wound inflicted upon her. The image reflected on the screen made Yalena wince. The gashes were ghastly, even hideous on screen. Again, gasps skittered across the clan members gathered at Zoe's. She lowered her shirt and waited until they quieted and continued.

"Don't even dare to mention that my King inflicted them. The traitors walk among you. My sister didn't just betray me; she betrayed all of us by partaking in Seth's scheme. Unfortunately, they will no longer be a part of this beautiful world." As Lena spoke, several guards surrounded Yazmine. Seth had already escaped as she spoke. She saw him but could do nothing at the moment.

"My Queen, how did you escape? We heard there were werewolves involved."

"Like this," she replied, opening her palm, and a flame ignited. Then she focused her energy and threw the fire to the fountain in the middle of the floor. Everyone scattered as the flame passed through the crowd and flames bloomed and grew over the fountain before them.

Ren closed the distance between them and encircled his arms around her. He kissed her cheek before taking the mic from her hands. Yalena leaned on him. Her body had not fully recovered, and the demonstration took more from her than she calculated. There was a lot still to be done. They would have to deal with the rest of the council. Well, Madeline, to be exact. The spotlight dimmed, and Yalena took a moment to close her eyes, trying to gather her strength.

"You don't have to stay," Ren whispered in her ear.

"Where else could I be? I will not hide and leave you to face this alone." Ren kissed her soft lips, forgetting that they were still the center of attention. The crowd below them cheered. Ren remembered himself and pulled away from his mate. Lifting the microphone to his lips, he began the announcement he had tried to avoid all year.

"I know it seems like we should be celebrating. As the gods have prophesied, it has come to pass. Clans around the United States are united. As we have been putting our future together, few have been working against us. Several council members have been plotting the demise of my Queen and myself. At this time, I need to bring to your attention that one of our long-time council members, Jonathan, has been executed in New Orleans for acts of treason." A deathly silence fell over the crowd. Then a scream sounded amidst the gathering.

"You murderer. I was right; he had him murdered. You have no proof. We have supported you all the way."

"Lies, Madeline," Ren replied calmly. "You lie so well. You had no interest in seeing the prophecy come to fruition. You planned to turn as many clan members from me as possible to start a war. As for proof, maybe the plot of treason would suffice as evidence." He signaled to Cell, and the voices bellowed throughout the club. Clear enough to identify the speakers. Madeline tried to step down from her perch to deflect attention from her whereabouts. She became separated from her beloved Carlos and her soldiers at that moment. So she was forced to remain.

"If you look around, more than our usual clan are among us. The outsiders are here with our trusted council person, Madeline. Her beloved son was the one responsible for Yalena's kidnapping. From this night on, we purge ourselves of the tainted blood. Either you stand with us, or you stand against us. If you stand against us, you can run, but you will be found and brought before the council."

"So you would hunt us down and kill us because we don't agree with you."

"Madeline, I would hunt you down for your betrayal. As for the others who wish to live your own life away from the rules we have established here in America, I suggest you find another place to call home. If we find out you are hunting humans and mistreating them for your perverse pleasure, you will be brought before the council provided that we don't have to kill you to bring you back."

"Do you hear him. He warns of execution. That is not the prophecy." There are a few murmurs of agreement, but not many.

"Madeline, my purpose here is to keep the order. To make sure that the growing vampire population isn't detrimental to the human population. At the rate we've grown, it would be dangerous for the human population if we revert to the old ways. Then what? If they are not here, how do you feed?"

"Enough of this bullshit! We want the right to live as we feel. Live free or die! Who cares if you hunt or treat your human to dinner before you feast." Ren nodded to Patrick, and he, in turn, signaled the other soldiers who barred the doors leading to and from the club. Those who had escaped couldn't return with reinforcements, and unfortunately, those who stayed were stuck. Ren had already noticed some vampires sneaking out their companions once Yalena lit the fountain.

Ren watched the crowd. The mutters and whispers slowly died as they began to realize that the doors were now bolted, and there were soldiers at every turn. The spotlight was out, and Ren and

Yalena were no longer on the balcony. Those who were left were primarily supporters of Madeline. No one uttered a sound for more than a few moments.

Ren was glad that Patrick had brought the reserve. He made Lena drink a pouch and then part of his. He knew that she would need the energy to fight and so much had already been taken from her to heal.

Chapter 28

When Lena and Ren entered the main door of the building into the club, everyone seemed to be startled. Lena walked towards the raised dance floor with Ren by her side. Patrick and Kiyoshi followed them. Those who remained watched silently. Lena looked around at the few hundred vampires and others who stood before her and around her. They looked like everyone else., but the energy pulsed around her. She was anxious and scared. They were fighting for their way of life. She had five children that depended on her to keep them safe.

Lena could feel the anxious energy in the club. She turned in a circle, meeting the eyes of those close to her and observing their soldiers at the doors. Finally, she turned toward the one who came in with Madeline. "Carlos, I presume," said Lena to the tall tanned vampire. Carlos stepped out of the crowd and bowed slightly before Lena. "Am I to assume by your presence here that you are supporting Madeline?"

"Nothing escapes you, my Queen."

Lena didn't reply, but the left corner of her mouth twitched. "And what is to prevent me from slaughtering you all?"

"I was under the impression that you are a fair ruler, although perhaps not as lenient as your mate." Lena smiled and wondered what the consequences of slaying him immediately would be. Her arm slid to her side and began to unsheathe her sword. Before she could uncover more than an inch, Ren gently put his arm around her and prevented any further action.

"So it would appear the news is more than true; we're at an impasse. I don't wish to stand around all day. So let me help you decide what to do." In one fluid move, Carlos stepped back, and a wolf jumped in front of him. Lena had barely enough time to unsheathe her sword. She managed to draw and slice the beast in half. That began what she and Ren had been avoiding for the last year. Lena watched as people who she thought were normal became human sized wolves.

With her first opponent dropped it signaled the soldiers to begin dismantling the forces Madeline brought with her. With Ren at her back, they began to take on the vampires and wolves together. At the same time, their soldiers fought the forces that gathered around them. The club erupted in clanging of metal and growls. Sounds of rips and tears echoed around the room. Yalena started to look for Madeline and Yazmine. They ran but wouldn't get far with the soldiers at every exit.

While she was looking for the two ladies, a werewolf thought he would catch her off guard. But, unfortunately for him, she could smell him coming before he stood in front of her. So she parried ahead of it stepping inches before her.

"You killed my brother."

"Wait, I know this line. It goes, 'my name is something that starts with an M, you killed my brother. Prepare to die'."

"You won't be laughing soon."

As Lena lunged forward, she said, "I'm sorry you don't like my line. I've been waiting more than a decade to use it." By the time Lena had finished speaking, she had struck the final blow that ended the wolf.

After him, they seemed to keep coming. Wolves and vampires together, one after the other. There was blood and mayhem all around her, yet it appeared that they lined up to fight her. As fast as she killed them, two more replaced them. After two fights with four people, she could hardly stand. Her injuries had taken their toll and it was amazing that Ren's reserve had gotten her this far. She called to her great great grandmother for the energy she needed. Lena could hear her laughing as a burst of energy hit her.

Lena smiled at her next opponent. They thought they had worn her down.

Finally, she was able to take a breath. Kiyoshi came to stand by her side and tore the head off the last two. He bowed before her. Lena nodded and returned his bow. His eyes sparkled before he turned to fight another. Lena looked around; they were in the throws of the final battle. The floor ran with blood and combatants. Only a few still fought, wolf on wolf and soldier on wolf. The clanging of blade on blade punctuated by broken glass and smashed furniture and walls. She wondered how they knew the difference. As she thought, she walked over to Yazmine and Madeline. It was unfortunate that Seth was nowhere to be found.

"Well, ladies, it would appear you're caught, and Seth has left you behind."

"But I am." Carlos glided over and leaped towards Yalena, who yawned while she stepped aside. In three strikes of her sword, Carlos was dead.

His last words were, "Madeline, you're the death of..."

"Now where were we? Oh yes. This is over."

"We can go? We'll be good," pled Madeline

"No words from my dear sister. You won't even beg for your life," asked Lena.

Yazmine scoffed. "Fuck you, little sis. Wouldn't want to live under your rule, bitch."

Lena laughed. "You know it takes a lot of energy for the soldiers at the door to stay so still." Yalena glimpsed Ren across the room, who had just finished fighting another wolf. He nodded. "Our soldiers need sustenance. Feed!"

Once said, all the soldiers left their post, they converged on Madeline and Yazmine. Those who were fighting fed from the dying vampires who could not escape. Half of the soldiers were dead or lay dying when the fight was all over. None of Madeline's forces or herself remained. The club's dance floors and couches ran rivers of blood, and the soldiers, Lena and Ren stood in the midst of it all.

"Soldiers leave. Seek refuge. Patrick will return for you." The soldiers hurried and limped through the doors into the night air. "Yalena, we must destroy it all. Nothing must remain."

"Where will they go? Are you sure, Ren?"

"To the penthouse and underground. And yes."

"I will be of no use afterwards."

"I got you. You'll be safe." Lena smiled sadly. Zoe's meant so much to Ren. He had spent centuries building it up. Now it was over. At least for a time. Once he assured her, she began to set the club aflame. First, the curtains that hung all around the club and over the beds and chairs. Once the curtains caught, the linen on the beds began to burn. Then, like a wildfire, it spread throughout the club. Yalena collapsed against Ren, and he swept her into his arms.

As Ren walked out carrying Yalena, the club burned around them. Cell followed them onto the street as well as Patrick and Kiyoshi. They had just made it out before the ceiling caved in. Both Yazmine and Madeline were dead, drained by the soldiers. Whatever remained was ablaze. The existence of vampires in the city for over two centuries smoldered behind them.

Chapter 29

When Yalena awoke a few days later, she lay in a massive bed among numerous pillows. She stretched and looked around the room, trying to remember where she was. She was more than delighted when her mate came into the room with Tehuti and Tahira in his arms and Tendai on his back. The rest of her beautiful children were walking in front. Oh, how she had missed them. Her heart ached a little, knowing she had been away from them. As each child came in, it hurt a little more as she thought of the danger their lives were in.

Kissa and Kamau jumped into the bed to hug her. Ren placed the triplets on the edge of the bed, and they crawled up to join in a big hug. It was apparent that they missed her too. Ren came around to the side and sat next to Kissa after putting Tendai on his lap. They were a growing happy family.

"They've missed you Yalena."

"I can see that."

"Kamau and Kissa were worried. They cried the first night. It's as if they knew something was keeping you from them." Lena hugged them tight and kissed each head before Kai came into the room. She was happy they were all safe. Ren had made sure of that. Lena sighed and touched each child. She felt warm wrapped in the arms of her children. She could only imagine how they felt.

"Alright, all of you out. Your mother needs her rest and time with your father."

"But Aunt Kai, we just got here."

"Yes, Kamau, but she'll be here. Come on."

"Aunt Kai."

"Kissa, go on," chided Ren. "Once your mother's up, we'll spend some time in the family room with everyone and help Kai with the triplets."

"Yes dad," Kamau replied as he grabbed Tehuti and walked out of the bedroom door, followed by Kissa and Tahira.

"I will give you two some time," stated Kai as she picked up Tendai, who whined when taken from her mother's arms. Kai soothed her by telling her she'd be in her mom's arms soon before closing the door behind her.

"Oh, Ren I missed them so."

"And they missed you my love." Ren nuzzled Yalena's neck before trailing kisses down to her shoulder, "and I have missed my wife." As he said this, he lifted her breast from her top and took it into his mouth. Yalena gasped for breath as one of her arms encircled his head. The other ran up and down his arm and over his back.

"I take it we are going to have our last brood?"

"I can no longer wait for you. I must have you now." Ren's hand slid under the sheet and up her thigh, stopping at the apex briefly before parting them and plunging his fingers inside.

"Ren," Yalena whispered. She and Ren were waiting for her body to grow stronger. It had been months since Ren touched her. Still, she died a little each day with anticipation of this moment.

Ren didn't wait long before he allowed her to sheathe him. Yalena's body, ready to accept his intrusion, bucked up against Ren. He rallied her response, taking her hard with need. Yalena screamed his name, unable to control herself. He punished her body for being away from his, as though his life depended on the ecstasy they shared.

"Don't ever put yourself at risk again. I cannot take it."

"Are you punishing me Ren?"

"I didn't mean to do so, but I have missed our intimacy; the way your body accepts mine." Ren continued to pound into Yalena, pushing himself deeper each time. He lifted her legs so that they were straight in the air and against his torso. Each movement sent him deeper into her. As he leaned down to kiss her, her body folded in half, taking his total weight. Ren took possession of her mouth and tongue, sucking and thrusting his tongue into her mouth.

Their passion was wild and fierce now that it was unhindered. With everything that had happened, they had won. Ren and Yalena were together and their children were safe from harm, even if for a time. As the two of them came, they stilled, gazing into the eyes of each other. Lena moved her legs so that they could wrap around her love. Then she folded them and pulled him closer.

"Well you wanted me pregnant, you shall soon get your wish." Ren laughed. "I can feel them Ren. I haven't before. I don't like how it feels."

"Doesn't matter, just relax. If you focus on that, your body will fight. Don't think about it." Ren kissed her once again and turned so that she straddled over his legs.

"Your turn."

"I love you, Lorenzo."

"And I love you, Yalena."